CLOSE YOUR EYES AND COUNT TO 10

Also by Lisa Unger

Angel Fire
The Darkness Gathers
Twice
Smoke
Beautiful Lies
Sliver of Truth
Black Out
Die for You
Fragile
Darkness, My Old Friend
Heartbroken
In the Blood
Crazy Love You
The Whispering Hollows (novella)
Ink and Bone
The Red Hunter
Under My Skin
The Stranger Inside
Confessions on the 7:45
Last Girl Ghosted
Secluded Cabin Sleeps Six
The New Couple in 5B

LISA UNGER

CLOSE YOUR EYES AND COUNT TO 10

PARK
ROW
BOOKS

PARK
ROW
BOOKS™

ISBN-13: 978-0-7783-3336-4
ISBN-13: 978-0-7783-8772-5 (International Trade Paperback Edition)

Close Your Eyes and Count to 10

Park Row Books
22 Adelaide St. West, 41st Floor
Toronto, Ontario M5H 4E3, Canada
ParkRowBooks.com

Printed in U.S.A.

For Violet,

Wiser than your years, smarter than you know,
bright, beautiful and loved beyond measure.

This one's for you.

Love,

Aunt Lisa

<u>Part One</u>

Close Your Eyes

Count 1 to 10
You go hide! And then I seek!
I promise not to peek.
You are good at this, where did you go?
Are you here? Yes, yes, yes...no!

NURSERY RHYME

The Game

A bolt of lightning cuts a jagged line in the night sky, casting the abandoned hotel in a brief, white-hot flash. A violent thunderclap follows, rumbling the ground. The twisting man-made walking paths snaking all around the hulking structure have turned to rivers. Viscous, muddy water rushes, taking with it debris, its force sweeping away the campsite, toppling the tents, filling the fire pit. Wind bends the trees into painful, straining arcs, howling. Branches splinter, falling.

If you circled up, up, up into the storming sky, you'd see them, the players, scattered.

A woman is unconscious, bound in a subbasement of the crumbling hotel.

A muscular man rappels down an empty elevator shaft filling with rainwater. He might be too late to save her, or himself.

Among the other sounds, buried beneath the roar of the weather, a terrified keening. A woman, clinging to a balcony separating from a small structure perched on the edge of a steep cliff, is about to fall into the volcanic lake below her. Her grip is slipping, strength failing.

Rain sheets, unrelenting, a hundred timpani drums beaten by a cosmic drummer.

Someone who was hiding runs in the direction of the terrified scream-
ing. Her body is strong and fit, even as she fights the current of the rush-
ing water, the weather raging all around her. She climbs over a fallen tree
as lightning cuts another electric swath through the night. She stumbles,
coming to the ground hard, gets up, keeps running.

The hotel Enchantments, once grand and luxurious, now a ruin,
groans. The rushing water, the impossibly powerful wind, the shifting
ground is destabilizing the very foundation of the beast.

Inside, a beam falls, crashing to the ground, echoing with the next
explosion of thunder.

In the middle of it all, someone waits. Stillness in chaos. Patience.
There was a plan.

Plots were hatched. Agendas run. Deception. A game. A stunning
betrayal. A murder. All the things that people do best. But that's all
done now.

Now there is only the storm, nature in all its fury, doing what it
does best.

Cleansing.
Washing away everything that doesn't belong.

1

~~~~~~

ADELE

Blake slouched beside Adele, holding a frosty-blue ice pack to the bridge of his swelling nose. He'd already handed her his shattered glasses, and she held them in the palms of her hands like a wounded baby bird.

Principal White, balding, bespectacled, leaned toward them earnestly over his orderly desk. He was saying something about how the school had a zero-tolerance policy when it came to bullying but that he wasn't going to be able to help unless Blake told him who had hit him. *Who* had punched him in the face so hard that his glasses were in pieces and that he'd likely have two black eyes?

"Blake?" said Adele, trying to keep the emotion from her voice. "Who did this?"

The skin on Blake's face was an angry red. He shifted his body away from her, wouldn't meet her eyes. Silence.

"I'm concerned," continued Principal White gently. "Because, as you know, this is not the first time Blake has been targeted.

There was the incident in gym class before break. The fight in the cafeteria last May."

Adele found that she could barely focus on his words, thinking about how when Blake was small, she could gather him in her arms and make anything that was wrong right again. Now at nearly fifteen, her six-foot son towered over her. In fact, he towered over most people. But soft-spoken, with a floppy mane of untamed dark hair, those thick glasses, and his quiet bearing, he was unwilling, it seemed, to stand up for himself in any way. He was, as his older sister, Violet, liked to put it, *bully bait*.

"It was an accident," Blake said finally, voice low. "I ran into a locker."

Principal White's chair issued a creak as he leaned back, ran a hand over his shiny head. He had sparkling blue eyes, a wiry, runner's build. They'd been friends once; his wife had worked with Adele's ex-husband. Birthday parties and barbecues, company picnics, holiday gatherings. But that was *before*.

Probably the kid, or kids, who had hurt Blake had been friends once, too. Likely they'd been to Adele's home, swum in their pool, slept over. She might have helped them open a juice box or even bandaged a scraped knee.

They didn't have as many friends now. Or any friends, really.

Blake pushed himself up from his slouch, stood up, and tugged at his father's tattered Harvard hoodie. His jeans were too baggy, gathering over his Converse high-tops. The kid was huge. If he put up his fists and fought back, whoever was doing this would surely go running. Not that she advocated violence. But sometimes you had to teach people that they couldn't hurt you and get away with it, right?

"Can we go?" he asked, voice husky. "I didn't do anything wrong."

He picked up his backpack from the floor, still keeping the ice to the bridge of his nose.

Adele's daughter, Violet, was full of fire, her anger volcanic;

they were working on dialing that back. Blake folded in onto himself, locked up. Which worried her more.

"Okay, Blake," said Principal White, resigned. He rose, a full head shorter than the teenager. "My door is open if you want to talk, okay? Anytime. Why don't you wait outside for your mom?"

Blake lumbered through the door and closed it behind him. Adele released a sigh.

"Who do you think it was?" she asked.

"I wouldn't like to speculate," Principal White said with a slight shake of his head. He removed his glasses and cleaned the lenses with a little cloth he took from his pocket. "But I have some ideas."

Adele had some ideas, too. She felt a familiar flicker of anger, but she quashed it. She was more like her daughter than her son, though Adele had better control over her emotions—most of the time. Blake had her ex-husband Miller's temperament: reticent, slow to anger, his silence containing volumes.

"Things haven't been easy," said Principal White. "I know that."

Another rush of emotion; her cheeks burned, and she looked away from him. His education degrees from Rutgers were displayed on the wall of his office. A wooden shelf held a slew of track-and-field trophies, framed pictures of his family.

"First Miller," he said, clearing his throat. "Then Covid. All the kids are struggling to find their footing right now. But Blake has been through that much more."

Like she needed to be reminded of how much her kids had suffered because of the things their father had done, was still doing in some sense. Her shoulders hiked, aching. She forced them down. Why did expressions of kindness so often feel like condescension? Wasn't there a note of superiority? His secure position, his intact family, offered a stark and obvious contrast to the mess of her own life.

"I want this to be a safe space for Blake, for all our students. I need him to talk to me, though."

Adele slipped the broken glasses into the side pocket of her tote. She stood, smoothed out the pleats of her skirt. Both the skirt and the bag were expensive, designer pieces, each about ten years old. They still looked nice, she thought, maybe showing their age a bit. She couldn't afford anything close with her salary now.

"I'll talk to him," she said, tucking her bag under her arm. "Thank you, Principal White."

"Ken," he said, smiling warmly, walking around the desk.

"Ken, of course." She moved toward the door, eager to take Blake home. The air in the sunny office, with the view of the football field outside, had become overwarm. Stifling, in fact.

"Hey, Adele, I just wanted to say..." He seemed to search for the right words. "We don't hold anything against you. What happened. Everyone knows it had nothing to do with you."

Well, that wasn't strictly true. Not everyone knew that. The fact that they were still talking about *what happened* nearly five years later was a reminder of how present it still was in this town. Maybe they should have left, started over someplace else. But they hadn't, for a million reasons.

"Thank you, Ken," she said. She forced herself to meet his eyes and smile. What did she see behind the understanding smile? Judgment, clear as day.

Outside the office, Blake had found another place to slouch in one of the chairs beside the door. School had already let out for the day, so the hallways were mercifully empty.

"Let's go home, kiddo," she said.

He nodded, rising, followed her to the car.

"So you're really not going to tell me who did it?" she asked as they took the winding, rural road back to the house. She chose the long way home so that they wouldn't have to pass the house they used to live in on the way to the place they rented now in a very different part of town. If he'd noticed, he didn't say anything.

"Does it matter?" he asked.

"I think it does, yeah," she said. "Because people should not be allowed to hurt you, Blakey."

He turned those dark eyes on her, Miller's eyes—wise, seeing, too old for his years. And now ringed with purple. He opened his mouth to say something, then seemed to change his mind, looked out the window into the golden late afternoon instead.

"Just drop it, Mom, okay?"

She tightened her grip on the wheel, saved her breath. Because she knew that her son was a locked box. There was no prying him open until he was ready, and that might be never.

He was out of the car before she even turned off the engine, disappearing through the front door as she stepped into the chill. The sound of the screen door slamming was as loud as a gunshot, causing her to startle. She glanced around at the trees that surrounded their house, the next place a few miles up the road.

A chill moved down her spine, the strange sense that she often had of being watched.

Paranoid. That's what Violet would say.

She wished she could chalk it up to that.

"Why are you protecting them?" Violet was in Blake's face. "It's not going to make them *like you.* You get that, right? It makes you their *doormat.*"

"Take it easy, Violet," Adele said as she plated the savory beef stew from the Crock-Pot.

"You know I'm right," her daughter countered, the seventeen-year-old firebrand. With her wild red hair, flashing blue-gray eyes, searing intelligence, she was a force. Adele found herself often in awe of her daughter's ability to stand up for herself.

"Those glasses," Violet went on, "cost eight hundred dollars.

We can barely afford that. At the very least, that little fucker and his filthy-rich parents should be paying for it."

"Language!"

Blake would have to wear his old prescription for a while. The fact that Violet knew that, that it concerned her, was a source of shame for Adele. She'd leaned too much on Violet; as a result, her daughter had had to grow up too fast.

"Let's put a pin in this until after dinner," said Adele, setting their dishes on the table while Violet got the water, and Blake, who hadn't said a word, placed the napkins and silverware. Her heart ached looking at him. Those shiners were growing darker by the second, the surrounding skin pink and raw from the cold of the ice pack.

Anger. It was always on simmer inside her. She'd used it—to get her act together, to get in the best shape of her life, to find work, to pursue a degree, and to take care of her family in the wake of Miller's crimes. But sometimes it threatened to overwhelm her. She'd need to go a few rounds with the punching bag suspended from the rafters in the garage when the kids were doing their homework.

They sat and ate. Their nightly ritual of sitting for dinner, no matter how late everyone got home, was a comfort to Adele. It was one of the few things she knew she'd done right.

As hot as Violet's temper ran, it passed just as quickly. Soon, she was talking about how she did *okay, not great* on her biology test, how her best friend Coral got in trouble in gym class for beaning (accidentally!) one of the mean girls with a volleyball, how all the boys in her school were *disgusting*. Her chatter was a salve. Even Blake seemed to relax as he scarfed down his meal. He may have even smiled.

She watched them. How could two kids from the same parents be so different? Blake's black hair a striking contrast to Violet's fairness, his deep brown eyes against Violet's sometimes stormy gray, sometimes sky-blue. Blake had his father's high cheek bones, serious brow. Violet had Adele's bisque skin, long nose. Adele's maternal grandparents were Scandinavian. Her father's mother was Japanese, his father from Nigeria; they met in the Peace Corps. Miller was Russian on both sides. In her children's faces she saw the blend of all these places around the world. They were true American kids, their heritage a vibrant mosaic. Violet was all light, high energy, optimism. Blake was her worrier, her old soul. *That's the Russian in him*, Miller had said when Blake emerged from the womb with a furrowed brow.

"And—*ugh*—I'm so PMS," concluded Violet. "I'm getting my period any minute."

"Jesus, Violet," Blake finally spoke up. Violet's smile told Adele that goading her brother had been exactly the point.

"Grow up, you big baby." She elbowed him. "Women *menstruate*."

Blake dipped his head in his hand, blushing. "Seriously, V?"

Adele laughed, the tension of the day easing some.

Then the doorbell rang.

They all froze, looking at each other. Not a normal response to the ringing of the doorbell. But they were not a normal family. They were a family always waiting for the next bad thing to happen.

"Probably just a delivery," said Adele, rising. "Sit."

But no. There was an electricity to the air, an energy of something about to go wrong.

When she looked through the glass at the top of the door, she saw a form that had become too familiar. Tall, broad-shouldered, close-shorn hair, hands in pockets, stance wide. *What now?* She released a sigh, opened the door.

"Why doesn't *anyone* ever seem happy to see me?" said Special Agent Sean Coben. He offered his hand, which she reluctantly took. It was strong and calloused in hers, his grip a little too firm.

"What can I do for you, Agent Coben?" She drew her hand back, kept her body in the doorjamb.

"I wanted to let you know," he said, peering past her into the house, "that we have a lead on your husband. A sighting in Tampa that we think might be legitimate."

She leaned against the frame. Was this day going to get any worse?

Agent Coben was the most recent in a long line of FBI agents looking for her husband, who had been on the run for the last five years. Coben was definitely the youngest and most energetic of the agents, fresh to the fight, bringing an uncommon enthusiasm to the hunt for a man accused of fraud and embezzlement. Miller's company, a biotechnology firm that developed prosthetics, among other things, was—*had been*—a major employer of the town in which they still lived. Due to his alleged activities, the company went bankrupt, employees lost everything, and Miller was said to have absconded with untold millions of dollars, leaving Adele behind to pick up the pieces of their shattered life.

"I have some footage I'd like to show you," Agent Coben said, rubbing at his clean-shaven jaw.

She swung the door open finally, and he walked inside, standing in the small foyer.

"We're eating," she said. "Would you like to join us?"

He smiled, maybe intuiting that it was a polite invitation that would be impolite to accept, lifted a palm. "Thank you. I'll just wait here until you're done."

The kids were standing inside the kitchen door when she returned.

"Did they find Dad?" asked Blake, childishly hopeful.

"If they'd *found* him, he'd be in jail," said Violet, face stone-still, eyes sad.

The pain that her husband had caused his children was a knife in her gut every single time.

"He's not going to jail," said Blake. "Because he's innocent. He was *framed*."

"You," said Violet softly, moving toward the sink, "are an idiot."

Blake glared but stayed quiet.

"Violet, in this family we treat each other with respect," said Adele, the words sounding weak even to her. "No name-calling."

Violet shook her head, mouth pressed into a thin line, stayed silent. No back talk, but no apology, either.

"Kids," she said, clearing her dish. She'd lost her appetite. "Finish eating and go work on your homework. If there's any news, I'll talk to you about it when Agent Coben leaves."

After Blake and Violet went upstairs, Adele sat with Agent Coben at the kitchen island. On his iPad, he showed her footage of a man walking down a city street, the image black-and-white and grainy. It could have been Miller. Baseball cap, mirrored glasses, light jacket, and jeans, it could have been anyone.

"We got a call, then pulled area footage. This was all we found."

"Why Tampa?"

"That's what I was hoping you could tell me."

Adele and Miller met in Florida; Miller had always talked about returning there someday. He loved the beach lifestyle, boats and warm weather all year. The last alleged Miller sighting had been in Majorca; before that, Greece. But if he had any connections in Tampa, any reason to go there, Adele had no idea what those might be. Her husband was a stranger to her, maybe in light of everything that had happened, even after ten years of marriage and two children, he always had been.

"Has he reached out to you?" asked Agent Coben, keeping his dark, girlishly lashed eyes on her. His gaze was warm but unyielding.

"You'd know if he had, wouldn't you?" It was no secret that she was still under FBI surveillance. It was subtle, but she knew.

"People have their ways," said Coben easily.

"He hasn't. And if he had, I would have called you. I would like Miller to come to justice, even if just for closure for my kids."

"You've said that before."

"But you don't believe me."

Something flashed across his face. Empathy maybe. "Love is complicated."

She gave him an assenting nod. "I haven't heard from him. And I couldn't swear that the man in your footage is him. It could be anyone."

He froze the image and zoomed in on the man on the lonely, gray street.

"Are you sure?"

She tried to call to mind an image of her husband: his fine features, his strong body, his carriage. Instead, all she could remember was his scent, the feel of his arms, the timbre of his deep voice, how loved, how safe he had always made her feel. Those were the things that she missed, even now, desperately. The image on the screen was ghostly, distant. Possibly Miller. Maybe not.

Where are you? she wondered for the millionth time, the question more physical ache than words.

"I don't know if that's him," she said, rubbing at the fatigue behind her eyes. "I don't think so? I'm sorry."

She wondered about Agent Coben, not for the first time. He seemed young, no wedding ring. Polite, not hard like some of the others; he didn't appear to judge her. There was something about his quiet but determined way that put her at ease. She wanted to ask him questions. *Why this work? This case? How did it get assigned to you? Do you think you'll find him?* But she stopped short of that. The next time the bell rang, it could be someone else there.

"Are you sure I can't get you anything?" she asked, chronically polite. "Coffee?"

He shook his head. "Thank you. No."

One last look at the image on his screen. She shrugged again. Coben nodded, then took his device and got up to leave.

In the foyer, he stopped and turned around. "Most people get caught, you know."

She didn't say anything.

"Life on the run is no life. There's no comfort in it. People start to miss their families. Regret sets in. Usually it's weddings or funerals where we get them. Calls on birthdays or anniversaries. Even people in witness protection, whose lives depend on staying hidden, can't always stay away forever."

Adele found herself shaking her head. "Miller won't come back."

Now it was Agent Coben's turn to stay silent.

"He doesn't care about us," she said. "If he did, he never could have done this, or stayed away so long."

Upstairs she heard heavy footsteps down the hall, a slammed door. Blake had been listening in. Maybe he needed to hear it.

"I'll be in touch," said Agent Coben. Then he was gone.

In the garage, Adele wrapped her hands to protect her knuckles underneath the boxing gloves. The heavy bag hung from the rafters.

She thought about going live for her followers.

Her WeWatch channel where she had chronicled her journey back from loss, losing weight with a nutrition and workout routine of her own creation, and a return to competing in half-marathons and the Tough Be-atch obstacle course competitions was steadily growing.

Once upon a time, she used to be a marathon runner, before she had her kids and had slowly allowed the tide of life and motherhood to take her away from the physical strength and fitness she'd once considered her birthright. Then, after the brutal months of grieving and trying to convince the FBI that she hadn't been an accomplice in Miller's crimes, terrified that she would go to jail, leaving her kids all alone and devastating her

He came down the few steps, leaned on the workbench where she'd propped up her phone.

"I'm sorry," he said. "About my glasses."

She put a tender hand to his cheek. "It's okay, Blakey. It's not your fault."

"I know they're expensive," he said. "And I know—money's always tight now."

Shame again, sadness, washed up hot. She'd be punching that bag all night and still never get rid of that feeling.

"I have an idea," he said. "It might be a little crazy."

He held up his iPhone.

"Maverick," Blake went on. "He's doing another game."

Maverick Dillan was Blake's idol, a WeWatch celebrity and founder of Maverick's Extreme Games and Insane Challenges. Wild man, philanthropist, and athlete, he and his posse did stunts around the globe and hosted games where other influencers competed live for their followers.

"The prize is a million dollars," said Blake with a note of awe.

She felt a tingle of unease. Hadn't there been something during one of his competitions? Some kind of accident? A girl gone missing?

"Mom," said Blake, more urgent, "a *million* dollars. Plus, think of all the followers you would gain from participating in the challenge. You'd achieve influencer status, for sure. That's big money on WeWatch."

"Okay, wow," she said. "What's the game?"

He raised his eyebrows, flashed her a grin. "Extreme Hide and Seek, at an abandoned hotel on some remote island."

How many of those had she watched with Blake? Truthfully, it all seemed a little fake and hollow to Adele, not quite real, something done just for the cameras. People hid in abandoned buildings—supposedly haunted houses, deserted hospitals and prisons, dilapidated asylums—all the while broadcasting live. There was never any real danger. Just some jump scares for the camera, some created drama between contestants. The kids loved it, though.

And Maverick—sometimes he came off as a little unhinged, doing things that were unsafe and reckless. His so-called fail reels—devastating slope wipeouts, precipitous falls, and bone-crunching skateboard crashes—were terrifying. But he always seemed to walk away unharmed. There was something, though, tapping at her memory...something bad had happened during one of the stunts or games. She'd have to search it.

"When does it start?" she asked, her curiosity piqued.

"Two weeks. There's a spot for one more hider."

Blake held out his phone for her, showing the page on Extreme's website where the text was in big red type against a black backdrop.

Maverick's Extreme Games and Insane Challenges

PRESENTS

The most INTENSE game of hide and seek EVER!
The biggest prize offered in the history of Extreme!
The winner walks away with ONE MILLION dollars!

Influencers,
APPLY HERE NOW!

She was surprised by a little jangle of excitement.

She wasn't really thinking about this, was she? She'd have to get time off work. Figure out who was going to take care of the kids.

No. It was really not even an option.

But—a million dollars? That would be a game changer.

And she wasn't sure how it all worked, but she knew the more followers she had, the better. Lately, she'd been hearing from

WeWatch, with tips and advice on how to grow her audience, monetize her page with advertising, sponsor content (known as *spon con*). She'd even been approached via DM by a couple of companies for small sponsorships, but nothing she believed in. An energy drink filled with sugar and chemicals. A vegan protein bar which she'd sampled and hated. She'd passed on both.

It was like a new world she was trying to navigate. She knew people were making money as WeWatch influencers. Lots of it.

But. There was *no way* she could fly to some abandoned hotel in the middle of nowhere to play a game of extreme hide and seek, right?

"Mom," said Blake, watching her intently, "you really slayed at that last Tough Be-atch competition."

She'd come in third in her age group, beating her time on the obstacle course by a full minute. She'd crossed the finish line, bleeding from a scraped knee, drenched in sweat, and totally pumped.

Blake went on, "All you have to do for this challenge is hide and not get found. It's like a no-brainer. Zero risk, huge reward."

Impossible. Moms didn't do things like that.

Or did they?

Maybe it was the trip to the principal's office, the sight now of Blake's black eyes, the visit from Agent Coben, that grainy image of a man who might or might not be Miller. She felt so lost sometimes, so powerless to right the wrongs in her life, in the lives of her kids.

"You can do this," Blake said, clamping a bear-claw hand on her shoulder. "I believe in you."

There was something so excited and electric in his gaze, and it connected to something buried within her.

Before she could think twice, she tapped on the bright red link.

2

MAVERICK

"Oh, *hell* no," Hector said from the back seat of the Ranger Rover.

Maverick, at the wheel, could see Hector's worried expression in the rearview mirror. His old friend ran a hand over his thick mop of dark hair, a thing he did when he was stressed, his doughy forehead moist and crinkled. Hector was *often* stressed. "That's a hard pass, Mav."

Maverick brought the SUV to a stop in front of a towering graffiti-covered sign very clearly warning them away. *PELIGRO! DANGER! GO BACK!*

"Aw, come on," said Mav, looking back at Hector with a smile. "Don't be such a baby."

"Why is it that when something says *danger* or *go away*, you view that as invitation?" asked Hector.

Riding shotgun beside Maverick, Gustavo was loose and easy, tattered hiking shoes up on the dash. Gustavo laughed and held out a fist which Mav bumped with his. "Because he's Maverick."

"One of these days you're going to get us all killed," complained Hector.

It was their shtick, their routine. "But not today," Maverick answered. Hector grinned at him in the mirror.

As they passed the towering sign and rounded the bend in the road, the abandoned hotel rose before the vista, windows yawning black, overgrown foliage leaking from the roof, deep fissures in the concrete walls. It was a great shadow looming at the precipice of a steep cliff overlooking a glittering volcanic lake.

The last light of the day glinted on the still water.

Maverick felt that familiar excitement, that electric current through his veins. His whole body vibrated with it.

The dark structure hulked, a huge concrete dare. Man, how he loved the broken thing, the jagged edge, the crumbling ruin. It thrilled him to see how things broke down.

"Holy shit," said Gustavo, dropping his feet and leaning forward. He was lean and muscular, with a square jaw, and long black hair that he pulled back into ponytail, a bandanna over his head. That toothy smile, a wide arc of mischief and joy. It always connected Mav to his inner adolescent boy. "*This* is going to be extreme, *brah*."

"This is going to be *nothing* if we don't get a permit from the town council," said Angeline from beside Hector in the back seat, tapping on her phone.

"We'll get it," said Maverick. They locked eyes in the mirror. "Trust me."

"Like Mav doesn't *always* get what he wants," said Alex from the too-small third row of the vehicle. He'd been mostly quiet on this trip, except to chime in with something negative. "In the meantime, he's going to bankrupt us if we keep having to pay everyone off."

"It's not a *payoff*," said Maverick. "It's a *donation* to build a library for the town. Just trying to grease the wheels."

"Hmm," said Alex. "Okay."

Mav looked for Alex's indulgent smile, the one that made him feel like everything was okay, but his friend was staring at his phone. Frowning. His vibe was off. Trouble at home, maybe. Alex and his wife, Lucia, had a new baby, and Mama was not too happy about this outing.

I can't just pick up and go at a moment's notice anymore, Mav, Alex had complained before the trip, which he had vigorously opposed.

And that was *exactly why* Mav was never having kids or tethering himself to a woman who wanted to settle down. Angeline had an adventurer's heart. He glanced at her in the mirror again. She and Alex had identical postures, heads bent over their respective screens, faces glowing in the light. If Angeline thought about marriage and kids, she'd never said so.

He pulled the vehicle to a crunching stop and stepped out. The air was so fresh that it made his lungs ache, everything around him a dripping, fecund green.

Maverick held up his phone and tried to frame the view before him on the screen. But there was no way to capture any of it, its beauty, its drama. The deserted structure sucked in all the light. The mineral green of the water, the hyperorange and gunmetal gray of the sky, and the rolling mountains beyond were made flat and dead by two dimensions. Even his eyes could barely take it in. *You can't squeeze the whole world into that rectangle in your hand,* his dad, who refused to carry a smartphone, liked to say.

That's not what he was trying to do. The phone—it wasn't a box. It was a portal. He was trying to *give* something to his followers, many of whom rarely left their gaming chairs.

"It's perfect," Mav said, the silence swallowing his words. But it wasn't really silence. The movement of the trees, the wind, the calling of birds, the rustling of undergrowth wove a chorus of whispers, a landscape of sound.

No one answered him.

Angeline was on her phone again. Having exited the vehicle, she moved purposefully toward the tilting gate at the grand entrance. Her form was a slim shadow, tiny against the towering old-growth forest.

Though he had the urge to call after her, bring her back closer to him, he stayed quiet, watching her. Her voice, but not her words, carried on the night. She sounded angry. But then she was usually angry, or at least annoyed. As the chief operating officer of Extreme, she was constantly in the middle of his circus, cracking the whip. Making sure things worked, that the haters stayed at a safe distance, that his plans came to life.

Gustavo and Hector already had the gear and were moving toward the open corpse of the hotel, laughing, their voices echoing. Gustavo Bello, or Tavo as they mostly called him, with Hector's reluctant help would rappel down the empty elevator shaft to inspect the foundation. Extreme's social-media director and main sidekick, Tavo *could* and *would* climb in or out of anything with agility and grace. As thin and powerful as a galvanized-steel cable, his body was seemingly not beholden to the laws of gravity that others had to obey.

Hector Cruz's role—his official title at Extreme was producer—was to stay on the sidelines telling them to be careful, identifying potential threats, managing safety. He was the one holding the rope, pulling them out when things went FUBAR.

Alex Tang, number cruncher, was still in the vehicle.

"You coming?" Mav called.

But Alex gave him a wave, pointed at his screen. Maverick pressed down a rush of annoyance, their last conversation—fight, really—still lingering.

The numbers don't work, Mav. We're in major trouble.

It's your job to make the numbers work, isn't it?

I'm the CFO, not a fucking magician.

Mav hesitated another second, then followed Hector and Tavo, watching the beams of their flashlights dancing around the near darkness.

When he was closer, he spun around and flipped the camera

so that it was his own face he saw, turned to put the hotel and the vista behind him. He knew that he should tell Angeline that he was going live, but instead he just pressed the button.

"Hey, guys."

He was supposed to say *folks* or *y'all*. *Guys* was misogynistic or at least neglectful of the fact that not everyone in his vast following was male. Though, most were. Most were *boys* to be honest, teenagers, young adults. But he had his passel of teen girls, too. Apparently, he even did well with the ClickClackers who skewed a little older. According to Tavo, who knew about all things web and social, the ClickClackers were hot for Mav.

The likes and comments started streaming in.

ManSplain: Mav, where are you dude?

Kittycatxxx: You're so so hot

Fairywings: I luv you mav

Glittergrrl: Marry me

Joshwuzhereyo: Douchebag

"Behind me you see the shell of what used to be Enchantments, a resort here on beautiful Falcão Island that sits in an archipelago the middle of the Atlantic."

That wasn't the actual name of the hotel. It's original name was Esperança. But Mav kept stumbling over the right pronunciation, so he changed it—against Angeline's wishes. But no one would care, right? The hotel went out of business long ago, and there was barely anything about it online. The word *Enchantments* sounded better to Mav than *Esperança*, which meant *hope*. And that had clearly died here long ago. It was depressing. *Enchantments* was optimistic, magical.

Pokemaz69: Looks like a dump

Climbergirl: Holy shit that's scary

Bloxman: What are you doing there, man?

He usually didn't read the comments, too distracting. But lately he'd been keeping his eye on them, looking out for one person in particular. Someone he kept blocking but who kept popping up under different accounts.

Maverick went on, walking backward, the hotel growing larger behind him.

"Built in the 1980s, this place was supposed to be the epitome of luxury, an isolated, hundred-acre paradise for the very wealthy with a grand ballroom, spa, stunning suites, private casitas, trails, tennis courts, three swimming pools."

He paused, panned the camera around so that his viewers could catch the whole vibe—dusk, the decrepit hotel, the isolation. He lowered his voice an octave.

"But because of outrageous debt and poor management, the inaccessibility of this tiny island, and a series of, um, *unfortunate incidents,* Enchantments went out of business in under five years. So this place has stood empty for four decades. Ravaged by time and by looters, Enchantments is a ghost of its former glory."

There were ten thousand people watching now. He watched as a flood of hearts streamed up the screen, name after name, a full rainbow of comments from praise to trash-talking. The whole mess of humanity scrolling by. It wasn't long before he saw the comment he was waiting for. This time it was *MavIsALiar* with three skull emojis. Formerly it was *MavSucks* or *FUMav.* That's how Maverick knew: those three skulls with their gray, menacing faces and holes for eyes.

MavIsALiar: Liar, liar.

He ignored it and continued.

"This is the location for my next challenge. The contestants are already on their way, and the game begins tomorrow. The winner will walk away with—wait for it—one million dollars, our biggest prize EVER."

Alex was in his head again.

Mav, we do not have a million dollars to give away. You can't promise people that.

We'll have it when the challenge is a success. Trust me, brah.

We're running on fumes.

But Mav shook off the negative vibe. He knew something that Alex didn't seem to. Money was magic. You could manifest it from the universe. If you asked it to come, it would come. And he was asking.

Pokemaz69: Holy shit.

Wildonez55: A cool million!

Byteme$$: I'm so there

Climbergirl: Where do I sign?

MavIsALiar: He never actually gives the money he raises for charity.

Truthteller09: Aren't you being investigated for fraud? Unfollow this loser.

ExtremeHottie: Ignore the haters, Mav. We know you're a good guy.

Violenceisblue: Love you, Mav.

Eleven thousand people now.

What a rush. He pressed a button on his phone, and people from all over the world tuned in to hear what he was saying. Him. A kid from New Jersey, a college dropout. He'd tried to explain that to his father. But the old man just didn't seem to get it.

What's a follower? his dad wanted to know. In his language, *follower* wasn't a good thing.

Fifteen thousand people now.

"We have some *sick* sponsors for this event," he said.

Over his phone, he saw Angeline marching toward him, tiny but mighty. A furious pixie with close-cropped jet hair and a face of hard angles: high cheekbones, arched brows, big heavily lashed dark eyes.

"What the fuck, Maverick," she mouthed, lifting her palms. She wouldn't screw up the live broadcast, though; he knew that. He gave her a grin, and she shook her head, put her hands on her hips.

"And I'll be announcing those sponsors and our players soon."

He moved in close, lowered his voice to a conspiratorial whisper.

"This place is *crazy*, you guys. The locals say it's cursed. And you know what?" He made a show of glancing around. "I think they may be right. The energy is electric, and this is the perfect place for Extreme Hide and Seek. More to come. Peace and love."

He cut the live, but not before he saw the comment from MavIsALiar:

Keep playing, Mav. But you will pay for what you've done. Where is Chloe Miranda?

"I *told you* we weren't ready to announce, Mav," said Angeline when she knew he was done. He tried to shake off that last comment from MavIsALiar, but it had hit dead center, echoing one of his dad's many wisdom sound bites: *What comes around goes around, son.*

He pushed it down deep, turned to Angeline. "Just getting people excited."

She had the flush on her cheeks that she got when she was mad, that glint to her eyes. It was hot. Really hot. It gave him a little jolt when she was angry, all her attention trained on him and whatever thing he'd just done. He loved the fire in her.

"We don't have permission from the island yet," she said. He tried to take her into his arms, but she shifted away, lithe as a cat. She was frowning, but underneath it he knew there was a smile, just a little one. "They could kick us out of here tomorrow."

She worried too much. Angeline and Alex, they were always on about what Extreme should and shouldn't do. Always worried about money and what was right.

"They won't," he said.

"How do you know that?"

He blew out a breath, held up his phone to show her the post with all its views and likes. "Because the internet has turned *us all* into publicity whores. Every single person, entity, and destination wants a piece of what we're offering. The guy from the tourism council was practically drooling."

He heard his own voice: knew he had a gift for sounding confident even when he had no idea what he was talking about. Angeline just held him in that gaze, the one that saw through all his bullshit and cared about him anyway. Or maybe it was just because he paid her a fortune. And she cared about that. Whatever. She was out of his league in every way. He'd take what he could get.

He put a hand on her shoulder, and she softened, looked up at him. There she was. She let him snake an arm around her waist, pull her close. "Chill, Ange. It will all work out. It always does."

Tavo, somewhere in the bowels of Enchantments, whooped with joy.

This place was his find. Gustavo spent time on Falcão Island growing up and had always been fascinated with the hotel. During the summers he spent with his grandparents, the condemned building was forbidden ground. Haunted, cursed, the locals said. At the very least dangerous, parents warned their children away. But, of course, the kids were always sneaking in there—exploring, later throwing raves and getting high. Gustavo was stoked to be back here, though his family had all moved away.

"This shit is off the chain, Mav! Even crazier than I remember."

The words echoed and bounced around the concrete, making Mav smile. Of all of them, Tavo was the only one who was—what? The same. Yes, the same as he had been when this all began. Wild. Always down for whatever, endlessly enthusiastic and optimistic. Alex had always been a bit of a nerd, but also a crack-up and a clown. Now all he cared about was money, how there wasn't enough, how to increase revenue and cut expenses. Hector's anxiety about their safety was reaching an annoying level. Angeline was hyperfocused on their charitable work.

Things were undeniably less fun than they had once been.

Life is not a game, son. His dad's old lecture. *Life is life.*

What did that even mean? Mav preferred the quote from his favorite grunge rocker, Beckett: *I'm gonna get my thrills before this crazy, spinning orb implodes.*

Hector's voice floated, echoing out of the darkness. "Okay, come on back up, Tavo. Did you hear that? That groaning noise? It sounds structural to me. And that's a lot of water down there."

Angeline frowned at that, opened her mouth to say more, but the rumble of an approaching vehicle caused them both to turn toward the entrance.

Overbright headlights cut through the night, moving closer.

Gustavo and Hector came up behind him, their laughter cut short as they approached. Alex, who hadn't even bothered to leave the car yet, forever bent over that goddamn laptop, emerged from the back to join them.

The five of them stood as a beat-up old Jeep rolled up within a few feet and then came to a stop, sat idling for a moment. Finally, two bulky men clad in black cargo pants and tight T-shirts climbed out, door slams echoing in the night. They were armed, grim-faced, thickly muscled.

"Damn," said Hector, with a nervous laugh. "What's all this?"

Maverick could feel Hector's anxious energy without even looking at him. Gustavo came to stand silently beside Maverick, his presence steadying, calming. His friend could always be counted on in a fight.

One of the big men opened the door for an older woman in robes, her face obscured by a headscarf. Short and wide, she seemed to glide through the darkness, followed by her tough-looking companions.

Mav felt a dump of dread in his middle. The armed men, the dark, their isolation. Bad things had happened before; they were still picking up the pieces.

The older woman pulled down her scarf, revealing a deeply lined face, haunting green eyes, a wan smile. She looked like a doll, a creepy doll that would sit on your chair during the day, come to life at night when you were sleeping.

"Angeline," she said, her accent heavy.

Angeline met her with a hand outstretched, and the old woman took it in both of hers.

During their meeting in the church in town yesterday, where they'd negotiated for permission to use the Enchantments site for the challenge, the old woman had only spoken to Angeline, seeming to dismiss Maverick and Alex altogether. Hector and Tavo didn't come to high-level meetings.

"What can we do for you tonight?" asked Angeline.

"I see you have ignored my advice," the older woman said, her eyes glancing around.

"Not at all." Angeline's voice was respectful but firm. "We're still just gathering information."

Petra nodded, but her expression showed that she didn't believe Angeline.

"Forty years ago, I stood on this very spot and spoke to a young man, told him that he was making a big mistake to build his hotel on this land. He laughed at me, called me a crazy old crone, said I was living in the past, afraid of progress."

Petra lifted a crooked finger toward the hotel. "This place. It destroyed him."

Wasn't this like a thing? Wasn't there always some old person telling you that you shouldn't or couldn't do the thing you wanted to do? Usually, it was his dad. *How long can you go on this way, just playing these stupid games?* he'd asked over pizza the night before Maverick left the country—on his *private jet.* Last year, Extreme had grossed more than his father had *ever* made in *all* his years working in construction *combined.* But that didn't seem to matter to Mav's father. Now it was this old woman, Petra Arruda, the *town elder,* whatever that meant.

"She's a spiritual leader. The people listen to her," Anton, the head of the tourism council, had told them. Everyone on the council had treated her with a kind of frightened reverence during the uncomfortable meeting where she withheld her blessing from their venture. Mav didn't get it. What actual power did she have? Apparently none. Anton had assured him that permission was forthcoming.

Now the old woman was back on her soapbox.

"Over the centuries, people like you have come here to *take.* Land, resources, people. But this island doesn't allow itself to be pillaged. The first European settlers left within a season. The trees, which have stood here since the dawn of time, refused to let themselves be cut down. The people refused to be enslaved or to sell themselves to corporations."

Insert eye-roll emoji here. What was she even *talking* about? Angeline had told him a bit about the history of the island chain, but he hadn't really listened. He wasn't much of a student, and history was like a movie you'd already watched. Boring. Over.

Gustavo was always going on about its natural beauty, the laid-back community of climbers and adventure-seekers who had made the place their home because of its affordability and the plentiful jobs catering to active tourists since it had become a destination for spelunkers, hikers, kayakers, and divers.

Petra went on, "This island *will* protect itself."

"We're not hurting anyone," said Maverick. He didn't love how his voice came up an octave, making him sound like a defensive teenager. He consciously lowered it. "We're not taking *anything*. We'll be here for a few days, a week tops. And then we'll be gone. And when we're done, *waayyy* more people will know about this island, which will be great for tourism and good for your economy. It's a win-win."

But Petra wouldn't even look at him. Even her thugs didn't seem inclined to glance in his direction. He felt invisible, voiceless as a specter. Which he hated more than anything. Oddly, he suddenly remembered standing outside the door of his parents' bedroom, peering into the dark and finding no one there. That feeling of being alone, abandoned, which used to make him cry, made him angry now. It was a tickling rage that started at the back of his throat and made him feel like he was breathing through a straw.

Then he heard Hector snigger behind him. Maverick turned to see Hector and Gustavo, who had dropped back, whispering to each other, laughing, and felt some of his tension release. Alex stood with arms folded, legs akimbo. He wasn't huge, but there was an inherent steel to him. He'd never backed down from any fight that had come up, and there had been a few. The guys. Whatever their flaws, they were more family to him than anyone related by blood, except his mom.

Petra looked to Gustavo, who stopped laughing abruptly. "A native son. You should know better than to dishonor this land."

Gustavo put a hand to this heart. "I have only love for this place," he said. But she didn't seem to hear him.

Petra was still holding Angeline's hand in both of hers. "It's too late for them. The sickness has already invaded their spirit. But it's not too late for you."

What the actual fuck? He felt the guys move in a little closer.

"We don't mean any disrespect to you or this land. Truly," said Angeline. The earnestness in her voice caused Maverick to stare at her. "Our games raise millions of dollars for charity. We've built schools and libraries around the world, helped folks rebuild after natural disasters. We've taken sick kids to Disney, helped their families pay medical bills. We have an ongoing initiative to clean plastic from the oceans. We're doing good in the world. I promise you that. These games are just a means to an end."

Angeline was good at that, making Extreme Games and Insane Challenges sound like a force for good in the world. She wasn't wrong. They did all those things and more. Well, *she* did. Would he have done as much without her influence? Probably not. When all of this started it was just about him and Gustavo having fun, showing off, getting laid all over the world. He'd just started giving money away because his publicist at the time told him it was a good way to get tons more followers. And she'd been right.

Petra just smiled at Angeline as if she was a child trying to explain why she believed in Santa Claus.

"Cleaning up the damage created by others is a noble but ultimately fruitless act. Because the destroyers simply grow bolder, less accountable for their actions. They leave others to pay the price for their depravity."

Ouch. That was harsh. He was a WeWatcher, a gamer, an influencer with millions of followers. He'd been called a man-baby, a douchebag, selfish, lazy. *Destroyer* seemed a little overly ambitious, like he was some Marvel villain looking to take over the world.

"Brah," said Hector, drawing the word out long and low in disapproval. "That's messed up."

Finally, Petra turned that kryptonite stare Maverick's way. He held his ground, stuck out his chin and his chest, but he shriveled a little inside. She saw him. All of him.

"You play your games. And people get hurt, isn't that right?"

Tension jacked up his bad shoulder. It was almost an exact echo of the letter from one of the mothers suing him. A group had banded together to ruin him: MAM for Moms Against Mav.

Maverick stayed silent.

"And what about Chloe Miranda, the girl who went missing during your last misadventure?"

"That had nothing to do with us," he said, his heart stuttering. "We have fully cooperated with police and been found not responsible."

That phrase was directly from his lawyer, the thing he was supposed to say every time questions came up. The look she gave him—it was almost pitying.

"Listen," he said. "All we want is to play the game and go."

"And all the world wants from men like you, Maverick Dillan, is just to be left alone."

A lash of anger.

"We're not leaving," he said, his voice a whip crack in the quiet. "And you can't make us. Anton told us that permission was forthcoming from the town council, and we've been given provisional access while we wait. So for the time being at least, this site belongs to me."

Another patient smile.

"*Nothing* belongs to you," Petra said quietly. She moved a little closer, and he had to fight the urge to take a step away. "A thing men like you never understand until it's too late."

She turned back to Angeline, leaned in close and whispered something in her ear. Then she turned, both the men behind her stepping aside so that she could walk between them, and they all returned to the vehicle. Once they'd climbed inside, the vehicle idled another moment. Then it spun around and roared out of the gate.

"What did she say?"

Angeline looked up at him. Usually, she was all fire, his biggest defender. But tonight, she looked tired and scared.

"She told me to save myself." She wrapped her arms around her middle, looking after the disappearing taillights.

He blew out an annoyed breath. "From *what*?"

Somewhere in the foliage a bird called, long and low. "From you."

Maverick laughed, his booming voice echoing back at him from the trees, the building. Tavo cracked up, too. Hector and Alex less so. When he looked back at Angeline, she wasn't laughing at all.

Enchantments loomed behind her, its windows like so many watching eyes.

elderly parents, she decided to channel her fear, anxiety, and rage into getting her body back.

Blake, her WeWatch fanatic, did all the setting up of her account, teaching her how to post and go live. She thought it was silly at first; she wasn't native to living her life online. But it turned out that her message of reclaiming yourself and coming back from adversity resonated. And having that virtual community of supporters, helping people who had suffered even worse fates than hers, kept her focused.

Instead of going live, she decided to record for later.

She propped up her phone, pressed Record, donned her gloves.

"This is a great way to blow off steam and burn some major calories," she told the camera. "Jab. Cross. Hook. Upper Cut. Again."

When she'd done this a few times, she looked back. "Better the bag than the person you *really* want to punch."

She threw a few more combos.

"Don't get even. Get in shape."

Then she turned off the camera and cranked her music, lost herself for a while. Tried not to think about the fact that (jab) her Visa card was nearly maxed. That (cross) her small savings account dwindled every month rather than grew. That (hook) her expenses regularly outstripped her earnings as a school counselor, a job she'd only landed because of a favor from a friend. That (upper cut) she had no idea how she was going to pay for college for Violet and then Blake without taking on even more debt. That (again) in the years since Miller left, she'd battled sometimes crippling anxiety and insecurity, even as she pretended to be strong for her kids.

Jab. Cross. Hook. Upper Cut. Again. Again. Again. Again.

"Mom."

Blake stood at the door that led from the garage to the house.

"Hey," she said, mopping the sweat from her brow, slipping off her gloves.

3

ADELE

Adele knew that Falcão Island was in the middle of the Atlantic and that its tourist season came to an abrupt stop at the end of September, but she'd still somehow expected to step out of the airport into balmy salt air. She'd envisioned blue skies and swaying palm trees.

Instead, as she moved through the automatic doors, hauling her pack, back stiff from the long flight, the sky was a moody dove gray, the air cool and damp. The airport, low, flat, and tiny, was quiet, a stark contrast to the bustling behemoth that was Newark Liberty International. Violet had dropped her off at the terminal in a honking river of other travelers, navigating the flow like the cold-blooded pro she was at pretty much everything. After hugging her daughter tight, then watching the Kia pull away, Adele spent the next couple of hours at the gate thinking she should just go home, that this was by far the most reckless thing she'd ever done.

But here she was.

The churning gray sea was only visible in the distance; she

couldn't hear it or smell it. It seemed flat and far away like an image in a postcard from a place you'd never visit. Her flight had been less than half full. Falcão Island, *falcão* Portuguese for *hawk*, population 150,000, was an emerging destination for adventure tourism, but only in the summer months. About half the local residents lived in Ponte Rico, the largest city in the island chain. Its history was storied, at least according to the internet—earthquakes, volcanic eruptions, European invasion, war. Apparently, it was home to one of Blake's gamer buddies—that's how her son had learned about the challenge. What was his name? Hugo? A spelunker, apparently, Hugo's application for the challenge had been declined. Blake had entered Hugo's contact information in her phone, saying she could call if she needed anything. Which was sweet, but what she *needed* was for the game to start, for her to win, and to get home to her kids.

Adele glanced around for the car that was supposed to pick her up, but there was no one there for her. A slender young woman with long skinny braids and stylishly torn jeans who'd been on Adele's flight stepped into the embrace of an older man, then dipped into his waiting car. A middle-aged couple wearing matching navy blue windbreakers, hauling big backpacks, hopped into the single waiting taxi. A group of four fit, young, outdoorsy types piled into a van, their voices bright, laughter loud, making Adele feel inexplicably lonely.

It had taken her a while to get her own oversize pack, stuffed with all manner of gear, from the baggage claim. Now she was the only passenger waiting for ground transportation. She didn't see another taxi or even any airport workers. Over the loudspeaker, a voice echoed. Even though she'd been studying Portuguese on Duolingo, she didn't understand a word. She zipped up her light puffer jacket against the chill.

Adele checked her phone, decided to wait a minute before she texted her contact. She didn't want to seem anxious. Finally, she lugged her heavy pack to lean it against a bench and sat, taking the opportunity to FaceTime Violet and Blake, although she knew it would only weaken her resolve for this whole enterprise.

She tapped on the app, then pressed their last call on the screen. She stared at her own image, fluffed up her wavy dark hair, pulled a smile so that she didn't look quite so tired; her dark eyes were shadowed by fatigue, skin dull. It was only a few moments before she saw her daughter's face.

"You made it," said Violet with her big, heart-melting smile. "What's it like?"

Adele looked around. Desolate. Deserted. That was the vibe. On the map, it was just a tiny green dot in a sea of blue. Twenty-five hundred kilometers from the US, fifteen hundred from Europe. The quite literal middle of nowhere and nothing. After October there were no more big commercial flights to and from the island.

"A little chilly," she said, then tried to brighten it. "Quiet. Pretty."

"Hi, Mom." Blake pushed his face next to his sister's. "Mav went live on Photogram and announced the game."

Blake was the official steward of this enterprise, keeping Adele abreast of everything he read and watched about it online.

She still couldn't believe she was here. It wasn't even two weeks since she'd tapped that link, been accepted, requested time off work, jumped through all the Extreme hoops, including a psych evaluation. Which she'd passed apparently. She'd dusted off her camping gear, bought a bunch of new equipment that she couldn't afford. Reconnected to her inner adventure-seeker, who she told herself was still in there, just dormant since she'd graduated college, married too young, and had two babies by the time she was twenty-five.

From where Adele sat on the bench, she could see a long, winding road heading off toward the horizon. As she watched, a black SUV crested the slight rise and glided toward the airport. That must be her ride. The sight of it moving toward her set her heart to racing. This was it. No turning back now.

"How are you guys?" she asked. "Miss me yet?"

She'd never left her kids before. Certainly, she'd never left them on their own. But together they'd convinced her that they could make meals, get to school, and not burn the house down. It was just a few days at the most. If she won. If she lost, she'd probably be home sooner. With nothing to show for this venture except more bills.

"We're good," said Violet. "We're *fine*. I just made breakfast. Blake's been studying *diligently* for his math test tomorrow. It's okay, Mom. You can do this. *We* can do this."

Another clench on her heart. The SUV drew closer.

Above her, the big sky swirled, black, gray, and white, with fierce patches of blue, a slight drizzle that was more like mist. Off in the distance the swell of low mountains, a rich deep green–black forest.

"Mom," said Blake, pushing his sister off the screen. "That place, the old hotel. It looks scary. Like even scarier than the other places they've done these challenges."

She and Blake were on some kind of a mom-kid loop—his anxiety could amp up her anxiety and vice versa. Violet was her own entity and always had been from the moment she was born. Violet's self-possessed newborn gaze told Adele that her daughter would be her own person, separate, distinct. When she looked into Blake's eyes, it was like she was looking into her own soul.

"*Of course* they're going to make it look as scary as possible," said Violet off-screen, ever the pragmatist. "No one would care if it looked easy."

"Mom," said Blake, leaning closer to the camera. "The other contestants—remember Wild Cody?"

How could she not remember Wild Cody? She and Blake had watched every episode of his nature show when Blake was small. But for Blake a few years was a lifetime. For Adele it was about five minutes ago that she and her kids used to curl up on the couch and watch documentaries about every place, animal, and planet in the solar system.

"He's an extreme survivalist now," Blake went on. "He's lived off the grid for like five years."

Wild Cody. Hadn't he been canceled for some messed-up thing he did on WeWatch? Didn't they call him Killer Cody now? Adele dug through the recesses of her pop-culture memory, but she couldn't access it. There was too much other life debris over the last few years for anything trivial to be stored there.

"Then there's Malinka Nicqui," Blake continued.

"O.M.G. *love* her," Violet chimed in. "Her Yes I Can clothing line is epic. A little overpriced, though."

If Adele won, she was going to get that Yes I Can hoodie (*Two hundred and fifty dollars? Seriously?*) for Violet, the one Adele knew Violet wanted but hadn't even asked for. Ads for it kept popping up on Adele's computer when she was working, just like the Ghost longboard that Blake coveted. Her kids were so good, so mature, that they didn't even hint at their material desires, knowing that they were barely making ends meet. But the internet wasn't so kind. Every time she saw one of those algorithmically generated ads, it broke her heart a little.

"She's twenty-five, and she's already climbed the Seven Summits," Blake put in. "She was the youngest woman to do that at eighteen."

"Well," said Adele, "good for her."

"Anyway, so what, *Blake*?" Violet again. "It's *hide and seek*. Not mountain-climbing."

He was trying to conceal it, but doubt had etched itself all over her son's sweet face. "They're all adventure influencers."

"Blake!" snapped Violet. "Wasn't this *your* stupid idea?"

"I'm an influencer, too," Adele said. "Remember?"

Just barely.

"Yeah," answered Blake. "Of course. But they've—done lots of stuff."

And you're—just a mom, he didn't say but was obviously thinking.

"Ha," said Adele, summoning a bravado she did not feel. "They've got nothing on a single, working mother of two. A mountain summit would be like a vacation. Extreme survival? That's just Tuesday."

Blake cracked a rare grin.

"You got this," said Violet, shoving Blake aside. "You're going to slay, Mom. There's no one tougher than you are."

"You know it," said Adele, and part of her even meant it.

"Anyway," Violet said, "I heard that Malinka's dad practically dragged her up some of those mountains. She didn't do it alone. And Wild Cody? He's like *for-real old*."

She was about to say that she thought she and Wild Cody were probably about the same age, when the SUV pulled to a stop in front of her. A lean but muscular man with long, inky curls and a stylishly stubbled jaw climbed out, offered a big wave.

"Adele?" he called. "I'm Gustavo. Sorry I'm late."

He had an easy kind of affability. And wow—he was super-hot in his tight black T-shirt, distressed hiking pants, tattered boots, like he just fell out of an REI ad. Rugged, capable, *ripped*.

"My ride's here." She turned the phone around so the kids could see.

Gustavo waved again, smiling. "Hey, that must be Violet and Blake."

"Oh, my god," she heard Blake say. "That's *Gustavo*."

She knew from Blake constantly talking about Extreme that Gustavo was the sidekick, one of the main pals in an entourage of guys who performed their crazy stunts and challenges all over the world—BASE jumping from buildings, parkour courses in abandoned prisons, mountaineering, survival challenges. Gustavo was Blake's favorite. *He'd be Mav if Mav wasn't Mav.*

"Hi, Gustavo," called Violet. Her voice was high and flirty in a way that Adele rarely heard, then she started to giggle—the same bubbling sound she'd made since she was a baby.

"Don't worry, kids," said Gustavo, cracking a heartthrob grin. "We'll take good care of your mom."

How old *was* he? she wondered. At least ten years younger than Adele, right? Not that she was interested in distractions like Gustavo. She was here for one reason only.

She turned the phone around and Violet had her eyebrows raised. "O.M.G.," she mouthed, cheeks flushed. Adele felt herself blush, too, gave Violet a wink.

"What are you guys talking about?" said Blake, annoyed at being left out.

"Nothing, shut up," said Violet, nudging him with her shoulder.

"*You* shut up. Mom, Violet's being Violet again," he said without heat.

"I'll text you when I get settled," she said, another big wave of anxiety pulsing through her.

"I'll be keeping my eye on everything," said Blake, eyes still faintly purple, pushing his new glasses up his nose. "The weather, the other contestants. I'm sending you a WholeEarthNow shot of the hotel site."

She had no idea what that was.

"You're a dork," said Violet. "He acts like he's running a command center. Like—what's he going to do from his bedroom?"

"Be good to each other," she said. "Love you."

Blake dropped an arm around his sister. Violet scowled at him.

"Love you," her kids said in unison.

They waved as the screen went blank. That feeling—when they walked into school for the first day, or slept over at a friend's house, or rode their bikes away down the street, finally one day taking off in your car—it was some mingling of pride and sadness.

She steeled herself. She was doing this for the right reasons. Her kids could handle themselves because she'd taught them how. She could handle this because she'd built herself back up from a woman deceived and abandoned by her husband into a competitor. She was no so-called adventure influencer. But there were plenty of people who had been inspired by her journey.

And that was something.

Gustavo moved over to grab her huge pack and effortlessly shouldered what took all her strength to carry. She should tell him that she could carry her own bag; after all, this was not a vacation. But he was already moving with the agility of the very athletic toward the car, and she trailed behind.

Was she going to be the only mom type on a roster of out-doorsy young hotties and off-the-grid survivalists? It didn't matter, she told herself as she climbed into the big SUV. She was a survivor. She knew that much about herself, at least.

Gustavo opened the passenger door of the Range Rover, and she climbed in, catching immediately the faint odor of cigarette smoke clinging to the upholstery. It turned her stomach a little, reminded her of Miller. It was the smallest of his lies, that he smoked. But somehow now that stale, acrid scent awoke an irrational anger. She quashed it.

"Why do you think that bothers you so much?" her therapist had asked. "Of everything he did, why do we keep returning to that?"

"Because... I had no idea. I never smelled it, never caught him out on the back deck late at night. How did he hide it so well?"

Adele's phone vibrated in her pocket, jolting her back into the moment. Before she even looked at it, a tingle of dread. When she glanced at the screen, she saw a number she didn't recognize and a message.

It's not too late. Go home. The game is dangerous, and you're not safe. Go back to your kids.

Who is this? she typed back quickly, feeling her blood pressure go up.

This was not the first time she'd received a text like this. Since she'd been accepted by Extreme, she'd received three. All from different numbers. No answer to her questioning replies. No one picking up when she tried to call back.

Adele stared at the screen another moment. Gustavo tossed her pack in the trunk and slammed it closed with a final thud.

She glanced back at the low concrete airport, the churning waters beyond. *It's not too late.*

Was someone messing with her? Maybe even a tactic by Extreme to throw her off-kilter—something for which they were supposedly famous?

Or was it a real warning? If so, from who? Since Miller's disappearance, she'd received so many nasty and threatening texts that she was actually a bit inured to it. Her number was out there. It had been on the company website. She never changed it. Because—not that she would admit it to anyone—she wanted Miller to have a way to reach her. If he had an attack of conscious, or one of those weak moments Agent Coben talked about, she wanted to talk him in. For herself, for the kids. Even, on some level, for the man she used to love.

Block. Delete. Fuck off.

She stowed the phone, took a breath. She wasn't going to let anyone get inside her head.

Climbing in beside her, Gustavo grabbed his own phone and stared at it a moment, shook his head just slightly, then pocketed it. He sat a moment, frowning ahead.

"Everything okay?" she asked.

He seemed to snap from his thoughts, then gave her a warm smile. "Just life, right? It's a puzzle sometimes, isn't it?"

She blew out a breath, gave one last look at the airport. *Wait,* she almost said. *I'm going home.* "That's for sure."

Gustavo started the car, and the big vehicle roared away from the airport, winding up that long road.

"Mind if I do a quick live?" she asked.

"Be my guest. That's what it's all about, right? Views, views, views."

Was there an edge to his tone? She decided to ignore it if there was.

She took out her phone and held it up so that she could see her face in the camera. Not bad, some lines debuting around her eyes, a little fatigued, hair a bit frizzy, but she never fussed over herself much, wore too much makeup, or filtered her image. *What you see is what you get.* It was one of her big messages. *Beauty is not about perfection, it's about being unapologetically yourself.*

She was new to this, but she was getting the hang of it. She pressed the button.

"Hey, friends, I'm finally here—on stunning Falcão Island."

She turned the camera to Gustavo who dutifully smiled and waved.

"This is Gustavo from Extreme. He's picked me up from the airport, and we're headed to the site. I'm tired and a little nervous but super excited."

Hearts and thumbs-up flooded the screen. The comments started rolling in a stream of *You got this!* and *You go, girl!* and *Slay, queen!*

"Look at this place," she said, turning the camera.

The screen filled with the fecund green of the trees, the riot of color from the wild hydrangeas, the swirling white, gray, black of the sky. It looked like an oil painting.

"Isn't it gorgeous?"

It *was* gorgeous, in a kind of moody, feral way. She felt something shift inside her, the way she always did when she was in nature. It was like her body remembered that this was where she belonged. That everything else was just the theater the world had created.

She changed the camera back to capture her face.

"Wish me luck, guys. I'm as prepared as I can be. And I'm going to do my best. I hear that the competition is fierce. But you know what we do when the trail ahead is rough and unpredictable? Take one step at a time."

Phoenix**: You can do this.

PowerBarb: There's no one tougher than you.

JenJenxoxo: I'm cheering for you, my friend.

VioletsInBloom: Love you, Mom!

She smiled at the camera and clicked off.

Silence again.

Ahead was a swath of deep green, the rise of the low mountains, that strange sky, which seemed equally about to open into
rain or wash into a sunny blue. A light, misty rain fell and the
windshield wipers pumped as the road wound out of town and
twisted dramatically up a rise, the airport disappearing in the
rearview mirror. Another riot of hydrangeas bloomed along the
roadside. Falcão Island was always temperate, she'd read. Never
hot, never cold. The famous hydrangeas bloomed most auda-
ciously in spring and summer, a fragrant watercolor, but could
be seen all year.

The light suddenly faded from the sky; she looked out the
window to see big thunderheads up ahead.

"Weather looks like it's about to turn."

He laughed a little.

"Here we say if you don't like the weather, wait five minutes. It's dramatic, changeable. Even if the skies open, in an hour
you'll have sun again. If it's sunny, you might find yourself surprised by sudden rain."

"Like life," she said.

He cast her a look she couldn't read, finally nodded.

"Are you from here?" she asked.

"I had family here, spent summers on Falcão Island as a kid.
It feels like home in some ways."

Gustavo had a serious aura, but it was lightened by an air of benevolent mischief, like the boys she found most frequently in her office at school. Not the troubled ones, the ones she worried about, but the wild ones. The boys for whom the structure and schedule of school was a kind of torture. They weren't bad as much as they were out of place, needed to be ranging through the woods somewhere instead of being chained to a desk. Gustavo seemed like someone who might get into trouble but talk his way out of it. Then get in trouble for something else.

"My son has a friend here, someone he met on *Red World.*"

Gustavo nodded. "There's a trend of people from other countries settling here. There are good jobs for hiking, climbing, and canyoneering guides, surfing teachers, hospitality, too. It's cheap to live, beautiful. But isolated. The island can close in on you sometimes."

In the distance, she saw the town on the coast, Ponte Rico. It was bigger than she'd imagined, looked bustling and clean. But then it disappeared behind a swath of deep green.

As they kept driving, she glanced at her phone a couple times to see if there was another text. But no. She breathed, forced herself out of her head and into her body.

"Tell me about a time you were under pressure and how you handled it," the very young, bespectacled Dr. Garvey had prompted during the Zoom psych evaluation she'd done to qualify for the competition.

"How often would you say you lose your temper? Do you ever feel like you're out of control?

"Have you experienced clinical depression, or any other kind of mental illness?

"Would you say you are an introvert or extrovert?"

She'd answered all his questions as truthfully as she could. She remembered how her heart thumped during that session, though Dr. Garvey had been kind and nonjudgmental.

As a result of those sessions, an extensive questionnaire, no doubt an exhaustive internet search, a background check, and the essay Violet and Blake had helped her write, Maverick and his Extreme team probably knew more about her than anyone else did, including her children.

They had all the tools necessary to mess with her—if that was part of the game. Texting from burner phones, telling her to go back to her kids. That would be easy.

"There it is," said Gustavo, pointing ahead.

She leaned forward and saw it. A giant concrete structure thrust itself out of the fecundity around it. A man-made thing, all hard angles and gray surfaces, unwelcome to the eye in the natural beauty of its surroundings. Even from this distance she could see that the windows were hollow of glass, that parts of it were crumbling.

"Enchantments," she said.

It was not in the least enchanting. It looked like a prison, or something from one of the ruined civilizations in the dystopian novels that Violet favored.

"That's what Mav has been calling it," said Gustavo with a tight smile. "But the original name in Portuguese was Esperança, really."

She knew enough Portuguese to get the irony.

"Hope," she said. "It means *hope*."

Gustavo nodded, and he looked up as well to the looming structure. It seemed to stare back at them. Then as they grew closer, it vanished from view.

He took a sharp turn off the road, and they were plunged into the blackness of the thick tree cover overhead. The road grew rougher. Adele jostled in her seat, grabbed for the handle above the window.

Gustavo flipped on the headlights, the beams carving through the darkness. Around the next bend, there was something in the road. Something big.

He brought the Rover to an abrupt stop. "What *is* that?" he said.

It was a huge pulsating mass in the dim light. Adele couldn't make it out right away. Gustavo climbed out of the vehicle, grabbing his phone. But he didn't approach the thing, staying behind the open car door, pointing the phone camera lens at the road.

Adele leaned closer to the windshield, and the form took shape.

It was an enormous bird of prey, its ferruginous wings extended, flapping, its end feathers wide and tilting up like the spread fingers of a hand. In its yellow beak it held some kind of small mammal, hanging limp, dead.

The bird dropped the carcass to the road and proceeded to tear it apart. Adele found that she couldn't look away as the bird used its razor-sharp beak to rip away pieces of flesh. There was no frenzy to the eating, the predator's cool yellow eyes glowing, glancing at them occasionally.

Her stomach turned as the bird tore into the bloody flesh.

That's the way of it, she used to tell the kids during nature shows, even though she too cringed as the lion took the gazelle or the shark ate the seal. *If the predator doesn't catch his prey, he dies.*

Another bird, lighter in color but greater in size, swooped in, and a terrible, shrieking dance occurred as both animals spread their flapping wings, screeching until finally the first bird flew away, the echo of its cries carrying angrily on the night air. The other bird snatched up the prey in its talons, then it, too, flew away.

Adele leaned forward to watch it disappear into the trees.

Gustavo climbed back into the driver's seat. "Buzzards. A male and a female. Looks like she won that fight."

"She probably has some babies to feed," said Adele, watching it disappear into the sky.

"The female is usually the strongest," said Gustavo. "In any species. Buzzards are the islands' only natural predator." She didn't interrupt him, though she already knew something about the birds. "They're not vultures, which are commonly called buzzards in the US, but hawklike birds in the kite family often

confused with goshawks. In fact, *Falcão* Island is a bit of a mis-
nomer. The early settlers probably mistook the birds for hawks.
The symbol of the goshawk figures prominently in the island
heraldry in spite of the mistake."

She'd read that buzzards were seen in some cultures as a symbol of transformation and change, the ability to release the old
and embrace the new.

In others, a harbinger of destruction.

She felt a chill move through her as the light grew dimmer,
and Gustavo started driving again.

They came to a stop at the grand entrance, the rusting gate
swung wide.

A towering, graffiti-covered sign greeted them.

PERIGO! it read in bold, black type, though someone had
turned the *O* into a comical frowning face. *Na Entre*, it went
on. And then for good measure, a translation: *DANGER! Do
Not Enter!* An enormous black hand was encircled by a red pro-
hibited symbol, a circle with a slash through it.

"They don't mean us, right?" said Gustavo with a mischievous grin.

Adele snapped a picture and watched the sign disappear behind them on the twisting road to Enchantments.

4

~~~~~~

MALINKA — Live on WeWatch

The Game

The camera is focused on a winding path through dense forest, the foliage cast in a bouncing light. Labored breathing is ragged and uneven, drowning out the sound of running footfalls.

A voice beyond the scope of the lens. "Will you look at this place?? Oh, my god, you guys! It's unreal."

The camera sweeps, and Enchantments is a light-swallowing shadow in the semidarkness. Rain has started to fall, and the waxy plants and towering trees sheen, glittering an eerie viridescent black. The footfalls come to a stop, and the camera pans around again.

A young woman's face with delicate, pale features, a smattering of freckles across a button nose, with shining, thickly lashed eyes, fills the screen. Her gaze darts, looking around off camera. Her breathing slows, raindrops dot the camera lens. She releases a sigh, gazes intensely at the lens now.

"Hello, my friends," she says, her eastern European accent heavy. "Most of you know me. But for those of you who don't, I'm Malinka Nicqui, the first woman to climb all Seven Summits by the age of eighteen, and the founder of the Yes I Can clothing company. And I'm here

on Falcão Island, participating in a game of hide and seek sponsored by Extreme Games and Insane Challenges."

Malinka's eyes drift off camera, then come back. She's breathless, flushed.

"The countdown has just begun, and the other hiders have scattered, looking for their spots. The game is officially on."

She leans in closer, lowers her voice to a conspiratorial whisper.

"For those of you who have been watching as I've broadcast live over the last couple of days, you know that shit has gotten truly weird here on the island," she says. "Someone is missing. And I don't think we're alone on this site. I think someone is…trying to hurt us. Like this is getting real."

Malinka's eyes are wide now.

"And this storm."

A loud clap of thunder punctuates her point. The rain comes down harder.

She seems to steel herself, puts a hand to her forehead. "But I'm here, and you guys know I don't give up. So—come with me while I find my hiding place."

The camera turns back to the path ahead.

"We can hide anywhere on the property," she says, off camera now. "Not just in the hotel. So, I've already done my research, and I have a few ideas."

The sound of jogging footfalls continues, the path bouncing.

"During my recon, I found the perfect place. I'm going to cover the camera for a moment. Maverick and the Extreme team are not supposed to be watching our feeds. But you never know who is and who isn't playing by the rules."

The camera goes dark. When she uncovers it again, Malinka is moving through a creaking door. Inside, the space is trashed, debris on the floor, furniture toppled, graffiti on the walls. The room is cast in a ghostly white as Malinka shines her light around the deserted structure.

"In here," she says softly, panning the recording. "I'm glad you guys are here with me. I couldn't do this alone."

She walks slowly into a small room and closes the door behind her, turns the camera back to her face.

"I shouldn't have come here. I see that now," she says, taking a shuddering breath, "now that it's too late. Maybe I always knew it, though."

She sinks against the wall, comes to a crouch.

"My dad used to say that certain places on the planet don't want you. The depths of the ocean will crush you. The tops of mountains will steal the oxygen from your blood, make you so ill that you'll wish for death. And I can promise you that's true. You feel it. How nature tells you in no uncertain terms that you don't belong, that you're selfish and arrogant to even try to push the limits."

She shivers. There's a loud crash of thunder. Rain drums on the roof, creating an ambient hiss.

"But that never stopped my father. There was no place that he felt was sacred or off-limits. Even as he lay dying, he was ready to forge into that final, forbidden place. I swear his eyes were gleaming."

She shakes her head, her own eyes glassy, remembering, then looks back at the camera.

"Maybe that's why I came here. Not for the money. Not for the views. Not for the game. But because I knew that it was another one of those places. Guys, this is how Chloe Miranda disappeared. She hid and was never found. Not here, but during a challenge just like this. What was supposed to be a game became real for her."

A loud crash startles Malinka, her blue eyes going even wider.

"The storm is raging, guys." A tear trails from her eye. "I don't know if I'm going to make it through the night."

Another sound outside the closed door. Malinka puts her hand to her mouth, her breathing coming in sighs.

"Oh, my god. What was that?"

The camera feed goes dark.

Wingedkitty: Malinka, you hot grrl

Mel333: You're my hero

Buttons&bows: You changed my life

Ellalove99: I paid $285 for that hoodie and it's fraying at the seams like some cheap p-o-s. Your clothes are a rip-off. And you're a poser.

Minecraftguru: You go, grrl. U gonna win this

MavIsALiar: Yes I Can is being investigated for fraud

MavIsALiar: Extreme too

Badmonkey21: You're all liars and losers

Hellokitten444: Love you, Malinka

YesICanFan: Tell us about your new line of lingerie.

Climb3rB0y: I heard her dad like dragged her up Everest literally had to tie her to his pack to get her to the summit.

7SummitGrrl: For real, dude. I was there. She barely survived it.

Angelwings: Omg your hair. So gorge.

Buttons&bows: Malinka! You okay, grrl???

5

~~~~~~

ADELE

Night was falling. Enchantments, just up the drive from the campsite, was a presence, something looming on the edge of Adele's consciousness.

"Are you sure that you don't want to spend your first night at the off-site hotel?" Gustavo asked, having helped her get settled and heading toward the waiting SUV.

"No," she said, though the idea of a real bed after the long flight was tempting. "I think I'm good."

She glanced over at her tent. She'd spared no expense on most of her gear, running up her already blisteringly high credit-card balance, knowing that it might mean the difference between winning and losing. After careful research, she'd decided on the CloudDome 6 for its sturdy build, weather protection, and reflective detailing to help you see in the dark.

She'd posted about it and immediately got an offer in her DMs from the company for sponsorship that nearly covered the cost of the tent, which was nice. Now, all set up and glowing orange from the interior light she'd turned on, she took a photo for her socials, filtering it so the greens and oranges in the image popped.

Ready for my first night on Falcão Island. The CloudDome 6 was supereasy to set up and is very comfortable inside. Highly recommend!

Was that stupid? Too prosaic? Should she try to be funny or cool? Whatever. She clicked to post.

The air felt fresh and clean, filled her lungs. Adele *wanted* the night on the site, to get the lay of the land, and to remember what it felt like to be outside again. Really outside. It had been years since she'd slept in a tent.

Her parents had taught her to climb, to camp, to live for days in nature with just what you'd brought and what you caught or foraged.

We're supposed to live like this, her father used to say. He'd open his chest and his arms to the sky. *This is home.*

They'd traveled the country, Adele and her sister, in the back of their beat-up old minivan, Dad singing along to the radio, Mom reading in the front seat. She still loved that feeling of sleeping under a blanket of stars, home being wherever you pitched your tent that night.

"I never sleep indoors when I can be out," Malinka said, coming up beside her.

Adele had liked the girl at first sight; there was something, an instant connection. Bright, fresh-faced, able, she'd greeted Adele with a big hug, immediately chipped in to help Adele get settled. Malinka's own tent was one Adele had seen online and knew that it cost well over a thousand dollars; she'd already strung some fairy lights around the entrance. Very *photogrammable*.

"Are you sure?" Gustavo asked again. His eyes, trained on Adele, seemed to hold some kind of deeper invitation. But maybe he was just that kind of guy, the kind who knew how to look at a woman, make her feel seen. "The hotel is nice—big showers, hot tub, the whole thing. The next few days are going to be rough."

"I'm sure it's lovely," said Adele, with a nod. She looked around at the trees and up to the stars. "But this is why I came."

"Me, too," said Malinka, her Polish accent heavy, pleasantly lilting. She gave Adele a wide smile. "Girl power, right? We got this."

Adele nodded her agreement, even though she was not a *girl*, far from it. Nor was she a fan of the phrase *We got this*. Something about it almost sounded like a taunt. Like a dare to the universe. *Here comes that hard fastball like a cannon-shot, grrl! Don't fumble.*

Still, she shared a high five with her new friend.

Adele would have to remind herself that Malinka—not a girl, either, but a woman and world-class athlete—was the competition. They'd both come here for the money, not to make friends. It was Adele's fatal flaw to open her heart too wide, to not see the truth that was right in front of her. She promised herself that this time she'd be tough, a competitor. Cold, even, if she had to be.

"Okay," said Gustavo, clapping his hands together, the sound echoing. He went to the Range Rover and pulled out a pack, held it up. "All provisions from our sponsors. If you have a chance to post about any of it, that would be great. Vege Fuel Protein Bars, Atomic Turkey Jerky, Nut Case Dried Cashews and Fruit, Quench Energy Drink.

"And here are two big canteens of water," he added with a smile. "Sponsor mother earth. No need to post."

Adele took the pack; Malinka held on to the water.

"Have a good night, and we'll see you bright and early."

Then he was in the SUV, disappearing down the drive.

Was there a shadow of something on Malinka's face when Gustavo drove off, leaving them and taking all the light and noise with him? Adele knew that she felt a tingle of self-doubt. More than a tingle.

Though the signal was strong on her phone, she felt again, profoundly, how she was an ocean away from her kids, camping for the first time in nearly twenty years.

Fearless. That's what Adele's mother had always called her. Sometimes she said it in admiration, sometimes in anger. Either way, Adele had always worn it like a badge. She remembered it whenever she was feeling anything but, and it made her stronger. Like now.

You're fearless, she told herself, felt a calm settle.

The truth was that Adele hadn't been any such thing since she was her parents' child, living in their care, cabled to them for safety literally and figuratively. And if she'd been so then, it was only because she didn't know how hard, how unforgiving, how deadly the fall could be.

"Let's get the fire going," said Malinka, voice bright.

"Great idea."

Together, they had it roaring in no time.

They both took a seat on the ground and dug into the pack of provisions. They ate some jerky and looked up at the sky, stars obscured by the thick cloud cover. In the middle of the Atlantic Adele had imagined a wild light show, but no, just a heavy black ceiling of night.

Their conversation, light and easy, ranged from injuries incurred during Tough Be-atch competitions, to the loss of their fathers, their love of the outdoors, favorite equipment, Malinka's little brother, Adele's kids.

After a while, Adele noticed that the charge was dwindling on her phone. And was dismayed to find that even her power bank was running low.

"Oh," said Malinka when Adele mentioned it. "Come with me."

The inside of Malinka's tent was strung with lights, everything color coordinated, a stack of books and journals by her puffy sleeping bag, even a little jute rug. It looked more like a stylish teen bedroom than a tent. In Adele's own tent, there was barely enough room for her pack and her sleeping bag.

Malinka kneeled down to one of the hard cases over in the corner and opened the lid. It was filled with tech gear—lights, chargers, adapters, camera and lenses, a variety of wires.

"Here," she'd said, handing Adele a large white rectangle of plastic with multiple ports. "This one is solar-powered and still has some juice. Use it to charge your phone and power bank, then put it in the sun tomorrow."

"Thank you so much," Adele said, a little embarrassed by Malinka's generosity and by her own gear failure. "I'll give it back to you tomorrow."

Malinka waved her off. "Keep it. I have like three."

Adele's eyes fell on a photograph lying on top of the pile of books. Malinka cheek to cheek with a sweet-faced, dark-haired girl who looked vaguely familiar to Adele. She tried to place the face but couldn't. Malinka noticed her looking and quickly slid the photograph underneath the leather cover of the journal.

Adele was about to apologize for her inadvertently prying eyes, but she was interrupted by a strange sound, long and low off in the distance. Not an animal. Almost mechanical, it was something she hadn't heard before, impossible to identify.

"What's that?" asked Adele, listening for it again.

Malinka looked up at her, slipping the journal beneath her other books. "That's Esperança—Enchantments. It's groaning. Some say it won't be standing in another year."

Adele had read that the structure had been condemned, hence the giant sign warning visitors away. It was slated for demolition, but the project just kept getting put off for various reason of politics and funds. Extreme had assured contestants that it had been tested and found perfectly safe for the time being.

"I've heard it a couple of times now," Malinka said. She rose easily from her squat and shouldered her pack.

"Ready for the tour?" she asked, giving Adele a friendly shoulder nudge. "I've already been through. Let me show you."

It was exactly what she'd planned to do tonight. She was happy enough not to have to do it alone.

"I'll get my gear."

The towering entrance to Enchantments was a gaping mouth breathing a fetid odor of decay. Water wept from the ceiling, streaming down the walls, pooling on the floor. Tendrils of foliage snaked in through the windows and cracks in the walls, hung like corpses from the exposed landings.

"What do you think?" asked Malinka, coming up beside her. "Pretty crazy, right?"

The wind howled and moaned, traveling through hallways and stairwells, swirling down elevator shafts. Adele didn't believe in ghosts, but if a place could be haunted, this would be it.

It was precisely the kind of situation she'd warn her kids to stay away from, but there she was, stepping into Enchantments with Malinka. She scampered over a fallen beam in her path, looking up to see where it had come from. The ceiling, high above, was riven with holes, the sky visible.

A high chain-link fence obviously erected to keep people out had been cut down the center and rolled back to either side. Another huge sign reading *Keep Out* in three languages had been cast to the side and was covered in spray paint and grime. They moved past the jagged remains of the fence, careful of the sharp edges.

Excitement was an electric current through Adele's nerves, dread a drumbeat. When was the last time she'd felt so *alive*? Not lying in bed worrying about how she was going to take care of her kids; not sitting in a car line or in her windowless office trying to help students who often didn't seem to want help or to even be paying attention; not struggling to complete her online degree so that she could keep the job that she wasn't *quite qualified* to do when contracts were reviewed and re-upped at the end of the year.

Here in this wild place, a dormant part of herself was stirring from slumber.

If she closed her eyes, she could imagine the grand past of Enchantments: luxury cars purring in the circular drive, wealthy guests entering, doors held wide-open for them. The glittering chandeliers, the lobby music, the pop of champagne corks.

Once a glittering, hidden destination for the very rich, now a ruin. Mysterious. Dramatic.

"Look at this," said Malinka. She had a powerful light on her pack, and she shined it around the space. "Over here."

They stood now at the empty elevator shaft where Adele saw a deep crack in the concrete.

"There are others," Malinka went on. "There. And there."

Her light fell on more wide fissures, rising from the floor, traveling up the walls.

"That can't be good," said Adele. "How long do you think before it collapses?"

Malinka shrugged, tracing one with her finger. The walls were covered with graffiti: names and dates, declarations of love, defiance, anger, warnings, cartoons, illegible scribbles. On the back wall of the empty elevator shaft, someone had spray painted *Free Candy* with an arrow pointing down. Creepy but funny. Adele snapped a picture for Blake, who would definitely find it hilarious.

"Hopefully not in the next couple of days?" said Malinka, offering Adele a confident wink. The very young. They didn't know how unstable the world could be. How very unforgiving the consequences of missteps. Adele envied her, not a little.

You'll die here, someone had written in red scrawl.

Surely the people at Extreme had been telling the truth when they claimed to have inspected the site and found it safe enough for their challenge. Right?

Adele flipped on her own pack light. The winding concrete staircase leading upstairs seemed solid enough if slippery with mold and wet earth. Were those footprints? Yes, large boot tracks leading up the stairs. Probably the Extreme team had been all over this place, and Malinka said she'd already been through. Adele headed up.

She'd had a few moments to check out the satellite views of the property that Blake had sent of the site from WholeEarthNow.

Probably the hotel itself is not the best place to hide. Too predictable, and Extreme has likely scoped out every inch of that place, he'd advised via text. **If it was me, I'd go for one of the casitas.**

Adele had seen on the images how paths from the hotel led past the pool to a smattering of small houses in the woods. Inside the hotel now, she knew that Blake was right. Things were too wide-open here, many of the hallways exposed to the grand lobby, sounds carrying.

Still, she'd check it out. She climbed carefully up.

At the landing, a long hallway unspooled into darkness.

"Have you been up this way?" she asked. But Malinka, who she could have sworn was right behind her, was gone.

"Malinka?" Adele's voice bounced off the concrete walls.

No answer. Some distant sound carried on the air, but Adele couldn't make it out. She couldn't worry about Malinka, who seemed as intrepid and courageous as Adele wished she still was.

It was nice to have company, but truthfully, she should do the recon on her own. After all, when it came down to it, she'd only have herself to rely on.

She pointed her light ahead.

Doors punctuated the hallway that seemed to have no end.

She pushed into the first one, heaving it against the heavy draft coming from the open glassless window frame. As she walked through the abandoned guest room, she found it stripped bare—all fixtures, furniture, and decor gone, a grim concrete shell like a jail cell. Graffiti on every surface, water dripping from the ceiling.

She stepped through the room onto the balcony and looked out.

The sky was a dramatic black. The volcanic lake below glittered like it had been scattered with jewels, ringed with deep black-and-green foliage. She took out her phone and snapped a photo, but the image didn't capture the wild, breathless beauty around her, its dimension and movement lost on the screen.

Why, even now, did she think of Miller when something moved her? He'd abandoned them, ruined all their lives, and yet she still wanted to share everything with him. Wanted to hear his thoughts, his laughter. *Isn't this amazing?* she wanted to tell him. *Look at where I am.*

If she was better at WeWatch, she'd be using this moment to go live. But she didn't. She just wanted to be present.

Somewhere a structural groan. Then, maybe, the sound of a voice carried on the wind. Adele pulled herself away from the view, moved back out into the hall.

"Malinka?"

There. Something moved. A bulky shadow.

Her eyes grappled with the changing light. What *was* that?

Then, at the end of the hall, a thick, dark form seemed to spill from the black, moving fast. Toward her? Away? She couldn't tell.

"Hey," she yelled, alarmed. "Hey!"

Then it disappeared through one of the doorways.

Fear like the strum of a guitar string vibrated on her nerve endings.

"Who's there?" Her voice wobbled, betraying her.

No answer.

She flashed her light around, scattering the night. Behind her, nothing, just the ambient glow from the stairway, ghostly and gray.

She should leave. *Walk away from danger,* she always told the kids, *not toward it.*

But she kept moving. The hallway felt like a nightmare tunnel, growing longer and longer. A perpetual moan of air moved through cracks and openings in the structure, kicking up dust and debris, snapping at the legs of her cargo pants, tossing the free strands of her hair.

No door on room 704. Empty but for that view again. Her breath was ragged, throat dry.

"Hello?" Some joke maybe. She'd seen enough of these on WeWatch to know how they would manufacture scares for the camera. Malinka would suddenly jump from one of the doorways and scare Adele for her followers.

But no. The girl with her still features, her serious bearing, didn't seem like a prankster.

Room 706 was also empty. She kept moving.

The door to 708 stood slightly ajar.

"What scares you the most?" Another question from Dr. Garvey. "And how do you deal with that fear?"

"Not being able to take care of or protect my kids. I just keep working at it. One day at a time."

"What else?"

"Secrets and lies. People who pretend to be one thing and are really another."

"Those are all existential. What else? What about heights or enclosed spaces?"

She'd thought about it. Violet was terrified of snakes: anything that *looked* like a snake—a hose in the backyard, a stick on a hiking trail—could make her scream. Blake couldn't handle bugs, even ants had him running in circles batting at himself. But Adele? There was nothing, not really. Not having good health insurance…that was scarier than most things she could conjure.

"Well, when I was a kid, I used to be afraid of the dark. But aren't all kids afraid of the dark?"

Her light flickered, came back to life, then flickered again. Of course. Because unlike with her tent, she'd cut costs and purchased the one that cost nineteen dollars instead of the one that cost a hundred and thirty-nine. She knocked it on her palm, and it came back to full brightness.

"The dark in the closet. The dark under the bed. The dark behind a closed door. Where things hide," she had replied to Dr. Garvey.

At the door, she paused, realized she was holding her breath.

"And how do you handle your fear?" said the doctor.

"Malinka?" she said again.

"Head-on," had been her reply.

She pushed the door open fast, slamming it hard against the wall. The sound echoed, reverberating down the hall.

Nothing. No one.

But this room had a ratty mattress on the floor, was littered with trash and debris, a tattered sneaker, a fallen chunk of plaster, a pizza box rotted and covered with mold, a crushed, faded condom box, a cracked purple bong. She thought of those boot prints, who they might belong to.

What had she seen? Was someone hiding in one of these rooms?

She kept moving toward the double doors at the end of the hallway. They seemed to breathe, opening and closing just slightly. Shining her light, she pushed inside.

Her pack light flickered and went out.

The sudden loss of brightness left her blind.

Her eyes slowly adjusted, forms taking shape. Then a shadow loomed from the black, moving fast toward her, heavy footfalls echoing. She lifted her arms as she was knocked back. Slamming hard against the wall, her head smacked on the cement. Then, stumbling, she lost her footing and went down onto concrete as the form ran past her, disappearing, footfalls still echoing off every surface, heavy on the stairs.

"Hey," she yelled, struggling to her feet.

She gave chase, tripping again, then getting up. By the time she reached the stairs, Malinka was coming up.

"Did you see that?" Malinka asked, breathless, eyes wide. "Who was it?"

"I don't know," Adele managed, still reeling.

"He knocked me down," said Malinka. She rubbed her arm. "But he's gone now. He ran out the back."

Adele put a hand to her forehead, brought back fingers bright with blood. Her heart pumped in overdrive, adrenaline making her shake.

"Oh, God," said Malinka. "You're bleeding."

Malinka sifted through her pack, came out with a white cloth, which Adele held to her head. Adele leaned against the wall, breathing still shallow.

"Where did he come from?" Malinka asked, peering into the darkness.

"Down that way," Adele answered.

After taking a moment to catch their breath, they walked back down the hall, Adele looking over her shoulder in the direction the shadow had disappeared. "In here."

Adele's light decided to come back on, dimmer than before. *Note to self: never get the cheap stuff.*

Inside what must have been the biggest suite in the hotel was a tatty old tent. Shining their lights, they saw that someone had boarded up the windows. There was a small camping stove in the corner, a pile of magazines, what looked like a tangle of old rags.

Malinka carefully pushed back the tent flap to reveal a cot, a camping light, a faded sleeping bag.

"Someone has been living here," she said.

She lifted up a pack of cigarettes, a lighter. A paperback, *Walden* by Thoreau. She let the things drop back on the cot.

Adele stared, her stomach clenching. The cigarettes—Marlboro— Miller's brand. Or so she came to discover after he'd gone when she found a carton in his desk. *Walden.* His favorite book, which she knew well because he was always quoting it. *To stand at the meeting of two eternities, the past and future, which is precisely the present moment,* he'd say.

She wondered how he justified the things he'd done against the principals he'd supposedly held dear.

"What's your greatest disappointment?" Dr. Garvey had asked.

She didn't have to think about that for very long. "My husband. My ex-husband."

Coincidence, of course. The book, the cigarettes. Or just the universe fucking with her as usual.

"Are you okay?" asked Malinka, coming in close and putting a gentle hand on Adele's arm. Her skin was dewy with youth, eyes bright.

"Yeah," Adele said, forcing a smile. "Just spooked."

Malinka inspected her cut with tenderness. "The bleeding stopped. It's not too bad."

Adele gave another look inside the tent, shone her light around the space, but there was little else to see. Just a collection of empty booze bottles in the corner. "Some squatter, probably."

Who would live here? Why? Someone on the run. Someone with no place else to go. She was still quaking slightly, felt chilled.

Not a ghost. Not someone with nefarious intent. Not… *Miller.*

Right? Her thoughts went back to her last conversation with Agent Coben. *Even people in witness protection, whose lives depend on staying hidden, can't always stay away forever.*

Adele felt her heartbeat in her throat.

"Whoever it is, we scared him off," said Malinka, maybe reading Adele's worry. "He won't come back."

The young woman sounded so certain. But how could she know that?

"There's more to see. Are you up for it?"

"Yeah," Adele answered. "Of course."

Malinka exited through the double doors, and Adele gave the room another pass, her light falling again on the crumpled pack of cigarettes, the tattered paperback.

"What else scares you?" Dr. Garvey had wanted to know.

"That he wins."

"Who?"

"Miller. That he never comes back, that he gets away with it. That my children and I spend our lives wondering what happened to him."

What she didn't say was that she was equally afraid of what she would do if she *did* see him again. There was animalistic rage that lived inside her, that had fueled her survival. She kept it caged. Who would she be and what was she capable of if it got loose?

Finally, she followed Malinka out the door.

Later, Adele drifted off to a fitful sleep. In her hypnagogic state, she was chased by the dark form through endless hallways, only to come upon Miller lounging on the cot, smoking.

"You don't belong here, Adele," he said with his familiar disapproving frown. "You know that."

Then Malinka leaped out at her, and she was startled awake.

Adele shrunk into her sleeping bag. Who was that shadow? Where was he now?

Off in the distance, she heard the sound of Malinka's voice, bright and talking fast. Then a long low groan from the hotel.

Esperança—that's what Gustavo had called the hotel.

Hope. It was a tricky thing, powerful enough to lure you across an ocean, and so easy to lose.

6

ANGELINE

Milky light diffused into the dim of the room; she stared at the white of ceiling where a faint crack looked like a bird. Dawn. Angeline loved the moment *before*. The pristine, quiet edge between what was planned and what would be.

The permits, as Anton had promised, had come in late last night. The generator and the trailer, both of which had been a bitch and a fortune to acquire, were fueled and ready. She glanced at the faint green glow of the clock. Gustavo should be on his way to the airport soon to pick up the last two contestants.

She took a deep breath, released it.

The game would start today as planned. In spite of her many misgivings.

"Wild Cody? Are you fucking kidding me, Mav?" she'd railed yesterday, her voice too shrill, anger and disbelief getting the better of her.

"What?" His eyes had widened with innocent surprise, a look he had perfected. "He's cool. I looovved him when I was a kid."

Mav had leaned back in the big chair, legs spread, arms winged behind his head like a cobra, the very posture of arrogance. There was no way he didn't know how messed up this was, right? She stared at him.

"Do you know how huge this will be?" he'd asked. "People will tune in *just* to see him."

She'd tried for that patient voice she sometimes had to use with him. Outside a light rain had been falling from the too-blue sky, the tall grass of the field swaying in the wind that seemed to be picking up. There was a storm coming, according to Gustavo and Hector, a big one. But Mav didn't seem worried about it.

"Wild Cody was *canceled*," she'd said, heat coming up her throat. "For killing *a lion*. At one of those fucked-up big-game hunting properties."

Maverick blew out an annoyed breath in response. "That was bullshit. Total CGI fake news."

She'd wondered, not for the first time, Was he really this clueless?

"It doesn't matter whether he *did it* or *not*, Mav. People *think* he did."

Maverick leaned forward, face earnest, fatigue purpling his eyes. "He's like the original conservationist and survivalist. He was doing that shit before anyone else, before WeWatch. Like he was *really* doing it, not just for the cameras."

Mav tapped something out on his phone and held it up for Angeline. It was Wild Cody's *Times* redemption piece. *Wild Cody Goes Back to Nature: After addiction and rock-bottom, the adventurer turned climate-change activist returns to the deep love of the planet he's held since childhood.*

"*And* he's like an environmental activist now."

There was a big color picture of Wild Cody, his long blond-gray hair pulled back. He looked different than she remembered him. Once he was a kid's-show character. Now he was chiseled, eyes serious and thoughtful, jaw stubbled. Was he actually…hot? How old was he even? Had to be ancient—like in his fifties.

She could tell, just by the smile that teased on the corners of his thin mouth, that he was trouble, a loose cannon.

It didn't matter, though she grudgingly acknowledged that this might, in fact, be good for views. It was only a question of time before Wild Cody screwed up again. Please, please, please let it not be on her watch.

She pushed the phone away. "You're not supposed to make decisions like this without talking to me."

"Ange, come on."

"I remember Wild Cody," Hector had chimed in.

He'd sat at the long dining table they'd been using as command central upon which there were three open laptops, two standing mics, ring lights on tripods, a stack of paperwork that Anton had dropped off, Angeline's pile of books about the islands. Boxes of other equipment—tile trackers, wireless mics, body cameras, spare phones, camping gear of all kinds, most of it given by companies that wanted mentions on their broadcasts—were stacked around the room.

Under the table, there were two big duffel bags that Mav wouldn't let anyone touch. Some big surprise. Angeline had found herself staring at them on and off, trying to discern from their heft what might be inside.

"Man, I wanted to *be him*," said Hector. "You know, like *out there*, one with nature and shit. That hat. Remember that cool hat he wore?"

"I thought he was dead," said Gustavo, who'd made himself comfortable on their couch, considerate enough to keep his tattered Merrill climbing shoes off the fabric. He was scrolling on his phone, the case covered in worn, faded stickers. "Didn't he like OD?"

Angeline looked around her at the men.

Boys.

Only Alex had matured, become a husband, a father. And where *was* he?

She could feel him drifting from their group, and it scared her. Because a lot of times he was her only ally, the only one who seemed to get that there was more to running a company than just following whatever idiotic impulse you might have.

"Anyway," Mav had concluded, his tone final, "Cody's already on his way. Adele Crane and Malinka Nicqui are on-site. *And* we got Scotty G, the gamer kid who won the contest. Man, he's got mad followers. More than I do."

"Kid?" asked Angeline.

"You know, like nineteen or something."

"Legal? You're sure?"

"Of course," he said. "Do you think I'm an idiot?"

"Don't make me answer that."

"Damn," said Hector, pulling out the syllable, mock-serious.

None of this was unfamiliar, the tension before every event, the tug of war between Angeline and Mav, the barely controlled chaos of each situation. Sometimes, right before a challenge, she got an eye twitch. Or her jaw might start to ache from unconscious clenching. This time it was both. Also, she'd bitten her nails to the quick. The cuticle of her right index finger was raw and bloody.

But maybe they all thrived on it a bit, even Angeline, little as she cared to admit it.

Maverick, bare-chested, now snored loud and rumbling beside her. He had a deviated septum, one of the many injuries from stunts gone bad. *Face, meet concrete*, he liked to say.

The reels of Mav's many fails got far more views than any of his successful stunts. It *was* funny when he wiped out, only because he was one of those people whose natural athleticism was so astounding. There was no game that he could not play, no sport at which he didn't excel. To watch him on skis or a snowboard was mesmerizing, not only because of his grace and strength but because of his daring. And to see that powerful, six-foot frame go toppling when it met with forces beyond its control was undeniably amusing, even when it was terrifying.

And he was good at laughing at himself, one of the things Angeline had first loved about him. How he got up with that sheepish smile, dusted himself off and was at it again right away. Except that he was really tearing himself up, and it was starting to take a toll on his body: a badly healed broken foot, a knee that gave out, his back, headaches. Which worried Angeline. He'd had three concussions since she'd known him, and last time the doctor had been stern.

Life is not a video game, Mav. You don't get another body when your luck runs out. And it will.

He'd laughed then, too. But she thought that maybe the words had resonated. He got that look, that kind of sad crinkle around the eyes he sometimes had. It was the look that told her there was more to him than his Extreme Maverick persona. The adventure hound, the thrill-seeker, the adrenaline junkie. Laugh too loud. Play too hard. Hurt himself for a laugh.

After that doctor's visit, in the limo on the way back to their place in Hudson Yard, he'd been contemplative.

Maybe it's time to slow down, Ange. What do you think?

But then the next week Mav took off to Argentina for heli-skiing, leaving Angeline behind to run the company. Which was fine: she was no daredevil. And someone had to do payroll, manage the social media team, and deal with the lawyers. The lawsuits—currently there were three. The conversation with the doctor was forgotten as soon as he was feeling better. It was almost as if he *couldn't* slow down.

Angeline rose from the bed now, heavy fatigue clinging to her eyes, her stomach queasy. She pulled on a robe over her tank top and undies. She couldn't remember a time when she'd felt more tired.

After this, Mav had promised, *we take a vacation. Just you and me—rest, relax, restore. Pick your spa, anywhere in the world. It will be all detox, yoga, and meditation. Couple time.*

She didn't believe him, not at all. But she wanted to. Because there was a guy she got to see when they were alone, when the cameras were off and the entourage had fallen away. Someone tender and kind, someone who gave with his whole heart—to her, to causes, to his friends, to his followers. He gave away millions of dollars a year, had a staff member solely devoted to answering personal pleas for money: *my mom needs surgery; my car broke down and I can't get to work; my brother has cancer and he's never seen the ocean.*

That was the guy Angeline wanted Petra to see. Though why Angeline should care what the supposed town elder thought about her and Mav, she didn't even know. Anton, slim and smarmy with a pencil mustache and heavily-lidded gaze, obviously had all the power. He wanted what Extreme brought to their little island. Eyes. Tourist dollars. Mav had obviously been right about that. Might didn't make right. Money did.

She pushed from the bedroom into the large living room suite. "Ange."

She issued a startled cry. In the corner, a form hunched in the dark. A light flipped on. Alex.

"Jesus," she said, releasing a breath, nerve endings tingling. "Why are you sitting there in the dark like a weirdo?"

"We have to talk."

Something about his expression, a mingling of anger and sadness, struck at her center. He was slim and boyish, with big glasses and a wide mouth, every bit the nerdy CFO. He wore what was basically a uniform for him: gray zip-up hoodie over a graphic T-shirt, baggy jeans. Alex looked as exhausted as Angeline felt.

"What's going on?" she asked. She didn't have the bandwidth for more problems.

Alex was worried, Angeline knew that much. They'd gone

over the books recently, and things were…not great. Revenue
was falling precipitously. Followers were dropping off by the
thousands a day. There had been some bad press, rumors of an
FBI investigation into Mav's charitable giving. The investigation into the disappearance of Chloe Miranda was ongoing, the
case being amped up by a popular podcaster.

"Is this about the lawsuits?"

There were several, including complainants who claimed they
were injured during stunts they'd mimicked from Maverick's
escapades. The online group Moms Against Maverick was vigorously campaigning for WeWatch to drop Maverick altogether.

One of the founding mothers had a kid who would be in a
wheelchair for the rest of his life. No amount of money offered
so far would satisfy his mother or get her to stop campaigning
against Extreme. Her last email had been scathing, sizzling with
rage and heartbreak.

**You're a role model to young boys. They worship you. Look
at my son. He had everything ahead of him. Now he can't
walk—won't walk again. Ever.**

Before they'd left the country, Alex had doubled their pre-
vious offer. The family of the injured child had not responded.

"No," he said. "Not the lawsuits."

He ran a hand over the crown of his head, didn't seem to
want to meet her eyes.

"Then, what?"

"Yeah, Alex."

Maverick came up behind Angeline; she felt his heat on her
back. He dropped a hand on her shoulder.

"What's going on?" Maverick's tone was heavy and dark, unfamiliar. Angeline turned to look at him and didn't like what
she saw on his face. Maverick was slow to anger. But when he
lost his temper it was a train wreck.

Alex rose and folded his arms around his slim middle. On his

T-shirt, a chubby cat held an enormous bloody knife, eyes innocent. *What?* the graphic's text read.

Then Hector came in through the suite door. He was trying to be quiet, looked up, startled to see everyone.

"What's going on?" he asked.

"Alex thinks we need to talk," said Maverick.

"There's no time to talk," said Hector, pushing inside. "We're T-minus twelve hours. Permits are in, contestants arriving. Time to pack up and go to the site."

Angeline and Alex locked eyes. She felt a little jolt of dread.

"We can talk later," he said. "Just administrative stuff."

"Alex," said Angeline.

"It's cool," he said, still not looking at her. "Later."

Then he pushed by Hector and was gone.

"What's his problem?" asked Hector, looking back and forth between Angeline and Maverick.

"He needs to chill," said Maverick. "All he does is worry these days."

"There's a lot going on," said Ange, wondering if she should go after Alex.

"Don't *you* start, too," Mav said, an unpleasant edge to his voice.

She was about to throw down, but then she just ran out of steam.

Last night, after Maverick had fallen sound asleep, she'd logged onto WeWatch at two in the morning and started digging through the comments on the live broadcast, looking for the one that had upset Mav. Because when you couldn't sleep it was always a good idea to go on social media and seek out the people who actively hated you and everything you stood for.

After scrolling for a while, she finally found it. MavIsALiar with the three skull emojis.

MavIsALiar: Keep playing, Mav. But you will pay for what you've done. Tell the truth. Where is Chloe Miranda?

Then, because she was truly masochistic, she went hunting for news on Chloe Miranda. But there was nothing new. That famous podcaster was investigating. But he wasn't going to find anything, nothing that could hurt Extreme. Because they'd fully cooperated with police, and there was nothing left to tell. She believed that with her whole heart.

"Ange," said Maverick now, putting a hand to her cheek. "You look wrecked. You need to try to get more sleep."

Before she could respond, he looked at Hector. "Are we ready to do this?"

"Yaaas!" said Hector, drawing out the word long and deep the way men do when they think they're being cool but are really just being douchebags.

She gave one last look at the door, wondering what was wrong with Alex and what he wanted to talk about. Should she go after him?

But then, like everything with Maverick, the tide of events swept her away and she turned all her focus on him and the game ahead.

It has to be bigger, scarier, better than anything we've ever done.

And if everything went as planned, it would be.

Mav grabbed the two duffel bags, shouldered them with effort.

"Are you going to tell me what's in those bags?"

She'd asked him twice what was inside. But all he'd offered was that mischievous grin.

"You'll see," he said. Then he was walking out the door.

Hector started packing up the rest of the stuff. Angeline turned to look at him.

"Go ahead," Hector told her. "And I'll get the other Rover packed up and follow you guys with the luggage and all the equipment."

"Are you sure?" she asked.

"Of course," said Hector, with a smile that didn't quite reach his eyes. "It's my job."

He'd taken the Chloe thing the hardest. It was his job to keep everyone safe, and he took it seriously. The fact that Chloe Miranda had hid during one of their games and was never found was something he carried. A kind of permanent look of sadness had etched itself around his eyes.

"Call if you need help," she tossed behind her as she hustled after Mav. It would not be out of the realm of possibility that he'd take the car and leave her behind with Hector.

When she turned to look at him one last time, just to make sure he was really okay, he was already at work packing up the equipment.

7

BLAKE

In *Red World*, you could never die.

As the game began, you were dropped in the middle of a dystopian universe of your choosing. You might choose Urban Hellscape, a crumbling city populated by zombies, or Jungle Warfare ruled by militant apes. There was a universe that consisted of only sewer tunnels called What Lies Beneath, WLB for short. Eyeless, white troglobites ruled WLB, using their sonar to find you. Blake's personal favorite was Death Mall, an abandoned five-level shopping center that also included an additional two levels of subbasement, if you found the right door, access always changing. Here, hot Stepford-mom robots with glowing green eyes and bouffant hairdos were the ones to kill.

No matter which world you chose, no matter how horribly your avatar was maimed in any of these places, or if you got trapped somehow and couldn't escape before the red circle closed around you, or even if you got your head chopped off or chopped off someone else's head, you always returned to The

Locker Room, where you could choose a fresh skin, new weapons, and start again.

Tonight, though, Blake was headed to Haunted Amusement Park. He hadn't been there in a while and supposedly there were some sick new upgrades.

Violet was in bed; he could hear the white noise coming from her room, a sound she always needed to sleep. Her homework was long done, of course. Because she was *perfect*. Blake still had some math to do, and it was nearly eleven o'clock.

But just one more round.

If Mom was home, she'd have already checked on it to make sure it was done. No gaming until schoolwork was finished: that was a hard-and-fast, as Mom liked to say. But Violet couldn't care less. *It's your business if you want to fry your brain with that stupid game.* Violet, when she lowered herself to play with him, slayed at *Red World*, like she did at everything.

Blake checked the various computer windows he had open to monitor his mom.

There was the weather tracker, where he watched an unnamed storm in the Atlantic move slowly toward the island.

There was a window he thought of as *Find My Mom* that showed Adele's location, in the middle of an island, in the middle of the Atlantic.

He had an alert set for any news about Extreme and the challenge.

Malinka's WeWatch page was open in one window, Mav's in another. He had enabled notifications in case either of them went live. He'd been toggling between the open windows, texting any new info to his mom.

He did a quick check—all quiet. He watched the recorded live broadcast his mom had done when she was riding with Gustavo to Enchantments. She looked happy, if a little tired, maybe a bit nervous. Seeing her, he felt some relief. Like she was close by instead of so far away.

He had a catch in his throat as he thought about his mom out there, hiding in some abandoned hotel.

This whole thing had been his idea.

If anything went wrong, it would be his fault.

He got up to shut and lock his door, then he donned his headset, turned off the lights, and pulled up to his desk. The controller was heavy and cool in his hand.

He dropped into the game, dropping out of real life and all the things he couldn't control.

In The Locker Room, he chose his mohawk helmet, black leather jacket, ripped jeans, and heavy boots. He took his virtual machete, rocket launcher, two guns, and a first-aid kit, which always came in handy. Not everyone had one of those; it was a high-value item. He could use it to heal himself or others if he was so inclined. The kit had earned him a reputation with the other players: they came to him for help all the time. And as a result, a lot of people owed him favors.

In the upper-right corner of the screen, a timer counted down. You had twelve minutes to gather as many prizes and supplies as you could and then find the doorway to the next level before the Red Cloud descended, ending everyone still in the game.

He entered Haunted Amusement Park by the roller coaster, a towering purple-and-black behemoth where a runaway coaster roared by every few minutes with riders screaming in terror.

As soon as he was boots on the ground, he had to react quickly and behead two skeleton bikers, the resident evil beings of Haunted Amusement Park. Afterward, he got moving fast. He grabbed two canteens, a gold ingot, and a bag of magic beans, shoving them into his pack. He hadn't had beans in a while; they got you out of all sorts of messes.

There were a lot of other players here tonight. He recognized a couple of kids from school. Blake's avatar was big and muscular, with a chiseled jaw, huge fists, and broad chest, a far cry from his doughy and essentially wimpy self, named The Beast. Vio-

let had snorted at that. But that was fine. Everyone's avatar was
somewhat aspirational. There was Tisha. In life, she was cute,
a bit pudgy with thick glasses and braces, a bookish strawberry
blonde who sometimes sat with him at lunch. In *Red World*, she
was Pink, a leather-clad babe with thick powerful thighs and
huge boobs, and heavily armed rocking a knife in a leg holster.
She was a friend, and he could count on her in a pinch, unless
they were competing for the same thing. Then she'd kill him
without a second thought. He'd learned that lesson the hard way.

The only person who looked exactly like herself in *Red World*
was Violet. And just like in the hallways at school, if she saw
him in *Red World*, she ignored him. But she wasn't on tonight.
Her avatar name was Violent.

He spotted some of his *former* friends. He avoided them, kept
moving.

And then there was Marco. Blake's former best friend turned
archnemesis. Marco's avatar, called Savage, was a bald, hulking
prison escapee in an orange jumpsuit and a hockey mask. His
smile was a metal grid. He wielded a gleaming machete. The
bridge of Blake's nose ached just thinking about him. Sometimes
he dreamed about Marco punching him in the face, smashing
his glasses. He'd cried in front of those guys; the pain and the
shame had been too much. *You fucking waste. Everyone here hates
you and your whole family.* The words were on a loop in his head.

That's why he never told on Marco and his former friends.
The shame of it all. How small and helpless and how sick it made
him feel. And how maybe there was a part of him that felt like
he deserved it.

Blake kept to the shadows. He was just here for the prizes,
for the game. He didn't want to engage with anyone. He was
on an ongoing quest for the golden peach. If you found it, it
quadrupled your Red Coin balance and unlocked a whole new
wardrobe of skins, as well as the ultimate weapons cache.

He watched as his friend Gregg dropped in. Blake rushed

over to help him kill off a few more skeletons. Gregg, or Bone
Breaker on *Red World*, was a ninja, slim and shadowy. He was a
master with the Chinese stars, preferred hand-to-hand combat.
Gregg was a senior at another local high school. They'd even
met at a football game in the real world. Gregg's parents got
him a new Bronco, and he'd shown it to Blake.

"Thanks, brah," said Gregg now. "I can always count on you."

Then he took off. Everyone was looking for that peach.

Blake was about to follow when he heard Marco's voice over
his headset. Their avatars were still connected from all their
years of playing, so Marco didn't have to request permission to
engage with Blake.

"What are you doing here, loser?"

The glasses incident had happened at lunch. He'd accidentally bumped into Marco on the cafeteria line, tipping his tray
to the ground. Marco had spun around and punched him hard,
knocking his glasses to the ground and then stepping on them
for good measure.

Blake, true to form, had just stood there staring, weirdly remembering how when they were in kindergarten Marco still
sucked his thumb. It was like a math equation he just couldn't
solve no matter how hard he puzzled over it: How could someone who was your friend once just stop being your friend? How
did they suddenly hate you?

"Your dad did a bad thing, and people judge us for that. Some
people will stop wanting to spend time with us," his mom had
explained.

"He didn't do it."

"Yes, he did, Blakey. He stole a lot of money from his company. People lost their jobs and their savings. And then he disappeared. He left us behind. I'm sorry, but that's the truth."

"That's the way it looks, but it might not be the truth. What
if something else happened?"

His mom got that look, a kind of sad patience. "Maybe," she said. But she didn't mean it.

"Just playing," Blake answered Marco now.

"Play someplace else. That peach is mine."

"Go fuck yourself, Marco."

It wasn't Blake who spoke up. It was Pink. He hadn't seen her come up beside him. "He has as much right to be here as you do."

"He has no right to be *anywhere*," said Marco.

With one swing of Marco's machete, Pink disappeared into a cloud of glitter.

Blake might have been next, if he didn't think to grab his stun gun and blow Marco back into a stone wall where he fell hard, rocks piling on top of him. Marco would have to stay there for a second to recover his energy.

Blake took off into the woods that surrounded the amusement park, hoping that would be the end of it. He didn't like to fight in *Red World* any more than he did in the real world. He felt bad for Pink: she'd be raging right now. She hated Marco almost as much as Blake did. He'd get her a cookie at lunch tomorrow.

He refocused himself on finding the peach. You were supposed to look for the doors to an underground bunker, hidden near a twisted old oak and a creek.

Blake made his way through the thick trees, using his scythe to clear a path.

"I'm coming for you, Blake."

Marco in his headset again. Behind him, Marco was running, so Blake picked up his pace.

"Just lay off of him."

Gregg was back, squaring off as Marco caught up to him at the creek. But then Marco threw a grenade, and Gregg was blown to pieces. Blake was on his own.

Marco's hulking avatar panted, arms akimbo.

"We used to be friends," said Blake pathetically.

"Used to be," said Marco. "Before my mom lost her job because of your dad."

That was true. A lot of people used to work at Dad's company. His dad had invented a new kind of prosthetic that was cheaper, lighter, and more comfortable for the wearer. But, according to police, his father had embezzled millions of dollars over the years, hiding money in offshore accounts. Then, just as he was about to get arrested, he took off, bankrupting the company, leaving his family, and disappearing without a trace. A scientist from the company stepped forward to claim that the original prototype had been her invention, that he'd stolen even that.

"He didn't do it," Blake said to Marco now. With all his heart, he still believed that.

Marco lifted his rocket launcher, and Blake prepared to return to The Locker Room. He didn't want to play anymore anyway.

But then it was Marco who disappeared into a cloud of green.

There was a man dressed all in black with combat boots and a shorn head standing behind Blake's avatar. He had stubble on his cheeks, muscular arms. His *Red World* name was Charger.

In the real world, Blake didn't have any truly close friends. But on *Red World* he had a few.

"Thanks," he said.

Charger, who was part robot, part soldier and who mostly stayed silent, saluted him. Beside Charger, another player dropped in.

Hugo was an Extremist like Blake, King Killer on the game, and the one who had told Blake about the challenge on the island.

Hugo actually lived on Falcão Island, sharing a house with a bunch of adventure guides. You never knew who was telling the truth on *Red World*. But Hugo's tip about Extreme's hide and seek and how there was an open spot had been true. And Hugo had given Blake some sweet intel about the casitas on the hotel property. Blake still had to verify.

"How's your mom doing?" Hugo said over Blake's headset.

"She arrived today," said Blake.

"Sweet," said Hugo. "Heard it's going to get hairy on the site. Bad weather moving in."

"She's pretty tough," said Blake, feeling his anxiety ramp up a little. He took a quick click through the sites he was monitoring.

"Cool, cool. Well, if she needs anything, I'm not too far from the hotel."

It was crazy—this person who he'd never met in the real world, who lived an ocean away, was more friend to him and his family than some of the people he'd known all his life. Of course, Hugo didn't know about his dad, didn't hate Blake because of what Miller had done.

"Looking for the peach?" said Hugo.

"You know it."

Hugo laughed. "Not if I get there first."

He took off then, disappearing into a wormhole.

"You've still got seven minutes to find it," Charger said. "Let's do it."

The sky was already turning pink, indicating that the Red Cloud was closing in.

"How'd you know where to find me?" Blake asked.

"I know lots of things, Blake-Man," he said. "And I'm always looking out for you. Don't forget that."

It wasn't the first time, or even the second time Blake had met Charger here. They talked a lot this way.

"Let's do this," the big man said, jogging off toward the twisted oak.

Blake waited a second and then followed.

8

VIOLET

When Violet thought about her father, which she tried not to do very often, she felt a kind of unpleasant heat come up from her center. Sometimes there was a rushing sound in her ears. Always there was a kind of tension, like she was holding her breath for too long.

Memories of him could surface suddenly, taking her by surprise. Like the smell of burnt toast made her remember the time they tried to make a surprise breakfast for Mom and the smoke detectors went off. Or the scar on her knee reminded her of the day he taught her how to ride her bike. She fell, and he carried her back to the house, where her mom bandaged the wound and they both kissed it better, while Blake cried because he thought she was really hurt. She'd gotten good at batting those memories away, making herself hard inside and swallowing the tide of feelings they brought up.

Dreams she couldn't control. In her dreams, her dad pushed her on the swing set in the backyard of their old house, the one they couldn't afford anymore. He sang her silly songs horribly out of tune, until she nearly peed her pants with laughter. Helped her, always patient and encouraging, with her math. *You can do this, little V.* And when she woke from a vivid one—like now—she might be crying or laughing. She might be reaching for him to take her into his arms and swing her around.

The familiar shadows of her room took shape—her dresser, her big purple beanbag chair, her backpack slouched by the door waiting for morning—as the image of her father baking cookies, which he had never done in real life, faded. She grasped for it, but it slipped from her consciousness like sand through her fingers.

Then she remembered. They were alone, Blake sleeping down the hallway. She was in charge.

She reached for her phone and checked her mom's location. Adele's red dot pulsed in the middle of a green dot, in the middle of a wide blue nothing. Violet felt some measure of relief, though of course, all it meant was that Adele's phone was on and charged. But there was no dot on any electronic map for her father for Violet to watch, to know he was somewhere, probably okay.

He was gone.

It was four in the morning. Her mom called it *the witching hour*, the time when you woke and were most likely to stay awake worrying about everything and nothing until morning. She lay a moment, listening to the darkness.

Before bed, she'd checked every door and window lock, dutifully set the alarm. Had there been a sound? Something that woke her?

She listened longer. Nothing.

Finally, she slipped from the warmth of her covers, bare feet hitting the hardwood floor, the cool air on her skin raising gooseflesh. She kept her dad's old baseball bat by the door. Just after he'd disappeared, there'd been threats, people calling at all hours; once, a woman turned up on their doorstep holding an infant on her hip.

He ruined us, she'd shrieked at Adele through the door she wouldn't open. *We've lost everything.*

I'm sorry, Adele said through the glass. *So have we.*

Blake had clung to Violet, his arms around her waist. "Who is she? Why does she hate us?"

She hadn't known how to answer.

Violet grabbed the bat before stepping into the hallway. Blake's door down the hall was ajar, the faint blue light of his various electronics glowing. She moved down the stairs, careful not to step on the one that creaked, gripping the gritty, taped handle of the bat.

She'd never said so to her mother, but there were things she liked about this house better, even though it was small, not grand with high ceilings and big glittering chandeliers. There was no pool or game-slash-music room with a pool table and Dad's drum kit, no giant U-shaped sofa in front of the home-theater-sized television. Her room was not even half as big. But in that house with its endless hallways and poured-concrete floors, her parents had seemed so far. Their bedroom suite on another level from Blake's and Violet's rooms. Here, they were close to each other. In the night, she could hear her mother talking on the phone or punching the bag in the garage. Blake and all his annoying noises—his allergic sniffles, his unexplainable grunts and groans, the creaking of his gaming chair. She liked knowing where everyone was, what they were doing. There couldn't be any secrets this way, right? Her mother couldn't be one thing and then suddenly be something else.

Violet stepped into the open-plan kitchen, eyes sweeping the space. Her mom's whiteboard calendar with all their various activities color-coded—purple for Violet, red for Blake, green for Adele—hung next to the refrigerator. Violet kept everything clean, just like her mom did. No dishes in the sink, every surface

wiped to a shine. The coffeepot was set to brew at six o'clock—
not that either of them drank coffee, but Violet liked the smell.

She walked through the cozy living room, everything plush
with big pillows, photos and Violet's and Blake's framed art-
work. In the old house, everything had been digital: pictures
on the screen saver of the television, on frames that changed
every few minutes.

She peered out the door to their fenced-in backyard. Just the
table and chairs, the grill.

It wasn't until she walked down the short hallway to the front
door that she knew something was wrong. The alarm pad that
glowed red when it was armed was green. The front door was
ajar. She froze, lifted the bat. Her throat went a little dry, her
shoulders hiked.

Call the police. That was the first thought.

And *before*, she wouldn't have thought twice. Of course when
there's trouble you call the cops. Because they were the good
guys, and their job was to protect you. But that was *before*. There
was a certain look that people got *after*—the police, the FBI,
people who used to work for her father. It was the stern, hard
look of disapproval, of judgment. And it was a kind of violence, a look that made Violet shut down, want to run away and
hide. Because that look, it was a closed door. It was the look of
people who wanted to hurt, not help. Like Agent Coben, who
pretended to be nice but really just wanted to arrest her father,
could take her mother away, too, if he wanted to.

One thing she knew for sure since her dad disappeared: Violet, Blake, and Adele were on their own.

She steeled herself. *Be brave, be wild.* That's what her mother
told her when Violet was worried or afraid. Violet crept toward
the door, mind racing. If the alarm had been disarmed, someone
knew the code. If the door was ajar, was there someone in the
house? She gripped the bat so hard that her knuckles ached, the

tape abrading the skin on her palm. Outside the door, a shuffling sound. Was that the sound of an engine?

The door opened slowly.

She ran toward it, bat high, issuing a warrior yell, which she hoped would scare whoever it was and wake her brother. A lumbering figure filled the door.

"Violet!"

She swung the bat and missed, went whipping around with the force of her own thrust, the bat flying into the kitchen, crashing against the kitchen island. There was a shout, hands on her.

"You could have killed me. Are you crazy?"

She stared, the face before her coming into focus.

"Oh, my god!" yelled Violet. "Blake, what are you doing?"

The sound of an engine had her running past him, just in time to see a pair of taillights disappearing up the drive.

She turned back to her brother. "Who was that?"

"No one," said Blake, picking up the bat. "None of your business."

"It's definitely my business," she said. "Did you sneak out? Where did you go?"

"You," he said, picking up the bat from where it had fallen, "are not Mom. I don't have to tell you anything."

Blake held up the bat, gave her a look, and then stuck it in the closet. "Why would you be walking around with that thing?"

She grappled with the situation. Who was that? Where did Blake go? He didn't have a single friend except all the other gamer dorks on *Red World*, and most of them he'd never met in real life.

"Fine," she said, her heart rate slowing, hands still shaking. "I'll tell Mom that you snuck out."

"You won't." Blake moved into the kitchen. "Because if you do, she'll come home. She'll lose the game. And then we'll be in worse shape than we are now."

She stared at him. His face was blank, unreadable. Adrenaline abandoned her, leaving her vaguely nauseated. He was right. She wouldn't tell Mom.

"Just tell me." She sounded dangerously close to begging.

Blake opened the refrigerator, casting himself in a buttery rectangle of light. He took out the pizza they'd ordered for dinner last night, grabbed a slice, and stuck it in his mouth, practically inhaling it.

"Whose car was that?" she pressed.

No answer. He took a seat at the kitchen island, opened his laptop, his back to her. Finally, without looking around, he answered.

"I just went out, okay? With Gregg. We just drove around."

"Who's Gregg?"

"He's a senior at Lake Forest. I met him on *Red World*. You don't know him. He got a Bronco for his birthday, so we just tooled around. Did you know the McDonald's in Chester is open twenty-four hours? We didn't do anything."

She didn't believe him.

"What's his Photogram ID?"

"No way. You're not following him."

She locked the front door and set the alarm. She'd change the code so that he couldn't get out again without setting the alarm. Then she sank into the couch, defeated, listening to him clattering on his keyboard.

He wasn't going to tell her anything else. She decided to drop it, and she'd do some detective work. Gregg from Lake Forest High with a new Bronco. What did a senior want with a freshman? Especially a giant nerd like Blake?

Cruising through the various social platforms, she didn't find anything about a Gregg, but she saw that her best friend Coral had posted a silly picture of herself up too late studying for their chem exam. Her friend, with her wild, pink-tinged hair and thick glitter eye shadow, clutched a can of Red Bull.

#APchemsucks #thestruggleisreal

Violet watched again the video of her mom arriving on Falcão Island, riding next to Gustavo, the foliage all around her impossibly green. Violet froze the frame on Adele's face: she'd never seen that expression before. Her mother looked young, unfamiliar; her features were lit with excitement. *Not* her mom, who was always kind, loving, but often worried or stressed. The woman in the video looked confident and free, someone on an enviable, *postable* adventure.

Anxiety thrummed. *Mom*, she wanted to write. *Come home.*

Verbally, Violet was all positive vibes and support. Inside, she was not a fan of this endeavor.

She scrolled through Malinka's WeWatch page and Photogram account, looking at the beautifully curated and filtered images of Enchantments, Malinka's tent, the lush green forest, and wild blooming hydrangeas. Malinka's Yes I Can gear was epic—that fluffy sleeping bag, the ruffled hoodie, the purple polarized sunglasses, the glittery fairy lights. So expensive.

Then Violet did a news search on Extreme, just to see what, if anything, other people were saying about the challenge.

But the first link that popped up wasn't about the game, it was for the podcast *Stranger Than Fiction*.

"New Leads in the Chloe Miranda Case."

She clicked and was greeted by the face of a beautiful girl with big dark eyes and a mane of honey curls. She smiled, but there was something distant, something sad about it. She had a delicate tattoo on her collarbone: *Mom*, written in a looping cursive followed by a tiny black heart. She looked familiar. Underneath the image, some bold type read, **Where is Chloe Miranda?**

Violet's mouth went a little dry as she started to read.

Twenty-five-year-old influencer Chloe Miranda went missing last year during a hide and seek challenge hosted by Maverick's Extreme Games and Insane Challenges.

As we approach the one-year anniversary of Chloe's

disappearance, the Miranda family has raised the reward amount to five hundred thousand dollars for any information leading to the truth about Chloe. Predictably, this has led to a number of calls from around the country from people who have claimed to see her. None of those leads, so far, have panned out.

For those of you new to this case, Chloe Miranda went missing during a hide and seek challenge hosted by Extreme Challenges and Insane Games. A longtime fan of Maverick Dillan and a graduate of New York University, Chloe Miranda signed up to participate in the Extreme Haunted Hide and Seek event at a supposedly haunted site called Eaton House for the cash prize. She hid with the rest of the contestants. And was never seen again.

Wait. What?

"Hey," she said. Blake turned to her. "Did you know about this?"

She read the passage aloud.

"Chloe Miranda?" Blake answered. "Yeah, of course I knew about it. What are you, living under a rock?"

Violet felt her mouth drop open. "She *hid* and was never found. She's *still* missing."

Her brother, who was an even bigger worrier than Mom, somehow seemed unconcerned about this. He blew out a breath. "Everyone knows it's some kind of scam."

She shook her head. "Who knows that? There's an actual police investigation. Harley Granger, that true crime guy, has picked up the case. There's a *podcast.*"

She kept reading aloud, *"'Chloe had a history of depression and had survived two suicide attempts, one in high school after the death of her mother, one in college after a painful breakup. Her family reached out to Extreme and asked them not to accept her application, but Chloe was one of the chosen influencers for the event.'"*

"See?" said Blake. "She was like messed up. Mom passed the psych evaluation."

Violet kept reading, *"In recent years, Chloe's podcast and Photogram feed focused on helping people deal with mental-health issues, focusing on self-love, body positivity, and ACT therapy. She was open about her ongoing battle with depression and had earned over three hundred thousand followers. Her desire to participate in the Haunted Hide and Seek Challenge was about "facing your fears, putting yourself out there, and taking risks.""*

That sounded a lot like Mom, who Violet knew hadn't just gone for the money. Adele wanted to prove to herself that she could do it. That she could take charge and win. She'd said as much.

Violet kept reading, not sure if Blake was even listening.

"'Chloe disappeared with the rest of the contestants at the start of the event. But she was never found, even after an exhaustive search of the property. Maverick Dillan claims to have no information about what could have happened to Chloe but declared her the official winner and donated her prize to NAMI, the National Alliance for Mental Illness.'"

"Okay," said Blake. "But there are plenty of people that think this is just some kind of stunt. Listen to this... *'Her credit card was used to buy gas at a New Jersey gas station the day after she was declared missing. A woman who could have been Chloe—same height and build, but in a hoodie and sunglasses—was captured on security footage, but the car was not hers, and the plates were not visible to the camera. A series of ATM withdrawals totaling nearly five thousand dollars over the next week, all in the same five-mile radius around the hide and seek event site, indicate that she might have been preparing for flight. Again, the woman caught on the ATM camera sought to hide her face behind glasses and a hoodie. Family members and friends disagree on whether it was Chloe or not.'* It's a total stunt," Blake concluded.

"Why would someone do that?" asked Violet.

Blake looked at her, and neither of them had to say anything to know that they were both thinking of their dad.

"Why do people do anything?" he asked. "She wants views. Her followers have doubled since she disappeared. Extreme wants the publicity. Or she wanted to get away, from something, from someone. Maybe she killed herself."

"Blake!"

He offered an exaggerated shrug. "I mean, who knows?"

Violet kept scrolling through the article. "It says here that during the investigation, it was revealed that Maverick and Chloe knew each other from the extreme-sports circuit. There are rumors they were together, something that Maverick at first denied, then admitted was true."

"So what if they *were* dating?" said Blake. "What does that prove?"

How could he be so cavalier about this?

"If you knew about this, how could you suggest that Mom go?" Violet asked, her voice coming up an octave. "How was Extreme even allowed to do another challenge?"

"That's my point," Blake said. "If it was real, they would have been shut down, right?"

She used to think that, that there was some force in the world that kept people from doing bad things over and over. But the news of the world proved that it wasn't so—the opioid crisis, the war in Ukraine, the planet dying, and corporations running amok. The truth was that no one stopped the worst things from happening.

"What if Mom is…in actual danger?"

Blake gave her that blank look he seemed to have perfected. He wore it when he didn't want to talk, or when he thought she was being stupid, or when he was just being a jerk.

"Mom," said Blake, "is fine. *Mom* is badass."

But so was Dad, she wanted to say. He ran a company. He coached her soccer team. He chased away the monsters hiding in her closet. And now he was gone. Missing like Chloe Miranda. What kept Mom tied to them, especially now that she was off on some adventure, wearing an expression that Violet had never seen on her face? Or what if she wasn't as strong as she seemed?

But she didn't say any of those things. Like everything else she was afraid of, she kept it inside. With a last look into the sad eyes of Chloe Miranda, she clicked off the page.

"Mav is going live soon. I just got the WeWatch alert," said Blake.

She didn't say anything, the things she'd learned on a spin cycle in her brain. Finally, he grabbed his laptop from the kitchen counter and came to sit next to her.

Usually, she'd push him away, but instead, still feeling shaky and so tired, she shifted closer as his fingers danced across the keyboard. The Extreme WeWatch page came up with a big countdown clock at the top. They were going live in just under ten minutes.

9

~~~~~~

ANGELINE

They made the turn onto the narrow road up the mountain, Maverick driving too fast as usual. Enormous thunderheads piled black and menacing as thick fingers of pink and orange light reached through the clouds. It took Angeline's breath away, the quiet of this place, its untouched beauty.

Up in the sky huge birds were circling the hotel, slow, graceful, gliding. Angeline thought of Petra again, the feeling she'd had when the old woman took her hands. As if Petra had grown from the earth like one of the ancient trees and was the voice of the island itself.

Please, she'd pleaded when the others couldn't hear. *Take these men and leave here. They don't belong.*

"What the fuck is this now?" Mav said as the Rover approached the hotel.

She didn't like the edge in Mav's voice. Lately as the pressure mounted at Extreme and Mav was getting his way less, making lots of compromises, his tantrums had amped up in volume and frequency. She felt her shoulders hike, checked the urge to soothe him.

There.

A line of men stood dressed in black and thick flak vests, with assault rifles cradled in their arms like babies, arms bulging with muscle, faces blank. In front of them another five men sat on mud-caked black-and-red ATVs, similarly clad and armed.

Petra stood at the apex of the grouping, looking severe, taller, and more powerful than she had during their last meetings where she had just seemed old and exhausted. Angeline drew in a breath.

The fierce old woman held a fighting stance, her expression grim.

"That bitch is *not* going to fuck this up for us," said Mav, his voice tight. He clenched the wheel, face taut with anger.

Angeline tried to put a calming hand on his arm, but he moved away quickly as he brought the SUV to an abrupt stop, killed the engine, and climbed out, slamming the door. She followed, moving swiftly past him so that she was the first one to greet Petra.

The old woman stood firm, a patient smile etched on her face. The humming engines of the ATVs buzzed like a swarm of angry bees, menacing and low. To their right the trailer and the generator sat waiting for fueling and setup.

Angeline turned to see the other Rover approaching with Gustavo at the wheel and Wild Cody riding shotgun. Great. Perfect.

Adele and Malinka walked around the formation unhindered by the men and over to join Mav and Angeline, eyes trained on the armed gathering.

"What's happening?" said Adele, brow furrowed with concern. "Who are these people?"

"It's okay," Angeline said. They'd yet to meet formally, but this didn't seem like the moment for introductions. "We'll handle it. Just some local opposition to our event."

Adele was younger, prettier than she'd seemed in the pictures and video Angeline had seen. Hard to believe she was a mother of two teenagers: she was fit and fresh-faced, eyes bright, dark hair shining.

"Uh," said Malinka. Angeline was not a fan. The girl was full of herself; she'd had a list of demands three pages long before she agreed to do this. But they needed her huge following, so they'd acquiesced. *"That's a small army."*

Why are you here? Why are you doing this? Angeline wanted to ask each of them. Malinka at her young age had already accomplished so much. Adele was a mom with kids at home. What did they need with a game like this?

But, of course, there was only one answer ever: money. People, she learned, would do just about any asinine thing for it, especially if they didn't have to actually earn it.

She turned away from the two women and focused her attention on Petra.

"Take your men and get out of here," said Mav, getting in the old woman's face. She stood her ground, though he towered over her. Two of the armed men stepped forward, and Mav took a step back, lifting his palms. "You have no right to do this."

"Petra," said Angeline putting herself between Maverick and Petra, keeping her voice calm, respectful. "I'm sure Anton told you that we've been granted our permit."

"He did," said the older woman. "Your permission has been granted. Legally you have a right to be here now, and there's nothing we can do to help that."

"Then, what is this shit?" Mav pressed behind Angeline, thrust his arm toward the obvious show of force Petra had mobilized.

Petra looked at Maverick with strained patience and barely concealed disgust, like he was the worst spoiled brat.

"A final warning," she said directing her gaze to Angeline. "This land is—" she seemed to search for the right word "—*unwell*. It has been scarred, damaged by greed, by murder, untimely death, accidents. Nothing good can happen here again. That's why this hotel sits rotting, never cleared, never rebuilt. It's a tomb. It stands as a warning to stay away."

The mean, white sun slipped suddenly behind clouds, the temperature dropping.

Petra's words echoed another earlier warning. *My daughter Chloe is not well. Please reject her application to this challenge. For her sake and for her family's sake.*

But Angeline pushed it aside, took a breath.

Focus.

"Please, Petra. I am going to have to ask you and your men to leave. I promise we'll do no harm. Our money will help you in your conservation efforts."

She knew that was important to the old woman, conserving the island, keeping it safe from encroachment. She spoke to that. "And we'll be gone before you know we were here. I know how important this island is to you. We won't hurt anything. It's just a game. Just for fun."

The high-pitched cries of the birds carried down. They were lower, their wingspans enormous.

Petra lifted a gentle hand to Angeline's cheek, and Angeline found herself thinking again of her abuela.

"You don't understand," said Petra. She brought her hand back, clasped the other at her heart center. "I'm not worried about protecting this island or the land. It can take care of itself. It has and will, long after I'm gone. Just as the earth will be here and will heal itself after it has ejected the virus that mankind has proven itself to be."

Angeline shook her head, folded her arms around her center. "Then, what do you want from us?"

The look of pity on the old woman's face cut Angeline deep.

"I'm trying to keep you from hurting yourselves."

It happened fast.

Maverick pushed past Angeline, rushing toward Petra, yelling, pointing his finger at her, aggressive. Angeline grabbed for him, his powerful arm filling her grasp. She couldn't even make out what he was saying. He was roaring. Petra didn't give an inch, staring him down.

But then two of the men were on him, moving with speed and intensity, bringing him hard to the ground while Maverick kept raging. She heard her own voice screaming in protest. Time pulled and slowed.

She tugged with all of her strength at one of the men, trying to get him off Mav, but he was like a slab of concrete, didn't even acknowledge her efforts.

Gustavo moved in, yelling, too.

But he was blocked by two other men who were now pointing their guns.

Gustavo lifted his palms, stopping short, face ashen.

Her heart stuttered with terror. It was chaos. Anything could happen: she braced for the sound of gunfire. Then Adele moved in.

"Hey, hey, hey," Adele said like she was on a playground somewhere, reprimanding unruly children. "Let's take this down a notch, gentlemen."

Angeline felt her tension build until she exploded.

"Stop," yelled Angeline at no one, at everyone. "Stop this right now!"

Her voice, clarion and strong, seemed to cut the gray morning. Everyone froze.

An eerie silence fell, leaves whispered in the wind that was picking up, blowing up dirt from the ground.

"Please," she said, her voice softer, directed at Petra. "We truly don't want any trouble. But we're not leaving."

Something passed between the two women. She saw Petra acquiesce without submitting, a kind of wise retreat. Understood between them: things would move forward. There was nothing either one of them could do, really. Except be around to clean up the mess. Men, *boys*, would have their way. It had always been so.

Petra said something in Portuguese that Angeline didn't understand. But then the armed men who were pinning Maverick climbed off him. They were calm, unruffled as if they'd exerted no effort while Maverick thrashed and raged, scrambled to his feet, breathing hard. Both with close-cropped hair, identical thick mustaches, along with the other men who had come forward they moved back into their formation, still pointing their guns. Maverick came up behind Angeline.

"You are going to fucking regret that," he said, his shaking voice betraying how scared he was.

"Regret," said Petra, still with that patient smile. "You know the taste of regret already, don't you? How it's an acid in your throat."

What was that supposed to mean? The way she looked at him, with such disdain, like she knew something about Maverick that Angeline did not.

"You don't know shit about me," he said weakly.

"Stop," snapped Angeline.

"What?" said Mav, quieter like a chastened child. "She doesn't."

Petra kept Maverick locked in her gaze. "You go back again and again, try to rewrite the truth. But the past won't be rewritten, no matter how hard we wish it."

Maverick swallowed hard, looked away.

Then she shifted her attention to Angeline. "This is your last moment to make the right choice. You can't save them. But maybe you can still save yourself."

A breath, a beat where anything could happen.

A breath, a beat where Angeline could go climb in the Range Rover and drive away, back home, back to the life she had thought she was going to have.

But no. She stood her ground beside Maverick. Why? She didn't even know. Maybe it was love. Maybe not.

Finally, a sad nod from the old woman, and then another quiet command. The ATVs roared to life, and moving with agility and grace, Petra climbed on behind one of the bulky men.

Their exit was loud, with some of the men making big circles, whooping loudly around them, then heading off down the road, the roar fading in the night. The other men followed on foot, slowly, footsteps rhythmic, a metronome of warning.

And then they were alone.

Adele, Malinka, Wild Cody, Tavo, Angeline, and Mav stood in a loose circle, stunned, staring at each other. They'd all stowed their phones. Adele looked the most worried. Malinka seemed like a child, confused, not smart enough to be scared. Wild Cody, who was younger, taller, more ruggedly good-looking than Angeline had imagined him, had a *seen-it-all-been-there-twice-and-got-the-T-shirt* set to his lined and ruddy face. He wore that stupid wide-brimmed leather adventure hat that Hector had been on about.

"Okay," said Mav, dusting himself off and flashing a wobbly smile to Angeline, who felt so dizzy she wondered if she might pass out. White stars danced in the periphery of her vision.

Maverick cast his eyes around to the silent group, dropped a strong hand on Angeline's shoulder. His palm was hot, slightly shaking. But when she looked up at him, he had pasted on that grin that hid everything from everyone but her. He was Extreme Maverick, up for what was next, no matter what kind of wipeout had preceded the moment. She loved and hated that about him, in equal measure.

"So," he said, "are we ready to go live?"

10

~~~~~~

ADELE

The Game

The game had begun, the hiders all scattered. It felt primal, like a hunt beginning. There was a deep thrum of excitement, even though Adele knew she was the prey.

She was alone, running up the wet path.

The storm, wild, raged around her, lighting and then darkening the sky like someone flipping a switch on and off. She felt the thunderclaps vibrate beneath her feet. What was supposed to be a game now felt very real.

Was she going to die here, an ocean away from her babies?

She kept running, digging deep. Outrun the storm. Don't get struck by lightning. Hide. Pray that morning comes. I'm sorry, she told her kids, God, herself. I should have known better.

Legs pumping, she moved deftly around fallen debris. Her feet struggled for purchase on the slick ground.

Where were the others?

They'd moved in opposite directions, unhesitating when Mav gave the word. As soon as the game began, it was everyone for themselves. Any connection she'd felt or imagined to the others was sundered when things started to get real. First the violence, then the vanished man, then the storm.

Was there even a game anymore? Or would she just hide out here like Chloe Miranda and never be found, her kids left with no answers about either of their parents?

Stop.

She couldn't think like that. It would only weaken her. She would get back to them. She had to get back to them.

Keep running. Keep moving.

Around the bend, the small casita she'd found during her recon rose white and ghostly, nestled in foliage. She felt a measure of relief as she jogged up the path. It wasn't the farthest one from the hotel, nor was it the biggest. But it was the one on highest ground, the only one intact.

Mom, when it rains, the lower part of the property will flood. This casita is high and dry.

That was the last piece of advice from her son.

She pushed through the door, stepped inside, and relished the blessed relief of being out of the rain. She was soaked through to the skin, her gear dripping. The rain beat on the roof, water leaking in from several holes in the ceiling, the scent of mold heavy in her sinuses.

She found the spot she'd staked out. A closet or crawl space where the door disappeared into the wall when it closed. Inside was the pack she'd left with supplies: water, some jerky, an extra light.

Her breath came easier; she settled into her space. She pulled her phone from her pocket, even knowing it was dead, staring at that black screen, willing it to life. Her only connection to her real life, the one she lived for Blake and Violet. For Miller, once. She'd sacrifice anything now to go back there. Had she really come here, risked everything—for money?

Those warnings. Who had been on the other side of those texts? Whoever it was, they were right.

She hardened herself. No tears. Sinking into sadness and fear was death.

Just breathe. Hide. Wait for morning or to be found. Win or lose. Just make it home.

She wrapped her arms around herself against the chill, shivering. She thought of home, dinner at the table with the kids, her cozy bed. She closed her eyes. Sometimes she would say to Violet, Be brave, be wild. *Not wild like reckless or mindless. But wild as in untamed, connected to the strength of the natural world. Her heart rate slowed.*

There. What was that sound?

She sat up, listening to the storm.

Was someone coming? Had they found her already?

A high-pitched cry.

Those birds again, always circling, always waiting for someone or something to die?

There it was again, connecting to every nerve in Adele's body.

The very sound of terror. Someone screaming. Again. Again.

What was it? A trick. Something to lure her from her spot?

No, that was a sound that could not be faked. Someone was in mortal danger or terrible pain.

Adele didn't have to think about it very long. She left her spot and started to run through the storm again in the direction of the sound.

11

~~~~~~

ADELE

What was she doing here? She'd had this feeling before, a kind of vertiginous tilt to her perception. Once on her wedding day, when she'd stood at the altar with Miller, their friends and family—everyone she'd ever known in her life—watching, expectant. Smiles, happy tears, all eyes on Adele in a stunning silk confection from Paris upon which Miller had insisted, though it had literally cost more than her first car. On Miller's side, there had been just a scattering of a family: a cousin from Duluth, an aunt and uncle from New Mexico, and the rest all friends and colleagues. She liked to think of them as the adoring hoards, people glamoured by Miller's genius, his wealth, his magnetism. They came to each posh party and fundraiser, hanging on his every word. Wasn't the wedding simply the most extravagant event he'd ever launched? And Miller. His wide grin, moist eyes, the way he looked at her, with such adoration. *Who is he looking at?* she remembered wondering. *Who does he see?*

Do you take this man? the Unitarian minister had asked.

And the world tilted. *What am I doing here?*

I do, she'd said, voice barely a whisper. The kiss, the cheers and rose petals, the drift down the aisle—it was like it was all happening to someone else.

Then on the day that Violet was born, a brutal natural childbirth had her experiencing altered states, not recognizing the sounds of her own anguished moaning. Then this little creature in her arms. Someone for whom she was totally responsible, expected to know things, to do right, protect, nurture.

Now a lifetime later, every illusion about love and parenthood shattered, here was that feeling again. A wobble, a tilt, like a glitch in the programming.

The retreating ATVs filled the air with a deafening swarm of sound, a powerful scent of fuel and burning rubber. Maverick, who Adele had only ever seen smiling for the camera, was bleeding from the mouth, his anger, his fear a palpable energy on the air.

This was not right.

They'll call the game off, and I'll go home. Disappointment and relief mingled.

Miller's admonishment from her dream: *You don't belong here, Adele. You know that.*

She did know that. On some very basic level she knew that she had forced herself into a situation that was inorganic, untenable.

"Are you okay?"

She found herself face-to-face with Wild Cody, another person she'd only ever seen on a screen. Taller than she'd imagined, with a rugged, earthy look, rubbing at a chiseled jaw, he had a hand on her arm, as if to steady her.

"I think so," she said, too stunned, too in-the-moment to be starstruck. "What *was* that?"

He shook his head, looked over at Maverick and Angeline, who were huddled, talking in low tones.

"Hard to say. Maybe theater?"

Malinka, who was holding out her phone, talking excitedly,

had obviously gone live during the—what?—the attack? Yes, that's what it was. Armed men, a physical fight, guns drawn. Not theater.

Real danger had not been part of Adele's plan.

Her phone was blowing up with frantic texts from Blake and Violet, who had, because this was the way of it now, watched the whole thing live on Malinka's WeWatch channel.

It's good. It's fine, she thumbed out. **I'm sure it was just for show.**

"These things are always...unpredictable. Cody," he said and offered his hand.

"Adele," she said, taking it. His grip was warm and solid, his skin slightly calloused. Should she tell him that she was a fan, that she and her son had watched every single episode of *Wild Cody*? He held her eyes, seemed to examine her, size her up. Something about his energy had her tongue-tied, awkward.

The sky had gone nearly dark with cloud cover, and Adele felt as though she'd been doused in ice water, every nerve ending tingling. She knew in her gut that whatever had happened, it was definitely not for show. The bad vibration still lingered. She glanced down the road. Those men—would they come back?

It looked real, texted Violet on their three-way text chain. She could imagine her kids sitting side by side at the kitchen bar, not speaking, just staring at their phones.

No way, wrote Blake. **Obviously planned to ramp up views. Mom. Don't freak out. It was just an act. They do stuff like that all the time. You're good. We're good.**

Adele wrote back, **Totally. It's fine. 100%!**

Then Maverick plastered on a big smile. Voice booming, he asked if they were ready to go live. There was a nonreality to it, a filtered strangeness, as if she were watching it all on-screen, not quite believing any of it.

What am I doing here?

She took a breath, pulled herself up tall. She wanted her kids to see her strong, ready for whatever came next. Not afraid and ready to bail, the way she actually felt. She wasn't going to be another disappointment in their lives, another person who failed them.

"Did that just happen?" asked Malinka, coming to stand beside Adele and Cody. Mouth in a grim line, forehead furrowed, hair in tight braided pigtails, Malinka was just a few years older than Violet. But today the young woman's eyes were as old and tired as any soldier's. There was a mettle there, but also a sadness. For some reason, Adele's mind flashed on the photograph she'd seen in Malinka's tent.

Adele pressed back the urge to drop a comforting arm around Malinka's slim shoulders, the way she would if Violet was panicking about whatever and trying not to show it.

"You took a video, right?" said Wild Cody with that enigmatic smile. "So it must be real."

"*Sheet,*" Malinka said softly. Her English grammar was as perfect as any native speaker, but Adele found her accent somehow soothing.

They exchanged a look, and Malinka, maybe unconsciously, moved a step closer to Adele.

"Wild Cody," said Malinka. Eyes wide, she put a hand to her heart. "I watched every episode of your show when I was kid. You probably inspired every single person here."

He touched the brim of his leather hat, offered a grateful nod. He was an odd one, and Adele couldn't stop looking at him.

And then Maverick approached, Gustavo holding the phone camera. Angeline raised her voice and announced, "We are going live in one, two, three…"

Mav seemed to grow an inch and come to life like some animated version of himself.

"Hey, Extremists! We are *live* from Enchantments!"

Maverick was huge, broad, and powerful through the chest, towering over Adele, hands like bear claws, skin dewy with youth, eyes rimmed with fatigue. He moved like things hurt

him, and Adele remembered those fail reels that Blake loved
so much—all those falls, body bending, thrown, landing hard.
Life. It takes its toll, leaves its scars.

"Malinka Nicqui, the youngest woman to climb all Seven
Summits and the founder of the Yes I Can clothing line, a portion of proceeds devoted to empowering women and girls all
over the world. Welcome to Extreme Hide and Seek at Enchantments."

"Hey, Mav," Malinka said to him. "Long time. Congrats on
all your success."

Was there something icy there? An edge to her tone and her
gaze?

"Thank you so much," he said as if he'd said it a million, a
billion times. Not insincere but practiced. Malinka kept an unreadable stare on him, but he didn't seem to notice, talking directly to the camera. "I don't have to ask if you're ready for the
challenge. You were born ready, right?"

Malinka stuck her chin out, put her hands on her hips. "That's
right."

"Do you have any strategies or plans?"

She smiled, her eyes narrow. Was there history? Did they
know each other? "If I did," she said, falsely bright, "I wouldn't
share them with you and the Extreme team, would I?"

His laughter boomed. "Fair enough. I've seen you compete
at the Tough Be-atch competitions. No matter what the haters
say, Malinka is the one to beat."

Was that a dig? Malinka seemed to think so, her expression
going dark, even though she managed to hold on to a tight smile.
Adele remembered reading that some people felt that her summits shouldn't count because her father had helped her. Knowing what Adele knew as a parent and a school counselor, she
knew that Malinka's relationship to her father must have been
complicated. A teenager driven to achieve what she had must

have had someone behind her pushing hard. But she didn't have time to contemplate Malinka's history.

"Adele!" Maverick turned his attention to her.

If she hadn't witnessed him being tackled to the ground by those men, she never would have guessed something so traumatic had happened just minutes before. She'd seen that before, too. Children of abuse or neglect were often good at hiding their pain. Was that his story? "Your kids wanted you to apply for this challenge, right?"

The question reminded her that Extreme knew just about everything there was to know about her. Thinking back to the scare in the hotel last night, she realized that it wouldn't have been hard for them to cross-reference, to discover what Miller's favorite book was. He'd certainly mentioned it in interviews. Maybe the cigarettes were a lucky guess, or maybe she'd said something to Dr. Garvey and didn't remember.

"They did." She matched his tone, keeping it light and easy. "That's right. My son is a big Extreme fan."

"You were quite the runner, right? Back in the day."

"That's right," she said again with a smile. *Back in the day. Before half your viewers were born.* Gustavo had his camera trained on her. "Then life got in the way. Marriage. Two kids."

A lying con man of a husband who was currently on the run from federal authorities.

Maverick gave her a bobbing nod. "I hear you. I know how it is."

No. He really didn't. Maverick—was he even thirty? He knew literally nothing.

"And look at you now," he went on. "Killing it. I've been watching your WeWatch channel. All those half-marathons, climbing walls, the Tough Be-atch wins. You went from Lunch Mom to Super Mom in like a year."

It wasn't condescending, exactly. It was just that he was young and privileged, and he didn't know how painful adult life could be. He couldn't understand how hard she had worked, and what was at stake for her now. Maverick Dillan seemed to float on a cloud of arrogance, looking down.

"It was hard work," she said, holding her smile. "But worth it to be here."

"Not everybody could overcome the things you have. Your husband—he left you, is accused of embezzlement and other crimes, and is still on the run from the law, is that right?"

She found she didn't trust her voice. Why were they talking about this?

Finally, she managed, "We can't always control what happens to us. But we can control how we respond."

"Hey," he said, clapping her on the shoulder. "I *like* that attitude. Maybe *you're* the one to beat, Adele."

"Thanks for the opportunity."

He laughed. "Don't thank me yet! You might want to punch me out before we're through here."

In fact, thought Adele still smiling, *I'd like to punch you out right now*. But he was already turning his attention away.

"Wild Cody! Man, you are the OG. Thanks for coming out."

"I'm glad to be here," he said.

"You've been open about the challenges you've faced over the years."

Oh, right. There was something. A fall from grace, a scandal. It came rushing back. Oh, God. The lion! She still remembered the disturbing image of the bony carcass with Wild Cody standing beside it, boot on its haunches, a rifle strapped around his chest.

He nodded. "True," he said with a nod. "I've made mistakes. I've battled demons. But I'm working to make amends to people I have hurt."

Maverick nodded. The wind picked up, whispering through the trees. Up above, the same three buzzards that had been circling for a while still drifted, hunters patiently waiting. Adele flashed back to the bird ripping apart the carcass on the road, its sharp beak tearing. Its yellow eyes glowing.

"If you win, the money will go to the One Planet, One Love Foundation, dedicated to preserving the wild, untouched places so near to your heart."

"That's right," he said. "Wild places, like this island, deserve our respect and need our protection."

Maverick put prayer hands to his heart and bowed his head. "So true." When he looked back at Cody, he wore a big grin. "Think of all the good that million dollars will do if you win. Think of all the *lions* you can save. Amiright?"

Okay, wow. Maverick was definitely messing with each of them, destabilizing, undermining, antagonizing. Adele guessed it made for good viewing, for drama.

Wild Cody seemed about to say something, but then the camera was back on Maverick. And he was talking about sponsors and about another contestant who still hadn't arrived.

Malinka and Cody stood on either side of her. Cody had his arms folded around his middle, eyes trained on Maverick. Malinka was watching Maverick's WeWatch live broadcast on her phone rather than actually looking at Maverick. For that generation, it seemed like the online world was more real than the actual one. They weren't her allies; they were her opponents. But somehow after those interviews, it felt like them against Maverick.

Maverick was still talking.

In her pocket, her phone vibrated. Probably the kids, telling her how she did.

But no.

Another strange number.

Go home before it's too late. You're not safe.

There was that feeling again. That strange out-of-body wobble. Very faintly in the distance, Enchantments groaned.

What was she doing here?

Maverick's voice boomed in the dim. "The next time we go
live it will be game time. Ready or not, Extremists, here we
come!"

12

~~~~~~

MAVERICK

Sometimes when shit got really hairy, Maverick went some-where else inside his head. As if there was a little room inside his brain that he could climb into and work the big Maverick puppet from a control center. No matter how scared or sad or afraid he became, or how badly he was hurt, that part of him-self, the one that could still feel, made himself very small and hid away, pulling all the right levers and strings so that the Mav puppet could face the world with a smile. *Never, ever let them see you cry.* That's what his mother had taught him. When the cam-era went off, that was the time for tears if necessary. And even then, his mother had little patience. *Walk it off,* she'd tell him, no matter what had happened. *Pain is inconvenience, nothing more. It's a construct of your mind.*

Was it, though?

At the end, his mother drifted on a morphine cloud, a liv-ing ghost of herself, barely conscious, eyes staring past him into a place only she could see. His whole body shook sometimes when he allowed himself to think about her final days. He almost never allowed himself to, only when he was really hurting, like now. That's when he missed her the most.

She'd pushed him to be his best self, too hard sometimes. But no one else on the planet had ever loved him so much. He was someone special beneath her gaze, which was also the camera's gaze. He was a star through her lens.

That tackle to the ground, those two men on top of him, crushing his chest. The breath leaving him. One of the men had a deep scar under his eye, his expression blank as if violence was routine for him, like he didn't even care. The other kneeled on Maverick's bad arm, kneecap digging into tendons. He had been pinned, powerless, hot rage turning to a chilling panic. How were they so strong? He was screaming at them, but he felt that part of himself retreat to the control room. And then he just went still, defeated, staring at the bigger man who stared back, blank.

Now he was on his feet again, the men roaring off on their ATVs, the hum disappearing into the trees.

Everyone was looking at him. They needed him to be strong, to keep going. That's what his mom had needed, for him to keep going and going, no matter who or how much he hurt. In the control room, he punched all the right buttons. *Dust off. Shake it off. Smile. Big smile. Never let them see that the crazy old bitch and her goons scared the shit out of you. That they got the best of you in that moment.*

He turned to Malinka and Adele and did his thing. But he wasn't there. They weren't there. They were just NPCs in the game of his mind, part of his universe but only just, only for right now.

Then Angeline turned on the live stream, and he felt himself settle a little. The dread receded and he was on, back in his body. Talking to the thousands of people who wanted to experience the next Extreme challenge from the peace and comfort of their homes. He kept his eyes off the comments. Or tried to.

KittyX25: Where is Chloe? We know you know.

Engine49: Closure for the Miranda family! Time to face the music, Extreme. Where is she?

ChloesDad: Where is she, Maverick?

MavIsALiar: Ready or not. Here I come.

But they just floated by him. The Maverick at the controls entered *Ignore the haters*.

"So that's everyone," he told the live stream. "Or almost. Grrl Power Malinka, Super Mom Adele, the OG Adventurer Wild Cody. There's one more surprise hider. He's someone most of you know and love, *Red World* master gamer, and WeWatch celebrity. Stayed tuned for the big announcement right before we begin the game."

Angeline held up a single finger.

He knew that this meant: spon con package number one. This package cost the sponsor fifty thousand dollars for an embedded product mention, in this case Extreme Quench, named after Mav's company. It also included a visible product placement, like one of them drinking from a can in way that seemed unplanned, one reel, and two posts over the course of the challenge.

Gustavo tossed him a can, and he caught it with one hand, held it up for Angeline. She was smiling now. She was happy again, back in the zone with him. That was childishly important to him.

He took a long deep swallow and tried not to gag.

"Wow! I just love this stuff. Have you guys tried Extreme Quench?"

Another swallow, thinking, *Damn, this stuff tastes like ass.* The first time he tried it, he literally thought he was going to vomit. He was on the toilet for an hour after the Bonkers Banana flavor.

"I mean, you know when you hit that four-o'clock slump, and you're just like, man, I don't have the juice for the gym, or a couple more hours of productivity, or my side hustle. Whatever it is?"

Off camera, Angeline was nodding. Gustavo was sticking

his finger down his throat and pretending to spew. Mav tried not to laugh.

"Just one of these—look how small it is!—and wow, I'm not kidding, it is *rocket fuel*. Whatever you need to do, you can do it with energy to spare. And even better—no sugar, tons of vitamins and antioxidants—and no disruption to your sleep later. Kooky Coconut, Manic Mango, Bonkers Banana, Brain Blaster Berry, and five other great flavors."

The comments scrolled and scrolled: heart eyes and star eyes, hearts, flowers, party horns. Marriage proposals, declarations of love. He was getting fat. He was superhot. He looked tired. Some slags on Extreme Quench: *rotgut, poison, gave me the runs*.

MavIsALiar: Do you even listen to yourself?

Ignore. Ignore. Ignore.

When he looked up from the screen, he caught Wild Cody's eyes. The older man was staring at Mav with this weird smile, as if he had a secret. As if he knew Mav's number. Angeline was right, maybe. He should have checked with her before answering Wild Cody's publicist, Brett, who was an old pal from the neighborhood. Brett was one of those guys you hired when your brand was in the toilet. For Wild Cody, the toilet would be a step up.

"The next time we go live it will be game time. Ready or not, Extremists, here we come!"

And then it was quiet again, and Angeline came to him, wrapped her arms around his middle. He looked down at her. She was the whole package: brains, beauty, kindness. No, he did not deserve her, and he knew this with every cell in his body. He held on to her anyway.

"Are you okay?" she asked, keeping her voice low.

He wanted to tell her *no*. That he wasn't okay and hadn't been for a while. And was there any way they could pull the plug on this? Maybe on everything? That he was tired and hurt, that shit was catching up with him in a big way. And he didn't know if he had what it took to play the game tonight or any more games ever. And could he just have a moment to figure out who he was off-screen, with her?

"Yeah, yeah," he said instead. "I'm good."

"Mav."

"For real. As long as you're here, I can do anything."

That was going to be the big finale, another proposal. He had it all planned for right before the last of the final two contestants were found when viewership was highest. The ring was *insane*, a two-karat cushion-cut pink diamond. He'd already returned two to the jeweler, each new one bigger than the last. This time, he felt certain she'd say *yes*.

"I'm here," she said. He leaned in to kiss her, and everyone cheered and jeered. Except for Cody, who kept that bizarre grin plastered on his face. Gustavo watched him and Angeline with an expression Mav couldn't read.

Just then Hector arrived with the big van, rumbling around the huge circular drive. As usual he was bringing up the rear, missing all the action.

"Are you ever going to say *yes*, Angeline?" teased Malinka, approaching them.

Angeline looked up at Mav. Those eyes, her full lips, the jutting cheekbones and dewy skin. The sound of her laughter. He'd never loved anyone or anything like he loved her. That's why he was going to be a better man. From now on.

Angeline smiled. His favorite look, the one that said she saw him, all of him, and loved him anyway. Malinka snapped a picture.

"We'll see," said Angeline.

13

ANGELINE

As she finished setting up their tent, Angeline was still jittery and agitated from the violence between Petra's men and Maverick. She kept seeing the men taking Mav to the ground. Petra's words echoed. And that moment when she thought about leaving came back to her again and again. But she pushed it all aside. Angeline was good at putting distress away; her life with Maverick necessitated it.

Maverick and Angeline were last to get their tent up after mucking about with all the other equipment in the trailer, managing the social-media shitstorm that followed Malinka's (unauthorized and in violation of their contract with her) live where Mav was attacked, and hundreds of thousands watched on their phones.

Just what they needed. More bad press.

On the other hand, the video *was* going viral. Six hours until game time. And truthfully, views and follower numbers *were* way up.

So why did she feel so sick? A pall had settled. And where was Alex?

He wasn't answering her texts.

Angeline sat on top of her sleeping bag, using her cellular hot spot to sift through a swath of emails from the lawyers, not to mention a nastygram from the CEO of Quench who claimed that it was clear to everyone that Mav's heart was *just not in* the content he'd broadcast for their shitty drink. Which everybody, like *everybody*, hated. But she'd written them an email that she hoped was soothing. She just prayed that Quench wouldn't go under before they made their final payment.

She called Alex again. Straight to voicemail. She didn't bother to leave another message.

Stress was a white noise that never went silent.

There was another sound now, too, a kind of rumbling growl. She hadn't noticed it at first, but now it leaked into her consciousness. She listened. What was that?

She clamped her laptop closed. Then something else, layered over the rumbling.

Voices. Someone yelling.

What now?

She cast about for her jacket, found it in a tangle on top of the duffel bags Mav had been hauling around. What was in there? She felt around for the zipper on one of them and discovered that it was locked. The other one, too.

What are you up to, Maverick?

She stared at the black bags a moment, frustration rising. She gave one a kick with her toe. Heavy but soft, malleable. Could be anything in there. Finally, she gave up. She'd find out soon enough. Or so Maverick kept promising.

Angeline stepped out into the cool, damp afternoon.

The other tents were pitched in a loose circle around the fire pit. Where was everyone? Probably scouting the site. That's what she'd be doing if she was participating.

Clouds swirled above. The fresh smell of the trees was a balm to her spirit. The dirt beneath her feet felt solid, as she crossed the campsite, heading to the trailer.

She felt Enchantments watching her. She stopped to stare at it a moment. It had a presence, an attitude. Petra's voice rang back to Angeline. *This land is unwell.* Did she believe that? That places could be sick, or haunted, evil?

She thought of Eaton House, where they'd staged their Extreme Haunted Hide and Seek. The place hadn't seemed evil as much as it seemed tired; bad things had happened there, horrible things. But as far as Angeline could feel then, there was no echo of past horrors, no lingering specters.

She decided standing there that Enchantments, likewise, was just a place.

People could be sick, haunted, evil, their deeds creating a terrible legacy. But, if anything, places were just impervious, indifferent. They just stood observing the folly, standing long after their inhabitants had returned to the earth. The trees whispered all around her, bearing witness to all their human madness and remaining unchanged.

Angeline moved noiselessly toward the human sounds that were coming from around the bend.

As she walked, she recognized the other sound she'd heard. The boys must have gassed up the generator for the trailer. The sound spoiled something about the place, disrupted the ancient beauty. And the smell of burning fuel hit her nostrils. They were pollution. Toxic. *We taint and ruin*, she thought before pushing that negative thought away quickly, too.

Mav and Gustavo were fighting, their voices carrying through the thin walls of the trailer as she approached, loud enough to be heard above the generator, which was *loud*.

God, people, nature. That's what Petra had said in their initial meeting and it resonated. Her abuela used to say in heavily accented English, *You can't fool Mother Nature.*

If that was true, and those were the only important things, then what the hell were they all doing? What would Mav say were the most important things? Thrills, views, money—not necessarily in that order.

She pushed in the door, and they didn't see her at first.

Gustavo was pointing angrily at his phone.

Hector was sitting with his head in his hands, like the abused kid forced to listen to his parents arguing.

On Gustavo's screen there was a big swath of red. He tapped it hard.

"This storm," he said. "It's coming, Mav. Tonight."

"It's a little rain. So what? It just adds to the atmosphere."

That cocksure smile, those folded muscular arms. How was he always so confident, even after everything? How had his life, a challenging one in spite of how it might look online, not brought him a shred of humility or self-doubt? For a moment she hated him a little. But it passed.

"What's going on?" she asked.

They all shifted their gazes to her, caught, like their mom had just walked into the room.

She was Wendy. They were her Lost Boys.

Mav lifted his palms. "Gustavo's freaking out about the rain."

"Angeline, it's not just rain." Gustavo moved over toward her. His dark eyes pinned her. For an adrenaline junkie, he was reliable, levelheaded. "It's a tropical storm. High winds, heavy rain. The hotel—the empty elevator shafts, the basement—it all fills with water. The land here, it swamps. It's dangerous."

Mav came over to stand beside him. He looked back and forth between them.

"Guys," he said. "We have forty-eight hours and then we have to leave. I don't have to tell you how much money is riding on this, do I? Spon con, advertising dollars, the WeWatch bonus?"

It was a balancing act, how much they spent on things like this and how much they earned. If they didn't get the views—and truthfully, until Malinka's live, they'd been losing subscribers at an alarming rate, views were down dramatically, and so was revenue—they didn't get the payout. Even the sponsors weren't paying as much for content since Chloe had gone missing and the Moms Against Mav campaign. All the mainstream brands had dropped them. Only places like Quench were still on board.

"Where's Alex?" asked Angeline.

He was the only one she could rely on to give her an accurate cost analysis.

"I think he's still at the hotel," said Hector, offering a shrug. He had raccoon rings of fatigue around his eyes. His black curls were wild, and there was a stain on his shirt. She had the urge to put him in clean pajamas and tuck him in somewhere.

No one said anything for a moment.

"He left," said Maverick. He looked down at his feet, shuffled them like a kid.

"What does that mean?" she asked, trying not to panic. "He *left?*"

"He, uh—he quit," said Mav, bowing his head and stepping back.

"What? No."

This was not happening. She thought back to Alex waiting in the dark of the suite for her.

Ange… We have to talk.

Then, too, the echo of another conversation with Alex before they'd left for the islands. "I found something in the books. Something I don't understand."

But she'd blown him off. *Look, let's just get through this challenge, and we'll have a serious financial meeting.*

He'd given her a look that she didn't understand. Now that she was thinking about it again, she realized that it was pity, maybe also anger.

"What happened?" she asked, squaring off to Maverick.

He kicked his right foot, kept his eyes down like a boy in the principal's office.

"We argued after the meeting with Anton," he said and rubbed a nervous hand over the crown of his head, something

he did when he was upset. "He didn't want to make the donation. He wanted to pull the plug on this. I said no. And he like
lost it a little."

Angeline felt a dump of dread, like the only other adult chap-
erone had left the summer camp, and she was alone with the
kids, outmanned, outgunned.

"He can't *quit*," said Angeline, a rise of desperation making
her voice shrill. "He's a partner."

"Yeah, we have to work that all out," said Mav, with a wave
of his hand. "Whatever. His loss. We don't need him."

He wore the Mav mask, the one he donned when he was
hurting.

"When were you going to tell me this?" asked Angeline.

"I'm telling you now." That was so Mav, to pretend that he
hadn't omitted critical information from her.

"*When* did he leave?"

"This morning. Before we left the hotel, I tried to talk to
him. We fought again. He said he was leaving." Maverick offered an elaborate shrug, palms raised.

"So we don't have a CFO."

"You know as much as Alex does, right?" said Mav to Angeline.

Did he really think that? That anyone could just step into the
role of chief financial officer of this shitshow? Did he not know
that Alex had been holding them together for the better part of a
year with a financial shell game that Angeline could barely follow, while Maverick continued to spend unchecked? The goddamn jet was costing them around a hundred thousand a month.

"No," she said. "I don't. At all. Like not even close."

"Look how well you managed that Quench asshole."

"That is not the same thing."

She saw it then. In Mav's eyes. Fear. He knew how fucked
they were. On some deep level, he knew. But the look was gone
quickly.

"It's fine," he said, with a deep exhale. "We'll deal with it when we get back. He probably didn't even mean it. He's just mad. He'll cool off."

Gustavo leaned against the trailer wall, watching her darkly. He'd stayed silent, but she could feel his eyes.

She took her phone from her pocket and called Alex again. No answer. She hung up, frustration and anger rising like bile. How could he do this to her? What would she do without him?

"We don't need him for this," said Mav.

Hector put his head down on his arms. Gustavo looked off into the middle distance.

"Guys," said Mav into the uncomfortable silence, "we *cannot* afford *not* to do this challenge. And it's going to be so epic. When we're done, all our problems will be handled."

Angeline was aware of a vein throbbing in her throat, heat in her cheeks. Nobody said anything. Outside, the sky grew light, then fell dark again. Was that lightning?

"Look," said Mav finally. He walked over to Angeline and took both of her hands. "I know things have been bad. But I promise you, when this is over, and we're flush with cash again, we'll go home and fix everything that's broken at Extreme."

She could see in his face that he really believed it. He thought that the problems Extreme had—falling revenue, lawsuits, the disappearance of Chloe Miranda, the upcoming IRS audit— he could just charm his way out of it. Part of her wanted to believe it, too.

The bill is about to come due for Maverick. Save yourself if you even can.

You can't save them. But maybe you can still save yourself.

MavIsALiar and Petra, people with no connection to each other, saying essentially the same thing, speaking directly to her.

Her abuela would say, *The universe speaks to us in all sorts of ways. Listen,* mija.

Mav was pleading. "Please believe in me, Ange. I'll fix everything, I promise. Just…let's get through this."

He turned to Gustavo, who was watching Angeline intently. "When is it coming? The storm."

Gustavo shifted his gaze back to Maverick. "Tonight, before midnight."

"See? That's perfect. We'll start at sunset. By midnight, we'll be packing up. We'll keep it tight."

Gustavo nodded reluctantly. "If things go as planned. If you find everyone fast."

Mav brightened. "Look, Hector is going to place the wireless cameras. Everyone is going to have a tracker. We won't look at their locations unless we have to, right? But we'll know where everyone is. So no surprises. Not like last time."

They'd been accused of cheating before. Of making sure certain people won to ramp up views, generate goodwill, please sponsors, or whatever. Like Benito, the gamer kid from East LA whose mom had died from Covid, or Tania, the Jamaican teen beauty-influencer who needed money for college. Angeline knew Mav's personal favorite for this challenge was Adele, the mom who'd been to hell and back, remade herself, and was working hard for her kids. Maybe he thought it would earn some love from the Moms Against Mav. That was Mav, always thinking.

"There are only twenty casitas, the pool house and cabanas, and the spa. The ramp down to the beach is way overgrown. No one's going down there. There's the hotel itself, which is like an echo chamber. Sounds carry. It will be easy to find anyone who hides there. All the doors are gone anyway. Everything is wide-open."

Another beat. Another breath. Another chance for her to say, *No, we're done here. I'm pulling the plug.* She was about to, really. But.

"Okay," said Gustavo finally. "If we're out by midnight."

Mav slapped him hard on the back. And Gustavo offered a reluctant smile.

Angeline watched them embrace, a big, hard-patting man hug. She moved toward the door, grabbed the keys from the table.

"Where are you going?" asked Mav, brow wrinkling, hand reaching for her.

"I'm going to find Alex, talk him out of quitting."

"Fuck him," said Mav. "He hasn't been *with us*, not really, since he had that kid. Let him go."

"I'll go with you," said Tavo to Angeline. She was about to decline his offer, but instead she found herself nodding.

She thought Mav might step in, say he'd go with her. But he didn't. What was that look on his face? It was new. "We'll stay here and get everything set up," he said, turning his attention to the equipment on the table. "In and out. Easy. You'll see. I—"

Angeline stepped out of the trailer, closing the door on Mav, who was still talking.

"Uh...okay, goodbye," he shouted through the closed door.

She looked up. The clouds above had cleared some; it didn't *look* like a big storm was coming.

She didn't say another word as Tavo followed her to the big SUV, climbed in the passenger seat. He knew better than to even suggest he might drive.

14

ADELE

Change is relentless, Miller used to say. *Even when things seem like they're standing still, they're in constant motion. The good. The bad. Nothing lasts.*

That's what Adele had loved about Miller first, his mind. No one would call him handsome in a classic sense. Tall and lanky, too thin, with a long nose and searing dark eyes. He wore his hair to his shoulders, was a distance runner. What he lacked in beauty he made up for in confidence, virility. It was his intensity, his passion, his appetites—for great food, for art, for invention and design—his ideas, that drew her in and kept her rapt. It was like the world was just this expansive buffet for him, wide-open, all-you-can-eat, there for the taking. And he took it with gusto.

They'd met at a half-marathon in Florida. Adele thought of it often. How she had just graduated from college, wondering what she was going to do with her English degree. She had been a middling student, restless, disorganized. She struggled to sit through classes, always looking for the next physical challenge, anything that would get her outside and into her body. She'd had the vague, childish idea that she wanted to help people. An online quiz pointed her toward psychology, and she was thinking about it. Even though she didn't know if she could take more school or even if she could get in after her mediocre undergraduate performance.

She finished well in the half-marathon, beating her personal best, and at the last minute decided to attend the after-party instead of crashing in front of the television in her cheap hotel room. It was a glittery night on Clearwater Beach, stars twinkling, palms swaying, the scent of jasmine on the cool air.

She mingled a bit, congratulated the winner, consoled someone who'd turned an ankle and was on crutches at the party. Then she'd wandered outside by herself to listen to the waves.

"You overpronate," he said to her, coming up and handing her a glass of white wine she didn't order. She'd been standing at the edge of the hotel pool deck, looking out at the Gulf of Mexico. Something about his smile. She took the glass.

"Oh?" she said. First thought about Miller: *What an arrogant jerk.* But in an amusing way.

"Yeah," he said, coming to lean on the railing beside her. "You turn your right foot out just a little when you run."

Because every woman loves a mansplainer.

"I know what *overpronate* means."

He regarded her, offered a nod. "It slows you down and will likely lead to injury. You're young, but if you like to run and want to keep doing it, I'd see a physical therapist."

"Let me guess. You're a physical therapist."

He laughed at that, a warm, generous sound that made her want to laugh, too.

"No," he said. "I'm a biotech engineer. I design prosthetics. So I know a few things about how the body works. Plus, I have my own overpronation to contend with, and the resulting injury from ignoring it."

They spent the rest of that night together, just talking about his work, about what she wanted to do with her life. Did he know she was unformed? Unmoored? She wondered about that later. Did he somehow sense that she was looking for direction, that she wasn't secure on her own path in life? Maybe it was just her youth, ten years younger than Miller, that told him the story about Adele. Her parents had bankrolled six months. "Find yourself," her father had urged. "Travel. Do the things you love, let them lead you now, while you're young and free. Once you get into the thick of it, work, family, life, it's harder to change course." That *find yourself* fund was running out.

The next thing she knew she was engaged to Miller, working at his company in human resources. She was good at it; it checked a box. She was helping people find meaningful work, counseling them when they struggled. Then she and Miller were married. Then she was pregnant with Violet. Miller wanted her to stay home for a year; she'd wanted that, too. Then there was Blake. Then she was corporate wife, full-time mom, hosting events, running charity auctions, sitting in car lines. The years ticked by.

"Was this what you wanted?" her father had asked during a visit. It was a gentle query, not a judgment. Though, it felt like one.

"What could be better than this?" her mother put in. "Look at her life."

The big house, the beautiful cars, the boat, the private school. She was blessed. Privileged. She knew that; it would be ungrateful to complain about anything. She was too busy to worry for long about whether or not there could have been something else for her. She told Miller what her dad had said.

"You're young," Miller said. "There's time for you to figure out another chapter when the kids are older."

That made sense. She saw so many people they knew struggle with two big careers and multiple kids. Marriages imploded under the strain; the kids were the collateral damage. She and Miller, their roles were clearly defined. He ran his company;

she ran their life. It worked until it didn't. Until he grew dark and started to pull away, subtly at first. Then disappearing on sudden trips, sleeping at the office, withdrawn, preoccupied at home with her and even the kids.

She thought maybe he was having an affair.

Then one night, he didn't come home from work when she expected him, didn't call to say he'd be late. She couldn't reach him. She still remembered that creeping knowledge that something was horribly wrong as she watched the kids sleep. She sat in the dim hallway outside their rooms, calling and calling him. Over and over.

The next morning the FBI raided his office and their house. She never saw her husband again.

She couldn't go there, to that moment when she felt like she'd built her life on quicksand and had no idea how she was going to get herself and the kids out as she sank and suffocated.

Never let them grab you by the throat. Another Millerism, as she'd come to think of it. Things that he said *before*, that meant one thing, that might have seemed funny or ironic or wise. But that seemed to mean something else entirely *after*.

She had that feeling now, of the air being squeezed from her, as the rest of the group seemed to take the violence and drama in stride and go about their business: pitching tents, and setting up the command center, starting the fire as the air seemed to grow cooler, damper. Only Wild Cody wore an expression that matched her concern, a kind of curious frown, as he expertly and quickly set up his small tent. He turned to look at her, and she blushed to be caught staring. But he just flashed her an enigmatic smile and disappeared into his tent.

Another Millerism: *Always take the time to examine your options.* What were her choices now?

The strange woman, the armed men, and their altercation with Maverick took the supposed game to another level. She'd come here to play hide and seek, to win money. Not to risk her life, leaving her kids with no one. She stared at the last ominous text. It seemed to pulse on her screen.

She could quit, get a ride back to the airport, where she'd book a flight home.

But then she remembered her maxed-out credit cards. The rent. The back taxes she still owed from the games Miller had played with the IRS. Her meager paycheck barely covered their monthly expenses. She had almost no savings. The slim earnings from the sale of their big house after the IRS garnished some of it, and she discovered Miller had borrowed against it, was almost gone. Every month she had less money, not more. There was college coming for both kids. Her own future to consider.

She couldn't go home. She couldn't face another failure. It seemed Extreme, or maybe circumstances, had her by the throat. There were no options. Only to play and win.

Malinka and the Extreme team had disappeared.

The trailer generator roared to life.

Adele wondered if she was the only one who was left feeling like a strange pall had settled over everything. Then she realized the difference between her and the others. She was a mom. The stakes, for her, were higher than they were for anyone else here.

Adele returned to her tent, shouldered her pack, light with just a bottle of water, some jerky, a small first-aid kit. She attached her backpack light and slipped from the tent, moving soundlessly toward the narrow path that led to the casitas.

Though they were just approaching noon, the heavy cloud cover and thick foliage made it feel like night. Somewhere a bird called, long and low. The trees and foliage seemed in constant motion, shifting, whispering in the wind, frequent scurrying in the underbrush.

A storm was coming. She was receiving weather updates from Blake, who was tracking the system as it made its way toward the island. But Adele didn't fear the natural world. People with

all their secrets and lies, hidden agendas, the masks they wore…
that's what scared her.

Check out the casitas for your hiding place, suggested Blake.
That's where I would hunker down if I was playing.

The paver stones were jagged and crooked as teeth, years of
neglect allowing them to settle unevenly into the red earth beneath. Thick weeds had pushed up; vines reached treacherously
across. Adele kept her footing light, her eyes on the ground in
front of her, knowing that one wrong step could lead to a trip—
a tweaked knee, a twisted ankle. Any injury could be the difference between winning and losing.

The path wound, studded by rusted ground lamps that no
longer worked. More movement in thick woods all around her,
skuttling.

Her own breathing was loud in the silence.

Up ahead, the pool deck. Porticos grown over, tables long
toppled covered with creeping vines, rusted chairs tilted every
which way, overgrown with weeds, the pool itself full of garbage, debris, even a small tree that had grown up through the
plaster bottom. Nature will take itself back. The made things we
leave behind will be slowly swallowed by the earth. Something
comforting in that, right? That we can only do so much damage. That the temporary nature of our existence limits our harm.

Just down one of the paths that slivered off the pool deck she
knew she'd find the casitas. Spacious cabins with multiple rooms.
She'd already been here, in a sense, using Blake's WholeEarth-
Now image to inspect the property from above. She knew the
place as well as she could from a distance.

It must have been stunningly beautiful once, a paradisial hide-
away for the very rich. She'd cast about for photos online and
found a pdf of a back issue of *Elegant Traveler* magazine. Gor-
geously appointed rooms, poolside cabanas with flowing gauzy
curtains, marble lobby with a tiered crystal chandelier. No expense had been spared in the pursuit of a luxurious setting.

Real-estate mogul Enrico Bello borrowed way too much money to build Esperança. He'd erected this behemoth in an effort to bring Americans and Europeans to a hidden paradise. But limited flights from the US and too-high prices for most European travelers had kept the property from prospering. Staff, unpaid, left their posts. Things slowly fell to seed. Less than five years from opening to abandonment. Now forty years later, it crumbled, a monument to failure.

She'd known men like Enrico, men whose ambition surpassed their means, their abilities. She'd married one. Adele was familiar with the feeling of picking her way through the ruins of a once-beautiful thing.

The sound of movement up ahead stopped her in her tracks. Not animal scurry. Footsteps, hard and quick. Adele shifted off the path and crouched in the foliage. She made herself still and small, willing herself to disappear into the heavy shadows.

"What are we doing?" A male voice. Tense and angry. "This is...wrong."

Hector. One of Maverick's crew.

He stopped just feet from where she had hidden herself. She held her breath and watched as he took something from his pack, which he wore on the front of his body like a marsupial pouch.

"This wasn't the plan," he said. "It wasn't supposed to be like *this*."

He was obviously on the phone, talking to someone through his earbuds.

"Alex is gone. Angeline looks like she's about to stroke out from stress. Mav is just...unhinged. It's not fun anymore."

Adele watched as he placed a small wireless camera carefully in the crook of a branch, affixing it with some kind of gummy substance. Expertly, he arranged foliage around the lens. No one would see it as they were passing by in the dark.

Okay, so the game was rigged. Good to know. She'd figured as much, she just hadn't known how. This was why her father always insisted on recon before any excursion. He'd study trails online, scan through hiker and climber reviews, get all the data he could about the weather, the area. He had taught Adele that knowing your environment was critical to success.

Hector, a bulky shadow, glanced around, uneasy. Maybe he sensed her staring at him. His eyes grazed over her hiding space but didn't stop.

Was that who she'd seen last night? Maybe he'd been setting up cameras in the hotel, or even planting the book and the cigarettes, to remind her of Miller, to throw her off-kilter. Another thought had occurred to her, too. Something Agent Coben had said, about how people on the run could rarely stay away. How they had their ways of getting in touch. But it wasn't possible. Was it?

"No," he said. "No. I'm with you. Of course I am. It's just—"

One of her superpowers since becoming a mom was the almost sixth sense she'd developed to detect when someone was lying. It hadn't kicked in with her husband until it was far too late, unfortunately. But with her own kids and those who found their way to her office for this or that infraction or issue, she was like a tuning fork that vibrated in the presence of deception. Was it the way his voice came up an octave? Or the tension in that second *no*? The way his words sounded like a plea. Who was he still with—or not? What was he talking about?

But then Hector kept moving up the path, back toward the campsite. His voice growing softer, words becoming inaudible. Adele waited.

She was about to shift in her spot when, down the path in the direction she was headed, she saw another figure step out in front of Hector. Slim, light-footed, and hooded, the form seemed to slip from the darkness between the trees, then stand in the center of the path, arms akimbo. Words were exchanged. Adele couldn't hear, though she edged closer, straining to catch the words.

Then the two figures came together. Were they fighting?

No. They were kissing, arms wrapping passionately around one another. After a moment, the two moved off down the path.

Okay. Who *was* that?

Malinka? Angeline? She waited a few moments, crouching in the silence, listening. Angeline was with Maverick. And Hector certainly didn't seem like Malinka's type.

So who was that? But they were gone now.

Adele puzzled over it another moment, then she continued down the path, determined to know everything she could about her environment, having learned more than she'd expected about the game.

After a while, she came to the place she'd been looking for. She'd seen it on the satellite image Blake had sent. A casita, nestled in overgrowth, not the farthest from the hotel but the one on highest ground. It was a ruin: a tree had fallen and rested against the tile roof, and the door stood gaping. The sun had disappeared behind a thickening cloud cover, casting the world in a dusky gloom.

Maybe this game was rigged, maybe it wasn't. Maybe she was fearless, maybe she wasn't. But Adele knew one thing for sure. She going to use every resource at her disposal, and for once, she was going to win.

And then no one would ever have her by the throat again.

15

~~~~~~

MALINKA'S Private Video Diary

The Game

"*I don't know if anyone will ever see this. I've lost service and the charge is running low. If I die here, maybe no one will even find my phone. So this might be pointless.*"

In the distance, the sounds of the storm are an oncoming train. The focus is tight on Malinka's bright, heavily lashed eyes. The area around her is dark. Her voice is low and urgent. She's crying.

"*The game has begun, and I am in my hiding spot. But the storm is out of control. And I don't know if anyone is coming.*"

She shifts, eyes red-rimmed. The wind howls, and there's a low groaning. She startles at a loud clap of thunder.

"*If anyone does find this, please, I just wanted people to know the truth. I haven't been totally honest about why I'm here. I came to play. But there were other reasons, too.*"

She takes a breath. "*It's been a full year of asking questions, digging deep.*"

For a moment she goes quiet, glances around her.

"*I came here to confront Maverick Dillan, to demand answers about my missing friend, Chloe Miranda. But I've failed her. I'm no closer to* understanding what happened to her than I was, except that I might be next. I might be the next person to hide in an Extreme challenge and never go home."

There's an unidentifiable noise off camera. Malinka's eyes dart around beyond the lens.

"Chloe and I met at a Tough Be-atch competition on Kauai a couple of years ago. We already followed each other on Photogram. I loved her body-positive, mental-wellness message, and she was a fan of my you-go-grrl empowerment stance, and an influencer for my clothing line. When we met...it was like an instant friendship connection. Like we were sisters separated at birth. Have you ever felt like that? Ever met a person that you felt like you'd known your whole life?"

Malinka wipes away a tear.

"I haven't had many friends. I didn't have a normal childhood, always so busy with the mission of summiting and tutoring for all the school I missed. Then my dad was sick."

She shakes her head, rubs at her forehead with her free hand.

"Then I started my company. So the few friends that I have are like family to me, you know. Anyway, Chloe and I bonded because we tied for third place, basically getting our asses kicked and emerging from the course injured. Her elbow, my knee. Who won that day?"

Malinka rolls her eyes at the camera.

"Angeline Alba. She finished the course a full five minutes before everyone else. Some people thought it was rigged, like she had a shortcut or something. But nah. She was one of the strongest, fastest, most focused competitors I've ever seen in those games. So hats off—even though she was fully five years older than we were."

Malinka pulls the camera out so that more of her is visible. She's wearing a tight red puffer jacket and cap. Around her the walls are cracked and covered with graffiti. That low groaning gets louder, and Malinka glances up at the ceiling.

"When I met her, Chloe was already a little obsessed with Maverick. She said that they'd hooked up in Colorado earlier that year and that he'd essentially ghosted her. But she was looking to rekindle whatever spark *there had been between them. She approached him at the after-party, where he was going to present the check to the winner later that night. From where I was sitting, he looked very happy to see her. Big hug, a quick kiss on the lips. It was all* hey, girl *and* it's been a minute."

Malinka disappears off-frame. The sound of rain is a ceaseless hiss.

"Chloe, she was—is—a beauty, with honey-colored hair and a bomb-shell body. She introduced Mav and me. He was personable, charming. She played it cool at first. Like 'Did you get my texts?'"

Malinka pulls a face and makes her voice deep to impersonate Mav.

"And he was all like 'Aw, no, sorry. I lost my phone. I have a new number.'"

The screen grows bright with another flash of lightning. Malinka looks up again.

"Even though I didn't know her well, I could tell she was starstruck, smitten. Their body language told me that there was a definite attraction— the way Mav leaned into her, how she kept touching him, her hair. For a while they disappeared, and I mingled about. Given the chemistry be-tween them, I figured they'd left together."

Malinka turns the lens around, and the new angle reveals the aban-doned casita. Her hand reaches into the frame, and she opens a closet door.

"But no, after a while Chloe found me again. I asked her what hap-pened, and she said that she and Mav were going to hook up after. We danced and drank, flirted with some other guys. I met someone, too. Looked like we were both going to get lucky."

Malinka's face fills the screen again. The frame bounces as she sits.

"Unfortunately for Chloe, that was the night that Maverick met An-geline. There was electricity between them from the very first moment. On stage together, when he presented Angeline with her prize and she donated it to Big Blue Ocean right there on the spot, you could see it. The chemistry. Fireworks."

Malinka makes a bursting motion with the fingers of her free hand.

"I remember the expression on Chloe's face. She saw it, too. That's *when I knew that she had more than a passing crush. She looked heart-broken. Later, Maverick and Angeline left together."*

Malinka stares at the camera, her expression intense, angry.

"'I heard he's a dick,' I told her as we walked back to the hotel. 'A womanizer. A liar. Bullet dodged, if you ask me.' She looped her arm through mine. We were both a little wobbly from our injuries and too much to drink, so we were essentially holding each other up.

"'I'm not giving up that easy,' she said. 'There's something there. And I'm going to make him see it.' I liked her fire, her determination.

"'You go, girl,' I told her.

"'You know,' she said, 'we meet guys and hook up at these things. And it's always a mess, right? But with you, I feel like I found a friend for life.'

"'You did.'"

Malinka's eyes fill with tears again. They spill, and she wipes at them, still looking at the camera.

"I dropped her off at her hotel room, stumbled back to mine. We had a heart connection, a soul-sister bond. But I didn't know a lot about Chloe at that time. I didn't know how obsessive she could become about things. How much she wanted Mav."

A loud crash off camera. Malinka turns, her face is in profile.

She's whispering now.

"I told her to let him go. But she just got more and more obsessed, even after he proposed to Angeline and made her the COO of his company. We started to drift apart a little. But I still loved her, hoped for the best for her."

More tears trail down Malinka's face.

"I didn't get picked for the Extreme Haunted Hide and Seek, even though Chloe and I had hoped to do it together. I tried to convince her to drop out, to let it go. But she wouldn't. The last text I got from her read, 'I know so much about Mav at this point. I am going to tell Angeline about us. And that will be the end of that. Will he be mad? Sure. At first. But then he'll see—we belong together. And next time it will be me with that big diamond ring she keeps turning down.'"

Malinka turns back to the camera. She's stopped crying and gazes at the camera now with steely resolve.

"He knows what happened to her. And now I might die before I make him admit it."

The groaning grows louder, the sound of the building straining.

"I don't think anyone is looking for us. The storm is out of control. This is not a game anymore. It's real."

Another crash, the sound of rushing water. Malinka looks off camera, her face a mask of terror. She starts to scream. The phone drops, and the screen goes dark.

16

BLAKE

In English class, Blake felt rough. Bleary-eyed, he tried to look like he was paying attention as Ms. Watson droned on about *The Catcher in the Rye*, which wasn't the worst thing they'd read. But he couldn't focus, was vaguely nauseated from the doughnuts he'd had for breakfast, another thing his mom would never have allowed. Violet just gave him a look as they'd climbed into the car and he was shoving a third doughnut into his mouth.

"Sugar isn't sleep, you know," she'd quipped.

"Neither is caffeine," he'd snapped back, casting a look at the big travel mug of coffee she'd poured for herself, even though he'd never seen her drink coffee before. She was just trying to be like mom.

"Shut it, Blake. I'm not even talking to you."

Violet looked equally exhausted, her skin even more ghostly pale than usual, purple circles under her eyes. She was mad at him, which he didn't love, not that he would ever admit it. But he couldn't tell her where he'd been. Couldn't tell anyone. What had been thrilling had become a secret burden. Something he was hiding from his mom and Violet. It had grown heavy, frightening.

Meanwhile, they were both edgy and worried about Mom. Malinka's live, the attack on Mav, had rattled them. The consensus online was that it was just another Extreme stunt to ramp up views. But it had *seemed* real. People seemed truly scared; Mav was like obviously not okay.

When the live ended and they'd texted with Mom a little, they had to get ready for school.

"This is your fault," Violet had hissed before heading upstairs. "You made her go."

"She *wanted* to go," he'd said weakly.

"Because of *you*."

She was right. It was his fault. If anything happened to Mom, it was because he'd told her about the challenge, encouraged her to apply. He didn't even answer his sister, just flipped her off.

"Nice. Real nice, Blake."

But underneath his fatigue and the weight of his guilt, there was a little joy. Last night on *Red World*, he'd vanquished Marco—okay, with help—and bigger than that, he'd found the peach. It had glowed rose-gold at the back of a long, dark tunnel.

"There it is," said Charger in his headset.

Blake was about to grab it, then hesitated. "You take it," he said. "I wouldn't have found it if not for you."

"No, kiddo," he said with a laugh. "It's all yours."

Blake had shoved it in his sack just five seconds before the red cloud closed around them and shunted them from the game. In his message box, there'd been a congratulations note from the game makers. **You have found one of three peaches in** *Red World*! **Good job.** His Red Coin balance was sick. He had a whole new wardrobe of skins, a bunch of new weapons and tricks. The real world sucked most of the time. But in *Red World*, right now, he was a king.

He raised his hand, asked for the bathroom pass. His stomach was churning. Ms. Watson handed it to him with a look. "Feeling okay? You look a little gray."

He nodded. Someone snickered. Then he was in the hallway, cool and silent, walking past the other classrooms. In the bathroom, he splashed cold water on his face. It was the right call: he felt better, some of the nausea subsiding. But when he looked up from the sink, he wasn't alone.

Marco was standing behind him. From his classroom he must have seen Blake walking to the bathroom.

Blake turned to face his old friend. Now his enemy. It was weird, because he had kind of a baby face, fleshy with pouty lips and big, soulful eyes. He *looked* like a nice guy. But he was a monster inside. So mean.

"I heard you got the peach," said Marco.

Blake stayed silent. Something in him was roiling. Not just his stomach. Something that came up occasionally and he tamped down hard. If Marco hadn't broken his glasses, maybe he wouldn't have felt bad enough to suggest the challenge to Mom because he knew she was always worried about money.

"Answer me. Do you have it?"

It washed up from his belly. Heat up his throat, coloring his cheeks. Anger. "What if I do?"

"I want it," he said. "Gift it to me on the app."

Blake laughed a little. "Yeah," he said. "Sure. I wouldn't do that even if I *liked* you."

A flash of surprise lit Marco's features. He put out a hand. "Give me your phone."

On his phone was the *Red World* app. If Marco got in, he could gift the peach and anything else he wanted to himself since they were still connected on the game. You could give your friends weapons and skins, anything you had in your locker.

"No," said Blake, squaring off. His mom had been teaching him how to punch on the bag in the garage. *People are not allowed to hurt you, Blakey. Sometimes you have to stand up for yourself.*

"Give it," said Marco, stepping closer. "Or I'm going to take it."

Blake squared off, put up his fists like his mom had taught him. Marco's eyes got wide, and Blake realized for the first time how much bigger he was than his old friend. Like a lot.

"Come and get it," he said, barely recognizing his own voice.

When Marco stepped to him, things went a little fuzzy. A kind of roar drowned out other sounds, his thoughts. All that anger he held back exploded. And the next thing Blake knew, Marco was lying on the floor groaning, blood gushing from his nose. He was crying.

"You punched me," he whimpered, looking up. "I'm bleeding."

Standing over Marco, Blake quashed the urge to hit him again. He didn't really want to hurt anyone, he just wanted to *stop hurting.*

"Don't fuck with me again, Marco," he said instead. Again, a voice he didn't know. "Next time, you won't get up."

Then he ran, getting back to class just as the bell sounded. He dropped the pass on Ms. Watson's desk.

"Everything okay?"

He hid his bleeding knuckles.

"All good," said Blake.

From his seat he grabbed his pack. Then, as he was heading toward the door, he got a message on his phone from the *Red World* app. It was from Charger. All it said was **It's time.**

He paused a minute, and everything around him seemed strange and new as the hallway filled with kids rushing between classes.

Finally he joined the throng, but instead of heading to his history class, he exited the building through the back doors of the school, stepping out into the bright, crisp afternoon. Blake was cutting school for the first time in his life.

17

ANGELINE

The small, stylish hotel was quiet when Angeline and Tavo pulled up in the Range Rover. They hadn't exchanged a single word the entire fifteen-minute drive on deserted roads.

The violence at the site, the red cloud of the approaching storm on the weather app, Maverick's unhinged (desperate?) energy, all of it had her jumpy, anxious. She needed to find Alex. He was the one who kept them all centered, grounded. Without him, it felt like anything could go wrong. The game was still five hours away; there was time to steady the ship before the hiders scattered.

On the drive from Enchantments, after they passed through the sleepy little town, which had a few small restaurants and bars, they hadn't passed another car or a single streetlamp. The island, unlike some other places she'd been in the world, slept a deep and steady slumber off-season. There were no glaring lights, no tacky billboards, no streets lined with revelers, no food delivery. New York City, the 24/7 candy store that it was, never closed its eyes, not for a moment. But this place gave you permission to power down, to take a breath. She pulled off the empty road, onto the even more deserted one that led up to the hotel, approaching slowly, gravel crunching, then killed the engine in the closest parking spot. They sat a moment, before Tavo reached a hand over and put it on her thigh.

Her whole body tingled at his touch.

"Don't," she said, her voice throaty. "Please."

"Angeline." Her name on his lips was a sound that made her go weak, crumbled all her resolve.

His other arm reached across, and she couldn't keep herself from leaning into him, his pull magnetic. His fingers in her hair, the scent of him, something woodsy and clean. His lips. Mav devoured her, aggressive, always wanted to go deeper, have more of her. Tavo explored, asked permission, invited her into the warmth of his energy. He gave as much as he got.

"Please," she begged.

But she was kissing him back, holding on to the strength of this arms, pulling him closer. It had been weeks since they'd been together. *I'm recommitting myself to Mav*, she'd told him after the last time.

Mav had been off with Hector somewhere in South America. They'd taken the jet for something decadent like a night out in Rio, and Mav planned to zip-line the next day. She was annoyed about it, for a lot of reasons. Then, in Hector's post, she'd seen Mav in the background leaning into some busty brunette in a low-cut leather dress. She knew that look, wolfish, hungry. She'd felt a lash of anger, even though Mav cheated all the time. He didn't think she knew. But she did. Someone like him, with so many appetites, so much freedom and money, he couldn't *not* cheat.

She'd revenge-texted Tavo, since she knew that he was in the city and not off with Mav. She and Tavo had been on-again, off-again for a while. He wanted more than she did. After her text, he was with her in under a half hour. Their lovemaking was passionate, gentle. Afterward, she felt guilty, told him that they couldn't be together again.

"He doesn't deserve you," Tavo had said. He'd said it without heat, a simple statement of fact. They both cared for Mav in their different ways, aware of his many flaws, their own. They were wrapped around each other on her living room couch— hers and Mav's.

"I know."

Tavo left for Falcão Island the next day, saying he respected her decision. But his texts came daily.

I can't stop thinking about you.

I love you, Angeline.

I'm here when you're ready to make a change. I'll wait. I know whatever this is between us might not come again in my lifetime.

While Angeline buried herself in work, closing up the Manhattan office, Tavo had been on Falcão Island for more than a month, location-scouting, reconnecting with old friends he'd grown up with, reaching out to the city council to set up meetings up for the challenge, staying away from her. She was glad he was gone, even though she thought about him every day, might catch herself thinking about him when she was with Maverick.

Now, she pulled away finally, decisively, and he respectfully backed off.

"I'm sorry," he said. He released a long breath, put his hands to prayer at his chest. "Forgive me."

Did she love him? Maybe. But not the way she loved Maverick. Gustavo wanted her. Maverick? He *needed* her. It was a subtle difference and one she couldn't even fully explain to herself. If she let Gustavo go, he'd go on to be a loving and devoted partner to some other lucky woman. If she left Maverick, he would fall apart. That she chose Maverick for this reason was, she suspected, an essential flaw in her character. She needed to be needed.

"There's nothing to forgive," she said. "But it's over, Tavo."

She sounded so weak and unsure of herself, but he just nodded. She slowed her breathing, gathered herself together, wanting nothing more than to move into his arms and weep. They both sat a moment.

Then Tavo said, "Let's find Alex."

"What if he's not here? What if he's gone already?"

Tavo held up his phone. She saw Alex's PopTalk icon, gathered close on the app to each of theirs. He had created an avatar for himself that was skinny and nerdy with big glasses and a beanie. They all followed each other on Pop, sending stupid messages and pics multiple times a day. The PopMap showed their locations in a cartoon world, each of them as animated versions of themselves. Angeline looked like a brunette Tinkerbell, small-waisted, big-bottomed, wearing a little dress and ballet flats. Tavo was stubbled and hauling a backpack. Hector wore, inexplicably, a miner's hat and jumpsuit. Maverick was a punk rocker, with a purple mohawk and leather vest, tight pants, and Moon Boots, ridiculously ripped, his mouth open in a perpetual rebel yell. She saw Hector's and Mav's avatars together at the site. She and Tavo were in a little animated car together, the app having deduced that they were driving. Alex was, she saw with relief, in his room at the hotel. His avatar was curled up in bed, with *Zzzz*s floating over his head, indicating that he'd set his phone for sleep.

It was not like him to be sleeping in the middle of the day.

Okay. She took a deep breath in and let it out. All was not lost. He was mad at Mav, but he hadn't left. Which meant he still cared. Or couldn't get a flight. Whatever. She could still beg him to hold on a little longer. One more challenge and she'd tell him about Mav's promise to fix everything that was broken. He would listen to her. He always did.

"Let's go," she said.

"Angeline," said Tavo, reaching for her hand, "I'm going to see you guys through this tomorrow."

She didn't like the tone in his voice. Sad. Resigned. She turned back to look at him.

He went on, "But when it's done, I have to go. Extreme... it's not a good place anymore. It's toxic for me."

She didn't say anything, just let the silence in the car expand. Finally, she pushed open the door. She could not deal with this right now. Things were falling apart, and it was up to her to keep it together for as long as she could.

"Let's talk about this later," she said, keeping her voice brisk like you'd talk to an anxious child. "After the challenge."

He didn't look at her, just stared out at something in front of them. Nothing. There was nothing there except for the trees and the stone wall edging a cliff that dropped into the tumultuous ocean below. The cloud cover was shifting from dove to charcoal, making it seem like dusk.

"Maverick is not the man I thought he was," said Tavo. "Or he's changed. He's not the man *you* think he is."

"Don't do this," she begged. "Not now. Just help me find Alex. I promise we can talk. When this is all over."

She reached for and squeezed his hand. It was warm, strong. He looked at her, and she saw all his goodness, his solid character, his kindness. That jaw, those cheekbones, deep soulful eyes. What was wrong with her?

"Okay," he said with a nod. "Let's go."

Angeline's key card still worked, which meant that maybe Hector never checked them out. Maybe he, like Angeline, was hoping for one more night in comfort before having to pitch a tent.

She let herself into the quiet, well-appointed lobby, wood

floors, a large fireplace, a simple desk with a giant computer monitor. There was no lobby attendant. No twenty-four-hour room service, just an after-hours emergency number you called if there was something you needed. It went straight to the owner's cell phone. The place was far from town, had the air of desertion, no other properties around for miles. Tourist season was well and truly over. For the last week, they'd been the only guests in the hotel, getting the star treatment from the limited staff, with all the facilities, heated pool, steam room, sauna, luxurious lounge bar with big comfy couches and stunning views all to themselves.

Angeline and Tavo moved through the courtyard that led to the pool, then passed under the stone tunnel that connected the main property to the rooms, their footfalls echoing. She ran her hands along the wall, relishing the cool rock, its solidity and re-silience. The property had stood here for hundreds of years, an old estate that the owners had bought in disrepair, then spent years restoring as a hotel just in time for the pandemic to hit. It made Angeline wonder what dream she'd had for her life. Was this it? Working for Mav? She'd always wanted to do things for others, to fix all the broken things, like Mav said. And she was doing that, most of the time. Wasn't she?

They were approaching Alex's door when Gustavo put up a hand to stop her.

"The door is open," he said.

She saw that it stood ajar. Something roared in the back of her head, but she ignored it, marching past Gustavo and com-ing to stand in the doorjamb.

"Alex," she said in a loud whisper. "Alex."

When there was no answer, she started pushing on the door, entering the dark space.

"Alex, you'd better be dressed. I'm coming in. We have to talk."

But the room was empty when Angeline flipped on the desk light. His suitcase lay open on the rack, everything neat and perfectly folded just like Alex, the most tidy and organized person she'd ever met.

The bed was made, and his charger was still plugged into the wall.

She turned to Gustavo, who was staring at the bathroom door, which was shut.

"Alex," she said, knocking hard.

Gustavo squinted at something and walked over to the patio doors. Outside was a private lounge area with a hot tub. He stopped at the glass, put his finger to it and drew it back quickly.

"What?" she asked, not waiting for an answer. She tried the bathroom door and found it unlocked, pushed it open, and flipped on the light.

Empty. Pristine white tile floor, veined quartz counter, enormous glass-enclosed shower. Towels fresh, every surface dry.

"Angeline."

She didn't like the tone of Gustavo's voice. She left the bathroom to join him and saw what he saw, a wide spray of viscous black-red liquid on the glass.

"It's blood," he said, holding up a finger smeared with bright red.

Her throat went dry. "Don't be stupid," she managed.

"It's *blood*," he said again, louder. "Angeline."

On the desk were Alex's laptop and phone. She picked up the phone and saw hundreds of unopened notifications: text, phone, email. She'd never in all her years of knowing him seen Alex without his phone in his hand. She'd rarely sent him a text or email that wasn't answered immediately, like he was just waiting to hear from her. Most of the messages were from his wife, Lucia, some from Gustavo.

"Do you have an area rug in your room?" asked Gustavo. The tone of his voice caused her to look up from Alex's phone. He was staring at the floor.

She followed his eyes.

There was more red splatter on the floor that ended abruptly in a straight line. As if it had continued onto an area rug that had once lain between the bed and the desk. One that had been removed, leaving the straight-edged absence of the stain.

Angeline nodded, something roaring in her ears.

The room was spinning, and she felt like she was breathing through a straw. She knew Alex's passcode, tapped it into his phone, scrolled through the endless messages, finding his chain with Lucia. She started reading. As she read, she felt the bottom dropping away from her world.

"I'm calling the police," said Gustavo, moving for his phone. She put a hand on his arm.

"Don't," she said, voice barely a whisper, heart thudding. "Just...don't."

18

STRANGER THAN FICTION
A True Crime Podcast with Harley Granger

The Disappearance of Chloe Miranda

Rough audio recording for editing

[A rustling sound.]

Harley Granger: Oh, wow. This place is sick.

[A car door slamming shut. Footsteps.]

Harley: I'm Harley Granger, host of your favorite true crime podcast Stanger Than Fiction. And on this blustery day, I am here at Eaton House in Upstate New York.

[Wind against the mic, more footsteps.]

Harley: The weather is about to turn, so we don't have much time.

[Another car door slams. A second set of footsteps.]

Harley: I'm here with my producer, Rog, who will not fail to remind you that he took a bullet for me when we were investigating a cold case not far from here.

Roger: Truth. I still have that bullet in me, my friend. Sup, y'all. Man. This place is creepy as fuck.

Harley: Eaton House. Built in 1916, it has been declared one of America's most haunted places by BumpintheNight.com.

Roger: *[laughing]* Bump in the what? That's the stupidest name I've ever heard.

Harley: You know I have to edit that out, right? They're a sponsor.

Roger: Sorry.

Harley: The owners, descendants of the original builders, rent the space out for parties and other events. Apparently, some couples like to spend their honeymoon at Eaton House. And once a year, Eaton House owners host an annual sleepover that attracts paranormal investigators from around the globe.

Roger: Huh. People are weird, right? But that's not why we're here.

Harley: No. Eaton House, a six-thousand-square-foot Victorian, is where Extreme Games and Insane Challenges held their Haunted Hide and Seek event on September fifteenth of last year, the day Chloe Miranda disappeared.

[Wood creaking.]

Roger: Maverick Dillan and the folks at Extreme say that no one saw Chloe Miranda again after she hid that night with the rest of the contestants. They have been investigated and cleared as suspects. But people close to Chloe say that she had a long on-again, off-again affair with Maverick. And they believe that he has something to do with her disappearance.

Harley: Eaton House has been thoroughly searched. But we pulled the property survey and discovered something that no one else has mentioned about the house. Even the property owners didn't know about it. We have obtained permission to check it out.

[The long whine of an opening door, footsteps echoing on hard wood.]

Harley: I'm filming now, and all this footage will be available on the website so that you can watch if you dare. Muwahaha!

Harley: Do you believe in ghosts, Rog?

Roger: I do not.

Harley: I don't, either. I believe that bad people do fucked-up things and then try to get away with it. That's what I believe.

[Another creaking door.]

Roger: Oh, look. A dark and creepy basement. What could go wrong?

Harley: After you. Watch out. Those stairs look a little sus, as the kids say.

[Tentative footsteps on the stairs. Then a scream from Roger, girlish and long.]

Harley: What the hell, Rog?

Roger: Oh, my God. I hate rats. I am so out of here.

Harley: Dude, do not leave me alone down here.

[Running footsteps fade away.]

Harley: Wow. That's messed up. You heard it, folks. Roger, my friend and producer, left me alone in the basement where people say that Chloe Miranda hid during the challenge. All right, well, I am not afraid of ghosts, or rats, for that matter. Here we go.

[Footsteps returning.]

Harley: Aaaannnndd he's back.

Roger: Let's just get this over with, for fuck's sake. Turn that thing off for a minute.

[Break in recording.]

Roger: Well, we've been down here for about an hour. And I guess the survey was wrong. There's nothing down here that police haven't found. There's no trace of Chloe Miranda.

[Some rustling.]

Harley: Hold up. Give me some light.

Roger: This place is giving me the creeps. Let's get out of here.

Harley: *[Coughs, more rustling.]* Look at this. Right here. Folks, I'm taking a last look at the land survey, trying to orient myself on the property.

[Sound of footsteps.]

Harley: Okay, okay, that's north. We're...right here.

Roger: If that's true, then there should be some kind of door, or a hatch in the floor. But there's just the staircase.

[A knocking sound.]

Harley: Listen. It's hollow. This area here. Look. A seam.

Roger: Holy shit. Push on it, see if it opens that way.

[A long squeaking sound.]

Harley: Whoa. It's a doorway to a compartment under the stairs. I'm taking some video. You'll be able to see it on the website when the episode airs.

Roger: It's empty. A dead end.

Harley: Maybe not.

Roger: Man, you can't fit in there. Harley, don't be crazy.

Harley: If I had a nickel for every time you said that...

Roger: They don't even make nickels anymore, loser. Harley, man, seriously.

Harley: *[Voice echoing.]* Oh, my God, Rog. Look at this.

Roger: Oh, shit. You were right.

<u>Part Two</u>

Ready or Not

"Small and hidden is the door that leads inward, and the entrance is barred by countless prejudices, mistaken assumptions, and fears."

CARL JUNG
Civilization in Transition

"Adopt the pace of nature. Her secret is patience."

RALPH WALDO EMERSON

19

ANGELINE

"Angeline," said Tavo, sitting on Alex's hotel-room bed. "What is it?"

She didn't answer right away, reading and reading again to see if there was any other way to interpret the texts. She felt like she'd swallowed glass—throat raw, stomach aching. Outside, the wind moaned, and even the shadows of the lawn furniture looked like crouched monsters waiting to pounce. She felt the heat of Tavo's gaze but kept her eyes on the screen swimming before her eyes. It was wrong, spying on a private exchange between husband and wife. But she read it again.

I'm going to do it. I'm going to confront him tonight.

Just come home, Alex. Please. The baby is sick. I miss you. Forget about Extreme. We'll get a lawyer.

I can't let this stand. I have to confront him. There are millions of dollars missing. He's stealing from all of us.

Maybe it's a mistake.

No. There's no mistake. I don't know how it took me so long to see it.

Look...just get out of there. You can report it and let a forensic accountant sort it all out.

Then we could all lose everything. I'm the fucking CFO. You don't think I'll be held accountable in some way if this goes to the courts, to the authorities? After all these years of putting up with his shit, we walk away with nothing? Worse. I go to jail with him? No. No fucking way.

Then, what?

I don't know. I talk to him. Make him give it back. I fix the books, and we take that offer from BoxOfficePlus and we all walk away rich.

But he said he'd never sell Extreme. That he'd never answer to a studio.

If I confront him about this, he won't have a choice. It's sell or go to jail.

Okay. But do it from here. Please. Just come home.

I have to give him the chance to do the right thing. To come clean to me.

People can be dangerous when you back them into a corner.

No. We're friends. Brothers.

Maybe you don't know him like you think you do.

I love you. I love our baby. By tomorrow this will be over, and we'll have a new life.

A few hours went by before Lucia texted again.

Alex? What was that whole mess at the site? I didn't see you.

What's going on? I'm worried.

Call me. Please let me know you're ok.

I'm calling Angeline.

Alex??? Where are you??? Please.

Angeline could feel Lucia's despair, her worry. She didn't like Lucia especially, but she knew what it was like to be on the worried end of a text chain. How many times had she waited by the phone when Mav was off on one of his *quests*, as he liked to call them.

"How do you live like this?" Lucia had asked Angeline one night at an Extreme dinner where they'd both had too much to drink. The boys were loud, swapping stories about Mav—Mav wiping out in Hawaii, Mav getting arrested in Mexico, Mav disappearing in Shanghai for a full day.

Lucia was a small woman, with big soulful eyes, a mane of dark hair. She and Alex had met in Brazil, and like any nerd who fell in love for the first time, Alex fell hard. Within a year, they were married, and Lucia was pregnant.

"Live like what?" Angeline had asked, surprised. They hadn't talked much. None of the guys liked her and thought that she was *changing Alex*.

But Lucia had just looked at her with something like pity. "Never mind," she said. "Not my business."

Angeline was about to press when Lucia rose, whispered something to Alex. A moment later they both got up, calling out their goodbyes, as the boys all jeered and tried to convince them to stay.

Then they left, Lucia giving them a wave and victorious smile as they went arm in arm.

"Bitch," said Mav. "She hates us. She's stealing Alex."

Through the restaurant window, she saw them on the street. Lucia peered up at Alex, brushing hair out of his eyes. He had a protective arm snaked around her back, smiled down at her. She was just starting to show. Angeline was surprised by a lash of envy.

"Don't use that word," she said.

He lifted his palms. "She is. She's stealing him."

At first, they'd all suspected that Lucia was looking for a green card, a big bank account, and a man she could control. Which was probably racist and sexist as fuck. Anyway, it had quickly become clear that she was as smitten with Alex as he was with her. They were inseparable, and then the baby came. And that's when Alex really started to pull away from the group. The truth was that they all viewed Lucia as a nuisance, an interloper, someone who made Alex less interested in them, in Extreme. Earlier that afternoon, Angeline had seen Lucia's call come in and ignored it. Lucia had made overtures of friendship over the years, which Angeline had rebuffed.

"Talk to me," Tavo said now.

She hesitated, then handed over the phone. She paced as he read, grappling with the words, trying to rearrange them into something that made sense. Anything that made a *different* kind of sense. Her own phone starting pinging. Mav.

What's taking you guys so long? Make Alex come talk to me. I see his Pop right next to you, so I know he didn't leave.

Angeline felt a chill move through her body, an unpleasant tingling of nerves.

Mav, she knew, was a cool and competent liar. A thinker.

"What is this about?" asked Tavo; he looked at her confused. "First, what offer?"

She released a long breath. The offer. The thing Mav and Alex had been fighting about for months. Mav would kill her for telling Tavo, but... "BoxOfficePlus made an offer to buy Extreme, turning it into a multiseason series and a video game. It was—is—huge, life-changing money. But Mav turned the initial offer down flat. They came back with even more money. It's still on the table."

Tavo stared down at the ground a moment. "Was he going to tell us?"

She shrugged, shook her head. "Mav has fifty-one percent of the shares. His vote rules. That's how you guys set up the company."

Alex had twenty-five, Tavo twenty, and Hector held the smallest at four percent. Those negotiations were before Angeline's time. She had no idea why the guys ceded so much power to Mav, or how they'd decided who got what, but the truth was that Extreme was Mav and Mav was Extreme. So maybe it was only fair. They all pulled hefty salaries; they each had their role in the group. It never really seemed equitable to Angeline that Hector had the smallest share but arguably did the most work. Even so, if the sale went through, they'd all be filthy rich, not to mention BoxOfficePlus wanted them all to be part of the show, so they'd continue doing the things they loved and still get paid for it.

As far as Alex was concerned, it was a no-brainer, especially since the last couple of years had not been great financially, and they were embattled on all sides. Mav just didn't want to cede control, to answer to anyone.

As far as a sale went, Angeline had no skin in the game, except

the golden parachute promised as part of her employment contract, which Alex had helped draft. She hadn't asked for shares
as part of her contract. Hadn't really known to ask for that at
that time. Her mind didn't work that way.

Tavo was still quiet. Then, "Is this true? Was Mav stealing
money from the company?"

"No," she said, the protest coming up from a deep place inside of her. "No way."

"How do you know? Do you think he's not capable of it?"

"Of what? Stealing money from all of his best friends? No.
I don't. Do you?"

Tavo rubbed at his chest like he had heartburn. "Honestly,
I don't know."

She was surprised to hear that, gazed over at him. His shoulders were hiked, face grim. He was angry: she could tell by the
set of his mouth. Everyone was a little angry at Mav, weren't
they? Everyone except for maybe Hector, who seemed to think
Mav got up and put the sun in the sky every morning.

"That's fucked-up, Tavo," said Angeline.

Tavo lifted his palms. "Alex is the most honest, trustworthy
person I know," he said. "The smartest. The person who has
been holding Extreme together for years."

He wasn't wrong. She felt the same way about Alex. "So...
he made a mistake," she said.

Tavo stood and walked over to the blood spray on the window.

"Then, what happened here?"

Angeline shook her head, her voice failing her. It was freezing in the room, she noticed. She was cold to her bones.

Her phone pinged. Mav again.

Heeelllooo? Are you guys coming back?

"We need to call the police," said Tavo.

"And say what?"

Tavo swept an arm around the room, his forehead wrinkled

with concern, like she wasn't thinking clearly. Maybe she wasn't. Maybe she could never think clearly when it came to Maverick, like he had her under some kind of spell. Her mother's words rang back to her: *You're someone different when you're with him.*

"That our CFO—our friend—is *missing*. That there's blood on the window and the floor. That the area rug is *gone*."

Maybe he was right. Maybe they should call the police.

"He's not *missing*," she said stubbornly.

"He's not? Have you ever seen Alex without his phone in his hand? His laptop under his arm?"

"Maybe he went for a walk," she suggested, desperately grasping at possibilities. "You know, to clear his head."

Her phone again.

Okay. I'm coming to you.

"Mav's on his way here," she said.

She opened the PopMap and saw his icon driving in their direction. He was already halfway to the hotel. Lately, she had the sense that maybe he suspected that there was something between her and Tavo. Something about the way he watched them when they were together. But she'd dismissed it. Mav wasn't subtle. He wasn't one to harbor secret suspicions. He was prone to outbursts, tantrums, rage. She couldn't think of single time when he'd kept a feeling to himself.

"Tell him not to," said Tavo quickly. "Tell him we're on our way back."

We're on our way back, she thumbed.

Stay put, came his quick reply.

Angeline didn't bother to answer again. She knew better. Mav would do what he wanted. Always.

"He's already on his way."

But Tavo wasn't listening. He was staring at something over by the door, moved in that direction. Angeline followed.

More dark spots, big dollops of blood-red. Tavo pushed the door open with a creak.

They stepped out into the hall, with Tavo sticking close to her. The trail of blood continued down the hallway. Blood rushed in her ears, a vein pulsing in her throat. She grabbed for Gustavo's hand. It was warm and strong; he held hers tight. His eyes, when he looked at her, were etched at the corners with worry.

Together they followed the trail down the darkened hallway.

20

ADELE

Adele slipped back toward camp. Exhilaration had her breathing deep and moving fleet-footed up the path, past the hulk of Enchantments. She'd found the *perfect* hiding space, something she hadn't seen on any map or on the WholeEarthNow images. This is why her father always insisted on recon. *There are things you can never know about a place until you've had boots on the ground.*

The stuttering rumble of the generator disrupted the deep peace of the site. It was an invasion of sound, and the area seemed disturbed by it. Again, she felt that stutter. That question. What was she doing here?

The answer was clear: money.

What do you need with all that money? her father, a true minimalist, would probably wonder out loud.

Peace, freedom, security, the knowledge that Blake and Violet will not want for anything, she'd tell him.

Things that can never be sought without, he'd surely offer. *Delusion.*

The world had changed, though, hadn't it? Since her dad was a young man with a family? In a postpandemic world where inflation ran wild, and even with a job her health-insurance premiums were a big chunk from her paycheck, and her grocery bill was shocking, and the kids didn't have a fraction of the things their friends had now. Or maybe it was just that they'd lost so much when Miller left them. Maybe if they'd never had so much, the absence of that security wouldn't be so frightening.

The things that kept her up at night: Could she pay for school for both kids if they didn't get scholarships or she couldn't get aid because of her abysmal credit history? What would happen if she got sick? Who would be there for her kids if she died? What would happen if she *didn't* die young? Would she ever be able to afford to retire?

That's what I need with all that money, Dad. The world has changed.

Some things don't change, he would tell her. She heard his voice so clearly; far more clearly than that of her mother, who was alive and well.

As Adele approached the site, she noticed the slightest flicker of light from inside Malinka's tent, making her big dome glow pink from within.

So was that *not* Malinka on the path?

Or had she taken another route and beaten Adele back to camp?

Whoever it had been out there, Adele hadn't seen the figure again or anyone else as she picked her way through the overgrown property, finding the established paved paths hiding beneath the fecund overgrowth.

Now Adele edged closer to Malinka's tent and heard the young woman's childlike voice. She was whispering something, but Adele couldn't make out the words. It brought her back home through a mental wormhole to standing outside Violet's closed door, listening to her daughter sing to herself or talk to her friends. Not eavesdropping or spying; she'd never had to do that with Violet. Just listening to her become, marveling at her smooth, grown-up singing voice, or how kind and wise she was with her friends, her word choices. She was so far from the little baby Adele had carried in her arms, and yet that essence was the same, somehow. Something uniquely Violet that stayed glowing at the center of who she was. Her essential self.

Violet's being Violet again. Blake always meant it as an insult. But Violet had *always* been Violet. And only a grown woman who'd been to hell and back knew what a gift it was to own yourself, to know yourself.

Adele strained toward the tent to hear better—yeah, eavesdropping this time. But try as she did, she couldn't decipher the young woman's words, just the tone. Urgent. Secretive.

What had Malinka discovered on *her* solo recon tonight?

Still standing outside the tent, Adele opened Malinka's page on Photogram. Nothing new. Then she checked her WeWatch channel. Malinka was dark, hadn't posted anything since the attack. Whoever she was talking to, it was offline.

A rustling in the foliage behind her caused her to jump like she'd been tasered, heart flying into her throat.

Adele froze as a huge black form emerged from the branches.

A giant bird, black in the shadows, with an impossibly large wingspan and kited tail, whooshed over her head, a shadow that lifted with great, silent flaps of its wings and then was swallowed by the clouds as suddenly as it had appeared.

The buzzard again. She imagined it with another feast for its chicks. Was it the same one? She felt a strange connection to the mama buzzard, hunting and fighting to feed her babies.

Her heart was an engine, and she breathed to calm herself, glad she hadn't cried out and revealed herself as listening outside Malinka's tent. She watched the sky for another glimpse of the bird. Falconers considered buzzards difficult to train and lazy because they were willing to feed on carrion. Adele thought that was a little unfair. They were survivors; she admired that. Being difficult to train wasn't necessarily a bad thing. Wildness was underrated.

Inside Malinka's tent, the girl had gone quiet. After guiltily hovering another few seconds, Adele turned to return to hers.

And smacked right into Wild Cody.

Her face came to his chest, which was hard and unyielding. He smelled of woodsmoke and sage. He lifted hands to her arms to steady her as she stumbled back. Then he smiled, released her quickly, and put a finger to his lips. *Shhh.*

He waved a hand, indicating that she should follow, then moved away.

She noticed that the two Range Rovers were gone. Did that mean that the Extreme team had gone back to the hotel? Was it only her and Wild Cody and Malinka on-site? The game was supposed to start in a few hours.

Cody crouched by the fire which had burned down to embers and coaxed it back to life.

Adele realized she was cold and felt herself drawn to the heat. Wild Cody (that was a stupid name; she couldn't call him that) nodded toward one of the logs that they'd pulled around as makeshift seating. And for no reason she could identify, she sat. He stared over at her with that clear, seeing gaze, and she saw something she hadn't expected: kindness. The warmth of the fire reached her skin, and the glow washed his face, softened the hard edges, filled in the landscape of lines.

Adele wrapped her arms around her center. He took a flask from his pocket, handed it to her.

Ew, had he been drinking from it? Postpandemic, that was pretty gross.

"It's not mine," he said, reading her expression. "I found it in my tent."

"What is it?"

She took off the cap and sniffed it gingerly. Bourbon, a good one, light and woodsy. It reminded her of Miller: the old-fashioned was his go-to drink. It wasn't Adele's favorite, but he'd always saved the boozy cherry on the bottom for Adele.

She remembered that sweetness, that biting alcoholic edge. She hadn't allowed herself a single sip of anything since Miller left. She felt strongly that she had to be present and in control for the kids at all times. She was tempted to drink from the flask but capped it instead. She tried to hand it back to him, but he held up a palm.

"I'm sober five years," he said. "But someone put a flask of booze in my tent."

"Who?" she asked, horrified. "Who would do something like that?"

He smiled, and for a moment, she flashed back to her father, face lit by the campfire, smile broad and relaxed.

"I think someone was trying to mess with me," said Cody.

She remembered the form in the hotel, the book, and cigarettes. She found herself telling him about it.

"Mind-fucking," he said with a nod. "I understand they're good at it. They like to keep you wobbly so you can't focus on the game."

She put the flask down, held her hands up to the fire, considering. That was pretty messed up. But she liked the explanation better than the idea that somehow Miller was here in this wild place, stalking her. She couldn't even imagine seeing him in the flesh again. He had become a ghost. A haunting.

She picked up the flask, unscrewed it again, and poured out the bourbon onto the ground.

"I'm sorry," she said. "They shouldn't have done that. It was wrong."

He looked into the flames. "Nothing surprises me anymore," he said easily. "Nothing people are willing to do anyway."

Adele heard resignation, a kind of awakened sadness. He used a big stick to poke at the stacked wood in the fire, and some embers crackled.

"So what did you find out there?" he asked.

Wild Cody's voice was gravelly, familiar. She'd heard it

before—a lot. His had been Blake's favorite nature show back in the day; probably it still was. She saw it turn up on the Box-OfficePlus Continue Watching queue from time to time. Usually after Blake had been bullied or treated badly by his former friends. It was her son's comfort show, something they'd watched together in a time when things were happy and good. Long ago, it seemed.

"Just what they said would be there," she lied. "The overgrown paths, the pool and clubhouse, the casitas. All in various states of disrepair."

He watched her. She found she liked the look of him—rugged, outdoorsy, ready for anything in the way that her father had been. She remembered when she'd watched with Blake that she'd liked his adventurous spirit, his ready laugh, the clear joy he took in animal life. Here beside the fire, he didn't seem unhinged to her at all.

"What were you looking for?" he asked. He poked at the fire with the stick; a log tumbled, and the flames danced.

Adele lifted her shoulders. She hadn't been looking for anything in particular. But she found it all the same.

"Nothing in particular," he answered for her. "Just recon."

She nodded.

"Smart."

"You?" she asked. "Same?"

He offered an assenting dip of his chin. The fire was roaring now, and Adele reached out her hands again, slid from the log onto the ground and leaned against the wood.

"I heard the game is rigged," he said. "That the winner is chosen before the game ever begins."

He took from his pocket what looked like a bag of leather strips. He lifted one out and took a bite. She was guessing jerky. Then he offered the bag to Adele.

Her stomach grumbled, and she took the bag, selected a small piece, handed the food back, earning another smile. She took a small bite, just to be polite. But it was actually good, meaty, spicy. She really hoped it wasn't lion or the flesh of some other endangered animal.

"I heard that, too," she admitted. Though she stopped short of telling him about the cameras. Knowledge was power, and you never knew how it could be used. They were opponents, here for the same reason. There could only be one winner. There would be no allies in this game.

They chewed in silence. The cloud cover was so thick that it seemed like dusk, though there were still hours before sunset.

"Then, why play?" he asked.

"In case it isn't?" she answered.

"It's a lot of money," he said, shifting down to the ground, as well, spreading his arms wide along the log.

"It is," she agreed.

"And you've got kids. A past to leave behind."

Even if Maverick hadn't skewered her with it during the live, it was all out there for the world to see.

Anyway, she wasn't the only one here with a past.

"As do you," she said easily. "Why are *you* here?"

He bobbed his head again, took off his hat, his salt-and-pepper hair wild, but it was thick and lustrous. He was older than Adele, certainly, but definitely not old.

"Money doesn't mean anything to me," he said. "I'm on the redemption circuit."

Right. She'd seen a slew of articles about him recently, about how he'd hit rock bottom, was clawing his way back to wellness. How he'd made mistakes and was sorry. Addiction. Rehab.

"My son, Blake, and I have watched every one of your shows," she told him finally. "He learned so much—so did I. About animals, the environment, insects, other countries and cultures. It was truly great."

He took another bite of jerky.

"It was a dream come true," he said. "Imagine getting to do

all that, get paid, see the world, everywhere you go kids love you. I was only ever at home outdoors in nature."

She was surprised by his candor. But she'd known some people in recovery before. If they were doing the work, they were wide-open. Honest.

She offered him a smile. "Swim with the dolphins, hang with the sloths, hunker down with the gorillas in Rwanda. Blake still wants to do all of those things."

"Turns out I could outrun the bulls but not my demons," he said. He held her gaze. "You don't get to run from those. Gotta face them down, apparently."

There'd been rumors about his addiction, sexual harassment on the set, exploitation of Indigenous guides. The show went off the air; Blake was heartbroken, watching the old seasons over and over.

Then the whole lion thing. Some video of Cody raging about a conspiracy to ruin his reputation. Wild Cody was canceled before canceling was a thing. It was long ago, or seemed so with the pandemic, and then the Miller nightmare, her father's passing, and she didn't remember all the details, just another man she thought was one thing but turned out to be another.

What she did recall from the show was how tender, how reverent he was with all the animals, even when he got bitten, attacked, and stung, how much awe and love he seemed to have for the natural world. How peaceful he seemed in his role.

"The *Wild* Cody thing didn't quite fit," she ventured.

He laughed, mirthless. "That was a marketing thing. It never sat right with me. But it stuck. I had pushed for Wilderness Cody."

She ran a hand through her hair, down the back of her neck which was aching from sleeping on the ground. She knew all about how if you didn't stand up for who you were early and often, then someone else could slap an identity on you that somehow became the truth. Corporate wife. Stay-at-home mom. Betrayed. Abandoned. Suspected.

She and Cody locked eyes. Blake had believed that the whole thing about the lion was a lie. And Adele humored him because he thought the same about his father's alleged crimes, and *that* she couldn't let slide. In the man by the fire she saw a sadness that she recognized all too well.

"I've never hurt a living thing," he said quietly, as if reading her thoughts, maybe still ruminating over the things Mav had said. "Except myself."

She was surprised to find she believed him.

"I'll just call you Cody, then?" she said, giving him a smile.

"That'll do."

The generator rumbled loudly, emitting some kind of grinding sound, then suddenly went quiet. But no one emerged from the trailer, which stayed dark.

"I heard people yelling earlier," said Adele.

Cody looked over in the direction of the trailer. "Trouble in paradise, I'm guessing, from the vibe around here."

"Yeah," Adele agreed reluctantly. There was a definite vibe. Not a good one.

"Just be careful tonight," Cody said, poking the fire again. "Once the game starts, no one here has any friends."

He glanced over at the trailer. Adele felt her stomach clench a little.

"And the only true prize in this world is living another day."

Then he rose and disappeared inside his tent without another word.

21

ADELE

The Game

As Adele ran from her hiding spot, the sound of the screaming grew louder.

It yanked at her like a chain attached to her heart. The mother in her, the counselor. She couldn't let someone suffer, struggle without reaching out to help. Even if it meant losing everything she'd come for.

Breathless, she clutched at the hard stitch in her side, kept running.

There was a moment in every marathon, a long, dark patch, where you thought you couldn't make it. Every runner knew that it was a matter of relying on your body, remembering all the past races you'd been able to complete, forgetting about the finish, and focusing on the breath. Right here. Right now. One stride, then the next.

The path was slick, the mud growing thicker, sucking at her feet. The rain was a beating drum, so omnipresent she almost doesn't notice; she was fully drenched. Keep going.

The sound of the terrified keening grew closer.

Trying to pick up speed, Adele tripped over a branch as large as a human leg in the path, fell hard on both elbows and knees, pain radiating. She struggled to her feet, bleeding from her skinned joints.

The voice carried on the storm kept her moving. Help! Help me! Please!

Who was it? Malinka? Angeline?

Limping now from the fall, Adele kept going.

Then, up ahead on the path, someone stood, blocking her way.

Terror cinched her throat, freezing her in place.

"Who is that? Who's there?" she yelled.

The grainy figure in photographs, the stranger hiding in Enchantments, the shadow in the forest. The ominous texts warning her away. Agent Coben with his suspicious gaze. That sense she's had of always being watched, followed. Miller and all his lies. That figure blocking her path—it was somehow all of those things.

Adele was tired of being afraid and ashamed. She felt it bubbling, that rage. Fear made you small. Rage made you strong.

"What do you want?" she said, this time her voice loud, deeper.

She didn't wait for an answer. She charged him, roaring as loud as the thunder.

22

MAVERICK

Mav gunned the Rover engine, taking the small winding road too fast. He felt this urgency to get to Angeline.

There was a feeling, something that tingled on his skin, when he knew that a challenge was going to go truly bad. He'd felt it the first time before that BMX jump, his first frightening, real accident. He remembered it, even now years later, standing there at the edge of the ramp, his mom behind her camera—as ever. He looked at that line of junked cars and thought, *This is not going to work.* There were nine cars. The jump was forty-eight feet; just a few farther than he had jumped before. The wind was high, the white flag flapping wildly.

He tried to tell his mom that he wanted to cancel.

Honey, she said. *You can't.*

She swept her arm toward the crowd of people who had gathered for the food-bank fundraiser. *These people all bought tickets to see you.*

He felt that notch in his throat, that deep desire to make his mom smile and laugh. He glanced at the crowd, looking for his dad. He wasn't there, had protested the whole thing and didn't show up on principle. Yeah, his dad had his principles.

He's not your show pony, Myra. Stop using him. His mom and dad had been divorced since before he could remember; still all they did was fight about him, about everything. He hated listening to them talk on the phone; their relationship was like a spoon in the garbage disposal.

Prior to that BMX, all his falls and skids, helmet knocks, tumbles on the slopes, and wipeouts in the waves had seemed like nothing, really. Get up. Walk it off. Stitch it up, bandage it. Laugh at the cosmic joke of it all when you get body-slammed by the planet and the forces that govern it. Because it's funny.

He didn't really remember the accident. But he recalled with clarity that final moment when he was on the top of the ramp with Hector. That feeling. Hector knew conditions weren't right, kept telling him to bail. But he'd done it before; the wind was at his back. He was going to fly. Sometimes it came back to him in dreams. When he looked at the video, his young face was grim and determined. Hector wore his signature worried frown, was holding on to Mav's arm as if he was trying to hold him back. That suit his mom got him, lightweight white leather, the striped helmet—dorky AF. But at the time he'd felt boss. Then he was flying. Then he was falling, bike twisting beneath him, ground coming up fast. Then nothing.

He could have been killed, Myra. You're lucky he's not in a wheelchair.

They love him. They cheered. He raised more money for the food bank than anyone ever has.

He was laid up for more than a month, playing *Red World*. His followership quadrupled. He quickly realized that people found it hilarious when you screwed up, or when nature took you down as she could and would so easily. They—the followers, the audience he'd been aware of all his life—liked it better when you failed than when you succeeded, it seemed. Because

everyone was wiping out, all the time. Anyone who tried to
do anything knew that you'd fail a hundred, a thousand times
for the one time you got one thing right, found the one thing
that worked. That was what people knew best: failure, disappointment.

It makes you real. It makes you relatable, his mother had told him.
If you were a superhero, they'd be looking for a way to take you down.
Better to let them see that you're human.

The long road twisted, went on and on, like someone's story
that didn't seem to have any end, any conclusion. It was empty of
cars, streetlamps, any sign of civilization. The island felt empty,
deserted, forgotten. He picked up speed.

He hadn't realized it at the time, but he'd felt that ugly tingle
the night he met Chloe Miranda. Where had they been? Aspen.
On the roof deck bar of The Little Nell. He'd been well and
truly high, the altitude, the gummies he swallowed, his killer
day on the slopes. He had done some amazing snowboarding,
got some footage that just slayed. Their followership was at an
all-time high. WeWatch was paying Extreme a fucking fortune.
More money than he'd ever imagined. At the time it seemed
like there was no way he could *ever* spend it all.

But he sure liked trying. Everyone, his dad especially, was always going on about money and how it corrupted, how it didn't
mean anything, and how it couldn't buy happiness. But Maverick *loved* being rich. Loved what he could do, what he could
give, how people treated him because he had it. Did that make
him shallow? Yeah. Probably.

When he looked back on that night right before he met
Chloe, he wondered, was that *it*? He thought about it again
now as he barreled down the dark road toward the hotel. Was
that the last, best day?

It was something his mom had said to him in her final week.

There's a day, she'd told him. *There's a last, best day. The day*
when everything is as good as it's ever going to be. And if you're not

*paying attention, you might miss it. It's the day when you're healthy,
and everyone you love is okay, and maybe the sun is shining, and you're
doing something stupid like making a cup of tea or reading a book on
the porch. And there's a whole list of things you want but don't have,
and that might be what you're thinking about. And not a single one of
them matters. Because everything that's important is right there. And,
Mav, it's so easy to miss it completely.*

He hated to admit that he checked out on her a lot during
that time. He left her on her own for days. Even when he was
there, he'd often smoke a bowl out in his car just to take the edge
off. He went to that little room inside himself and worked the
Mav puppet from the control panel. He was there, but not there.

It's okay, Mom, he assured her, not knowing what else to say.
You're okay.

But it wasn't, and she wasn't, and they both knew that. But
she just smiled and nodded, reached for his hand. Even now
he still remembered the milky light in that room and her frail
hand, her fading voice.

So maybe that was it. That day in Aspen just before he met
Chloe Miranda. He saw her from across the bar. Small, tight,
princess pretty with honey hair and almond-shaped eyes. She
had that look on her face that the fan girls get, wide-eyed, curious, a big smile like they're looking at the milky way in wonder of all its vastness.

"Check it," said Gustavo, who was gazing in her direction.
"The hot one. She's looking at you."

Mav had already clocked her, was thinking about what he
might say if he made his way over there. "Maybe she's looking
at *you*," he answered his friend, who blew out a breath. Gustavo
was also quite hot and had no trouble with the ladies.

Mav recognized her, an influencer—mental health or some
girl-power type thing. A competitor in the challenge. She'd
done well—third, he thought. Some cash and prizes. She looked
young, like *really* young. Was she legal? Must be: she held a pink

drink in her hand. She whispered something to her friend, keeping her eyes on him.

"Nah. No one's looking at me when you're around," Gustavo said without any hint of jealousy. They'd been friends
too long, and guys just didn't care about that shit. Gustavo was
happy enough if the girl of the evening came with a gaggle of
friends. Everyone in places like Aspen was a certain kind of hot,
in shape, moneyed. To Mav and his boys, then, one girl was as
good as any other for the night. That was before Angeline. That
was before Maverick knew what it was like to have the love of
a good, strong woman, love you had to earn.

Something happened when Mav locked eyes with Chloe that
night; a kind of sizzling energy passed between them. And although she was hot AF, he felt that chill, the one he had right
before the extra big fuckups that laid him up and forced him to
take a hard, cold look at his ceiling and his life.

But at that stage, before Angeline, before she'd turned him
on to yoga, meditation, and mindfulness—or tried to—he was
not about following his *inner voice*. He was all about following
his...desires. In fact, at that point, he didn't even realize there
was another way to live. It was only about *want* and *get*.

That night in Aspen, he made his way through the hard-
bodied, well-heeled crowd over to Chloe, and it was like they
already knew each other. Which was often the case, because
when you were internet-famous, people always thought they
knew you. Chloe was petite; he had to bend down to hear her.
That smile, it told him everything he needed to know about
himself, about her. Over the din, she said all the right things,
how she was a fan, how she'd been inspired to enter the Tough
Be-atch competitions as a way to combat her mental-health issues, because of him, because of Extreme. She reached up to
touch the deep scar over his eye where his forehead had met
the sharp edge of his metal wheel guard during a flail on his
BMX in Germany.

"I was watching when you did this," she said. "You walked it off like it was nothing."

What the cameras didn't see: Maverick puking in the trees. Passing out when they stitched him up in the med tent. The three days it took him to recover. The pain pills that left him foggy and not himself. How he felt himself disappearing into that Oxy cloud and liking it, and how if it hadn't been for Hector taking the pills and sitting on him for a couple of days, he might have found himself hooked.

"It wasn't nothing," he surprised himself by admitting.

Her gaze was thoughtful, knowing.

"Are you ever going to slow down?" she'd asked. They'd found a quiet booth in the back of the bar. Her friend was dancing with Gustavo. "I don't have the same followership as you do. And they're not rabid fans like yours are. But it's like a lot, isn't it, every day? Living for your feed, your WeWatch channel?"

"I don't know anything else," he admitted. "I've never lived another way."

Another thing he'd never said out loud. He'd taken too many gummies, obviously.

She nodded, ran a delicate finger around the rim of her glass. "The pressure gets to me sometimes. The highs and lows of it, the nastygrams in my DMs, the people you meet on the street who think they know you, for me all the girls in pain out there, writing to me for help with their depression, anxiety, eating disorders. Then when you go dark for whatever reason, you lose so many followers. And real life…"

She gazed around, and he recognized her expression, a kind of confused disappointment. Reality, the real world, it paled in comparison to the dizzying highs and crushing lows of a life lived online. Like sometimes, his online life seemed real, and reality seemed distant, inaccessible, frighteningly dull. The exhilaration of successes, the anger at detractors, the disappointment when a post failed, the money when you slayed, the roller coaster of it all was addictive. Later Angeline would teach him that there was only here, only now, only the breath. And he'd glimpse that, its essential truth. What he didn't—couldn't—tell Angeline was that it scared him to death.

Even now, Aspen far behind him, as he rushed toward the hotel on this tiny, nowhere island that didn't have a single nightclub, he had the urge to go live, to broadcast to his followers about something, about anything, just to get the reactions, even the bad ones. Just to have the *engagement*, anything but the quiet, dark truth of the moment. He was alone.

His night with Chloe was, should have been, just another highly pleasant sexual encounter in a five-star hotel, followed by a decadent breakfast in bed, and then, of course, his hasty retreat.

"Hey, keep the room," he told her. "I think we have it through the weekend."

She nodded, looked down at her cuticles, and he could see she was upset that he was going. She felt something that he didn't.

"I'm so sorry I have to jet," he said, leaning in for a kiss. Then deep eye contact. "Can I see you again?"

He always asked that. It helped ease his escape, made him seem like less of a dick. She brightened a bit. They exchanged numbers. But the truth was, he had mostly forgotten her by the time he made it to the plane. Hector and Alex were already there waiting. They were on to the next thing. What had it been? Now, he couldn't even remember.

Something about his encounter with Chloe stayed with him, though. A clinging unease, like he'd done something wrong. But he hadn't, right? They were grown people who'd shared a night together, and that was it. He didn't have to marry her. He didn't even have to call. She texted him that night:

That was special for me. I don't usually do things like that.

He ignored it. She kept texting.

I can still feel you on my skin.

Hey, I'll be at the Tough Be-atch in Cabo. Meet up?

Okay, wow. R U ghosting me?

When she called the next day, he blocked her. But not before he saw her final text.

I'm not like other girls, Mav.

That turned out to be true.

He almost missed the turn off the deserted road that led past crumbling, old houses and wide, empty fields, turning quickly and skidding into the parking lot. The whole island seemed like a beautiful ruin, wild hydrangeas growing over tumbling road-side walls, huge, estate-sized homes abandoned and falling to piles, barely populated towns. Angeline loved it. But something about it scared him, even before creepy Petra and her goons. His neck and the back of his head still ached. He'd twisted his arm in the fall. He felt a wash of the same impotent rage he'd felt when they'd pinned him to the ground.

Maverick slowed the vehicle, tires crunching on the gravel. The radio didn't pick up any stations, only static. The silence was oppressive. He realized he was gripping the wheel so hard that his hands ached.

The hotel came into view as he drove farther into the lot, a low white building. Above, the clouds had cleared. It looked like one of those VR experiences where everything was just shy of being real, elevated, colors filtered and popping, the movement of leaves and clouds just a little too perfect. What did they call it? *Uncanny valley.* When something was close but not quite close enough to the truth as to become almost frightening, just shy of being human or natural as to become unhuman, unnatural.

He stepped out of the car, the air heavy with the smell of salt and rain. He walked around to the back and popped the hatch and put his eyes on the bags he'd taken from the tent and stashed there. Seeing those bags, knowing what they contained, gave him comfort.

He shut the hatch, the sound echoing.

Then he walked over to the other Range Rover, put a hand on the still-warm hood, glanced at the PopMap. He saw Angeline's Tinkerbell avatar hovering near Alex's and Tavo's.

His throat was dry.

There.

A slender, dark form over by the stone wall that edged a cliff, a vertiginous drop into the rocky, churning sea below. Angeline said that someone had died by suicide from that ridge—a princess, was it? Some kind of island royalty, forced into an arranged marriage. He'd barely been listening but remembered thinking the name sounded like a flower. Jacintha. Angeline loved all that stuff: history, legends, ghost stories. There was a book about the doomed princess in the lobby. She'd been a poet, apparently. The book and all her poems were in Portuguese, but that didn't stop Angeline from poring over the pictures.

"Why kill yourself, though? Just put up with the guy. How bad could it be?" he'd offered when she told him the story.

That look. "Spoken like someone who has never been forced to do anything he doesn't want to do. That's what it is to be a white, affluent male in this world."

As usual, he felt like he'd fallen short of the mark Angeline used to judge everyone, everything.

"I'm just saying."

The form over by the wall stood stock-still, looking out at the surf or back in his direction, he couldn't tell. He waved an arm, but the figure was unmoving. Angeline. It had to be. That Tinkerbell shape, those narrow but erect shoulders. A dancer's bearing. A queen.

Twice in the last year he'd sensed that she wanted to leave him. After his last rejected proposal, he'd pressed her when the camera was off.

"Why won't you marry me?"

She'd hemmed and hawed, finally answering.

"You're not ready for marriage, Mav. It's not just a ring and a piece of paper. Not something you do for show. It's a union. It means that we put each other before everything else. In the little things, the day-to-day, and the big things. That takes a certain kind of...maturity."

"I'm mature," he'd whined.

But the next day, he and Tavo flew to a friend's new restaurant in Rio, and some jet-tracker asshole posted about it on Twitter. **While people all over the world starve, and climate change is an emergency for humanity, influencer Maverick Dillan takes his private jet to Rio for a single steak dinner.** There was an image of him stuffing his face, looking bloated and high. To make matters worse, he'd missed an important meeting with a sponsor, and Ange had had to cover for him.

She was mad. Madder than she'd ever been at him.

But then he tore his rotator cuff during a bad snowboarding fall the next week, and he was laid up in major pain. She softened then, like she always did when he was broken. She stayed. He'd made promises he intended to keep. It was time to slow down. After this challenge he'd make some wrong things right.

He walked toward the hotel, the form still unmoving. Maybe it wasn't a person at all. His phone pinged, and he looked down to see a text from Hector.

The generator just crapped out.

He didn't answer it; the generator was the least of his fucking problems right now. *Handle it, Hector. For fuck's sake, it's your only job.*

He let himself into the dim lobby, moved soundlessly through the elegant lounge with its low couches and tables, sprawling bar, fireplace with embers still glowing. The back wall was comprised entirely of glass doors that opened onto the stone patio, revealing the spectacular view.

The place felt deserted; they'd had it mostly to themselves like a staffed Airbnb. Behind Angeline's back, he'd asked Hector not to check them out. Keep the rooms. The plan at the time, before everything started to go FUBAR, had been to sneak back here to sleep. He had too many injuries to sleep in a tent like he used to.

He stepped outside, and the ocean was a roar. The form he'd been chasing was gone. Nothing, no one there. But there had been. He was sure of it.

The wind whipped at his hair and his clothes as he tried Angeline again. He felt small, inconsequential against the endless sky and the wild surf below. As a kid, he remembered loving that feeling. Now it scared him. In the real world, he was nothing.

No answer. But this time, faintly, he heard Angeline's ringtone from off in the distance, that riot of chimes she favored that sounded like manic fairy bells. He followed the sound, hung up, and dialed again, the sound of the chimes getting louder as he approached the stone passageway that led to the guest rooms. On the air, he heard the high-pitched calling of a bird.

But no, he thought, coming to a stop, listening. It wasn't a bird. Someone was screaming.

Angeline.

He ran with everything he had toward the sound, pounding on the rough stone pavers, calling her name, following the sound of her screaming, the chimes of her phone.

The world around him swam, colors punching. For a blissful moment, he imagined he was in *Red World*, none of it real. He was immortal, and the consequences of his actions were virtual: no matter what he stole, or who he killed, or what kind of prizes he banked, it was only real in that universe where everyone was just a player in his game.

But no, he felt the unyielding concrete against his feet, the damp rough stone of the outdoor corridor brush his shoulder. Hard surfaces, no give.

When he found Angeline, she was standing at an open door, Tavo holding her back from entering the room. He came up behind them and grabbed her away from Tavo, and she fell into him weeping. "OhmygodohmygodMavohmygod."

"What the fuck? What did you do to her?" he yelled at Tavo, holding her tight.

But Tavo just shook his head, staring, like he couldn't speak. His face was ashen, eyes wild with confusion.

Mav followed his gaze to the concrete floor of the utility closet and saw what they saw.

Alex.

Head bloodied, misshapen, neck unnaturally bent, ghost-white. Broken. Maverick could barely take in the sight, felt the world tilt and fade around him. Alex. Gone.

Not Alex. Not anymore.

23

ANGELINE

"Help me get him out of there."

Mav's voice sounded as if he was on the other side of thick glass, desperate, pleading, muffled beneath the roaring in her ears and the chaos of her thoughts. There was a stunned feeling that had her limbs heavy; she could barely process the scene, what was happening. She leaned against the rough, cold wall, badly needing to sit or lie down. Bile burned its way up her throat.

"We should leave him," said Tavo faintly. "We need to call the police."

His words seemed to come out very slowly and hover on the air.

She wanted to agree but couldn't seem to find her voice. As much as she didn't want to leave Alex, her friend, lying broken in a utility closet, alone on the wet stone floor in the dark, that was undeniably the right thing to do. The other day she had watched him eat a slice of pizza with gusto. She punched him playfully on his bony but fully alive shoulder, listened to him laugh at some joke she had made about Mav.

"Fuck no, we're not calling the police," said Mav, angry.

No, *scared*. She knew that pitch, boyish, wobbly.

"Do you have any idea what kind of a shitshow we're talking about here?" he went on. "We're in a foreign country. I barely made it out of Mexico, man."

Tavo blinked at him, his brow knitting.

"*You're* in a foreign country," said Tavo. "This is my home."

There was a truth in that, and it made Gustavo seem other to her all of a sudden, not part of what was happening here, maybe not an ally. Maybe there had always been something other about him. He didn't grow up with the guys. He'd met Maverick at NYU. She watched him now: he seemed like a stranger.

"Shut up and help me," barked Mav.

The three of them just stared at each other for a long moment, Tavo's eyes were wide with grief, confusion, shock. Angeline had no frame of reference here, no idea *what* to do. She never thought she'd be a person who froze in an emergency. But here she was, a statue. Still, already beneath the shock and terror, other thoughts had started to churn. *Who did this? Why?*

Then, the texts she'd read scrolled back on the screen of her mind. The BoxOfficePlus deal. Which Alex wanted and Maverick did not. The confrontation Alex had planned. Lucia's concern that he wasn't safe.

And then, horribly, unbelievably, Maverick and Tavo were lifting Alex in the rug that had been missing from his room, using it like a stretcher. And Alex looked so small, like a boy with knobby knees and skinny arms, but the two of them struggled with the weight as they edged down the long hallway. And Angeline thought about Lucia and their baby and *ohmygod* this is a dream, and it isn't happening. *Please, please, please.*

"What are you *doing*?" she hissed, finding her voice. "Where are you taking him?"

She took in their surroundings—the dark exterior hallway, the empty courtyard. She knew there were no guests, that there was not as much staff at the hotel in the off-season. The kitchen and bar crew arrived later to start meal prep; the cleaning people came later in the morning. The owners were sometimes on the property and sometimes not. In a moment of clarity, she scanned the dark corners of the courtyard. They were alone. No cameras.

"Taking him back to the room," Mav grunted, straining with effort. "So we have time to think."

How was he so calm? Shock. He was in shock, right?

Mav and Tavo maneuvered the body back into the hotel room and dropped it clumsily onto the floor, where it landed with an unsettling thud. Angeline stared, horror mounting. The only dead body she'd ever seen was her abuela, nicely dressed and made-up, laid out for the endless wake where legions of relatives and friends filed by the casket offering respects, showing their grief. It had been sad but orderly. None of the wild grief of tragedy, merely the expected passing of an old woman. Her body was stiff and unnatural, like a doll. A doll of her abuela laid out so that people could say goodbye.

This? This was chaos, mind-bending, reality stuttering. Alex was dead. Gone. Murdered.

Maverick took the Privacy, Please sign from the knob and hung it outside, pulling the door closed with a decisive click.

The smell—too much blood, something else. Angeline ran for the toilet, barely made it, heaved everything she'd eaten in a disgusting spray. She hung over the bowl, clinging to its coldness, dry-heaving, weeping.

Maverick came in to stand beside her.

"Ange."

She looked up at him. His face was uncharacteristically still, serious. No hint of his usual smiling mischief. Without the smile, bluster, and bravado he was like someone else. A darker version of Mav. And he looked huge, ripped, muscles straining against his T-shirt. She felt small on the floor at his feet.

"Ange," he said again, voice icy. "I'm *really* going to need you to pull yourself together."

What did you do? she wanted to ask, but she couldn't force out the words. She couldn't go there. Once she did, there was no going back. Instead, she pulled herself to her feet and followed him out to the bedroom, where Tavo sat on the bed with his head in his hands, and Alex's body was covered by half of the rug. She had to keep her eyes off it, off Mav. She walked over to the window and stared at her own reflection. *Who are you?* she asked the shadow of herself in the glass. *What is happening?*

"I think we should take him to the plane," said Mav.

"What?" said Tavo. The energy in the room was electric.

"Just until after the challenge."

"After the *challenge*?" said Tavo. He blew out a disbelieving breath. "I think the challenge is off."

"It's not," said Mav, still in the same cold, hard tone. "It can't be. We can't afford not to finish the challenge."

Angeline turned back to them, and Tavo was staring, incredulous. Mav was right beside Alex's body. And for a second, Angeline saw the image of Wild Cody with his foot up on the flank of the dead lion, hunting rifle in hand. She pushed the image away, her stomach starting to churn again.

"We're like a month of expenses away from total bankruptcy," he said quietly. "We're running on fumes. Without the We-Watch bonus and sponsor payments, we won't make it another sixty days."

"How are we talking about this?" Angeline yelled, the volume surprising even her. "About money? About the challenge? Alex is *dead*."

"I know," said Mav, voice coming up an octave. He moved toward her, and she took a step back, hitting against the cold glass.

"*Someone* killed him," said Tavo, rising, looking at Maverick, dark eyes searing. "And *you* don't want us to call the police."

Maverick looked back and forth between them, put a hand to his heart.

"Wait. Wait."

The silence in the room was deafening.

"You guys think *I* killed him?" he said when neither of them said anything.

All their eyes fell on the Alex lump on the floor between them. Angeline felt the rise of bile again, pushed it back. She grappled with the scene before here, Mav's demeanor, his words.

Finally, she took Alex's phone from her pocket and started reading off the text chain between Alex and Lucia.

"No, no, no," he said, interrupting her, lifting his palm. "That's all bullshit."

"Why did he think you were stealing money from Extreme, Mav?" Tavo's voice was gentle, but his gaze was unrelenting.

"I—I," Mav started, then stopped to take a breath, his eyes falling on Alex. "I have no idea."

He moved over to Angeline, took both her hands. "You know me. You *live* with me. Do you think I would steal money from the company I built? From my best friends? Do you really think I could ever...hurt *anyone*?"

But it happened all the time, didn't it? It was probably the most common white-collar crime, embezzlement. The big personality responsible for the initial success of the company thinks that the accounts and the lines of credit are there for his fun and pleasure, to indulge his vices, and starts skimming off the top. Still, when she looked at Mav, she couldn't reconcile it. Immature. Irresponsible. Okay, yes. But not a criminal. She took another glance at the rug. Not a killer. No way.

She shook her head. "No," she said. "Of course not."

Mav looked to Tavo, who stared for an awkward moment, then shook his head. Mav seemed to deflate with relief.

"Then, who did this?" Tavo asked. "Why?"

Maverick sank onto the bed, and Tavo rose, creating distance.

Angeline could read his tension in the stiffness of his shoulders, the way he clenched his right hand.

"Did he confront you? You said you fought. Was it about this?" Angeline asked.

Mav nodded reluctantly. Angeline and Tavo exchanged a look.

"I haven't told anyone," he said. "I didn't want to scare you guys."

He had that blank look he sometimes wore when things got too much for him. When he was too hurt, or too stressed, when he talked about his mother, sometimes even when they were making love. It was like he just kind of checked out.

"Haven't told anyone what?" Tavo's voice had an impatient edge.

"Someone's been threatening me. Threatening Extreme."

"What are you talking about?" asked Angeline.

"In social, in the comments, on Pop. That person, you know, MavIsALiar with the three skulls? Whoever it is? They've been threatening me."

He fished his phone from his pocket, tapped it a few times, and showed it to Angeline. There was a file of emails, the scroll of subject lines filled with vitriol.

I'm coming for you.

Liar, liar, pants on fire.

I am going to expose all the fraud at Extreme.

You killed Chloe Miranda. And I can prove it.

I'm going to hack my way into your company and destroy it.

Countdown to the end of Maverick Dillan.

Extreme is a virus.

You're a dead man.

Ready or not, here I come.

It was an endless list of threats and accusations and the dates spanned nearly three months. Angeline felt a shiver, as if the malice leached from the phone into her skin.

"That wipeout at the skate park in Venice Beach last month? Someone loosened the trucks on my board," he said.

It had been bad. He'd dislocated his shoulder which had needed to be painfully snapped back into place. The doctor said he was just lucky he hadn't broken his neck dropping into the bowl.

"Before that, when we were skiing in February in the Italian Alps, Tav, and the weather got bad? I skied the black-diamond trail run, barely made it down the visibility was so poor, and got in trouble at the bottom because it was closed?"

"Yeah," said Tavo. "They were pissed."

"Except that there was no closing net at the head of the run to say that it had been shut down. Later, they told me that someone took down the sign. They found it in the trees. They thought I did it, wanted to fine me."

Tavo dipped his head. "I remember."

"You were there," said Maverick. "Both times. Then, the scuba-equipment failure in the Keys?"

Tavo was nodding slowly. "Your regulator broke apart in your mouth during the night dive. We had to buddy-breathe to the surface."

"You saved my life."

"What are you saying?" asked Angeline.

"I think," said Mav, "that someone's trying to kill me. And if they can't kill me, they want to ruin me."

He stared at Alex. "Alex confronted me about the money. I told him what was happening. Alex...he didn't believe me. But he wasn't going to turn me in. He said he was going to get a commercial flight home, and we'd deal with it next week. When the money flowed in from WeWatch and the sponsorships, he was going to fix the books, and we were going to bring you guys the BoxOfficePlus deal, decide what to do."

"I thought you said you'd never sell."

"I don't want to," he said. "But...I think we have to. It's time. We all get a big payout, and we still get to do the things we love, more or less."

Outside, the wind picked up and knocked some branches against the glass. They all startled at the sound, Mav hopping to his feet.

"He told Lucia that you were blocking the deal," said Angeline.

"I had been. I had an angel investor in my pocket, thought with the bonus we could dig ourselves out. But then Alex showed me the financials and said it was sell now or hold on and maybe lose everything."

Maverick ran a thick hand over the flop of his dark hair. "When I left him earlier, he was fine. He hated me. Thought I was lying. But he was going to stick it out and try to fix the books so that we could make the deal. He was..."

Mav's eyes fell again on the lump, and this time they filled up. She'd never seen him cry. Never. His voice faltered, and he batted angrily at his tears. "He was fine. Angry but fine."

She wanted to move to comfort him but didn't, feeling Tavo's eyes on her.

"Oh, my God, this is not happening," Mav said quietly. "He can't be gone. He can't."

"Who did this?" Tavo asked again.

They'd talked about everything else, but that was the big question, wasn't it? If not Maverick, then who? Why? And where was that person? Angeline was still holding Maverick's phone and stared down at the string of angry emails.

"Whoever wrote these, I'm guessing," she said, handing the

phone to Maverick. "*Ready or not?* Does that mean he was planning to come to this challenge?"

Maverick looked stricken suddenly, turned toward the door. "I saw someone when I was heading to the room. Someone on the property—just now."

Angeline felt a jolt of alarm. "Who? Where?"

"Out by the wall, just standing. I thought it was you, but when I got there—no one."

"So someone small?" asked Tavo. Angeline clocked his skepticism. Tavo didn't believe Maverick. In fact, Tavo had been subtly edging closer to her so that he stood between them now, like he was getting ready to defend her.

Did *she*? *Did* she believe Maverick?

"I guess?" said Mav, rubbing at his eyes with the heels of his hands. "I don't know."

They all stared toward the door, as if they were waiting for it to burst open, some crazed assailant rushing in.

"In fact," he went on, "I've felt like—a couple times—like maybe someone was following me. You know that feeling that you're being watched?"

"You're always being watched. You live for it," said Tavo, an angry edge to his voice that Angeline hadn't heard before. If Maverick heard the tone, he ignored it.

"Not like that. On the subway, someone was watching through the cars," said Mav. "Once when I was heading home late from a bar, I heard footsteps behind me, and when I turned, someone ducked into a doorway. Once when I was leaving the gym, early morning, I thought I felt someone come up behind me, but when I turned—nothing."

Since when did Mav ever take the subway? They hadn't ridden the trains together since before Covid.

"You never said anything," said Angeline. "About any of this."

"I know. I just…hoped it would stop?"

That tracked. Mav generally took the bumblebee approach to all problems: ignore them and hope they'll go away.

More scratching at the window, the wind picking up. It was nearly three o'clock. Stress, a deep fatigue, a thrum of fear. The room was tilting with it.

"So you think this person threatening you is the same person following you," said Tavo, his accent thicker than usual, which happened when he was drunk, or passionate, or upset. "This *person* is also stealing money from the company. And this person followed you to Falcão Island?"

He moved a step closer to Mav. It was aggressive. But Mav, much bigger than Tavo, hung his head and took a step back.

"This mysterious *person*," continued Tavo, "killed Alex?"

Mav shouted, "I don't know! I don't know. Fuck, I have no fucking idea. But it wasn't me. It *wasn't*. I *loved* him. He was one of my *oldest friends*."

Angeline stepped between them, a coolness, a calm settling over her. It was suddenly clear what needed to be done. What Alex would surely do. He would act to protect Extreme first; she knew that. He would cover the theft, whoever was responsible, and make the deal.

"We need to get rid of his body," she said.

"What?" said Tavo. "*No*. It's bad enough that we moved him from the closet."

But Maverick was nodding.

"We finish the challenge, make WeWatch and all the sponsors happy. When we're flush again, we'll fix the books." She looked over at Alex's laptop. "He was probably already working on it."

"What about *Alex*?" Tavo's voice was a shocked whisper. He looked at her like she was a stranger. *Who are you?* his eyes asked.

"He can't have died here," she said, surprised at her own coldness. "Not right now."

"What are you saying?"

"Right now, everyone here thinks he went home, that he quit Extreme."

"Except for Lucia," said Tavo, tapping hard on the phone. "She's frantic."

Angeline picked it up and started typing, tears falling. Who *was* she?

Hey, babe, so sorry. I had it out with Mav and crashed hard. So stressful. On my way home. Talk to you when I get on the plane. Love you and the kiddo.

She felt like she captured his syntax, the way she'd heard Alex talk to Lucia. He always used correct punctuation in his texts like a true nerd.

She held it up to Mav who gave her a nod and then she pressed Send. The whoosh sound echoed like an accusation. Had she just done a thing that she could never, ever undo? And why? What was she now? An accessory to murder? Could you be an accessory to murder if you didn't know the identity of the killer?

Only if they got caught.

"When the challenge is done, we'll report him missing," said Angeline.

The phone was ringing then, and a picture of Lucia and the baby popped up on the screen. They all looked at it; she could hear Tavo breathing. She let it go to voicemail. After a second it started ringing again.

"With the money from the deal, we'll take care of them," she said. "They'll be set for life. That's what Alex would have wanted us to do."

Tavo looked like he was going to be sick. Mav had retreated to whatever place he went when things got hot.

She went on Alex's Pop account and turned off his location. She did the same with his Find My Peeps app. Then she shut down his phone.

"Let's go," she said, her voice sounding sure, strong. Which she definitely did not feel. She walked over to the door and peered outside. They were alone. For a moment, no one did anything. If Tavo freaked out, if he bailed on them, they were all fucked. But he, too, had a lot to lose.

She didn't have a plan past *get rid of his body*. What happened next had not been written yet. The publicity of his murder or disappearance would be a firestorm. There was no way around that. And Extreme being linked to another suspicious event was not good for any of them or their pending deal. She couldn't get them out of that, but she could delay it, maybe get them off the island before all hell broke loose. And maybe that would be enough to save Extreme, to save Mav.

"It's clear," she said, gazing out into the hallway one last time.

Tavo and Maverick hesitated another moment, then each took one side of the rug and maneuvered the body of their friend out the door.

"Where are we taking him?" asked Tavo when they were out in the hallway. He was crying, big tears trailing down his cheeks. But he was cooperating.

The plane was a bad idea. His body would start to smell and could easily be discovered by airport workers. And it wasn't the place they'd want him found.

"Let's take him over to the wall."

The cliff from where Princess Jacintha had thrown herself to escape a loveless marriage to a known brute. The cliff face was steep, with a hundred-foot drop into churning, rocky, deep water, no beach. The island was in the middle of the Atlantic, no other land mass except for the other islands for thousands of kilometers.

"What if there's someone else here? Someone watching us," asked Mav. "I mean I *saw* someone. They could be lurking just out of sight."

Angeline reflected on this a moment. Did she believe someone was following and had it in for Mav? There *were* a lot of people who hated him. Chloe Miranda's family. Moms Against Mav.

Petra and her army of thugs. The losers of his challenges that claimed they were rigged before it began. The vitriolic haters who commented on every live broadcast and post, whoever they were. Still, it seemed paranoid and just slightly narcissistic to think he was being followed, that someone had tried to kill him with so much subtlety and creativity from Venice Beach to the Italian Alps. And yet someone *had* killed Alex. So what did that mean? That Angeline thought *Maverick* killed Alex and she was doing this to protect *him*? She didn't love that version of herself.

"We're just going to throw him off the cliff?" said Tavo, ghostly pale, face drawn with strain and horror. "I mean, his body might never be found. What will we tell Lucia? His son?"

She looked between Tavo and Maverick, their eyes on her. They were weak, both of them. And honestly it sickened her a little.

"Do either of you have a better idea?" she snapped.

After a moment, both men shook their heads.

"Then, let's go."

Mav had a place where he went. But so did Angeline. There was a place in her brain that was cool and calculating, calm under pressure. They hadn't killed their friend; they were just trying to save the company. She was sure it's what Alex would have wanted her to do, because it meant that she could make sure Lucia and the baby would be set for life. She couldn't bring Alex back, but she could take care of the company and his family.

As they moved awkwardly toward the wall, Angeline followed, scanning the darkness for anyone who might be watching. Petra's words rang back to her.

It's too late for them. The sickness has already invaded their spirit. But it's not too late for you.

The old woman had been wrong. It was too late for Angeline, had been for a while. And even though part of her had been pretending it wasn't true, a bigger part of her already knew that.

24

~~~~~~

MAVISALIAR

If you watch something on a screen and don't see it with your own eyes, is it really happening?

Press Record.

Let other people decide if it's real or not.

These days we never know, do we? What's true and what isn't?

Three figures emerge from an exterior hallway that leads to a glittering lap pool. The dim light dances on the surface of the water. The three move slowly, two of them struggling with the weight they're carrying between them. Seen through this tiny rectangular screen, there are just shadows, all distinguishing features blacked out by the stormy sky.

One is slim, a woman, she moves out ahead. Says something. Her tone official, quietly commanding. The man closest to her is huge, tall and broad, muscular. The third is smaller, but lithe and quick on his feet, in shape, nimbler than the other man. They edge past the pool, knock against one of the loungers. A female voice cuts the darkness.

Be careful.

Then they move onto the grass and come to stand by the low stone wall.

The woman dumps her head in her hands, and the big man moves in to comfort her, her darkness disappearing into his. But she pushes him away. The third figure stands aloof, posture stiff. They all radiate a deep unhappiness, a kind of toxic sorrow.

What is evil?

Is evil doing *something*? Or doing *nothing*?

The woman speaks, the high wind whipping her words out to sea. The trees are starting to bend, and ripples move across the surface of the pool water. There's a storm coming. A big one.

Nature knows how to clean house. It keeps trying, doesn't it?

Mammoth hurricanes and cyclones, raging wildfires, a pandemic that kills millions, devastating earthquakes, tsunamis. Social media. Ha ha. That's a joke—but not really. Has anything hurt us more? Has anything unstitched the fabric of our humanity more than the things that we have devised to entertain ourselves? Humankind destroys itself with brilliant creativity, but everything comes from mother earth, even technology. There's nothing more brutally organic than the human mind and all its diabolical inventions.

The three just stand there for a moment. They look at their feet. They are statues. Frozen on the precipice. Finally, after long moments pass, the woman kneels beside the mound at their feet a moment and bows her head as if praying. Then she rises and nods.

The two men lift the load, heaving it with all their strength over the wall. The carpet unfurls and whatever was inside disappears over the edge. The wind is too loud to hear anything— a scream, a crash—but the skein of fabric flaps in the wind like a great flag.

They pull it in and fold it up into a square.

The big man crumbles. Even over the heavy wind, his wails can be heard.

The other two stand, unmoved.
What is the greater evil?
To commit a heinous act?
Or to do nothing at all?
The truth is rarely simple.
End recording.

25

VIOLET

Violet tried not to zone out as Mr. Fieldstone talked on excitedly about the six functions of an angle—sine, cosine, tangent, co-whatever whatever. She scribbled dutifully in her notebook.

Could someone please explain *why* math? What people would ever use any of it ever again after they took the AP exam? Mr. Fieldstone was famous for saying, *There is no why in math. It just is. Relish in that simplicity. Because for too few things in life is that true.*

Which made no sense at all to Violet. Because that was all she ever thought about: Why? Why did she have to get her period? Every single month? Why was her skin breaking out? Why were boys all so vacant, staring only ever at their devices?

Why was everything so...hard?

She used to enjoy Mr. Fieldstone and the geeky thrill he seemed to get out of numbers. Even if she didn't share his enthusiasm exactly, it was contagious. It reminded Violet of her dad and how excited he was about everything, especially science, especially any project she or Blake was working on. He was *into* it. He'd get this gleam, and his hands would fly when he talked about chemistry or geology, when they had to build something. And that energy made them excited, too. But then he was gone.

Her mom *tried*; she really did. But school projects were just another stressor after Dad left them broke, alone. Sometimes it seemed like he'd taken all the joy with him. All the fun, too. But Violet never said that to her mom because she knew how much that would hurt. Her mom was fun, too, in different ways. When Violet finally accepted that her father wasn't coming back and what everyone said about him was probably true, Mr. Fieldstone's math joy started to make her sad. She wasn't doing well, barely clinging to her low B.

To Violet's right, her best friend Coral, whose jet-black hair was tipped with hot-pink this week, was leaning her cheek against her fist, and her eyes were closed. Was she sleeping? Coral was doing even worse than Violet, despite her extraordinary aptitude, and Mr. Fieldstone had gently suggested that Coral either start paying attention or drop down to Honors or even Basic. Which she could not do because Coral's mother was the original bulldozer parent, still clinging to the idea that Coral was going to be a concert pianist, a professional soccer player, and an Ivy League student. Coral, it was pretty clear, would be none of those things.

Violet kicked her friend's stool, and Coral sat up blinking.

"Is it over?" she said too loudly, earning a frown from Mr. Fieldstone.

"No." Violet nodded toward the clock. Unbelievably they still had fifteen minutes to go. Had time stopped completely?

"For frack's sake," said Coral, who was trying to swear less since a guy she was talking to on Pop said that girls who use curse words was a turnoff for him. Which Violet thought was misogynistic and small-minded, and *that* was a major turnoff for her. But Coral was into him—though she'd never spoken to him, or even seen him on FaceTime. Sharif was a long boarder in Morocco according to his Photogram profile. Of course, he could be a housewife in Tacoma, or an incel in Miami, for all they knew. Still, it was a kind of fiction that worked for a while, since real, actual, flesh-and-blood boys seemed barely conscious—into VR or whatever girl they were talking to online or lost to *Red World* or some other game.

Mr. Fieldstone had stopped talking. Shoot. What had she missed? Now he was handing back quizzes. From the groans and heads slumped into hands, Violet deduced that things weren't going to go well. She hustled to scribble down the last of the notes on the board since she'd missed the end of his lecture.

"Oh, fraggle," said Coral, holding up her quiz emblazoned with a big red D.

Mr. Fieldstone handed Violet her paper. He was tall and doughy, wearing a perpetual sweater-vest in any weather, even though he was always perspiring a little. He stared at them menacingly over his round wire specs. "You can both do better."

She squinted at her paper, afraid to look. Finally, she focused her eyes. It was just a B, which once upon a time would have been surprising, even upsetting. Now she was just relieved that it wasn't worse.

"My mom is going to murder me," said Coral miserably. Glitter from the purple tutu she was wearing over black leggings and lug-soled Mary Janes was getting everywhere. She really did look like she might cry, even though Violet suspected that Coral enjoyed her mother's rage. Like it was some kind of theater performance in which they participated together, and maybe the only time her mother paid full attention to her.

"You can come live with us," offered Violet, a comforting hand on her friend's shoulder.

"Okay, yeah," said Coral, nodding as if this was an actual option. "Can I spend the night tonight? Watch the challenge with you guys?"

"Of course."

Just a few hours to go, Violet thought excitedly. Win or lose, her mom would be home tomorrow. Maybe they'd be richer and things would be easier for Adele. Her mom wouldn't have to worry so much every month as their expenses constantly outstripped their income. Or maybe they'd be poorer with more bills to pay. They'd run up Adele's credit card getting her the gear she needed. *Sometimes you have to spend money to make money*, Adele had told her in REI. Again, this made no sense to Violet. Didn't you have to *earn* money to make money? Or save money to make money? But what did she know?

Her phone pinged, and she pulled it from her pocket.

There was an update from her LifeTracker app: *Blake has left East Tanglewood High School.*

Violet stared at it. Huh? It was not even noon.

Violet had dropped her exhausted brother off at the lower school this morning. He had been super cranky and had eaten four doughnuts, which he definitely did not need. She knew the look of cybersickness when she saw it, when too many hours on a screen became a kind of illness.

"Were you up all night on *Red World*?" she'd asked him in the car.

"Not all night," he'd answered.

He'd slumped in the passenger seat looking like he was going to puke.

"Well, these are the consequences of your actions."

"Shut up, Violet."

While Blake was in the shower this morning, she'd loaded the tracking app on his phone, accepted her own request to track, and then removed the app icon from his phone's home screen. He had no idea she was tracking him. Mom tracked them both with the Find My Peeps app that came with the phones. For safety reasons only, Mom was quick to say, not because she didn't trust them. Violet and Blake both knew how to trick that app, with another app called Teleporter that let you mask your true location.

But LifeTracker was more comprehensive, including things like whether you were driving or on foot, how much charge your phone had left. Violet only thought to put it on Blake's phone because of what happened last night. Who had he been with? Where had he gone? she asked him multiple times over the course of the morning until he'd stopped speaking to her altogether.

She held up the phone to Coral.

"That little brat," said Coral, outraged. "How does *he* get to cut?"

"He's in someone's car," said Violet, a kind of hole opening in her middle.

Blake is moving at fifty miles an hour on Oakhurst Road, the app announced.

Panic had her stomach tumbling, her throat dry. She started to call him, but Coral put a hand on her arm. "If you call him, he'll just lie. Maybe he'll find the app and turn it off."

"What do I do?" she whispered. Mr. Fieldstone was talking to students at his desk about their quizzes. He got up to the whiteboard and started writing. "Tell the office? Call the cops?"

"I'm sorry," said Coral, dark eyes wide in inquiry. "Are you *a narc* now?"

"No," said Violet. Coral didn't get it, an only, the worshipped center of her intact, two-parent universe, she'd never been responsible for anyone else. And Violet's mom was trusting her, counting on her to keep them both safe while she went to try to make life better for all of them. Her mom had only done this at all because Violet convinced her that she was up to the task. "But what if he's been like *abducted* or something?"

Coral rolled her eyes. "No. Who would abduct Blake? He's like six feet tall already. He's off getting high somewhere."

"With who?" Violet said. "He doesn't have any friends. He's only fourteen. Who does he know with a car?"

She remembered what he said last night. That guy Gregg with the Bronco from Lakewood?

Coral shrugged. "The kid is a dark horse. He's got *way more* going on than anyone knows."

"What does that mean?" Violet was pretty sure that wasn't what *dark horse* meant. But whatever. Violet got the point. And Coral was right. What did her brother have going on? Something.

The bell rang, and Coral stood up, shoved her quiz in her tattered denim pack. "Let's go find out what he's doing."

"You mean...follow him?" asked Violet, rising. Next to her friend, Violet looked like a boy, in torn jeans, Converse sneakers, and the tattered sweatshirt that used to belong to her dad.

Coral leaned in close. "Why should that little turd be the only one who gets the afternoon off?"

Cutting class. That was a new low for Violet. Her mom would flip.

But what else could she do?

She didn't want Blake to get in trouble. She just wanted to throttle him with her own bare hands. And she wanted to—no, needed to—find out who *the frack* he was with.

Meanwhile, the game was starting in a few hours.

Violet and Coral didn't speak another word to each other, just marched toward the side door and exited into the bright afternoon sun.

26

AGENT COBEN

It wasn't a hunch. Coben didn't believe in that. What he believed in was patterns, the way seemingly disparate pieces of information were connected. When they were, there was a kind of vibration that he perceived. Lies had a certain kind of energy, something high-pitched and chaotic. So did the truth, low and somber.

He sat in the souped-up Crown Victoria and sipped from a truly terrible cup of coffee he'd picked up at a local diner. There was no excuse for coffee this bad—weak, bitter, in the pot too long so that it had that burnt note. The lady who'd served him had what seemed to be a permanent scowl, as if it had etched deep lines in her face. His mother, who'd worked too hard at too many low-level jobs to support him and his brothers, had taught him to respect people in thankless service positions. But that woman had made being polite a chore. And the coffee she'd given him tasted like the attitude with which it had been served. He took another sip, then finally slipped the cup into the holder in the center console. Forget it. He didn't need the caffeine that bad.

He stretched his back: he was too tall, too big through the shoulders to sit this long. But sitting was part of the job. Tanglewood was every concrete educational facility in the Eastern United States, low and dull, this one surrounded by sports fields and, beyond, woods painted in their autumnal fire show.

He'd followed the kids from the house this morning. Violet Crane dropped her brother off at the lower school car line, then parked her mother's white Kia in the back lot, walking in through the doors just minutes before the starting bell rang.

From where his car was parked, at the head of a small rural road, he had a good vantage point. And so far, he hadn't been clocked by any helpful passersby. Because everyone loved to see a single man lurking in an older car, watching the local high school. If he was noticed, he could expect interference, a hassle, his position blown. He waited. It was a breezy day, sunshiny.

The Miller Crane assignment was a punishment. Well, not a punishment exactly. But the kind of assignment one gets when one has pissed off the wrong people. Coben, luckily, was used to being in trouble. In fact, he was more accustomed to it than he was to any other type of treatment. *Son, you could try the patience of a saint*, his tired mother said often with exasperation but not without love. In school, he was often on the bad side of teachers for asking too many questions. With women for not asking enough questions, or not the right questions, or for *not picking up on cues*, as his most recent ex had complained via text. At Quantico, one gun instructor had accused him of resting on his natural talent and not pushing himself to do better, just scraping by. If you peeked at his file, you'd see things like *bad attitude, insubordinate, arrogant*. But he was good at things, physically capable, a sharpshooter with fast reflexes, a gift for making connections.

After training, he was assigned to white-collar crimes, which was the last the thing he wanted. Definitely not the fantasy he'd had when he'd been recruited out of college because of his computer skills. He knew it was a message from the powers that be that if he didn't get his act together, his career in the FBI would consist of sifting through data, following up on cold cases, and long hours in the basement file room (not that he minded the file room so much—endless reading, a sea of facts to connect). Miller Crane was the case no one wanted. A flubbed bust that had let him escape the net and five years on the run, which was no small feat considering modern technology being what it was. It was almost impossible for the average person to disappear. It took cash, connections, a network of people with private transportation—yachts and jets. A capture would see Miller facing a slew of charges from embezzlement to fraud and, if convicted, a trip to the federal pen where he'd stay for a good, long time. If Agent Coben found him, it might save his career. But it wasn't that fact which drove him. There were far too many people getting away with far too much in the world. It was disgusting. So for the last six months, Coben had been like a dog with a bone.

He knew more about Miller Crane than anyone.

But the Tampa sighting was just luck. Or so he thought at first. That Miller Crane had come back to the US and had just happened to be on a street that had FBI surveillance by a camera that just happened to be running facial-recognition software. Due to its large, busy port, the local FBI office downtown, and MacDill Air Force Base in proximity, Tampa had more surveillance than one might expect of a small city. So the guy had just screwed up. Finally. Or had he?

And more than that, when he brought the grainy and unclear image to Adele Crane, she'd recognized it. Coben saw it in the little twitch of the right corner of her mouth. A smile. There and gone.

Then the next thing he knew, Adele Crane was off to an island in the middle of the Atlantic to play some game. She was leaving her kids alone. Coben had figured that if Miller was

going to approach her, it would be at one of those Tough Be-
atch competitions she participated in. So far, nothing. But they
had eyes on her in Falcão Island.

If she thought she was meeting Miller there and then taking
off with him to parts unknown, she had another think coming.

But he didn't think that was the plan. That would be an
anomaly in the pattern.

Because he knew Adele Crane even better than he did Miller.

In five years, she hadn't dated a single person. She'd never
been in touch with Miller. She'd fully cooperated with the FBI.
She'd got a job, a degree. She'd never missed a parent confer-
ence or a school event. Coben followed her on WeWatch. There
were eyes on the footage of every competition, every broadcast,
analyzed at the bureau. Adele was clean.

If anything, this was the moment when Miller Crane would
come for his kids. If Coben was watching Adele, so, he bet, was
her husband.

So since Violet Crane had dropped her mother at Newark
Liberty Airport, he'd been watching her.

The coffee had given him heartburn, an acidic discomfort
climbing up his gullet. The other day, Coben's boss had told
him that Coben was giving *him* heartburn.

Man, if you'd just check your ego at the door, you'd be a great agent.
Coben didn't get it. Weren't you supposed to believe in yourself? How could you do this work if you didn't?

Coben heard the high tone of the bell inside the school. It
reminded him how much he'd hated high school. All the arbi-
trary rules and pointless information. He'd spent a lot of time
in the principal's office.

After a few more minutes, he saw the back doors of the school
swing open, which didn't surprise him. There was a lot of cutting and screwing around going on at East Tanglewood High
School. Kids taking off in expensive cars they didn't deserve,
smoking down behind the parked buses. He watched one young

couple get it on in the back of a Jeep. Not that he could see anything, but the rocking vehicle told the tale.

He sat up, feeling a rush of adrenaline. There she was. Violet Crane and a friend, an Asian girl in a tutu and pink in her hair.

He watched as they got in the Kia and pulled away. Agent Coben gave them a little space and then followed. No rush. He had a tracker on her car.

27

ADELE

Crouching, Adele organized her pack. Rope. Flashlight. Jerky. Water. Wipes. She wouldn't need much. Outside, the wind had started to pick up; it pushed at the tent. She rolled up her sleeping bag, attached it through the loops. Not that she'd be doing much sleeping.

Her phone pinged, and she took a deep breath. But it was just Blake, his texts coming in quick succession.

That storm has picked up steam. Looks like they're closing the airport.

Was that true? The weather didn't look *that* bad yet.

That casita you found is your best bet. It's on the highest elevation.

But did Extreme already know about her recon? How many cameras did they have? Where were they?

All you need to do now is be the last person found and you win, Mom.

She tapped out a response: **I'm good, kiddo. Don't worry about me. Aren't you in Algebra 2 right now?**

She checked the app, just to be sure he was in school. She didn't want him cutting class because of this. She was comforted to see both Violet's and Blake's dots at the high school. They were safe, so she could focus. The butterflies in her stomach felt more like helicopters; she was so nervous she actually felt nauseated.

Mom, whatever you do, don't fall for their tricks. They'll do whatever they can to lure you from your hiding spot or to scare you into giving up.

I got this. I'll be home tomorrow. Win or lose.

Outside, a distant rumbling turned to a roar. The approach of vehicles. She stepped out to see Malinka emerging from her tent.

"Oh, no," said the other woman as she approached Adele, eyes looking past her.

The same ATV caravan from earlier roared into sight again; Cody emerged from his tent. With his hair pulled back and without his hat, he looked less like a kids'-show character and more like someone tough and rugged that you'd want on your team. But they weren't a team, Adele had to keep reminding herself. Everyone was here to win. That was all. He'd said so himself.

Adele and Malinka both turned to face the road as the engines grew louder.

Finally, the ATVs came into view, the smell of gasoline heavy on the air. The older woman—Angeline had called her Petra—climbed off the lead vehicle when they came to a stop. Adele found herself a little mesmerized; the old woman was kind of badass. A rare power radiated off her, though she was small, maybe just five feet tall, unapologetically wrinkled.

The door to the trailer opened, and the Extreme team tumbled out, looking exhausted and stressed. Maverick took the lead, Angeline behind him, and Tavo and Hector trailing. Someone was missing. Alex, the CFO. Adele remembered the raised voices she'd heard.

Trouble in paradise, Cody had said.

It certainly seemed like it. If they weren't in control of the game, who was?

Behind the ATVs, a small, official-looking gray-and-white Prius pulled up. Blue lights on its roof flashed languidly. As it came into better view, Adele read the words on its hood, *Policia Municipal*. Two slim men climbed out. Clean-cut and baby-faced, they looked like they were playing dress-up. Uniforms crisp, unarmed except for big radios buckled to leather belts.

Maverick strode over to meet them.

"Are you kidding with this right now?" he asked, his voice strained with annoyance.

Adele moved in closer, feeling Malinka and Cody flanking her.

"You should know that all incoming flights to the island have been canceled," said Petra, moving a step closer to Maverick. She was so much smaller than he was that she had to look up at him. Still, her approach forced him to take a step back.

"We're still waiting for a contestant," he said. His voice came up an octave, a boy not getting his way. "His flight was scheduled to arrive yesterday, but it was delayed."

"If he is not here, he will not be coming," said one of the officers. "Most likely his flight has been diverted to the mainland."

He seemed to be the more senior of the two, the other hanging back. On second glance, he was older than Adele first thought, hair graying at the temples. "And the last flight out is leaving our island in two hours. Air travel, including for private jets, will not resume until after the storm has passed. Our very strong suggestion is that your contestants evacuate."

Maverick blew out a breath and shook his head. "We're not leaving until the challenge is complete."

Adele felt her shoulders stiffen, her stomach bottom out. Please, she thought. As much as she wanted to go home, she couldn't face this challenge canceling, leaving here with nothing but more debt.

Maverick looked over to Adele, Malinka, and Cody. "We can still do this," he said. "With three hiders. That's still a good game."

Petra seemed not to hear him, spoke to everyone else. "We are here to offer you all safe passage to the airport. If we leave now, you can leave safely before the storm arrives."

No. No way. Adele had come too far, had too much at stake. She wasn't leaving here with nothing to show for everything she'd spent. She stayed rooted; the other two did, as well. She wasn't afraid of weather.

"There's more," said one of the officers. "Is there an Alex Tang present?"

Angeline stepped up. "He's not here. He might still be at the hotel."

"He's not at the hotel," said the other officer. "His wife has called to report him missing. She expected him to come home, and she has lost contact with him."

Angeline shook her head, looked confused.

"Who saw him last?" asked the senior officer. Adele was not close enough to see his name tag.

"I did," said Mav. "We had a meeting this morning. I left him at the hotel."

The older officer offered a slow nod, looked at the group. "His wife seems to think that there was some kind of fight or altercation."

Mav shook his head vigorously, lifted a palm. "No, nothing like that. Just a normal meeting between CEO and CFO."

"Was anyone else present?"

"No," said Mav. "It was just us. I should tell you—his wife? She's a little unstable, gets very, very antsy when she can't reach him. I would not overreact based on a call from her."

"So then, where is he?" asked Petra, her voice edged with suspicion.

"Oh, I'm sorry," said Mav turning to face her. "Are you *the police* now, too? Town elder, *spiritual* leader or whatever, and—cop?"

Petra's smile was an ice-water plunge.

"Look," said Angeline stepping in. "Maybe he left the island. Went home?"

The younger of the two officers stepped forward, seemed to find his voice.

"He did not leave on a commercial flight. And your jet is still in its hangar. The pilot said that no one from Extreme had yet contacted him about a departure time."

Adele found herself watching Tavo's face. Mav and Angeline were still as statues, poker-faced, but Tavo's eyes were wide, his hand rubbed at his chin. There's always one in the group of misbehaving kids, one good egg who can't lie like the rest, who wears his emotions on the surface.

"I mean, I don't know what to tell you. Alex is a grown man," said Maverick. "We're not in the business of keeping tabs on each other."

"Oh, hey," said Hector, taking out his phone. "We can check his Pop Map."

"Good idea," said Angeline, moving over toward Hector.

He took out his phone and tapped it a couple of times.

"Weird," he said after a moment, looking up at the group. "He turned his location off."

"His wife said that he texted her this afternoon, said he'd

text again from the plane. But never did," said the older officer. "Then turned off his location, which is apparently out of
character."

"Totally," agreed Hector with a frown. "It's really not like
him to be out of touch. He and Lucia talk constantly."

"It's true," said Angeline thoughtfully. Mav stared at her. "It's
not really like him. Were he and Lucia fighting, maybe? Maybe
he needed some space from her. Like Mav said, she could get a
little clingy. She wasn't thrilled about him taking off to come
here and leaving her with the baby."

Adele felt goose bumps come up on her arms. That sense she
had was firing on all cylinders. What the hell was going on?
She turned to look at Malinka who was watching the scene
with interest but surprisingly had not gone live on Photogram.

Petra turned to them, her back to the Extreme group now.
"If you are not part of Extreme, this is your last chance to get
off the island before the storm comes. I suggest you pack your
things and go with the officers. Go home to your families. This
site is not safe when heavy rains come."

Adele looked back at the hotel. It slouched, black with menace against the gunmetal sky. The clouds were moving fast, foliage wild in the wind.

Almost. She *almost* accepted. The deal *wasn't* that she would
risk her life for money. She knew that the kids needed her in
their lives more than they needed a million dollars. It was just
a game.

Was someone really missing? Again?

"I'm good," said Cody. "I'm staying. Hey, with one less contestant, the odds just went up for all of us."

A man with nothing left to lose.

"Me, too," said Malinka, sounding slightly less certain. "We
got this."

A young woman with no children, no one waiting for her
to come home.

The old woman's eyes fell to Adele. There was wisdom there, a kind of steely calm.

Almost.

If she left now, she'd be home in time to tuck the kids in tonight.

And then she'd have to face the sting of failure, the look of disappointment on Blake's and Violet's faces, even if they tried to hide it. Even if they said all the right things, and they would. She couldn't let them down on this one. Everyone else—their dad, most of their friends—had hurt or disappointed them. But not her. She was going to stay. She was going to *win*. Cody was right. The odds had just improved for all of them.

"Thank you," said Adele, her voice catching mutinously. "I'm staying, too."

Petra smiled sadly and nodded as if she knew the plight of all mothers everywhere, how you'd risk everything for your kids. Even when you were risking more than you had to give.

The old woman raised a gnarled, ringed hand. In response, the men on ATVs formed a line along the property's exit and killed their engines.

After the roar ceased, one of the officers spoke. "Now, we ask that no one associated with Extreme leaves this island until Mr. Tang's whereabouts are known."

"What?" Mav barked, outraged when just moments ago he'd refused to leave the site and the island. "That's ridiculous. I'll do *whatever* the *fuck* I *want*."

But Angeline had his arm, whispered something in his ear. And, finally, he lifted his palm.

"Fine," he said. "Let us know when he turns up. And, when he does, I expect an apology. And you can forget about *your fucking donation*. This island sucks."

Angeline stepped in front of him, speaking directly to Petra. "We'll make good on all of our promises. You have our word."

Then to the police officer, "And all of our cooperation in lo-
cating Alex."

The two officers moved toward their vehicle which was
parked on the other side of the ATVs, with access to the road.

"Finish your game," said Petra to Mav. She moved to leave
with the officers. "Whether you want to pay or not, the bill
will come due."

Mav lifted an arm toward the men on the ATVs.

"And what are these guys going to do if we try to leave?"
Maverick asked. "Shoot us?"

One of the men laughed, and Maverick glanced over at them,
ran a hand through his hair, tried and failed to look tough. The
men—were they soldiers of some kind?—all stood stone-faced;
Adele had no idea where the laughter had come from. Angeline
put a hand on Maverick's arm, but this time he shook her off.

The older officer turned toward them. "These men are empowered to detain you by any means necessary and bring you
to the police station if you leave this property. For your own
safety, we will be closing the roads and establishing a curfew
due to the storm."

"*By any means necessary?* But who are they? They're not cops,"
said Maverick. "Are they soldiers? What is their authority?"

"Maverick," said Gustavo, coming to stand in front of him.
"Stop."

"But seriously, right? They can't keep us here. *Who* are they?"

The police officers and Petra climbed in the car, and it
hummed away.

"So are they mercenaries, then? Like a private security force?"
Maverick obviously could not let it go.

"Look," said Gustavo. He tapped Maverick on the chest. "Do
you *want* your ass kicked again?"

"Hey, guys!" Maverick raised his voice, pushing past Tavo.
"Whatever they're paying you? I'll double it. Come work for
me. I want my own private army."

"What a tool," said Cody under his breath.

Not one of the men even looked in Maverick's direction. It was like they were behind a wall of glass.

Adele examined them. There were fifteen of them, all of different builds but similar in shape, muscled, with that ready posture of military. All armed, big guns at their waists. One man had a deep scar over his right eye. Another had an illegible tattoo on his hand. The only blond among them had his hair pulled back in a tight ponytail. The largest man on the far ATV was missing a finger.

Okay. Wow.

Who were these guys?

It was just the Extreme people who couldn't leave, right?

"Holy wow, you guys." Malinka was live. "The crazy factor on this challenge has just gone off the chain."

Adele turned to look, and Malinka was backing up toward the men, speaking into the camera. "A storm is bearing down, and these men don't want us to leave the property until it has passed."

"Stop her," said Angeline to Hector.

"Let her do it," said Mav. "We need the views, especially now that Scotty G can't come."

Hector looked worriedly between Angeline and Mav, a kid caught in the middle of warring parents.

"Stop her," said Angeline again.

But no one moved.

28

"And if that wasn't enough, you guys? Alex Tang, Extreme CFO, and longtime Mav bestie is, according to local police, missing. Another Extreme Hide and Seek Challenge, another missing person. Doesn't that seem odd? Let's ask Maverick what he has to say about this."

The camera turns to Maverick, who stands between Angeline and Hector. He's rubbing his eyes with thumb and forefinger. When he pulls his hand away to the camera, he looks bone-tired. The trees behind the three are thrashing chaotically in the wind. Angeline glares.

"So what's the deal, Mav? First Chloe Miranda. Now Alex Tang."

Mav steps forward, looks right at the lens.

"First of all, Alex is not missing. And I have nothing to say about Chloe Miranda that I haven't already said. One event has nothing to do with the other."

"Okay, but the police here seem to think there's a problem.

They've asked Extreme employees not to leave the island until Alex is found."

Mav shrugs dramatically, eyes drifting to the men on the ATVs.

"They're just doing their job, I guess. Alex will turn up, and everything will be fine."

"That's what you said about Chloe."

Mav puts a hand up. "Nothing more to say about Chloe."

"I wonder—does Angeline know that you were sleeping with Chloe? Like hooking up with her on the regular?"

Mav shakes his head in disapproval, blowing out an annoyed breath. Angeline folds her arms, looks down at her feet.

"The police know that Chloe and I were briefly involved before I met Angeline. I am not a suspect in her disappearance."

"You ghosted her."

Maverick steps closer to the camera.

"Chloe was…unwell. We had a single encounter before I met Angeline, but Chloe thought it was more than that. It wasn't. I'm sorry, but it wasn't. Angeline is the woman I love and the one I want to marry. Chloe had…a hard time understanding that."

"So why would you accept her for your Extreme Haunted Hide and Seek Challenge? If you knew she was unwell, that she was basically obsessed with you?"

Another shrug, a look to Angeline, who nods.

"She was a strong competitor. She had a big following. I hoped we could be friends. That was it. Maybe it was my way of apologizing to her, making amends for the misunderstanding between us."

"So what do you think happened to her?"

"The last I saw her was when she went off with the rest of the hiders. Someone matching her description was sighted a number of times in the area. She took money from her accounts. Honestly? I think she ran away from her life. She told me how much pressure she felt as an influencer, how she had a troubled relationship with her father. Maybe she just wanted a break."

"Did you know that we were friends?"

Angeline still hasn't lifted her eyes from the ground. Hector is looking at the camera, expression unreadable. Mav looks off to the side at something beyond the scope of the lens.

"I didn't know that. I'm sorry."

"I'm not going to stop looking for her. I think you guys know more than you're saying. I think you know what happened to Chloe."

"Malinka, maybe you didn't know her as well as you think you did."

"One thing I know for sure is that people associated with Extreme get hurt or go missing."

Angeline steps forward. "You're free to go, Malinka. I'm sure one of the charming mercenaries on the ATVs will drive you to the airport."

"I'm not leaving without the truth."

Angeline stares a moment, then abruptly turns and walks to the trailer. Maverick, Tavo, and Hector follow like ducklings. They disappear into the trailer, door shutting behind them. Malinka is back on camera, her face filling the screen.

"I mean it. I'm not leaving this island until I know the truth about my friend. Are you with me? Leave your comments."

Mel333: Where is Chloe? Mav is lying!

Wingedkitty: Oh, no she didn't

Buttons&bows: You go GRRRRL.

Ellalove99: So, what is this, a true crime podcast now???

MavIsALiar: You're a liar, too. Your company is about to go bankrupt. And this is just another stunt you cooked up with Mav to get more views.

MavIsALiar: You're all going to pay.

Minecraftguru: Don't let him off the hook.

Badmonkey21: I hate you. I can't wait to see how you all destroy each other.

Hellokitten444: Love you, Malinka. Get out of there grrl, before you get hurt.

7SummitGrrl: Your gear isn't even waterproof. And are those fake eyelashes?

YesICanFan: Tell us about your new line of skater pants.

Climb3rdude: This is such a mess. Do you guys not have a weather app? There's a huge storm coming. Ever met a "climber" less prepared for the elements?

Angelwings: You're beautiful, Malinka, and a hero to girls everywhere. Don't let them get away with it. Justice for Chloe!

Dragongrrl: Malinka, get out of there. Go home. If people are getting hurt and going missing whenever Extreme is up to their tricks, what makes you think you won't be next????

More comments, fade out.

29

ANGELINE

The air in the trailer was thick with tension, with the scent of sweat. Angeline felt as if her legs might give out beneath her, so she leaned against the long table in the center. It wobbled, gear knocking. She was overcome by exhaustion, horror at what they'd done. Fear, it was a kaleidoscope, bending reality. She forced herself to take slow, deep breaths.

What is real? What is true?

Had they really found Alex's dead body? Had they really dumped him and his phone off a cliff? It had seemed right, like the only option then. Now it seemed like what it was. Depraved. The actions of people not in their right minds. Who had killed Alex? Where was that person now?

Her eyes fell on Mav. It could only have been him. Who else? But she just couldn't believe that. She just...couldn't.

"That little bitch," hissed Mav, as if Malinka was their biggest problem. "She is *not* the winner. No matter what. Though, we'll probably get a shit ton of views because of that."

Angeline already knew about Chloe, the girl's obsession with

Maverick. It was not the revelation Malinka clearly had thought it would be. Angeline honestly couldn't care less about Maverick's little side pieces. She wouldn't have given Chloe a second thought if not for the horror show of her disappearance. Lots of girls wanted Mav, threw themselves at him, were obsessed with him. Maverick, she knew, only really wanted Angeline.

Angeline walked over to peer out the window. The hiders were in a huddle by the fire pit, talking. What were they saying? There was still time for them to leave. Would they? The sky was darkening. Petra's men stood statue-still.

How would they get out of this? How, *how*, had they *gotten into it*?

Mav sunk his head down in his hands. Gustavo looked off into the middle distance; he hadn't made eye contact with her since the wall. Hector was a cartoon character of stress hair a mess, eyes bulging, looking back and forth between them. His forehead was beaded with perspiration.

Finally, he blew. *"Can someone tell me what the actual fuck is going on?"*

They all stared at Hector as he went on. "All the cameras I set up? They're dead. I think there is someone out there. Sabotaging the game."

Angeline just felt numb, stared out the window at the armed men. She needed to get out of this trailer. It stank of sweat and dread.

"Look at this," Hector said when none of them spoke.

He opened an image on one of the laptops. A masked face filled the screen—bright white with button eyes and stitching for a mouth—lingered a moment, taunting, before the screen went dark.

"I told you," said Maverick, spreading his arms. "I *told you* there was someone out there trying to hurt us."

"I'm going out there," said Gustavo, moving toward the door. "I'm going to find out who's doing this."

"No," said Angeline, too quickly. She felt the heat of Mav's gaze. "What if Mav's right? What if someone really is trying to *hurt us*?"

"What do you mean?" Maverick barked at her. "*What if Mav's right?* Alex is dead—someone killed him. There's definitely someone out there. They're *definitely* trying to hurt us, Ange. They *are* hurting us."

Hector released a horrified sob. "*What?*"

Oh, shit. They hadn't told Hector about Alex.

"I'm sorry, buddy," said Mav, eyes filling. "We...found him at the hotel."

Hector shook his head rapidly. Angeline rose to embrace him as he started weeping uncontrollably. Now Mav was crying, too. Which made Angeline cry again. Tavo was the only one who stood stone-faced. He moved toward the door, put a hand on the knob.

"You told the police he went home," said Hector, his voice hoarse with emotion.

Maverick hung his head.

"Why did you do that?" Hector went on. "We have to tell them. We have to call Lucia."

"We *can't*," said Maverick, wiping at his eyes. Was he really crying? wondered Angeline. There was something blank to him, something empty. Had there always been?

"Not yet."

"*Who* killed Alex?"

"We don't know," said Mav. "Someone's been following me. Threatening me."

"Where is he? His...*b-b-ody*?"

None of them could answer. Angeline kept replaying the moment when they dumped Alex over the wall. Above the violence of the waves they never even heard it hit below, from that great height. He was just—gone.

"Honestly, Hector," said Angeline, soothing him, "the less you know, the better."

Maverick explained the situation to Hector, stopping short of their dumping the body, who just stared at him like he couldn't believe what he was hearing. "But—but—but."

"We have to complete the game. Trust me on this," said Mav. "Otherwise, we all lose everything."

"That doesn't make any sense," said Hector.

"We're broke, Hec. We survive this challenge, get flush, fix the books, and sell. And we all get rich. Otherwise, we'll be bankrupt inside a month."

Hector's face was a mask of confusion. Listening to Maverick talk, Angeline realized he was delusional. Maybe she was, too. There was no way back from where they were.

"All the money we made," said Hector, "where did it go, Mav? We worked so hard."

Angeline and Tavo locked eyes, both of them thinking of Alex's texts to Lucia. When she turned back to Maverick, he was watching them. His eyes. They were so cold.

"I don't know, buddy," said Maverick like he was talking to a child. "Challenges like this, I guess. We gave a shit ton away. Our expenses were high. We've been losing viewers. All the bad publicity. But if we can do this, we can fix it."

Outside, the sky rumbled, the small amount of light coming in through the narrow, opaque windows growing dimmer.

"But we've already lost everything," said Hector, his voice soft and frightened. "People know that something has happened to Alex, because of Malinka's live. We'll lose the sponsors. We-Watch will dump us. There's so much heat already because of Chloe, because of Moms Against Mav. The subpar sponsors that are still with us are already squirrelly as fuck."

Maverick shook his head.

"Views," he said. "They only care about views. If we give them that tonight, they won't do a thing except throw more money at us. I promise you that. That's the way the world works now."

How was he always so sure of himself, of his own rightness?

"Alex," Hector said, then started to cry again. Helpless. Like a child. Angeline felt the weight of his grief, something neither she, Tavo, nor Maverick had expressed, if they'd felt it at all. They'd gone from horror and shock straight into survival mode. What did that make them?

How easy it had been to haul Alex to the wall in that rug. To watch as Tavo and Maverick hefted him over the side. Like he was not a person, their friend, someone's father, husband. She was back there now, feeling the wind and sea spray. It hadn't seemed real even, like she was in a video game, the way you do things like cut off someone's head or slice them in half with a machete and it isn't real, it's just a game, just a simulation. That's how it felt.

But it was real.

She felt herself go weak inside, that childish churning of fear.

Stop it, Angeline. When the going gets tough, the tough get going. That's what her abuela always said. *When the worst thing happens, you don't curl up into a ball, you stand and fight.* She could grieve later. Atone later. They all could.

"Tavo," said Angeline, still holding Hector who had his head on her shoulder, clung to her like a little kid. It was a bit ridiculous as he was nearly twice her size. Still, she drew some comfort from being able to comfort him. "What is the deal with those men? With Petra?"

Tavo blew out an exhausted breath, rubbed hard at his right shoulder which she knew was injured. "Petra. She's—I don't know how to explain it—like a shaman, a spiritual leader."

"With an army?" said Maverick.

"Some people call her a *radical shaman*, like a fighting shaman, if that makes sense. She protects the island and its people from the encroachment of outside forces."

"What does that even mean?" asked Angeline. She thought

of the old woman, small, wrinkled, and still somehow power-ful. Righteous, a warrior.

"These islands were once untouched ecosystems with prime-val forests, populated only by people whose ancestors had been here for a millennium. Over the centuries, people from Europe settled the islands."

Tavo moved back toward them, went on, "In the eighties, the government allowed European companies to come in and clear-cut the land to raise cattle. We lost almost fifty percent of those ancient trees. Petra's father, whose family descended from São Miguel, sold a huge portion of their ancestral lands, and in doing so became very, very rich. They became the wealthiest family on the islands."

The trees. The thought of companies cutting down ancient forest made Angeline helplessly angry. How could be people be so blinded by greed?

Tavo went on, "Petra, in full rebellion of her father, became an environmental activist. She organized locals to make life very difficult for the cattle companies—staging sit-ins on land that was scheduled to be clear-cut, encouraging locals not to work in the slaughterhouses, lobbying the government not to allow foreign workers to be imported. She made life very difficult for the companies destroying the islands. One by one, they left. Now, her father dead, Petra uses her family's wealth to control the islands and keep them safe from—"

"People like us," said Angeline, feeling a squeeze on her heart.

Tavo offered a reluctant nod. "She and her team managed to eject the European companies, reclaim the land, and force the government to legislate against excessive tourism, any cattle ranching, blocking big corporations from building resorts and hotels, and resisting ports for cruise ships."

"That's nuts," said Mav. "Don't they want money? Look at this place. It could be a tourist mecca. Instead, it's a ghost town."

A ghost town. That's what Mav saw when he looked at this pristine and beautiful place. A reflection of his own emptiness.

"Not everyone is motivated only by wealth," said Tavo, voice low and cold.

"I haven't heard you complaining," said Mav. "You've never turned down your paycheck."

She didn't like the look on Gustavo's face. Nose wrinkled like he was smelling something bad, eyes narrow. It was pure disgust.

"Look," said Angeline. "We have like twenty huge, unsolvable problems right now. And if we're going to survive them and get off this island, we have to work together. Can we do that?"

The silence grew heavier, electric with all their dark thoughts and raging emotions.

Angeline's stomach bottomed out, a horrible sinking sensation. Nothing was ever going to be the same again. Before the last challenge, before Chloe, before she'd started sleeping with Tavo, they'd had a big anniversary party at Mav's place. They brought in servers, bartenders, a chef. There was a jazz singer, an endless well of booze and food. At one point late in the evening, she'd stood on the balcony with Mav, looking inside at the party. Alex and Lucia were dancing slow, madly in love. Hector was laughing uproariously about something. Tavo was hitting on one of the waitresses.

"We built this," Maverick had said. "From nothing."

"*You* did," she said.

"Nah," he demurred. "All of us. The guys have been here since the beginning. You gave us a soul, a mission. We're a family. And Extreme is the thing we all made together. We play hard, we give back. It's good, right? Like really, really good?"

"Yes," she said. "It is. Truly."

And she'd believed that.

"I love you," he whispered in her ear. He'd said it before, but he didn't say it often. "Thank you for making me a better man."

She loved him so much in that moment, his boyishness, his

passion for Extreme, his willingness to give credit to his friends, when everyone knew that there was no Extreme without Mav. That he needed her.

"I love you, too," she answered. She'd meant that, too, then.

And she remembered thinking that everything was so right, how could it ever go wrong? How could something so big, so powerful ever be anything less?

Now in the trailer, company teetering on the brink, Alex gone, what they'd done. There was a mercenary army guarding their exit. Maybe a killer or at least a saboteur stalking them. A challenge they had to get off the ground or lose everything. She didn't even want to look at social.

All the men—the boys—were looking at her.

"What are we going to do?" asked Hector. The wind was wild now. The first raindrops started to fall.

"The only thing we *can* do. Play the game."

30

~~~~~~

BLAKE

"Hey," Blake said, climbing into the passenger seat. The air outside was cool, and he glanced back at the school. He'd never cut before. Not ever.

"Any excuse to bail on bio," said Gregg with a slow smile. "And the least I can do after all the times you saved my ass in *Red World*."

The interior of the Bronco smelled faintly of weed, and David Bowie was soft on the radio. Gregg rested one hand on the wheel and gunned the Bronco as soon as Blake was strapped in. One last glance back. Would someone come running out after him?

He thought back to middle school, how the teachers brought you to your parent's car. How you needed a note to go home with someone else. How in the early days after Dad left, he knew the FBI was there watching. Would he come and try to take them? Blake always wished for it. But he didn't come then. Now, in high school, it was like no one cared. When the final bell rang, kids ran for the bus or drove themselves, walked, or rode off on bikes alone. No one knew how or if you got home.

"Never cut before?" ask Gregg. He had a deep, smoky voice.

"Yeah," Blake lied. "Lots of times."

Gregg just smiled, easy. Denim jacket, slouchy, longish sandy hair. He had this aura, both on the game and in real life. Supreme confidence, a kind of toughness under the chill exterior. Blake had seen him behead three players with a single sword strike in *Red World*.

"Gummy?" Gregg held out a bag with little orange sugar-coated circles clinging together.

"No, thanks."

He wasn't going to add getting high to his list of infractions, though he was tempted. And he really wished he was as cool as Gregg, who popped one in his mouth. Should he be doing that while he was driving? Blake stayed quiet. He didn't want Gregg to think he wasn't cool.

"It's the good stuff. I lifted it from my mom's safe," said Gregg. "My parents are rocked all the time."

"Sweet," said Blake. He'd never even seen his mom have a glass of wine, not since Dad left.

"Where are we headed?" asked Gregg.

Blake glanced at the map on his phone. "Just make a right at the light. I'll tell you where to go. Not far."

Gregg offered an easy bob of his head, shifted in his seat, and kept driving.

"Hey," said Gregg, as he made the turn, "I was going to ask you what you're going to do about those tools who are always bullying you on the game."

"I'm handling it."

He thought of Marco cowering on the floor of the bathroom, bleeding. He didn't want that. He'd avoided conflict as much as possible. But he wasn't sorry. Not even a little.

Gregg rubbed at his very faint blond goatee. "Sometimes you gotta bust some heads, you know?"

"I'm not much of a fighter," he said. But maybe that wasn't true.

Gregg shot him a skeptical squint. "I've seen you slay."

"*Red World* is not the real world," said Blake. He wished it was. He wished the gaming world was real and this one was the simulation. It was so much easier to navigate, so much easier to understand people and their motives, to defend yourself. The goals were clear. Punishments were harsh but temporary.

"Yeah, but the same rules apply," said Gregg with a laugh. "Don't let anyone push you around. Usually, you only have to do some damage once and they leave you alone after that."

Blake hoped that was true.

"I don't want to hurt anyone." *Anyone else*, he thought, hiding his sore knuckles. In *Red World*, no one got hurt, not really. No one died. If they disappeared, they came back the next round. In the real world, when you hurt someone, you couldn't help but hurt yourself, too.

"Even if *they* hurt *you*?"

Blake didn't know what to say. But he thought no, not even then.

"Cool, cool," said Gregg when he didn't answer. "A pacifist."

A wimp, a doormat, that's what Violet would say. What she *did* say. What was the difference? he wondered. He couldn't wait to tell Violet about Marco. He was probably going to get suspended. Fighting in the bathroom, then cutting. It was a lot.

They pulled past the supermarket, the big mall with the Target and the gym. The daylight looked funny, like on a sick day because that's the only time he was out of school during the week. Then they were on the wooded road that led out of town. They drove awhile, and Blake kept his eyes on the road behind in the side-view mirror. There were no other cars, hadn't been even once since they left town. That was good.

"So what kind of errand is this?" asked Gregg. On the radio Mick Jagger was unsatisfied. "You're not in any trouble, are you?"

"Up here on the right," said Blake.

Gregg shot him a quick glance. "There's nothing out here."

It was true. His destination was still a solid mile away. But he couldn't have Gregg or anyone driving him all the way. That's why he hadn't called an Uber. The rules were clear, no one could know where he was or what he was doing.

"I'm good," he said. "Really."

Gregg gave him a concerned frown but pulled over. Blake opened the door and lugged his big pack out. The leaves around them were turning yellow, red, brown, falling, the air crisp, smelling of wet grass.

"Brah, I don't love leaving you here. Sure you're okay?"

"I'm good," said Blake with a nod. "And—just—bro code, right? No one ever needs to know you dropped me here."

Gregg's hazel eyes were serious, if a little glassy. "Bro code."

"Thanks for this. I owe you." Blake shut the door, and the sound of it echoed in the quiet.

Gregg looked at him long through the window, then gave a quick nod. Blake waited until he was out of sight before shouldering the heavy pack and heading down the road.

After a while he dipped into the trees. He knew his way, and it was better to stay out of sight.

31

Okay, Extremists. As you may have seen on Malinka's live stream, things have gotten a little hairy here just as the challenge is supposed to begin. People are freaking out, and understandably so, because of Malinka's suspicions that we know something about Chloe Miranda. Now, my good friend and CFO Alex Tang is also missing. Right? That's what they're saying.

Well, look. He's not missing.

We had a disagreement—nothing big, just the usual CEO-CFO tug-of-war over money. And he decided not to stay for the challenge. So that's it.

Honestly? I think he just wanted to get home to his wife and new baby. You know how it is. I promise he's going to turn up at home and be like, *WTF you guys, I'm fine.* So we're definitely not worried about Alex, and you shouldn't be, either.

As for Chloe?

There's truthfully nothing left to say. You can find my statements on the subject in all the news coverage over the last year. No one here is a suspect. And no one has any more information.

So...just chill.

I'm sorry for Chloe's family. I wish I could give them closure. It's true, Chloe and I did hook up. Once. A looong time ago, before I met Angeline, who you all know is the love of my life. I care about Chloe, we all do, and hope that she's okay somehow, somewhere.

And, Chloe, if you're watching, please come home. Your family misses you and needs some answers.

If anyone out there knows what happened to her, please, please come forward.

Now, as for our challenge, the one you've all been waiting for.

We have our three kick-ass contestants. Wild Cody, everyone's favorite wilderness explorer and television star. Most of us grew up watching him and learning about the world and all its flora and fauna. He definitely gave me the travel itch. Welcome, Cody!

[A cool nod from Cody, thumbs-up.]

The superwoman Adele, who morphed herself from struggling single mom to Tough Be-atch champion. Lots of you have told me how she inspired you with her workouts and nutrition tips, her advice on overcoming terrible events in your life. She's here to win. Welcome, Adele!

[A tentative smile and a wave from Adele.]

And Malinka! Okay, we know Malinka is mad at me, thinks maybe I know more than I'm saying about Chloe. But I have to forgive her, and so should you, because she's a fierce and loyal friend, looking for answers to the mystery surrounding Chloe, someone we both care about. And what do we expect from the you-go-grrl maven who is the youngest woman to climb all seven summits and is the founder of Yes I Can women's athletic wear?

[A glare from Malinka, then a reluctant smile and
a peace sign for the camera.]

In disappointing news, megastar *Red World* gamer Scotty G
was not able to make it because an encroaching storm closed
the airports here. BUT he has agreed to stream our broadcast
on his page and offer running commentary. And I promise you
he'll be on board for the next one.

You think this one's sick??

Just wait for the next challenge. We've scoped out an awe-
some—well, never mind, we'll tell you all about it when we've
completed this one.

[Camera turns to the hotel. The sun is low in the sky, just a white ball
through the thick cloud cover. Wind hisses and
howls against the phone mic.]

Wow! The views are off the charts today. Look at you guys,
tuning in for what promises to be our most Extreme Hide and
Seek ever. Don't forget to leave your comments and tell us what
you love about Extreme and our adventures all over the world.

Look at the sky! Wow, Mother Nature in all her fearsome
beauty.

[Maverick turns the camera to reveal a threatening black-and-gray sky, some
drops of water hit the lens, the trees bend in silhouette.
Enchantments looms, windows black and hollow, entrance yawning.]

Oh, and these guys.

[Maverick turns the camera to the line of men guarding the exit.
They stand stock-still beside their ATVs.]

Apparently, we are not allowed to leave this property until

Alex lets us know that he's home safe and sound, and we're not allowed to leave this island until after the storm has passed.

Yeah, it's headed our way.

A big one.

But what's a little weather, right?

And these guys—I don't know what to say. They're not cops. They're not soldiers. They're some kind of private mercenary army beholden to a crazy cultist... I think. They are apparently empowered to detain us by any means necessary. I have no idea what to think about that. So folks at the US embassy here in the islands, maybe you want to look into this. Because honestly? It's a tad fucked.

[The camera stays trained on the men who don't move at all.]

But...whatever, right?

[Camera back to Mav.]

Right now, we have a game to play. And we're not leaving until it's over.

[Turns the camera back to Malinka, Adele, and Wild Cody. They stand, looking intrepid, determined, the sky and hotel behind them.]

Hey, hiders! What do you say?

"Let's do this!" says Wild Cody.

"Yes, I Can," says Malinka, raising both arms and an issuing a whoop.

"For my kids," says Adele, giving a smile and a thumbs-up.

All right, Extremists. Game on!

32

The Disappearance of Chloe Miranda

Rough recording for editing

Harley Granger: Are you comfortable? Can I get you anything?

Peter Miranda: I'm good. Thanks.

Harley: Tonight, I'm talking to Peter Miranda, Chloe's brother and the person spearheading the investigation and ongoing search for his sister. Thank you for being here.

Peter: Thank you for having me. And thank you for helping to keep attention on Chloe. It means a lot to our family.

Harley: Let's start with Chloe's frame of mind in the weeks before she headed to Eaton House for Extreme's Haunted Hide and Seek Challenge.

Peter: She was good, you know. Excited. Her career as an influencer was going well. Things haven't always been easy with or for Chloe. She battled depression. There were two suicide attempts. Some issues with substance abuse. But she seemed stable to me. Happy.

Harley: Still, your family had some misgivings about the challenge.

Peter: Yeah, we did. My dad, he thought it could be destabilizing. She had this on-again, off-again thing with Maverick. My dad thought she was a little overfocused on him, especially as he was clearly in love with someone else. And the stress of competition could sometimes be a lot for Chloe. He said she seemed tired and stressed to him. Personally, I didn't see it. But he was concerned that it wasn't a healthy undertaking for her.

Harley: And what did you think?

Peter: I thought that maybe Chloe was tougher than our dad might have believed. I thought she would be fine.

Harley: Your father contacted Extreme and asked them not to accept her.

Peter: That's right.

Harley: And how did Chloe feel about that?

Peter: She was pissed. Like extra. She claimed that he was infantilizing her, wanting her to be sick and vulnerable so that he felt like she needed him. They weren't speaking when she headed to Eaton House.

Harley: Was there any truth to her claims?

Peter: [*A heavy sigh.*] Maybe? I don't know. My dad loves us, wants to protect us, especially Chloe. Things haven't been easy since my mom died—for either of them. For any of us. I can see why he wants to hold on tight, to make sure we're well. And, well, now— he was right, wasn't he? If she hadn't gone to Eaton House, she'd still be with us.

Harley: What do you think happened to your sister?

[*Silence, a shuddering breath.*]

Peter: I'm sorry. I don't know. I think someone at Extreme...hurt her. Probably Maverick. We just want answers.

Harley: And what do you say to the people who think Chloe used this event to run away from her life?

Peter: They're wrong. She wouldn't do that to us. She just... wouldn't.

Harley: What do you have to say about the missing money from her bank accounts? The Chloe sightings in the area in the days after her appearance?

Peter: I don't have any answers. Maybe someone stole that money. Staged those appearances. I think in some ways those things prevented the police from really investigating the way they should have. There was always this underlying suspicion that she'd run off or hurt herself. Because she'd done those things in the past.

Harley: Rog and I visited Eaton House last week, looking for anything that might further the investigation. On the property survey, we found something kind of interesting. We're not sure what it means.

[The sound of paper being shuffled.]

Harley: Do you see this dotted line from the house out to the edge of the wooded area that surrounds the property?

Peter: Yeah. What is it?

Harley: It's a tunnel. We went down into the basement and found a space under the staircase. If you climbed inside, there's a door. It opens into this tunnel that leads away from the house and comes out through a hatch in the ground at the edge of the property.

[Silence. Throat clearing.]

Peter: So...what are you saying?

Harley: That it's possible Chloe used it to leave the house undetected. It was less than a mile from the tunnel entrance to the road.

[Silence.]

Harley: But there's another possibility, too. Someone used the tunnel to get into Eaton House undetected.

Peter: And take Chloe.

Part Three

The Game

"On Falcão Island, I think there was a moment when the game became reality. And the stakes shifted from who would win to who would make it out alive. But that's life, right? We think we're motivated by all sorts of things—money, success, fame. But when shit gets real, we're all reduced to praying for something as simple as another good day with the people we love."

HARLEY GRANGER,
Stranger Than Fiction: A Podcast
"What Happened to Chloe Miranda?"

33

~~~~~~

ADELE

"What do you want?" Adele said, this time her voice loud, deeper.

She didn't wait for an answer. She charged the strange figure in her path, roaring as loud as the thunder.

As she bolted forward, mud sucking at her feet, lightning flashing, the form stayed rooted. Fear, adrenaline seemed to slow time to a crawl. The person ahead of her raised his arms, yelled something. But she didn't stop, kept moving until they came crashing together.

He didn't yield and didn't fight. Strong hands held her back, and her warrior's yell died in her throat. The moment, the man came into focus.

Miller. For a moment, clear as day, she saw the face of her husband wearing that amused grin he used to flash at her when he thought she was being silly. She wanted to pummel him, to hold him tight, to rage, to weep.

But it wasn't Miller. He hadn't followed her here. He wasn't as Agent Coben suggested, looking for a way to connect with her. He didn't care. He'd left her, left their children, and never looked back.

"Easy there, tiger." The voice was a grumble, barely audible in the weather.

Wild Cody stood drenched, still holding her wrists. She sagged with relief.

"You're a badass, Adele Crane."

"What are you doing out here?" she yelled against the rain.

"I thought you were calling for help," he said. "I thought you were in trouble."

"What happened to *every man for himself*?"

He lifted his palms to the falling rain. "Well, I guess I'm as full of shit as everyone else around here."

She almost laughed. Then the screaming started again.

"Let's go," she said, running toward the sound down a path that led to one of the other structures.

The roof of the farthest casita had collapsed, just as she suspected it might when she'd explored it last night. She had been able to tell, by the water stains and the constant dripping, that there was already standing water trapped above the ceiling and that heavy rain and more water might finally collapse the rotting wood. Buena Vista was the biggest by far and clung to the edge of the cliff, once upon a time, she was sure, offering the best view. It was mere feet from the rim, the volcanic lake glittering below.

Why do we have to try to own it? Her father used to marvel at houses built on the coasts, near the forests, on the cliffs. *Don't they know they don't belong there?*

Adele stood at the side open entrance where the doors used to be.

"Who's there?" she called into the darkness, her voice taken by the wind.

Faintly, she heard an answer, gave a worried glance at the roof, then back to Cody, and raced inside with him behind her.

The floor was a pool of murky water pouring downhill toward the cliff edge. She took the rope from her pack and with Cody's help wrapped it around a pillar that didn't seem quite secure but was their only option.

She tugged at it, and it seemed to hold. Then Cody fastened the rest of the rope around her waist, tying an expert knot.

"Where are you?" Adele called. The ceiling above them was gaping, water pouring down.

"Oh, my God, thank God. Here! The balcony! I can't hold much longer. Please."

Malinka.

Adele backed herself into the flow, with Cody holding the rope, watching the water pour over her feet, up to her calves, and getting deeper. She could only pray that the pillar would hold and that Cody was strong enough if it didn't. Another flash of lightning, a hard crack of thunder that made the ground shake. Something got hit. Almost instantly she smelled smoke.

She backed toward the edge, keeping her gaze roving—the water, the ceiling, behind her.

There.

Malinka clung to what was left of the porch railing, water rushing past her, her body dangling over the edge.

"Adele!"

"I'm coming!"

She edged with the current toward Malinka. Just a few more feet. That's when she saw that the whole porch was detaching from the house, about to plunge over the edge of the cliff and take Malinka with it.

Adrenaline still pulsing, Adele got on her knees and started reaching for Malinka, relying all her weight on Cody and the failing pillar.

"Can you reach for me?"

"I *can't*," said the girl, panic clear on her pale face.

Adele could just see the top of her head and her eyes. Both of her hands grasped the wrought metal of the railing that was mostly missing. The entirety of her body weight was dangling. There was no way the girl was strong enough to pull herself up. And doing so might cause the whole porch to fall away.

Think. Think!

She rushed back against the current to Cody. "I can't reach her."

He untied the rope from the pillar, then grabbed another from his pack and tied it around her waist. "I'll hold on to you. You throw her this."

Was he strong enough to hold both her and Malinka against the rushing current of rainwater?

"Please! Adele! I'm falling."

No time to decide.

Adele ran back to the porch, lay flat on the casita floor in the floodwater and flung the rope, Cody holding tight to the one that was attached to Adele. The lifeline draped over the side, the water rushing past her and over the edge.

"Reach for it!" Adele yelled.

"I can't." Horror and desperation pulled the girl's voice taut.

Adele made her voice stern, like she was talking to one of her children. "Malinka, listen to me. You *have to* reach for it."

Adele edged closer, feeling Cody's strong grip on the rope. The porch creaked, the gap between it and the casita yawning wider, the structure groaning, water rushing.

"Just one hand," she yelled again. "Malinka, please! The porch is falling."

Malinka let go of a scream, and Adele saw one hand disappear, then she felt a hard tug on the rope around her waist. She grabbed onto it, felt Cody pulling her back.

"I got it," Malinka called, her other hand still grabbing the metal railing.

"Okay," Adele yelled. "Now the other hand. And I'll start crawling back."

She prayed that the knot Cody tied would hold. That she was

strong enough to pull Malinka's dangling weight back from the precipice. That Cody was strong enough for both of them.

What were the chances the girl could hold on to the rope? In the rain?

Maybe. Maybe she could do it if she was really a climber. Adele's father had always said that extreme survival often came down to being able to dangle by your fingertips. The full-body strength that was required to do that was very rare. It wasn't just about hand strength. It was upper body. It was core.

Malinka's other hand disappeared.

She imagined the girl falling, listening to her anguished scream as she plummeted to her death. Instead, the rope jerked hard. Adele felt it dig into her waist and back, pulling tight, burning her skin with friction. She reached forward to grab the rope with both hands, bringing her hips back to stabilize herself.

"I got it!" Malinka called over the edge, voice high with strain. "I'm pulling."

Adele used all her strength, feeling the rope jerking as the girl tried to climb. The porch whined, wanting to fall. If it did, they were both going over. This was it. She saved Malinka, or they both died. Right here in this place, right now.

She thought of Violet and Blake, everything that had been taken from them. Her heart nearly burst with grief, anguish. Her kids. Her babies. How was she getting back to them from where she was right now?

Fight. Win.

Another surge of adrenaline; she pulled harder.

Then Malinka let out a scream of effort, and Adele saw the top of her head again. She was doing it. Then she was slipping, her weight pulling Adele with her.

"I can't!" she wailed.

"Malinka! Yes. You. Can."

The voice boomed in the night.

It wasn't Adele. It was Cody. She almost sobbed with relief as he sat on top of her pinning her beneath his weight, stabilizing her. Then he reached over her head and grabbed for the rope. They both pulled together with all their strength.

The top of Malinka's head. Then her shoulders. Them pulling, Malinka climbing, wailing with effort.

Then had her.

They *almost* had her.

When the porch finally gave way, it fell with a final groan, the cracking of wood and plaster, then crashing over the cliff edge.

Adele closed her eyes, screamed with despair.

Cody yelled something, but she couldn't hear him. She was sobbing, thinking of the girl, her mother whoever she was. The incalculable loss of a vibrant, young life.

"Adele," Cody yelled louder. "Help me. We got her."

The porch was gone, but Malinka still clung onto the rope. With a final heave, the girl was inside the casita. She climbed into Adele's arms, where they clung to each other for a moment, weeping. Adele felt like she was holding Violet, keeping her close. "You're okay, kiddo. You're okay."

"You came for me," Malinka said, looking up at her, tears streaming, eyes grateful. "You saved me."

"We gotta get out of here," said Cody, standing. "Like *now* before this whole place goes over."

Adele looked up at him. He stood tall and rugged, and she'd never been so grateful to see anyone in her life. She took his helping hand up and then helped Malinka stand.

"Where are we going?" Adele asked as they followed Cody down the path.

"Follow me," he said.

With an arm around Malinka's shaking shoulders, she followed Wild Cody into the night.

34

~~~~~~

MAVERICK

The players had their hour to hide.

In the trailer, it had gone quiet.

Hector, who looked like he was sleepwalking, had disappeared for a while and, through some magic on his part, got the generator running again. That was one of his superpowers, to fix whatever gear was broken. So they had electricity, at least. Though, the generator was making an odd noise, a kind of strangled sound every few minutes. And the lights kept flickering.

Tavo and Angeline had gone to fix the cameras. Which seemed like a bad idea, given the circumstances. But just try to stop Angeline from doing what she wanted to do. She was a force.

Outside, the sky was growing ever darker, and the pressure in Maverick's sinuses told him that the barometric pressure was dropping fast. They'd handed out the tracker tiles to each of the hiders, explaining that it was just for safety and that they would not be tracked unless there was a problem. They were asked to put the tiles in the bottom of their packs, and they'd agreed.

Cody had given him a look, and Mav wondered how long it would be before he ditched the device. Whatever. Wild Cody was the least of his worries.

"All set," said Hector faintly, looking at his computer screen. "The blue one is Cody. Malinka is pink. And Adele is purple."

They had fanned out around the property.

He put a hand on his friend's thick shoulder, feeling the tension there. He really hoped that Hector wasn't going to start crying again. Maverick just couldn't handle it.

"Mav," said Hector, spinning in his chair so that they were facing each other. He looked different somehow, his eyes serious, dark. "Tell me what's *really* going on."

Hector and Mav had been friends the longest, growing up next to each other in identical split-level homes on the same suburban street. And of all the crew, they were the least alike. There was something grounding about that, the lack of competition. With Tavo, and even Alex, there was always all this jockeying for who was smarter, stronger, faster, more daring. Hector was the one standing on the sidelines, waiting with an ice pack. He didn't have to prove anything to Hector.

"I'm scared, Mav," said Hector, when Maverick stayed silent, struggling for the right words. "Things aren't right. We both know it. Haven't been for a while. Not since Chloe."

Hector's wide-open, nonjudgmental gaze made Maverick want to tell him everything, everything that had gone wrong since Chloe Miranda stepped into his life. That was the thing about Hector: ever since they were kids, he always just knew what to do, what to say. Maybe he'd have some magic fix for all of it, something that Maverick couldn't see because he was in too deep.

Something the old woman said rang back to Maverick. *The bill will come due.*

Didn't Maverick know, even before they'd come here, that it was true?

★ ★ ★

Maverick had been drunk the next time he saw Chloe. Like piss-in-your-pants, blackout drunk. She appeared as if out of an icy vision, a figure sauntering out of a blustery Reykjavik night as he stumbled from the rowdy bar up the quiet street toward the hotel. Hector and Tavo had both hooked up. Alex wasn't with them. And Maverick had been about to get lucky with a superhot plus-size model named Giselle—and what had happened? What words had come out of his mouth so that her smile froze, then dropped? Her eyes went cold. And she slid out from under his arm, excused herself to the bathroom and never came back. What had he said? It was a rare night when Maverick went back to his hotel room alone, slipping along a slick sidewalk, snow falling.

A woman shimmered and wobbled on the path ahead of him like a mirage. He squinted in the dim light; it had been dark since three in the afternoon and would be until after ten the next morning. The sun was only up for about six hours in the Icelandic winter. There was something so weird about that; he felt like they were on the moon. Angeline and he had had their first fight. She wasn't answering his calls.

"Not looking too good there, Mav," the woman said, coming closer. He knew her. "Can I help you get back to your hotel?"

He struggled for her name. He pointed at her. "Heeyy."

"Don't you recognize me?" she said, just the slightest edge to her tone.

"Sorry," he said. "I lost a contact. Can't see a thing."

Which was bullshit because he had perfect vision. What was her name? One thing was for sure: girls you'd slept with really got pissed when you forgot their names. And he knew he'd slept with her, and that her skin was smooth and warm, her body tight and lithe. *That* he remembered.

"It's Chloe, silly," she said. "Man, you're really drunk."

Oh, shit. He and Chloe had met in Aspen, hooked up again

in Cabo before he met Angeline. There had been lots of texts and voicemails, some of them angry. Now here she was in Iceland, where the cold was so bitter it actually hurt, snaking its way under Maverick's Patagonia puffer, biting at the skin on his face. And that vodka, cool and smooth, had gone down a little too easy.

"Yeah," he said. "The vodka here. Damn."

She laughed; it was sweet, understanding. "It's no joke."

She came up beside him, and he dropped an arm too heavily around her shoulders, nearly toppling them both. "Easy there, tiger," she said with a laugh. She was strong, held his weight. "Let's get you back to your room. Your hotel is right up there. Got your key?"

He fished it out of his pocket and handed it to her. The street, which had been packed with tourists all day, was deserted, shops and restaurants shuttered. At the entrance to the Tower Suites where he was staying on the top floor, the doorman held the door and gave him a knowing look. That old song—who sang it?—about how you can check out when you want, but you have to stay forever, played in his head, eerie and distant.

Then they were in the elevator, making out, the cold forgotten in the warmth of the indoors, the heat of her mouth on his, her hand reaching between his legs. When he closed his eyes, he imagined it was Angeline. And part of him thought he should stop himself, because he knew he had to be a better man to be worthy of the woman he loved. But this girl, the one right in front of him, was so good, and he was so weak against the wave of his own desires.

They stumbled giggling up the hall, crashed together into the door to his suite. She swiped his key card, and they fell inside. He lifted her, and she wrapped her legs around him. He carried her to the bed and laid her down. They shed their heavy coats, their clothes. He lay on the bed beside her, the room spinning. He did not want to pass out, not yet.

"I've missed you," she said, straddling him. "So much."

Wow, she was hot—abs ripped, tits high and tight, hips full, that honey hair cascading over her shoulders, mouth glistening. He remembered their nights together then—Aspen, Cabo. Also, all the texts. The phone calls and angry voicemails. It was a swirl of pleasant and unpleasant. Hot sex, then scathing reproach.

Probably not a good idea to sleep with her again. But then he was inside her and the sight of her on top of him, breasts bouncing, head back in pleasure...ah, it was good, very, very good. And Angeline had been super nasty with him, hung up on him, hadn't answered when he called her back.

"Mav," Chloe breathed, pressing herself deeper, deeper. "I need you so bad."

That's how he remembered his night with Chloe. Anyway, that's the *last thing* he remembered before a black curtain fell. When he woke up again, she was sitting in the chair over by the window, crying. The city lights behind her glittered, and she was curled up into a protective position, legs pulled into her chest, arms wrapped around her legs. There was a little blood on her lip; it was swelling and faintly purple.

"What? What is it?" he asked, sitting up. The room was spinning horribly. Why was she crying? "Did you fall?"

She shook her head, drew in some shuddering breaths. "You. You hit me."

"No, no," he said. He looked at his own hands, unmarked, as if they didn't belong to him. He'd never hit a woman; he had too much respect for his mother. Would never.

"I'm sorry," he said. It must have been accident, him flailing in his sleep. "I'm so drunk. I don't remember. Should we call for some ice?"

She got up, backing away as if she was afraid to turn away from him. She was still nude, her body toned and tan. She gathered up her clothes, keeping her eyes on him.

"I'm leaving," she said.

"Wait," he said and struggled to get up. And the speed of his movement was too much. He ran for the toilet, emptied out the contents of his stomach in a revolting rush of chemical scarlet. Red Bull and vodka. Never again. He knew he wasn't his best self when he drank like this.

When he managed to crawl back to the bedroom, Chloe was gone.

He remembered a blissful feeling of relief.

When he woke up in the morning to Tavo pounding on his door, he wasn't sure whether he'd dreamed it or not. A glance at his phone revealed two calls from Angeline. His head was pounding. He made it to the door, let Tavo in.

"What happened to you? Man, you look like ass."

"You guys bailed on me."

"Bro code," said Tavo. "If you can get laid, do it. Your bro will find his way home."

"Fair," admitted Maverick.

"You didn't hook up?" There was something about the way he asked it. A little surprised, maybe disappointed? Mav wasn't stupid. He'd seen the way Tavo looked at Angeline, like a kind of lovesick kid. Tavo would *love* it if Angeline dumped Maverick; he'd move right in.

"Nah," Mav said. "I flirted. But, you know, I'm all about Angeline. Even if she currently wants to kill me."

Tavo nodded, his eyes drifting to the mess of Maverick's bed. "Must be serious."

Reaching down, Tavo extracted from the twisted sheets a red lace thong, held it up, raising his eyebrow.

"Huh," said Mav, sheepish. "How'd that get here?"

"You didn't hook up with Chloe again, right? She's trouble. You know that."

"Brah."

Tavo lifted his hands. "Okay, man. Whatever. We gotta get back, right? Wheels up at noon?"

Maverick agreed, and Tavo left casting him a look that Maverick couldn't read. Maverick puked one more time, then ordered a huge greasy breakfast from room service, got in the shower, and tried to feel human.

When he got back to the phone, it was full of text notifications. Chloe.

Hey look, last night. It wasn't cool.

The next text was just a picture, her bloodied and swollen lip. Another: big purple fingerprint marks on her arm.

What? No. He *did not* do that. He grappled for memories of the evening. All he remembered was pleasure, her soft skin, her breath in his ear, his cock in her mouth. He'd been accused of a lot of things in this life, most of them true. But not this. He would never, ever physically hurt a woman. Never.

I'm keeping these pictures.

I have to give this some thought. I have to decide what to do next.

Then there was a notice that he had a PopTalk message. Chloe.

He clicked on her video message. She stared intently into the camera, her lip puffed up, looking swollen and painful. "You owe me, Mav."

The thing about PopTalk messages was that they disappeared right after you watched them. No replay, no record, no screenshots. It was just there, then gone.

You owe me, Mav.

"Mav, are you with me?" said Hector now, still waiting for his answer.

He wanted to spill it all, everything that had happened since that night. But it was so ugly, he just couldn't get it out. If Hector hated him, Maverick wouldn't know what to do.

"We'll be okay," he said again, patting Hector on the shoulder. He pushed away everything about Chloe, about Alex; it was behind a thick concrete wall inside him. "We always are, right?"

Hector looked like he was about to say something else, then just nodded. There was something odd about the way he looked at Maverick.

"Yeah, man," he said. "Sure."

Maverick adjusted his body cam and geared up. As soon as Tavo and Angeline got back, they'd go find the hiders. He couldn't do it without them.

Where were they?

35

ANGELINE

Angeline's knee always ached when a storm was coming. She trudged behind Tavo, who moved with the speed and lightness of a true athlete, seeming to leap along without the drag of gravity, ignoring her. She pushed the pain away. She'd thought that aching old injuries were just a myth until she'd started wrecking her body at those Tough Be-atch competitions. Now, her rotator cuff swelled when she was overtired. And when rain was coming—and it *was* coming—her right knee was a siren, high-pitched and relentless.

She dug deep, tried to keep up with Tavo.

She'd started training for the competitions after a guy tried to overpower her in a basement bathroom of a nightclub. Not tried. He *had* overpowered her, quickly, easily, as she'd emerged from the stall having broken one of her mother's cardinal rules: never go to the bathroom alone at a nightclub. Especially in New York City where the bathrooms were almost all in the basement, where the music upstairs was so loud that no one would ever hear you screaming.

He had been big, she remembered that much. His narrow brown eyes were blank, glassy, unfeeling. High, drunk. His mouth tasted like tequila as he pressed it against hers, pinning her to the cold tile wall with his body. She struggled, but her arms and legs were as useless as butterfly wings against his superior strength, his weight. She still dreamed about it sometimes, that feeling of utter powerlessness, the brutality of a man taking what he wanted, of being dehumanized by another person's desire.

If a group of girls hadn't busted in, laughing, yelling, oblivious, and startled him, he'd have raped her, maybe worse. He ran when they entered, thrusting past them, knocking one of them down. By the time they'd found the security guard, he was long gone. Between the four of them, they couldn't even identify him. Big, brown hair—well, maybe dark blond. Was it a black shirt? No, navy. A tattoo on his hand they'd all agreed, but of what? Angeline could still smell his cheap cologne on her skin.

She remembered the look on the security guard's face, not apathetic, not unkind. Just like *Yeah—well, sorry, girls. Nothing I can do.*

After that, Angeline had started training. Ran, lifted, hired a coach to take her from weakling to tough bitch. She learned how to defend herself. Never again. She'd never let a man surprise and overpower her again. Ha. Not physically anyway.

"Tavo," she said now, growing breathless. "Please."

He stopped, looked down at the ground. Angeline came up to see what he saw. One of the cameras smashed to pieces on the ground, glittering in the scant light.

The silence and growing darkness all around them took on a kind of menace. Angeline moved closer to Tavo, glancing behind them to make sure they were alone.

Was there someone else out here with them, hiding? The same person who'd killed Alex? Someone who wanted to hurt them all?

Were the broken cameras a trap, to lure them out looking?

She realized that they were all separated now. She and Tavo were out in the forest; Hector and Maverick were back at the trailer. *Let's not split up like this*, Maverick had said. She'd ignored him.

Her breathing was labored; she couldn't catch it. Fear, effort, a heavy fatigue.

Finally, she leaned against the rough, thick trunk of a towering tree. She was so tired. She couldn't stop thinking about Alex, his body in the closet, going over the edge. Oh, God. Oh, God, what had they done?

The trees, black and green, their movement in the wind making a kind of whisper, looked down on her. She was so small, so temporary. Her deeds, the things she held as important, her desires meant nothing in this ancient forest. The trees had seen it all, held a primal knowledge in their trunks, their roots, the mycelial network between them. Humans thought they ruled, but far from it. Angeline sagged heavily against her tree, relying on its strength to keep her up. Away from Maverick, away from the challenge, she saw what a sickness there was surrounding the company. They all had it. It was like a virus they passed back and forth.

Why hadn't they called the police?

Why hadn't they come clean when the police came to them?

Now there was no way out.

Tavo turned to look at her for the first time since before Maverick had showed up at the hotel. She thought he might take her in her arms, comfort her. But no. There was a new coldness to him, a distance. He'd seen something in her that neither one of them had known was there.

"I'm sorry," she said. "I'm sorry. You were right. We should have called the police."

He was slightly breathless, too, put his hands to his hips and stared past her.

"But we didn't," he said. "And now we're all fucked. You see that, right?"

She was about to reach for him when a rustling in the trees had them both spinning toward the sound.

She looked around, peering into the growing darkness, the shadows. Why wasn't she *more* afraid? Was it because on some level she believed that Maverick had killed Alex? Or was it because she'd confronted a terrible darkness within herself as they dumped their friend's body off a cliff in a futile attempt to save their game?

Maybe *she* was the worst person out here.

Nothing, no one, emerged from the overgrowth. There was silence again, just the sound of light rain on leaves.

Tavo moved off the path and into the thick forest. She didn't follow. When he came back, he held the broken bits of another camera.

"Mav was right," she said. "There's someone else out here. Fucking with us. They killed Alex."

Tavo was looking at her oddly, a tight smile spreading.

"Angeline," he said, "you're never going to see him for what he is. Are you?"

"We can't do this now." They'd argued about Maverick before. The truth was that she *did* see him for exactly who he was. Every layer, every flaw. And in spite of it all, she'd never loved anyone more.

"We can't *not* do this now," said Gustavo. "Time's up."

He grabbed her arm, hard. She struggled to get away from him, panic rising.

"What are you doing?" she asked. But he didn't answer, grabbed her other arm. Beneath the panic, there was rage. The rage of all women everywhere, tired of being bullied, overpowered, crushed beneath the will of men.

"Get your fucking hands off me."

She kicked him in the shin as hard as she could, freed herself from his grasp with an inward twist of her arms like her trainer had showed her. She was about to break into a run back to the site when a shadow slipped from the darkness ahead and blocked her path.

Angeline stopped short, heart thudding, throat dry. "Who's there? Who are you?"

The rain came down harder then.

She put up her fists, ready to fight. Instead, she caught a hard, stunning blow on the side of the face, sending her to the ground.

Tavo stood over her. Her head spun. Warm blood sluiced down her cheek. The world wobbled, white stars dancing. The pain, the brutality of his betrayal.

"I'm sorry, Angeline," said Tavo. But his voice was cold: he wasn't sorry. The other person came to stand beside him.

No. It wasn't—possible.

"Oh, God," she said. "You."

Then black.

36

MAVERICK

"Where are they?" asked Maverick, looking at the trees through which Tavo and Angeline had disappeared. He tried to manifest their return, imagining Angeline's smile, Tavo's serious frown. Hector didn't answer.

Outside, Petra's men stayed stock-still, unmoved, apparently with no intention of leaving their posts to take cover, even as the rain bore down. The sky was the color of dread, darkening, foreboding, and the wind pushed around the trailer. Still, the men stood sentry against the gloom, black-clad, straight-backed. On Maverick's phone, the huge swath of red weather was swallowing the island.

Tap. Tap. Tap. The rain slithered down the window in rivulets, blurring his vision outside. He had a thought then, resting his head against the glass. End it. Let the men take him. Let the company fold. Burn it all to the ground and see what rose from the ashes.

But it was too late for all of that.

The last moment to cancel had been when Alex confronted him in the parking lot of the hotel.

Maverick, we need to talk. Like now.

Looking back at it now, he saw the conversation for what it truly had been. His old friend was offering him a lifeline, a way out of the mess he'd made. But in the moment, he had felt like an animal in a trap.

Alex. Fuck. I'm so sorry.

Hector was silent in the chair, staring at his phone. "Hector, it wasn't a rhetorical question," he snapped. "Where are they? Are they on their way back?"

"Uh," Hector said, "we have a problem."

The rain beat a tempo on the roof in fits and starts, sounding like some giant was throwing great handfuls of pebbles at the metal intermittently.

"What now?"

"They're gone," said Hector. "They've turned off their locations."

Maverick moved over to his friend. Hector's hand was shaking as he held up the screen to show him the PopMap. Their icons were shaded gray. *Location unavailable.*

"Why would they do that?"

Hector just shook his head, rubbed hard at his stubbled chin with one hand.

"Mav?" he said. His tone had gone serious, his gaze direct. "You have to tell me, man. We've been friends forever, right? What the fuck is going on?"

Maverick was searching for something to say, some way to explain the absolute shitshow they'd found themselves in, when his phone rang. It rang and rang. *Caller Unknown.* He didn't want to answer it.

"I've made some mistakes," Maverick said to Hector, who had wide eyes on him. Hector, who always looked out for him and everyone. They made fun of him, but they needed him to take care of them. Because they didn't take care of themselves. "Big ones."

Where did it start?

The fail always had a discernible starting point.

He'd determined this back when he'd taken his first big wipe-out, all those hours he'd spent laid up. In that case, it had started the night before the jump. He'd been up too late on *Red World*, so he wasn't rested. Instead, he'd chugged three energy drinks in the morning, which left him jumpy and vaguely sick. That morning he knew conditions weren't right, but he went ahead with it anyway. Because he wasn't focused, he hadn't inspected the bike. If he had, he'd have seen that the wheel needed tightening. But maybe it started even long before that. That terrible need he had to please, to perform, to be watched, to be praised. Maybe that was the starting point that led to every crushing wipeout.

What was the starting point for this mess? Maybe it was the same. Maybe all the fails started at that original desire. Maybe that's why he couldn't stop fucking around. Why he lost his temper. Why he took bigger and bigger risks. And the money. Money and all the things it could buy was a kind of salve.

The phone kept ringing and ringing. FaceTime. *Caller Unknown.*

"Answer it," said Hector, urgent.

But Maverick was frozen. That feeling he got when something was about to go really wrong was a siren.

Finally, Hector reached over, took the phone from his hand, and answered.

His face was cast in the blue light of the screen. "Oh, God," Hector said, putting a hand to his mouth.

Maverick snatched the phone back from him.

He could barely process what he was seeing. On the screen, an unconscious Angeline was tied to a chair, a trail of blood coming from her mouth down her white tank top.

"Ange," he yelled. "Ange!"

All his nerve endings vibrated; he wanted to crawl through the phone and rescue her. *What happened? What was happening?*

Then a face in a black mask with jagged white stitching for a mouth and two big gleaming buttons for eyes like a horror-movie rag doll filled the screen.

"I have another hider for you, Maverick," it said. "You know, I thought she'd be tougher, would have put up more of a fight."

The voice sounded strange and mechanical. Maverick tried to look in the background to see where they were, but all he saw was graffiti-covered concrete wall. The light, wherever they were, was low. He squinted into the background. They had to be close.

"Don't you fucking hurt her," he said through clenched teeth. "Don't you dare. She has nothing to do with anything."

The rag doll shook its head, the movement exaggerated and slow. It shook a gloved finger at Mav.

"That's just another lie. I saw what you all did. I recorded you."

Maverick thought back to carrying Alex across the lawn, to the form he'd seen at the hotel. Had someone been there? Had someone seen what they did? Bile rose in the back of his throat.

"You never stop lying, do you?" it asked.

Was it a man? A woman? He couldn't tell. But there was something familiar there. Maverick kept staring. Hector still had his hand over his mouth and was backing away from the phone, almost comically afraid.

"Where's Tavo?" asked Maverick. "What have you done with him?"

A light, mechanical laugh. "You're on your own now, Mav. None of your team to help you. No one to enable you, to laugh at your jokes, to reflect back a self you want to see. Just Hector, who we all know is as useless as a kitten."

Mav retreated to the control room, started operating from the box inside his head. A weird calm came over him, even as Hector started to cry. Mav watched as his friend sank his head into his hands, whimpering. He really was such a baby. He wasn't going to be any help at all. The rag doll was right: he needed Tavo. They were the rough-and-ready team. Where was he?

"What do you want?" he asked the dollface. Because everyone wanted something, right?

"*There* he is," the doll said. "There's the cold, calculating Maverick we all know and love. Just curious, have you ever experienced a true feeling?"

The fog of fear dissipated, and a mental clarity settled.

Play the game. Save Ange. Save Extreme. Get the payout.

He leaned in close to the camera, made his voice low. He stared, too, at the graffiti on the wall. He'd seen it before. Where? "What," he spat. "Do. You. *Want.*"

The dollface moved in, too, taking up the whole screen. The voice became a hiss of menace. "I want you to *pay*, Maverick. I want you to answer for every lie you've told, every dime you've stolen, every person you've used or hurt, every person who hurt themselves trying to be like you. I want you to have nothing left. No love. No money. No adoring fans. I want everyone to see you for what you are."

The rage coming across the line was sizzling, unhinged. Was it one of the Moms Against Mav? In his experience, only moms could muster that much rage.

"And how does hurting the people I love accomplish *that*?" he asked.

"You don't need to worry about my agenda, Mav. All you need to know is that this game belongs to me now. You're just a player. Wow. Look at all these views. I'm live, Maverick. I have my followers, too."

"Who are you?" he asked. It was right there. Something familiar.

Hector seemed to come to life again, moved over to his computer, and started clicking. The rain on the roof was a chaotic drumbeat.

"You know me, don't you?" said the rag doll. "I've had a lot of names."

"MavIsALiar."

That mechanical laughter again.

"That's right. And *my* followers don't want money or prizes. They don't want thrills. In a world where the worst men run free, creating the most damage, they just want to see someone get what they deserve."

"You're hurting an innocent woman," said Maverick. "What does that make *you*?"

Maverick heard the echo of his own voice. He walked over behind Hector and saw his own face on the screen there, too.

MavIsALiar was live on WeWatch.

Thousands of people were watching, the comment stream a chaos of mean emojis and jeers. He watched, stunned at the level of vitriol and hatred that scrolled by—all the flames and devil faces. And wasn't there also that secret thrill? Because even when people hated you, they were still focused on you, watching.

"What are the rules? What is the prize?" he asked.

"I admire your focus. The rules? There are no rules, because men like you ignore them anyway. The prize? Angeline lives."

Panic was a distant siren, something he felt but managed to push down, away.

"What do I do?"

"It's hide and seek, Maverick. If you can find Angeline, and you admit *live* all the things you've done wrong, she goes free."

He'd been playing games since he was a kid. It was a thing he could do, something he understood. Except this time the stakes were his future and the only person he'd ever cared about. And he had the feeling that the whole thing was rigged. No matter how well he played, he was going to lose.

"Don't hurt my friends." He didn't love the sound of his echoing voice—whiny, desperate.

"You don't have any friends, Mav. You have employees. You have an audience. That's not the same thing."

Hector looked back at him, eyes strangely sad. Maverick could see on the screen that Hector was sharing the broadcast on the Extreme WeWatch channel, as well. Yes, that was right. Use it to get the most views possible. The game would go on.

"What about the other hiders?" Maverick asked.

He looked out the blurry window. Those men were still waiting, eyes on the trailer. The tension, the ruin, the high-energy vibration sizzled. Fear was a drug; it could be like rocket fuel.

The rag doll face filled the screen. Then it went black.

Then the power went out.

37

~~~~~~

VIOLET

"Where are we?" said Coral, sounding less confident than usual. "What is this place?"

Violet pulled the car up the rocky dirt road that wound deep into the woods. Was it vaguely familiar? Had she been here before? She felt like she was dreaming.

Wake up, she told herself and kept driving. The light dappled the road ahead, scattered by the thick tree cover.

"Violet," said Coral when Violet stayed quiet. "This is maybe not such a good idea. Like if this was a horror movie, we'd be screaming at ourselves to go back, call the police. Right?"

"But Blake's here," said Violet, gripping the wheel.

"In eight hundred feet, you will arrive at your destination," said the navigation computer.

Her heart was hammering, palms sweaty. Yes, it was familiar. Something about the light. She gazed at the blue pulse of Blake's dot on the LifeTracker app. "I mean, there's his dot. It says he's two minutes away."

Coral was quiet a moment, picked at the tiny hole in her leggings with her black polished fingernails. She was getting glitter *everywhere.*

"So like if he's been abducted, are we *rescuing him?*" she asked with a frown.

Violet didn't have an answer for that. She breathed through a throb of anxiety.

"I should call my mom," said Coral. With her pink-edged black hair and wild clothes, she looked like a rebel. But she was a good girl at heart.

"No!" said Violet, too loudly. She was surprised by a rush of emotion, tears welling. "We're cutting. He's cutting. If my mom finds out or thinks we're in trouble, she'll *freak.* She's all in on this challenge. And we're like totally screwed if she doesn't win."

Coral's worried frown deepened, and she reached for Violet's hand.

Coral just didn't get it. No one Violet knew did. All her friends, most of whom weren't her friends anymore, had never been without money, without security. They'd never lost a parent, listened to their mom crying when she thought she was alone at night. They didn't know what it was like to lose your dad, your house, everything you thought was safe and true about your life.

"I'm sorry," said Coral.

Violet knew what she meant. That she was sorry about everything that might be hurting Violet. That's the kind of friend Coral was: unwavering, down for the ride wherever it went. A couple of years ago, Violet wouldn't have said that Coral was her best friend. But that's because, before her dad disappeared, Violet didn't even know what real friendship was.

Coral's phone started to ring. "Oh, no."

"What?"

"It's my mom."

"Don't answer it."

Coral let it ring out and go to voicemail, staring at her phone in horror, like she wanted to toss it out the window. But it just started ringing again. Finally, Coral pulled a stoic look and be-fore Violet could stop her, she answered. "Hey, Mom."

Violet cringed listening to Coral's mom's voice, high and shrill in the air. Coral pulled the phone away from her ear, rolled her eyes seeming to recapture her cool self.

"Mom, *chill*," said Coral. "The geology field trip, remember?"

Violet gave a quick side glance at her friend, then shifted her eyes back to the road ahead.

"Yes, *you did* sign it," said Coral. "Call the school if you don't believe me. I am sure lots of parents forget about stuff like that. You've been so busy with work."

Wow. Ballsy. And so, so manipulative. If Coral got caught now, she'd be grounded for eternity. Violet had a new level of respect for her tutu-wearing friend. Violet couldn't lie to her mother, even when she tried. It was bad enough that she'd jig-gered her own location with the app. If her mom tracked her, she'd see that Violet was still at school.

"*Relax*, Mom," Coral went on. "I'll get a ride home from Violet after school."

Violet kept driving, taking the final turn on the long drive. There in the clearing. A small, contemporary white house.

"Okay," said Coral, after she'd ended the call. "We're good. For now."

Were they?

38

"The Disappearance of Chloe Miranda"

Rough recording for editing

Harley Granger: So this wouldn't be a true investigation unless we talked about some of the people who believe that Chloe Miranda has not been harmed by Maverick or anyone at Extreme. And that, in fact, she has disappeared by choice. So today, I'm here with Lizzie Burke who is a life-long friend of Chloe's, someone who has known Chloe and been close to her family since grade school. Welcome, Lizzie.

Lizzie: Thank you for having me.

Harley: So when did you first get to know Chloe?

Lizzie: We were in second grade, I think. Yeah, like really little, you know? And Chloe was such a tiny thing, so quiet. Some of the boys were teasing her, not giving her a turn on the swing set. And I stood up for her because, yeah, I was big for my age and the boys were a little afraid of me. From that day forward, we were friends. It was Lizzie and Chloe, Chloe and Lizzie—always. Grade school, middle school. We were always together, knew each other so well. When we weren't together, we were Face-Timing, gaming, or texting. You always think that kind of friend-ship is forever, don't you?

Harley: I'm not sure I ever had a friend like that.

Lizzie: Maybe you're better off.

Harley: How's that?

Lizzie: Because then you don't know what it feels like to lose her.

Harley: Did you?

Lizzie: Yeah. It's funny. In my memory of her, there are two ver-sions of Chloe. There's the girl she was before—when we were kids.

Harley: And then?

Lizzie: There was the girl she became after her mother died. *[Lizzie starts to cry here.]* Sorry. Can I have a minute?

Harley: Of course. Take your time. Let me stop recording until you're ready.

[Recording pauses.]

Harley: Ready to start again? Tell me about Chloe after her mother died.

Lizzie: She just kind of went dark, you know? Like all the light and laughter, all the goofy sweetness. It was gone. She started hanging out with a rougher crowd. There were rumors—drinking, drugs, bad boys. She ghosted me, essentially, before it was a thing.

Harley: Did you ever confront her?

Lizzie: Yeah, I went to her house one day. Her mom had been gone about a year then. Sometimes we still gamed together on *Red World*, so we were still connected that way. I just missed her so much. She had a boyfriend by then. This guy who everyone called Stash, a real loser who was supposedly a drug dealer.

Harley: What happened?

Lizzie: She came to the door, and she didn't even look like herself. She was all sunken around the eyes and so thin. She'd dyed her hair, and she had a hickey on her neck. She didn't even invite me in. I told her I missed her, asked if we could talk. But she just shook her head. And I'll never forget what she said.

Harley: Tell me.

Lizzie: She said that the Chloe I remembered was gone. That I was a part of her life that didn't exist anymore. She saw the world for what it was—random, unfair, dark. And everything we thought we knew was a lie. And that looking at me reminded her how silly, how young she'd been and that we weren't friends anymore. She asked me to leave and not come back.

[Soft sobbing.]

Harley: I'm sorry.

Lizzie: She broke my heart. I've lost other friends, broken up with boys, or been broken up with, and nothing else ever hurt that bad.

Harley: So what happened after that?

Lizzie: A couple months later, she overdosed, went to rehab for a while. She came back to school junior year. There were all kinds of rumors about her then. I'm not sure what was true.

Harley: Such as?

Lizzie: That she stabbed someone in rehab. That she was sleeping with this young, hot algebra teacher that everyone was crushing on, Mr. Pine. He got fired. I tried to reach out to her a couple more times, but she just ignored me.

Harley: Was any of that true? I tried to find her record in rehab, but it was confidential, locked because she was a minor. No one at the school would talk to me about her alleged relationship with Pine or why he got fired. And he wouldn't comment, either.

Lizzie: I don't know, honestly. But then it seemed like she got her act together. She went off to college. From her socials, it seemed like she was doing better. Then there was her whole influencer thing—mental health and body positivity, the Tough Be-atch wins. Then the whole Maverick Dillan thing. She was obsessed with him, always posting about him and commenting on his page. You could just tell by the way he didn't post about her, didn't answer her comments that it was one-sided. Then she disappeared.

Harley: What did you think about that?

Lizzie: Right away, I thought something was up. I saw all those pictures—from the ATM footage, the gas station. It was her. I know it was.

Harley: How do you know that?

Lizzie: She always did this thing, since we were little kids. She would put her left pinkie finger in her mouth and chew on the cuticle. Once she chewed it so bad that it got an infection. In both of the pictures, I could see that's what she was doing.

Harley: Lots of people chew on their cuticles. It's a pretty common anxiety tic.

Lizzie: When you know someone most of their life, you know things about them—like I knew the shape of her head, even the color of her hoodie, that sky-blue. That was always her favorite color.

Harley: But her own family doesn't think it was her.

Lizzie: Let me ask you something. Who knows you better? Your family—or your friends?

Harley: I take your point. So what are you saying?

Lizzie: I'm saying that the girl Chloe was before her mom died would never hurt anyone. She was good, sweet, goofy, openhearted. But the girl she was after? I could see her doing something like this. The teacher, the one she was sleeping with, who got fired, he claimed that she was blackmailing him. That she turned him in only because he refused to keep paying her.

Harley: But...do we believe a pedophile? I mean, he was having a relationship with a sixteen-year-old girl. He's lucky he didn't go to jail.

Lizzie: He was twenty-three, and she was very mature. And honestly, any one of us would have slept with Mr. Pine.

Harley: Still.

Lizzie: You know that saying? Hurt people hurt people? I think she became someone who liked to cause pain. Because she was in so much pain. I don't think she cares who she hurts as long as she gets what she wants.

Harley: Okay. Say that's true. What does she gain by staging her own disappearance?

Lizzie: What does anyone gain by hurting people? Who knows what she wants or what the agenda is? All eyes on Chloe, right, for like a year? Her whole family rallied around finding her. Endless speculation about what happened to her. Major damage to Maverick Dillan and Extreme. A podcast. Her Photogram and WeWatch channels, even though she hasn't posted a thing, have doubled in followers.

Harley: I'm still not following. So, you think Chloe used the Extreme Challenge to stage her disappearance—to get attention? To gain more followers?

Lizzie: Or something. She used it for something. And we won't know what it is until she's ready to show us.

39

ANGELINE

Angeline. Angeline.

Wake up.

Pain. Her head, her back. Her arms.

"Angeline."

Where was she? What was happening? She grappled for the night before. Had they partied too hard? Was this some kind of brutal hangover from a debauched evening out?

The smell of rot, of mold tickling her nose, her throat. Concrete all around her. The sound of water endlessly drip-dripping. The sweet, metallic taste of blood in her mouth. This was not a hangover. It all came back in a sickening rush.

The island. The game. Alex dead. Tavo, his face filled with hate. The dark path. The blow to the side of the head. Someone else. *Who* was there? Her memory churned, murky and gray. A face she knew.

"No," she croaked, forcing her eyes open.

It was dark except from some dim obviously battery-operated

light source over in the far corner of the room, and even that was flickering. Was someone standing there? Still. Watching.

"What's happening? Who's there?"

Maybe this wasn't real. Some kind of dream. And she'd wake up with Maverick in their bedroom back in the city. She loved the way the light washed in their big windows in the morning, and the city was spread out around them, the day waiting.

Graffiti on the wall. Debris on the floor. Everything tilting, groaning. The basement of Enchantments. *We just ask that you limit your time in the hotel itself. We can't guarantee your safety.* That's what Anton had said when he delivered the permits. *The building is slated for demolition.* She'd totally blocked that part out.

"Who's there?" she said, forcing her voice deeper.

She oriented herself. Bound to a rusting metal chair, arms behind her, her ankles were tied. Angeline struggled against her bindings, grunting, the metal legs scraping against the concrete floor.

Fear. Thick and hot in her belly, her throat. That feeling of being powerless, at the mercy of someone stronger.

"Do you think he'll come for you?"

A voice in the darkness.

"Or do you think he'll find a way to run?"

"Who?" she asked. But she knew.

"He's slippery. If there's a way out, he'll find it, right? With or without you. I think you understand that. You know him better than anyone."

"Tavo," she said, although it didn't sound like him. "Don't do this."

Angeline experienced a moment of clarity, the fog in her mind clearing. This was about Maverick. Something he had done. Of course it was. It was always going to come to this, wasn't it? With Angeline paying for things that Maverick had done.

"Do you know what he has in those bags he's been hauling around?"

She'd had her suspicions. After they'd dumped Alex's body over the wall, and Tavo had stormed away from them, Mav had grabbed her arm.

"Let's go," he'd said, eyes wild, desperate. "Right now. Let's get in the Range Rover and take the jet. We can go anywhere. Just the two of us. Just like you wanted."

"What about the challenge? The company?"

"Fuck it," he said. "It's just us. Just you and me, that's all that matters now."

And she could see that he meant it. And that he was terrified of what they'd done, and what would happen next, and of whoever was trying to hurt them. It lit up something primal in her, as well.

"We can't," she said.

"We *can*. I can take care of us. I made sure of it."

"What do you mean?"

"Just…trust me. Ange. Get in the car with me. We'll get off this rock. Wheels up in an hour. Anywhere in the world you want."

She didn't say anything, just let him take her by the hand and lead her back to the lot. Her mind was ticking through possibilities: go, stay, go to the police.

But when they arrived at the lot, Tavo was in the other Rover, the one Maverick had been driving. From the driver's seat, Gustavo cast them a look that Angeline couldn't read, then tore out, gravel spitting behind him.

"Wait!" Maverick ran after the car a few feet, then came to a stop. But Tavo was gone, heading back to the site. Angeline had the keys to the Rover that she and Tavo had arrived in.

"Fuck," Maverick yelled at the sky. "I must have left the keys in the ignition."

The look of despair on his face. That's when she knew what was in the bags. Their heft. Even the scent that came off them. It was like him to be suddenly careless, to leave the bags unattended even after he'd not left them out of his sight for a minute. Was it a form of self-sabotage?

"Let's go anyway," she said, feeling desperation tug at her, too. "Let's just go home. Face whatever comes next. Together."

He shook his head slowly, watched Tavo until his taillights were swallowed by the night. Finally, tired of waiting, Angeline got in the driver's seat. After another moment Maverick climbed in beside her, his big frame slumped.

"We need to get the other Range Rover," he said. "There's something in there that I need."

"We don't need it. We don't need anything. Let's leave it all behind."

He looked at her in the dim light, half his face in shadow. Now it was his turn to balk. "I...can't."

It was then that she'd seen how trapped he was, like the monkey with his hand in the candy jar. He would never be free because he could never let go of the sweets. The money, the toys, the views. There was never going to be a moment when it was just the two of them, without an audience, without the toys and the next big adventure. Because that Maverick—he simply didn't exist.

Here in this concrete dungeon, bound to a chair, she saw it all so clearly. Too late. The bill had come due, like Petra promised. And Angeline would be the one to pay.

"Why are you doing this? What do you want?" asked Angeline now. A sob crawled up her throat, anger, terror.

There in the corner, she saw a blinking red light.

"Are you...filming this?" she asked. "Are we *live*?"

No answer came from the form standing in the darkness.

40

MAVERICK

Maverick geared up, the image of Angeline unconscious, bound, seared into his brain. That feeling of powerlessness, helplessness that he had when his mom was dying swelled and expanded inside him, pushing the air from his lungs. He wanted to run.

"Where *is she*, Hector?" he asked again, shouldering his pack.

"The hotel?" he answered. "On the video, it looked like it *could be* the lower level of the hotel."

Hector was hunched over his keyboard, tapping. The power was out, but they still had battery life on the laptops, the cellular hot spot on the phone. Angeline's PopMap locator was off, so Hector was trying Find My Device, where all the company phones and laptops were registered. Nothing.

On the other screen, Maverick could see Malinka, Cody, and Adele, their tracker dots pulsing—even though he'd promised them that they wouldn't be tracked unless necessary. Their dots all went in different directions. It didn't matter now, when an hour ago the challenge was the only thing on his mind. All that concerned him now was Angeline.

"Oh, my God," said Hector. "The cameras I set up. I had them set to Record. Maybe they caught something before they went dark."

He rolled his chair over to the other monitor and tapped on the keyboard.

Maverick stood behind Hector as he fast-forwarded through recorded footage. Hector setting up the camera, looking comically into the lens, his fingers huge as he adjusted the camera like a boomer on Zoom.

"There," said Hector after another minute of scrolling. "There she is."

On the grainy video footage, Angeline was standing on the path, looking at someone off camera, her hands up, eyes wide. Maverick watched as someone came up behind her, unidentifiable in the dark. Then the dollface mask filled the screen, and the picture went black.

"Where is that camera?" asked Maverick.

Hector pointed to the survey they had open on the table near the computers. It was a proper command center inside the trailer, except that they'd lost all control of the game.

"Here," Hector said, pointing to the spot where the path veered in two directions, one trail leading to the casitas, the other leading to Enchantments.

"Okay. I'm heading out."

"I'm coming with you," Hector said rising.

"No. Stay here, Hec." He tried to be gentle with his tone. But he could not be dragging a quivering, out-of-shape Hector down into Enchantments. Tavo, even Alex would be an asset. But Hector's skills kept him in the chair. Out in the field, he'd just get hurt. "I'm going live. Stay with me that way. If things go bad, get help."

"How?" Hector said, sounding slightly panicked. "Who do you think is going to help us now, Mav?"

But Maverick was already out in the storm, heading to the hotel.

Outside, on the edge of the path, he hesitated.

The Range Rover stood off to the right of the campsite, gleaming in the rain. The keys were in his pocket, hard and cold. The duffel bags were in the back.

He glanced at the line of soldiers, still standing in the rain. They didn't seem real, like a mirage or projected CGI.

"Hey," he yelled, his voice faint in the storm. "Hey, we're in serious trouble here. My girlfriend—someone's taken her. Can we get a little help?"

Not one of them moved or even looked at him.

He looked back at the SUV.

Could he just start driving, smash through that line of soldiers with the big black vehicle? Get to the jet. Wait there until the storm cleared, then head...anywhere. If Tavo hadn't taken the wrong Rover, Maverick and Angeline would already be gone. It had been their last chance to escape.

He glanced down the dark path, covered now with debris, that would lead him to Enchantments.

The day his mother died, Maverick had left her.

Don't go, the hospice nurse had said. *She doesn't have much time.*

His aunt had been there. Her best friend Pauline. They'd been quietly taking care of her and Mav for days. Reading to his mom from the paper, bringing him food even when he said he wasn't hungry. Playing the podcasts she loved, talking to her about news events. She wasn't alone. He remembered the light in that room, a kind of buttery yellow though the drapes. The sound of her monitors. The hospital smell—antiseptic and illness. The scent of sadness.

There was an interview scheduled, a big network morning show to promote the upcoming challenge. It mattered in the way things like that mattered, and he knew if his mother was conscious, she'd tell him to go. She wouldn't want him sitting there crying, waiting for her to die. She would consider it a waste of time. After all, without her there would be no Extreme, there would be no Maverick Dillan. It was through the lens of her camera, her tireless efforts, that he had become everything that he was now.

He'd sat beside her a moment, held her hand, put it to his lips. He touched her wispy blond hair. She looked ancient, though she was just fifty.

Mom, he said silently. *I'll be right back. Just…stay awhile longer.*

Live your life, Maverick. He thought that's what she'd say if he asked her what he should do. *Go.*

And so, he'd left. The waiting Lincoln Town Car took him into the city. He sat in the greenroom, thinking about his mother, going through the motions. The interview—it had taken approximately four minutes—was a blur in his memory, bright lights, an impossibly made-up and coiffed interviewer, giant cameras like robots surrounding a faux living room set.

Lots of people saw it, posted about it, said all the things they always say when he was on television or in the paper for his challenges or his charity work. That he was a hero, a sellout, an angel; that he only did the good things he did for more money and more views; that he was hot, or a fat ass. His WeWatch followers jumped ten percent; a pop star tweeted that she was a fan. It was, by all accounts, a huge success and one of the things that took Extreme to the next level. Like a prize he found on *Red World*, something that shuttled him to the next layer of play.

And then in the car on the way back to the hospital, he felt the universe shift. To this day, he'd swear to it. The sun went behind the clouds, and the driver had the radio on, and his mom's favorite Stevie Nicks song started playing. And he knew.

He didn't cry.

Then, moments later, his aunt texted him.

She's gone, Mav. It was peaceful. She loved you more than she loved anything in this world.

What she didn't say: And you weren't here.

Maverick didn't cry, didn't make a sound. Didn't call a soul.

He just sat with it, listening to Stevie croon about her fear of change.

Back at the hospital, he sat in the room with his mom in that yellow light, the monitors finally quiet. One by one, the guys arrived. Alex, then Tavo, then Hector. They stood around him, a hand on his shoulder, a voice in his ear.

I'm sorry, man.

She was a good mom.

The best.

They each said their goodbyes, Hector blubbering like a girl. Then they just sat with him as afternoon turned to evening. Alex perched on the foot of the bed. Hector sat by the window, looking out. Tavo stood directly behind Maverick, a heavy hand on his shoulder.

Once the tears subsided, they started chatting, joking—the way you do when death comes. Because it feels like the end of the world for a while until you realize it isn't, not for you, not yet. If his mom could hear them, she would have laughed along with them because she always loved his stupid, crazy friends. They all stayed with her until the nurse told him it was time to take her body away.

And now standing on this path in the storm, he felt as he had then.

Afraid, alone, powerless. Like the world was too big, too complicated, and he was too small, not up to the forces working against him. His whole life was a battle against that feeling. And every wave, or jump, or climb, or obstacle course he'd faced was just an allegory for that struggle. Sometimes he won. More often he lost.

The only time he didn't feel that way was when he was with Angeline. When she looked at him the way his mom used to, seeing him, all of him, and loving him anyway.

He wasn't going to leave this time.

He broke into a jog toward Enchantments, wind so powerful he had to push against it, debris flying across his path, lightning flashing on the giant dark structure, illuminating it weirdly, light pooling in dark spaces, only to disappear again. Thunder like a freight train.

Inside the grand entrance, he thought things would get quieter. Instead, the wind whipped through all the open places, whined and moaned, slapped at his pants, his jacket.

"Angeline!" he yelled. "Angeline!"

His voice was taken by the noise. He spun in a panicked circle, and then he saw down the elevator shaft maybe the slightest hint of light leaking up from below.

He took out his phone and went live.

"Hey, guys," he said to the camera. "I'm live from inside Enchantments. And let me tell you what. It is scary AF. But I've got to find Angeline and then the other hiders. You can probably hear that the storm is raging. We're trapped here, and someone has Ange. This was supposed to be fun and games, but it's real now. Too real."

He propped his phone up against some debris, then he took his rope and fastened it around a pillar, checking its stability once, twice, three times, pulling hard.

"I think she's in the belly of the beast. That's right. Down this empty elevator shaft somewhere in the basement of Enchantments. I can already hear water running, lots of it. So I hope it's not flooded down there. I'll go live again when I get down. Wish me luck."

He ended the live, stowed his phone.

Then without thought, he rappelled down into the darkness.

Surf3rDud3: Oh, my god. Mav you are a wild man.

KillerCraig: What a tool. Ur gonna die.

Mavericksbride: I love you so much. I wish you were com-ing to rescue me.

Fr$4dsterNinja: This is so fake.

Sk4techick666: When's the next challenge, Mav?

More comments, fade out.

41

~~~~~~

VIOLET

"Who do you think is in there?" asked Coral.

They'd hatched a plan. Coral was going to wait in the car with the engine running, and Violet was going to ring the bell, then step back toward the vehicle.

"Blake, for one," answered Violet. She stared at the door. The house had the air of desertion; it was hard to imagine someone inside. Why was it so familiar, though? Had she been here? When?

So Violet would ring the bell, move back toward the car, and then if anything should go crazy-bad, if Violet couldn't get back to the car, Coral was supposed to call 9-1-1 and drive away.

It was getting late. The challenge would be starting any minute. Her mom was out there, probably worrying about why she hadn't heard from them. How could Blake do this? Why had he come here, to this place?

They weren't supposed to keep secrets from each other. That was her mom's number one rule. Secrets were poison, she said. They leaked into any system and corroded from within. When someone asked you to keep a secret, you had to question that person's motive. When you held something back from someone you loved, you had to ask yourself why. The answer, more often than not, said her mom, was fear. You were afraid of the truth, to tell it, to face it.

Violet had kept a secret.

A couple of months before her father disappeared, she'd awoken to hear his voice carrying up from downstairs. She was used to hearing her dad talk on the phone—his work voice, she always thought of it. The work voice was very different from the one he used with Violet and Blake or the soft, low tones he used with Mom. She couldn't say how it was different exactly, but the work voice was kind of like maybe he was on stage: passionate, sometimes a little angry. The voice she heard that night wasn't any of those.

He sounded…scared.

Violet crept from her bed and out into the hallway, moving silently past Blake's room, her parents' room where her mom was still sound asleep, breathing heavily.

Violet lingered at the top of the stairs, something telling her not to go down. And even now she sometimes wondered, if she hadn't gone down, hadn't heard what she heard, maybe nothing that followed would have happened.

But that wasn't true—that's what Dr. S. told her. That was magical thinking, he told her. That as a kid, she wasn't responsible for the mistakes her parents made. It was their job to protect her, not hers to protect them. There had been no mystical fork in the road as she stood at the top of the stairs, deciding whether or not to go down.

Then there was another sound, one she didn't recognize at all.

She found herself following it past all the family pictures that lined the staircase, past the front door where her and Blake's backpacks hung ready for the morning rush to the car. Her father was sitting hunched on the couch, head in hands.

He was crying.

The sight of it filled her with dread, confused her. Her mom cried all the time. If she was sad, tired, frustrated, even watching *Moana*. But dads didn't cry. Her dad especially. He was perpetually upbeat, never even angry with them.

Violet thought about going back to her room, but instead she came to sit beside him. He jumped, then looked at her, stricken. Batted at the tears coming from his eyes, pulled a fake smile.

"Violet," he said. "Honey, I'm sorry."

"What's wrong, Dad?"

He dropped an arm around her, pulled her tight. He smelled of soap and linen. "Nothing. Just some stuff going on at work. I'm...overtired."

What at *work* could make her dad *cry*?

"It's okay, Dad," she said. "Just make a list of all the things you have to do, and then it won't seem like so much."

He'd given her that advice a thousand times when she got stressed about school. He held her tighter.

"That's great advice," he said, kissing her on the top of her head. "How'd you get so grown-up?"

It was a question that didn't need an answer, so she just sat with him for a while, pressing herself against him, listening to his heart beating.

"Hey," he said, finally. "It's getting late. Let's get you back to bed."

He walked her upstairs, tucked her in, and kissed her on the forehead.

"Hey, V," he said. "Let's have this be our little secret, okay? Mom would just be worried if she knew I was upset."

She nodded, even though her parents had told her a hundred, a thousand times that no one good would ever ask you to keep a secret from one of your parents. But this was different, right? *Private* was not the same as *secret*. That was another hard-to-understand distinction. It was private that her mom had an ap-pointment for a bikini wax. It wasn't a secret, but your teacher didn't need to hear about it.

Later, after everything, she'd wonder again and again if things would have been different if she had told her mother that her dad was upset enough about something at work that he'd *cried*.

Why she was thinking about this as she approached the door, she didn't know. Just that it was another one of those moments when there were other, better choices. And she chose this one.

She rang the bell, once, twice, hard so that it couldn't be ignored.

Then she ran back halfway between the house and the car, Coral watching intently from the driver's seat, her cell phone clutched in her hand. Violet was breathless, a vein throbbing in her throat.

But when the door swung open, it was just her brother standing there. Not bound or gagged, not kidnapped.

"What took you so long?" he asked, moving back inside.

"What took me so long?" she said, following him.

She heard Coral yelling, *"Violet! Violet! What's happening?"*

"What the actual fuck, Blake?"

"You think I didn't know you put LifeTracker on my phone?" he called back, his voice echoing in the unfurnished space.

She stopped at the door.

She remembered: there had been a big sectional over there, a television mounted on the wall. Outside, visible though the sliding-glass doors, there had been a swing set, and down the path into the woods there was a tree house.

Coral came up behind her, smelling of bubble gum and lilac. *"What is happening?"*

"I have no idea," she said as she followed her brother inside.

As she turned the corner into the kitchen, she saw him.

Grayer, thinner than she remembered, than he appeared to her in her dreams. He had dark circles under his eyes, a salt-and-pepper beard. She stood staring, stunned. She opened her mouth, but no words came. Distantly, she was aware of a hurricane brewing—a terrible swirl of rage, grief, sadness, relief, surprise, joy.

She staggered back into Coral, who held her shoulders tight.

Coral issued a gasp. "Holy missing persons," she whispered.

"Hey, kiddo," he said, rising.

Violet lifted a hand, indicating that he should stay back, and he stopped where he stood.

"Hi, Dad."

42

MAVERICK

The bottom of the elevator shaft was already filling. Maverick splashed down and found himself ankle-deep in murky water, debris floating, an unpleasant smell drifting up. He stopped and listened to the darkness, felt his aloneness.

Leaving the rope dangling, he waded out of the shaft. In the ruined elevator lobby, he was about to go live again, then stopped himself. He was rarely without one of the guys, his audience, Angeline. There was always someone watching, someone to laugh at his jokes or to encourage him before a crazy stunt and to help him up when he wiped out.

Wasn't that everyone now, though? Wasn't *everyone* living their lives on display? It wasn't just WeWatchers and influencers. Everyone was curating and filtering the moments of their lives, posting them for approval, checking back to see what people thought.

"When you have a kid, that's when shit gets real," Alex told him. "All of this? You just suddenly see it for what it is. A game. A dream."

Alex had said it in anger. They'd been fighting outside the hotel.

"You're not even here anymore," Maverick had accused him. "Your heart is not in this anymore."

"You're right," Alex had answered grimly, surprising Maverick, cutting him deep. "My heart is with my family. My wife. My child."

"*We're* family, aren't we?" He pointed an angry finger back and forth between them. "Brothers."

"That's what I thought, too, Mav," he said.

"That's what you *thought*?"

"Until I realized that you were stealing money from the company."

Maverick felt himself retreating from the conversation, from reality. "Fuck you," he said. "How could you accuse me of that?"

But Alex got really still, quiet the way he was when things were serious. Maverick always blustered and yelled. Alex went calm. One of the ways they'd always balanced each other out.

"Where's the money, Maverick?" he asked. He sounded almost sad, patient, like he was talking to a child.

"*What* money?"

"Almost two million dollars," said Alex. "Small withdrawals, payouts to invoices I can't find, donations to causes that don't exist. All over the last two years. Since you've been with Angeline."

Maverick's stomach bottomed out. Then a red tide of rage washed through him.

"You're telling me there's two million dollars missing?" he roared. "You're the fucking CFO. Shouldn't *you* know where it went?"

"Maverick," said Alex, lifting his palms. "Talk to me. Before it's too late. While I can still help you. Help us."

The sky was growing dim, and at his friend's words the rage left him. And above them, those birds Angeline was always talking about circled overhead, gliding effortlessly on the air. Huge wingspans, graceful dips, and deep arcs. What was it like to be so free?

"Someone's been blackmailing me," he surprised himself by saying. The relief of speaking it out loud was so total that he literally felt his shoulders drop. His breath came easier than it had in years.

Alex shook his head, brow furrowing. "Who? How?"

Maverick bowed his head, couldn't answer.

"Maverick," said Alex, moving closer, "what did you do?"

Maverick confessed everything to Alex. That's what hurt now. Before his friend died, he knew the truth, the *whole truth*, about Maverick. That he wasn't a star, the ringleader of their wild circus of a life, the adventurer heading into the fray, the crusader for good. He was a flawed man, a coward, a liar...a thief. That was the last thing Alex would know about Maverick. Did it eclipse everything else they'd shared?

He'd expected Alex to lose it, but he didn't.

"I can fix it, Mav," he said instead. "I can fix the books, and we'll make the BoxOfficePlus deal. Okay? And then we're free. *You're* free."

"Free from what?" Maverick asked.

Alex looked at him like he was a poor student, someone to whom he had to explain a very basic idea. "Free from Extreme. From the camera. From all the demands on your time, your body. You can live your life with Angeline, maybe start a family."

Maverick smiled then, nodded. Because he knew that's what Alex wanted. Alex wanted to be free from Extreme. He just didn't realize that Maverick *was* Extreme, always had been, always would be. There was no Just Maverick. He didn't exist.

"Just get us through the challenge," said Alex. "And I'll fix everything else, okay?"

Then Tavo was coming out with the gear, and they were

moving toward the Range Rover. Alex stayed rooted, watching them load and go. And Maverick knew that everything had changed between them. The look on Alex's face—was it *pity*? He was still standing there as they drove away, getting smaller and smaller in the rearview mirror.

I'll fix everything else, okay?

He would have. Maverick knew that. He would have—if he could.

Now Maverick turned on the flashlight attached to his pack. Outside, he could still hear the storm raging. He was glad to have it in the background. Its raw power, the way the wind pushed things around, broke trees, the way the rain pelted, came down so heavy and fast that it turned the site into a swamp, unnerved him. Nature. What a bitch.

The standing water in the basement, which had been just over his ankle, was creeping up his calves. It was cold, gritty, the floor thick with viscous grime. The basement was a horror show of shadows and gaping doorways leading to nothing. Rusted, jagged pieces of rebar jutted out randomly like claws waiting to slice. He moved with deliberation, intention, pushing back panic, caging it where it rattled and screeched but was controlled.

Somewhere a sound, its echo. A yell? A scream? He stopped moving and listened.

In the video he'd recognized some of the graffiti on the wall from his recon down here, checking out all the places the hiders might choose. Where had it been? He listened to the darkness now, started moving in the direction of the ballroom.

When he turned the corner, he saw a light shining from down the hall. Was that a voice? Someone speaking low?

In his pocket, he rested his hand on the gun he usually kept on the plane. A flat black Glock he'd spent some time learning to use at a downtown gun range, just for the thrill of it. Not because he'd ever thought he'd need it. Not because he'd ever planned to hurt anyone.

But things had gone too far.

His mom was gone. Alex was gone. Hector was practically useless away from a computer screen. Tavo, Maverick could tell, had grown to hate him a little because Tavo was in love with Angeline.

All he had was Angeline, and in this moment, all she had was him.

It was time for him to be the man she wanted him to be.

He went live and started running toward the sound.

43

VIOLET

The night after she realized her father wasn't coming back, she'd torn up her room looking for the note she was sure he would have left her. When he went on trips, he always hid sticky notes in places she would find them. Inside the book she was reading, on the package of cookies she favored, in a shoe, between her pillows. They'd just say silly things like *I'm thinking about you right now.* Or *Give your mom a hug from me.* Or *I love you so much.* Or *You're my special girl.* Or it would be something funny that they had laughed about recently, like *I'm off to goat yoga!*

She never knew how he did it. How he knew where to hide the notes, how he did it without her knowing, since he often worked late, and she and Blake were usually sleeping when he came in at night.

Finally, she realized that the notes, though they were signed *Dad xoxo*, were from her mom. That she hid them for Violet and Blake after they went to school. It was Mom who knew where to hide them and what each of them most wanted to hear from their father.

When he went away for good, there were no sticky notes, just those she had saved, pressed inside her journal. He had left them without a word, as he always had. But this time, Adele hadn't thought, had the energy, or wanted to cover for him. She *couldn't* cover for him.

Violet remembered the feeling of shame more acutely than any other feeling she had when her father left. She remembered walking into the school the week after and feeling like everyone turned away from her. Like everyone could look at her and see that she wasn't enough to keep her father with them.

One by one, they lost their friends. Had to sell their house and move in with her grandparents for a time. Eventually, Violet and Blake had to leave the private school her mother could no longer afford, even though she worked there now, thanks to the job her best friend had gotten for her. There was anger, too. Sadness. Grief. All feelings she had learned to identify with Dr. S.'s help.

But mostly there was shame that her father was a bad man who had hurt people, and she was his daughter, so she must be bad in some ways, too. Otherwise, why would everybody hate them because of what her father had done?

"Holy shit," whispered Coral behind her, gripping her arm. "O.M.G."

Now the feeling that came up as Violet saw her father for the first time in years was rage. It was a hard knot at the base of her throat, a clench in her stomach.

"Violet," said Blake, moving in front of her, "don't lose it."

"What are you *doing here*?" The words felt like acid in her throat. The back of her neck and the palms of her hands tingled; her whole body quaked. If it wasn't for Coral's hand on her shoulder she might have fallen over. "I'm calling the police."

He looked so strange, haunted around the eyes. There were deep lines etched in his face. In her dreams, he was always smiling, color high in his cheeks. The man before her looked hollowed-out. He lifted a palm, bowed his head. "It's okay. You can do that. But let's talk first."

She remembered that about him, how calm he always was. How her mom would get angry, and how even Violet was prone to door-slamming and fits of temper. But her dad and Blake were always chill, easy, accepting of the circumstances whatever they were.

"First," said the faded version of her father, "let's make sure your mom is okay."

"What do you mean *make sure she's okay*?"

"There's a storm," said Blake, brow furrowed, cheeks flushed. "Her phone is dead. And there's some kind of mess happening on the island."

She'd been so caught up in Blake's drama, that she hadn't even checked in on her mom since the morning. But Adele, she knew, was tough, ready for anything. And this was just a silly game—less challenging than the Tough Be-atch competitions she participated in.

Blake worried about her, but Violet didn't as much. Her mom was the strongest person she knew. The steadiest. Not like her father. Even when Violet was small, even before her father left, she had the sense of him as ghostlike, always almost slipping away, almost not quite there—staring at his phone, or lost in thought, like whatever was going on elsewhere was just slightly more important than what was going on right in front of him. Adele was rock-solid, always present.

"What's *actually* happening?" she asked Blake.

She found herself staring at her father. He seemed like a stranger, not the person who lived in her memories or her dreams. Mostly, he just looked worn-down, like someone you'd see on the street and feel sorry for. The moment was wobbly and strange. How could she process all of this? She couldn't. A kind of mental fog was setting in.

Blake motioned for her to follow him farther into the house, and she did so hand in hand with Coral.

"This is crazy, V," Coral whispered urgently. "We need to call the police. Your dad is like a total fugitive from justice."

That was true. But he was still her father. A man who'd taken on mythic proportions since he left. He was villain, mystery, and heartbreak wrapped all into one. Violet had no idea what she should do, what she wanted to do.

On a table in the sun-washed kitchen were several large computer monitors, each one streaming a different site.

There was a weather site open on one, in which a big red swath was swallowing whole the island she knew her mother was on.

There was Extreme's WeWatch page showing Maverick live, about to go down an elevator shaft. Malinka's page was dark. Mom's LifeTracker listed her as *unavailable*. Meaning that her phone was dead.

Violet felt a notch of dread. Her mother had *never* been untraceable, unfindable, unreachable. It just wasn't a thing that happened with her mom. She'd never called her mom and not reached her, never needed her when she wasn't right where Violet expected her to be.

Instinctively she reached for her phone and called, though she knew it was probably futile. Predictably, it went straight to voicemail.

"Mom," she said, "please call me."

She felt an intense lash of fear and anger.

"This is your fault," she said to Blake. "She's there *because of you*."

"You didn't try to stop her, either," he said quietly. "You encouraged her."

She shook her head, tears welling, words jammed up in her throat. He was right. She could have stopped her mom. All she would have had to do was ask her to stay home.

"I left school so that I could help her," Blake said miserably when she didn't answer him.

"How are you going to *help* Mom sitting in front of a screen?"

What was this strange, yet somehow familiar, place? She turned her attention toward her father now. "And *you*."

Rage came up hot and wild, fueled by worry for Adele. "Why are you here? Where have you been? How could you do this to us and then just turn up? Who even *are you*?"

Her father bowed his head again, put his hands to his chest in prayer hands.

"I have screwed up big-time, Violet," he said, his voice a rasp. "Made too many mistakes to count. But I'm here now, to help you guys and your mom, to make amends. To answer for the things I've done—to you and to the law."

She barely recognized him: gone was all his light and energy. He was a faded, broken version of himself. She thought of something she'd overheard Agent Coben say. *Life on the run is no life.*

"What does that mean?"

Her father drew and released a breath, held her gaze. "It means when I discovered that your mom had left to go to Falcão Island, I knew I had to come home and be here for you guys. I didn't just ruin my life, I ruined yours and your mom's. That's why she's in this mess. It's not your fault or Blake's. It's mine. I did this, and I'm here to face that."

She couldn't stand to look at him, in her chest that terrible tangle of anger and love. She wanted to break things.

Instead, Violet moved in to look at each screen. And Blake filled her in on everything that had happened—from the missing CFO to the men on ATVs returning; from the storm and Malinka's last, desperate broadcast to Angeline's apparent abduction. The feeling of anguished helplessness was almost too much. They couldn't climb through the screen to bring their mother home.

"So what do we do?" she asked. That was her mom's thing.

When the going got tough, what specific action could you take to make things better? "Can we...call the island police?"

"I did that," said Blake. "I used the translate app. And they said all the roads to Enchantments are swamped. There's no way to get them now. They were warned to leave, and they all chose to stay. Including Mom. So there's nothing they can do now."

"What about those men, those soldiers on the site?" asked Violet. "Can't they help?"

"I asked that, too," said Blake. "They have nothing to do with island law enforcement. They're a private security team."

"Owned by who?" asked Violet.

Blake just shrugged. Then his lower lip quivered, and his eyes filled. "I don't know. You're right, this was my idea. If anything happens to her—"

"It's not your fault, son," said Miller. "You're all in the place you're in because of me."

"Well, that's the truth," spat Violet. She flung her arm wide. "What is *this* place? How did you get in touch with Blake?"

Her dad moved closer, like he might try to embrace her, and Violet reeled away from him. "Don't touch me."

"We've been talking on *Red World*," said Blake, voice soft, crying in earnest now.

The news landed hard. Violet played *Red World* all the time, and her father had never approached her there. She could see how easy it would be, to create an avatar and seek to connect. If he'd wanted to, he could have reached out to Violet, too. But he hadn't. Just Blake.

"For how long?"

Blake looked ashamed, like he was reading her mind. "A long time. In the game, he was Charger."

There were so many things to be angry about she had no idea which one to choose. Her head started to ache, and finally she sank into one of the kitchen chairs. *Think, Violet. Think.* But her head was a confused swirl of thoughts. Coral came up behind her, put her hands on both of her shoulders.

"*Red World*," said Blake, eyes widening.

"What about it?" Violet snapped.

"I know someone on Falcão Island. He's the one who told me that Extreme was coming to the island, about the hotel."

"Who?"

"His avatar name is King Killer."

Violet threw up her hands. "Perfect."

Blake spun and sat down at the table, fingers dancing across the keyboard. "Maybe he can help us."

"*Red World* is not the real world, Blake."

"Maybe it should be. Anyway, I have something he wants. Maybe that will motivate him to help us. He and his friends are all adventure guides. If anyone can get to the site, it's him."

Coral leaned in close and whispered so that only Violet could hear, "Violet, do you hear that? Are those sirens?"

Violet felt her father's eyes on her, and when she looked over at him, he smiled. His eyes were glistening. Did he hear? Would he run again? *I love you*, he mouthed. Violet couldn't say it back. Did she? Yes, but it was buried deep beneath anger, betrayal, grief.

A booming voice startled her. "Hey, Extremists!"

"Mav is live," said Blake, moving over to the other keyboard and turning up the volume.

They all crowded around to look at the screen.

"Oh, my God," said Coral. "Look at all those views. There's like a million people watching."

Maverick's face filled the screen, and the comments section was a rushing river of emojis, expletives, praise, anger, jokes.

"As you may know, everything has gone completely FUBAR here on Falcão Island."

He was moving backward, voice breathless, eyes wide.

"And the game has taken an ugly turn. We're trapped. The storm is raging out of control. Our hiders are off the grid, because back at the trailer we've lost power for our devices. So the trackers we gave them are useless now. I hope they're okay, and I *will* look for them soon. But before I do that, I have to save Angeline."

He pointed the camera down to reveal that he was wading in knee-deep water.

"I'm in the basement of Enchantments. And this place is flooding fast. And I don't know how much time I have."

His face filled the screen again.

"I think I may have found where whoever is doing this is holding Angeline. I'm about to go in. Wish me luck."

The screen went black.

Violet just stared at the emptiness. Coral dropped an arm around her shoulder and held her tight. Her father had put his head into his hands. He seemed beaten, no help at all. Why had he come back? She wanted to remember him how he was— before. Not like this, someone hollowed-out, deeply flawed.

Blake had his back to them and his headphones on. He was on *Red World*, presumably looking for King Killer.

What could go wrong?

44

~~~~~~

ADELE

Now, adrenaline abandoning her, she had to face the stinging bite of failure. They'd saved Malinka's life. But the game was obviously over before it ever began. Adele pushed away the disappointment. The foliage all around seemed to whisper, mocking. Malinka, limping, bleeding from a cut on her head, her hands raw from the rope, leaned heavily on Adele as they moved slowly together back to the casita on high ground. The storm had lessened some, but the ground was a swamp.

"It's the eye," said Cody, looking up into the sky. The clouds had parted, and a field of stars was visible in the velvet-black sky. "It won't last."

The girl was shivering in Adele's arms. "You shouldn't have come for me," she said, maybe picking up on Adele's despair. "I don't deserve it."

"Don't *say* that," said Adele. "You're okay. We're all okay for the moment. That's all that matters."

"You came here for your kids," Malinka said, her voice throaty. "To make a better life for them. And instead, you had to save me."

"The only thing that matters right now is that we all make it home." She meant it. She saw the whole enterprise clearly now for what it always had been. A social-media sham; a false idol. A game that was rigged from the outset. How could she have been so foolish?

Cody took Malinka's other arm and shifted her weight from Adele. Over the girl's head, they exchanged a look. Adele felt the energy of a smile.

Inside it was blessedly dry. Cody got right to work clearing away some debris. He took a blanket from his pack and handed it to Adele, who wrapped it around Malinka. They sat together in the corner of the casita, farthest from the window. The occasional lightning flashes were distant now, thunder muted. Outside, the view was clear, lit by the moon.

"It's so beautiful," whispered Malinka, looking up. Adele felt it, too, the gratitude just to be alive.

Cody took out a canteen of water, handed it to Adele who drank from it, then offered it to Malinka. She waved it away.

"Drink," said Cody. "Hydration is everything."

Malinka reluctantly took a sip. Then she leaned against the wall and closed her eyes.

"Now what?" said Adele.

Cody's face was half-cast in shadows. He stared outside at the view.

"Well, I think it's clear that the game is off, right?" he said after a moment. "I don't think anyone is coming for us."

As much as she didn't want to admit it, she knew he was right. Cody's clothes were soaked through like Adele's and Malinka's—their sponsored supposedly impermeable rain gear had been no match for real weather. But Cody didn't seem cold or especially rattled. His gaze was clear and focused.

"So the way I see it, we have a couple of choices." He sat cross-legged on the ground next to Adele.

"Okay. What are you thinking?"

"We take advantage of the break in the weather, head back to camp, hop in one of those Range Rovers and get off this site, head back to town or to the airport, and wait out the rest of the storm there. Those men aren't going to keep us here. They only care about detaining the Extreme team."

This appealed to Adele. She felt beaten. She remembered something that Cody said. *The only true prize in this world is living another day.* Thinking that she was going to watch Malinka die, that she might go over the edge with her, had her shaken to the core. She realized that the only prize she cared about now was seeing her kids again.

"Do we have the keys?" asked Adele.

"The last I checked they were in the vehicle," he said. So he *had* thought about leaving. "Right before the game began."

She'd thought about leaving then, too.

"What's the other option?" asked Malinka. Some of the color had returned to her cheeks. She took another drink from the canteen.

"We go along with whatever stunt Extreme is pulling."

"What are you saying?" asked Malinka, leaning toward him with a frown.

"Maverick is down in the basement of Enchantments looking for Angeline. If WeWatch is to be believed, she's been kidnapped."

"What?" asked Adele. "How do you know that?"

"He went live. I saw it."

He held up his phone to show the muted video of Maverick wading through the flooded basement, talking to the camera. It was recorded, playing on a loop. Maverick looked truly scared.

In all the videos Adele had watched with Blake, he always had this goofy, performative look on his face, as if all his emotions, from surprise to enthusiasm, were for the audience. The man on the camera was focused, determined, and very afraid. Or a better actor than he had a right to be. She read the captions: *I think I may have found where whoever is doing this is holding Angeline. I'm about to go in. Wish me luck.*

"So we follow," said Cody. "If it's for real, Maverick might need help. If it's theater, then at least we're there for the finale."

Malinka's expression was serious, but her eyes lit up a little.

"We might not get the money we came for. But think of the views," she said. "Look at that. Nearly two million views of that video since it posted. That's sick."

These days *sick* was a good thing, Adele reminded herself.

But it was also a little *sick*—not in a good way—to be thinking about views less than an hour after you almost died. In fact, the unwellness of all of it was starting to get to her, including her own. Maybe she and the kids never needed a million dollars. Maybe they just needed each other. She felt something that had been squeezing her heart release.

"I think..." said Adele. Both Cody and Malinka had eyes on her. She felt weirdly close to them, as if she'd known them for years. They'd been bonded by their extreme circumstances. When things went FUBAR, each of them had abandoned the competition to help the others. That was something special.

"I think I'm ready to go home," she finished.

It hurt because in her heart she was a competitor. Giving up felt like another failure. But the game was clearly rigged: people were missing. Even Mother Nature was angry.

Cody offered a slow nod, keeping his unreadable gaze on her. She figured he'd stay, but then he surprised her. "I'm with you."

She felt a little jolt of electricity when they locked eyes. He reached out a hand to her, and she took it. It was familiar, intimate. Then he looked embarrassed, drew it back, his heat lingering on her palm.

Adele expected an argument from Malinka, but instead she just nodded, looking as defeated as Adele felt. The heaviness of it all felt unbearable. She thought about asking for Cody's phone to call Violet. Let her kids know that she was okay and on her way back, however long it might take. But she didn't. She'd give herself a little longer before she had to call them and tell them she had failed.

Cody rose.

"Let's take advantage of this break in the weather and get back to camp."

Malinka, seeming stronger, led the way down the path, Adele right behind her, Cody taking the rear. They moved quickly, though they were all worse for wear—Malinka limping, Adele's back and shoulders aching. Cody had hurt his arm pulling on the rope. The night was humid and cool, rain slowed to a persistent drizzle, wind greatly diminished but still gusting as if to remind them that it wasn't quite done with its show. There was more in store.

"It's true what they say about me, you know," said Malinka, turning back to Adele.

"What's that?" she answered, coming into step beside the younger woman.

"That I couldn't have made the summits without my father. Especially Everest. I almost died up there. If he hadn't tethered me, I would have."

She could see the young woman's shame. Adele said what she had thought all along about Malinka's story, "You were a child, you know. Fifteen on Everest, right?"

"Almost sixteen."

"Still," she said. "Were you a climber because you *wanted* to be? Or to please your father?"

Malinka frowned at her, then looked ahead. "I guess I don't know the answer to that."

"Most therapists would hold that you weren't of the age of consent," Adele went on gently. "That you weren't old enough to know what you wanted past wanting your father's approval."

Malinka kept walking, looking at the path ahead.

"Most adults couldn't make Everest without assistance," Adele went on. "Even elite climbers have Sherpas hauling them up or hauling their gear. What you did, what you've done—it's extraordinary. No matter how much help you had."

Malinka laughed a little. "My company is about to go bankrupt."

Adele put a hand on her shoulder. "I have a feeling you'll figure out a way to save it."

"Maybe," she said, sounding unconvinced.

"You're a survivor," said Adele, looking back at Cody who was a few paces behind them. "We all are."

They kept walking, each silent for a few paces.

"I don't know why I'm telling you this. Maybe because you saved my life. When I was dangling there, and you were holding on, I wished you weren't risking everything for me. I wanted you to know."

Malinka blinked back tears.

"Here's the thing," said Adele. "We're worthy of life and love because of who *we are*, not because of *what we do*. You're enough, Malinka. I wish someone had told me that when I was younger."

Malinka reached for Adele's hand and gave it a squeeze. Adele wasn't sure if Malinka truly heard her, though. It was a lesson you needed to learn for yourself.

"And for the record," said Cody from behind them, "while we're playing true confessions, I *did not* kill that lion."

Adele believed him. The man she used to watch on-screen with her son, and the one who helped her save Malinka, didn't jibe with the images of him she'd seen in the media in the last couple of years.

"That photo was total CGI," he explained.

Malinka looked at him, eyes soft. "I never believed it. You were my hero, growing up."

He nodded sadly. "But the whole scandal, the loss of my show, all of it—I'm ashamed to say that I spiraled. My demons caught up with me, and rock bottom was waking up in an alley in New York City, high, broke, and no idea how to get well."

Adele remembered the mug shot that had made its way around the internet, thinking what a shame that a person so beloved by children could fall so far. "The person I was on the way down, even before that—the things I did, and the people I hurt—I'm not proud of who I was."

For a moment, there was only the sound their footfalls. Ahead, the turn to camp.

"You risked everything to save me. You both did," said Malinka finally. "Maybe who we were, the things we did before we came here, maybe nothing matters as much as what we do now."

Cody offered an assenting grunt. Above, the sky rumbled, the wind picked up.

"What about you, Adele? Anything you want to leave here on Falcão Island?" asked Malinka as Enchantments rose into view, the sliver of moon glowing behind it.

So many things. But nothing she could share right now because her secrets weren't hers alone.

The three of them stood at the edge of the campsite.

The men on the ATVs were gone. Was the storm too much for them? The trailer was dark and deserted. The two Range Rovers were parked, unattended, presumably with the keys in the car, if Cody was to be believed.

The wind picked up again, rain growing heavier.

A left turn offered a clear run for home.

A right turn brought them back to the darkness and danger of Enchantments.

There was no discussion, just exchanged looks between them. Adele felt the rush of adrenaline, and then they were jogging to the right.

As the storm began to rage again, the gaping mouth of Enchantments swallowed them whole.

45

~~~~~~

BLAKE

The Haunted Amusement Park was quiet as Blake dropped into
Red World. He'd used the app to ping King Killer, asking him
if he could play. But he'd received no answer.

Now he moved through the game, avoiding rather than killing a skeleton gang in a Hummer to conserve his energy. The sky
was dark here, purple lightning streaking the sky every so often.
If you happened to get struck, you got X-ray vision for a while.
But it was totally random, a gift from whoever was running
the game. Blake had never been struck; it was on his wish list.

He used a magic bean to grow a vine and go up high and
scope out the landscape. No sign of King Killer.

His breathing was shallow, shoulders aching. Violet leaned
over him. She was saying something, but he couldn't hear her
over the sounds of the game in his headphones. He ignored her.
She wasn't real at the moment. There was only the game.

He used the communication system to send Hugo a message.
"Hey, brah. I need a trade. You still want what I have?"

"What are you doing on here, loser?"

Marco. His hulking avatar moved from the other side of roller coaster. A car of screaming zombies raced toward them. Marco used his rocket launcher to blow it up, and it disappeared in a mushroom cloud.

"I don't have time for you, Marco," said Blake.

"Oh, really." Marco pulled out his axe. "Make time."

Blake *could not* afford to die right now. Then it would be at least another ten minutes before he could get back on the game. And that might be too late for his mom.

He remembered what Gregg said in the car. *Don't let anyone push you around.*

He pulled out his machine gun and squared off to Marco.

"When'd you get that?" asked Marco, envy pulling his tone taut.

"Walk away, Marco," said Blake. "Go play somewhere else. I don't want to kick your ass here, too, but I will."

"I'll make your life a living hell tomorrow at flesh school." But his voice sounded weaker, less menacing. Maybe Gregg was right; maybe you only had to get tough once.

"No," he said, "you won't. Because I'm never going to let you touch me again."

"Ooh, someone grew a backbone. I'm shaking." He lifted his axe and moved closer.

"I'm sorry," said Blake. "I'm sorry that your family got hurt because of my family. But I can't let you fuck with me anymore."

Blake felt something like relief move through him. Something about seeing his dad again, so tired and old-looking, about needing to be strong for his mother, Violet crying when usually she raged. They needed him. He couldn't let his shame and the Marcos of the world make him small. Not anymore.

Marco came hollering, axe raised high.

But before he could swing, Blake used the machine gun to obliterate Marco into a thousand green pieces, like confetti.

"You're dead, Blake," Marco yelled as he got shunted from the game.

Blake just smiled. He knew he dominated here, and now in the real world, too.

"Whoa," said King Killer. "That was sick."

Blake turned to see his friend. His avatar today was a scary clown, with a pile of rainbow hair and big red shoes. Hugo wasn't about violence: he was just there for the prizes, the Red Coin, and the skins. He never fought and had no weapons. That was one of the things Blake liked best about him. That, and he knew all about the secret doors and passageways in the game and was happy to share. Turned out he also knew about things like that in the real world. He was a spelunker. It was Hugo who told him about the casitas on the property. And how he knew a secret way in and out of Enchantments.

"I need your help, King Killer," Blake said. "In the real world."

"What's in it for me?"

Blake reached into his pack and pulled out the peach. It glowed in his hand and cast everything around him in a rose-gold light.

King Killer released a low sigh of desire.

"Name your price, brah."

46

ANGELINE

"Who are you?" Angeline yelled again at the still form in the corner.

The figure hadn't moved, and the red light kept blinking.

Was she losing her mind? Was she dreaming? Maybe this wasn't even happening. It was so bizarre that it didn't even seem real. The pain *was* real—her head, her neck, her bound arms and legs. She heard the distant sounds of the storm and dripping water. There was a heavy smell—mold, rot, age.

"There are people out there. Please," she said, desperation replacing anger, fear settling in. "What do you want?"

But the form stayed still, silent. Unmoved and unmoving. Maybe she was imagining it. Was there anyone even there?

"Is it money?" she asked. "How much?"

That earned a snort, but no words in response.

"Then, *what?*"

Silence. Which was somehow worse than anything else. The silence allowed her mind to race, thinking about all the reasons she found herself in this place. Her abuela had liked to get biblical: *We reap what we sow. What we put into this life is what we get from it.*

But that wasn't true, was it? How many evil, undeserving people were living lives of ease and luxury? And how many good people were toiling, suffering, struggling to get by? It was just another lie they told you to keep you obeying the rules, doing what *they* wanted. Do good, be good, and life will treat you well.

She worked to measure her breathing, clear her head from panic.

"You must want something," she said. "Everyone wants something."

More silence.

Finally, her rage and distress took over.

"Help!" she screamed to the camera, to the air around her. "Help me! I'm in the basement of Enchantments. I've been kidnapped."

A shuffle to her right caught her attention, but she didn't turn to look.

"He's going to come for me," Angeline told her captor. "Maverick will be here."

And then she realized that's what the person wanted. Too late it started to make sense. That's what they were doing. That's who they were waiting for. She was the bait; Maverick was the catch.

"Ange!"

Maverick burst from the darkness then, gun in hand, looking like some kind of action hero come to the rescue. Her heart flooded with love and relief. He hadn't taken the money and left her. He'd come for her.

"Over there," she said as he raced to her. "There's someone there. In the corner. There's a camera."

He turned to face whoever it was, putting his body in front of her.

"Who's there?" he asked, raising the gun. "What do you want?"

"Mav," said Ange urgently, "untie me."

There was a loud groan, the sound of the building straining. The powerful wind, the rising water—warnings from Petra loomed in Angeline's memory. *This land is unwell. Nothing good can happen here.*

She kept working her bindings, feeling them start to loosen. They had to get out of here.

Maverick pointed his gun at the figure in the corner. "What do you want?" he asked, voice shaking. "Who are you?"

"Put the gun down, Mav."

When the person stepped into view, Angeline knew her right away, before she even took off her mask. Still, when she did remove it, honey hair cascading down her shoulders, Angeline released a gasp.

It was Chloe Miranda. Thinner, but looking older, stronger than Angeline remembered her. She had an unfamiliar sense of purpose, a coldness to her.

"*Chloe,*" said Maverick, his voice holding all the notes of relief, anger, surprise.

And she wasn't alone. Another form moved out of the darkness. Angeline's scattered memory from the blow she took on the path came back into view. No.

"Tavo?" said Maverick. Angeline could hear Maverick's despair, his sense of betrayal.

"Put the gun down, Maverick," said Hector, coming in from the other door. Gone was the frazzled, anxious worry, the sweetness. The man before them was tall and upright, his face still and cold.

Hector, too? All of them?

"Hector?" said Mav. "What the fuck?"

The three of them formed a grim-faced line, all eyes on Maverick. Angeline struggled against her bindings, feeling them loosening more, panic swelling. That groaning. The yowl of the wind. Were they going to die down here? Was this it?

Maverick dropped the gun to his side, letting out an angry laugh. "What is this? An intervention?"

The guys just stood there, staring. Angeline's shock was only surpassed by her rage. How could they? The traitors.

"You hurt people, Maverick," said Chloe. She stuck her chin out at him, shoulders back, the very posture of indignation. How could she muster it? After everything she'd done. Had she just been hiding all this time, working with Hector and Gustavo to ambush Maverick? Her brain went into hyperdrive, remembering how Tavo had suggested the island, and Hector had eagerly supported. Was it all a ploy, from the beginning? It must have been.

Chloe even seemed taller than Angeline remembered her. There was a new hardness to her now, like she'd taken off her sweet-girl mask to reveal the woman she really was. "You take and you take. And you don't think about how your actions impact other people."

Angeline got one of her hands free.

"Oh, really," Mav said with a mirthless laugh. "And what about you, Chloe? Where have you been this year while your family suffered, police investigated, reporters chased us around wanting answers. There's even a podcast."

Chloe nodded slowly, had the decency to look ashamed. "I've made mistakes. I've hurt people, too. But *you* drove me to it. You're like a poison, Maverick. You make people sick."

"Okay, sure. I'm the bad guy. You were *blackmailing* me," said Maverick.

"That's a lie," Chloe said, raising her palms. "I never did."

"No one has been blackmailing you, Maverick. Everyone knows that you've been stealing money from the company," said Tavo. "How much, Mav? Two million?"

Maverick said nothing; Angeline saw his shoulders tense, his hand gripping the gun. Finally, Angeline got her other hand free. She kept both hands behind her back, biding her time, looking for the way out.

"You've cheated innocent people," said Gustavo, his voice

soft and sad. "Charities you raised money for with these challenges but never paid. Or like Moms Against Mav. You never even said you were sorry. All those kids hurting themselves because they were emulating you. You haven't given a dime to those families."

"All the girls you've used and abused, hooked up with, ghosted," said Chloe. "You use people, then discard them."

Then Hector. "The jet—for fuck's sake, Mav. The planet is dying. And you're traveling around on a private plane."

Maverick was shaking his head. He pointed his finger at them, accusing. "And you were all right there with me. You never turned down a single thing I offered you."

"Yeah," Hector said, sadly. "I've fucked up, too. I'm not proud. But Chloe's right. You're a sickness, Mav, contagious."

A thunder crash from outside. Another long, loud groan from the building. Angeline felt the electricity of bad possibilities. *Nothing good can happen here now. Everyone flawed, everyone broken.*

"The BoxOfficePlus deal? Were you even going to tell us about it?" said Hector. "We all would have been rich, even me with the piddling shares you gave me in Extreme."

"I *was* going to tell you," said Maverick, voice thin. "When I was sure it would be good for all of us."

The red light blinked in the darkness like a watching eye. Who was on the other side of the camera? There was an audience, had to be. Everything had an audience these days. But would any of those people act to help them?

No.

They'd just sit there watching, waiting to see what happened next. Voyeurs. WeWatchers. We *watch*, but we *do* nothing.

"Where's Alex, Mav?" asked Chloe sadly.

Maverick stayed silent a moment. Then, "Yeah, Hector. *Where's Alex?*"

Angeline flashed back to Alex's body in the closet, Gustavo and Maverick carrying him in the rug, dumping him over the wall.

Alex. Angeline felt another painful wave of regret and self-loathing. What had they all done?

Hector stayed quiet, too, clenching his fists.

"You were the last person at the hotel," Maverick went on. "*What* did you do to him, Hector?"

Angeline saw a flash of guilt across Hector's face; he pulled his mouth into a tight line, said nothing. Hector was the last person at the hotel after they left. Had *he* killed Alex? Sweet Hector. But he wasn't sweet. He was conniving, a liar, just like Chloe. Hector and Chloe exchanged a look that Angeline couldn't read.

"What did *you* do, Maverick?" Tavo was moving closer, voice booming.

"Alex was on *my side*," said Maverick, lifting the gun. Tavo stopped in his tracks. "You think I'd hurt him? I *needed* him. If something happened to Alex, it wasn't me. Which one of you? What did *you* do to him?"

"Stop it, Maverick," said Gustavo. "You're not slipping out of this one."

Maverick backed toward Angeline, waved the gun at Gustavo, who took another step back, lifted his palms.

"What do you *want*?" asked Maverick. "*Why* are we here?"

Hector stepped forward with Chloe by his side. He dropped an arm around her shoulders, and she moved into him. Both of them stared at Maverick. Oh, wow. Were they a couple? Angeline felt a rush of hatred so intense, she had to keep herself from raging. So self-righteous, so hypocritical. Even Tavo. What had she ever seen in him? All of them as bankrupt as Maverick and worse. Angeline's stomach roiled as she got one of her legs free.

"We want you to tell the world *all* the things you've done, Mav," Hector said softly. "You've put on this show of yourself, all your life, convinced the world you're one thing. Now we want you to tell the truth."

"You know the truth, Hector," said Maverick. "You've been with me—*every minute*."

"No, man," said Hector. "I've spent most of my life trying to help you. Trying to fix what you break. Trying to keep you safe. That's it. I'm tired."

"*Wah, wah*, Hector. Poor baby. You're cowards. What are you going to do to me with the camera going?"

Maverick put the gun in his pocket, turned his back on them, and helped Angeline with the rest of her bindings.

No one moved, everyone locked in place, frozen. When she was free, Angeline stood wobbly beside him. He propped her up, holding her tight around the shoulders, and turned back to face the group. She held on to him, the pain in her head a siren.

Maverick pointed at the group, at the camera. His voice wavered when he spoke. "I was never anything but what you all wanted me to be. I never did *anything* out of your sight."

Hector bowed his head, but Tavo kept staring him down.

They'd turned on Maverick, his friends. Chloe was crying, angry tears streaming, fist clenched. They stood there, making a spectacle for the camera. But none of them moved to do a thing. Because they were just watchers. Maverick Dillan was the only actor among them.

Angeline could only imagine the comments scrolling. It was true: Maverick was deeply flawed. Broken, even. But so was Angeline, so were they all. She decided right then and there, she was staying with him. They'd make amends for every wrong he'd done. They'd limp back into the light together.

She squeezed him around the waist, tugged at him.

"Don't you guys hear that?" she said. "The building is failing. We have to get out of here."

"What is this? What kind of sick game are you all running?"

They all spun toward the voice. Wild Cody, Malinka, and Adele behind him, looking like they'd been through it, too—bleeding, clothes torn and mud-caked. Wild Cody had lost his hat. Another wash of shame.

The people who thought they were here to play a game and

win, dragged halfway around the world—for nothing. There
was no money. Except what Maverick had in those duffel bags.
Which were...where?

The money.

Where was it?

Gustavo used the distraction to rush Maverick, crashing into
him hard and taking him to the ground with a grunt. The gun
went skittering, and the two of them were a tangle on the floor,
groaning, punching.

Angeline ran for the gun, but not before Hector knocked
her out of the way, sending her tumbling into the wall. She lay,
wind knocked from her, head spinning from the earlier blow,
tasting dirt in her mouth. Chloe came to stand over her, her
smile victorious. The room spun.

Hector held the gun now, pointing it at Maverick and Gustavo. Mav was on top of Tavo, hitting him hard again and again.

"Stop," Hector yelled, voice bouncing. But as usual, no one
listened.

"I was always going to win," Chloe said to Angeline. But Angeline had no idea what she meant. There were clearly no win-
ners in this insane game. Angeline saw the gleam of instability
in the other woman's eyes. An anger that chilled her.

"Chloe?" Malinka moved tentatively toward them. "Chloe?
What is this? I've been...so afraid for you."

An expression of sorrow, of shame, clouded Chloe's face when
she looked at Malinka. Malinka reached out a hand, and Chloe
took it.

"I'm sorry," said Chloe. "I have so much to tell you."

But before Malinka could answer, the sharp report of a fired
gun froze the moment. The building shuddered, plaster falling
from the ceiling in chunks. Then Maverick was tackling Hector, punching him hard in the face and easily taking the gun
from him.

"Enough," Maverick roared, struggling to his feet. He kept

the gun pointed at Hector, who lifted his hands from his place on the ground.

"We have to get out of here," yelled Adele. "This place is going to collapse."

Maverick ignored her, moving away from Tavo, who was also on the ground, doubled over, seemingly immobilized by pain.

Maverick walked toward the camera. Adele, Malinka, and Cody were moving toward the door.

Where was Chloe? Angeline didn't see her. Had she run? She was gone; she'd left them all.

"I am only exactly what you all want me to be," Maverick yelled at the camera. "I do the things you're afraid to do. I live the way you all wish you could live. I break myself to make you laugh."

He looked around, waited for someone to say something, but no one did. He spoke again straight to the blinking red light.

"I'm sorry. But if you hurt yourself to be like me, or if *your kids* do, that's on you. Who's parking them in front of their devices and letting them watch?"

Angeline moved over to him, grabbed his arms. A crash somewhere inside the hotel. Did she hear voices?

"If I make promises I can't keep...well, who doesn't? If I took money, it was mine to take. The point is, I am out here. *Doing* shit. Living large, sucking the marrow out of this life— climbing, diving, flying, falling. And if you hate me, it's because you're jealous. You *never stop* watching me. You never decline to come along for the ride. If you hate me for who I am, then ask yourself this: Who are *you* for watching me? Who are *you* for making me who I am?"

He swept the gun around the room. Everyone stayed frozen, speechless. Breathless.

"I'm leaving here with Angeline," he said.

And his tone reminded her why she had first loved him. He was sure of himself. He knew himself, where he was in the world, what he could do. Physically, he was sure-footed, athletic. He was right. He could fly. Only the most confident person could. Only the boldest person leaped into the air without thinking about the hard, unyielding ground.

"You've abducted an innocent woman," he went on. "To get *to me*. Derailed a game that was meant to help people. *One of you* is responsible for whatever happened to Alex."

He never lost sight of the agenda, even as it all fell apart.

Hector and Tavo were silent, helpless, both on the ground, bleeding. They thought they'd brought Maverick to his knees. They'd failed.

Were they live? If they were, Maverick had shamed them all and emerged unscathed as ever. Always on top. Always ahead. Always the winner of every game.

It was the camera that gave him his power. If they'd confronted him alone, he might have crumbled. But not with the eye on him. That's what his mother had taught him, from the time he was a little boy. *Never, ever let them see you cry.*

"And trust me, if you try to come after us, I *will* kill you. In self-defense."

It was at that moment that Enchantments offered its final protest. Somewhere deep in the belly of the beast, another crash. Outside the door, a great piece of concrete dropped from above, crashing into rubble. Adele let out a scream.

"Everybody, get out of here," yelled Cody, moving to usher people out. "We have to get up top."

They ran, Maverick holding Angeline's hand and forearm tight, half dragging, half carrying her really, as she struggled to keep moving. The place seemed to be turning to rubble all around them, debris falling, water gushing in. She could hear the others running, screaming behind her as pieces of the ceiling fell, crashing into the water.

They moved toward the elevator shaft, but it was blocked

now, filled with fallen debris, a giant plank of wood, chunks of concrete.

"This is where I left my rope," said Maverick, turning to her. "Ange, we can't get out this way. We're trapped. I'm sorry. I'm so sorry."

He moved toward her and held her tight as Enchantments started to crumble all around them.

47

ADELE

Enchantments was falling.

"Where's Chloe?" yelled Malinka as Adele dragged her by the hand down the long hallway toward the stairwell.

"Forget her," yelled Cody.

"She's my friend." Malinka came to a stop, looking back. "I...I love her."

Adele remembered the picture she'd seen in Malinka's tent of the two women cheek to cheek. Malinka had come to Enchantments for answers about Chloe. Now she had them. Unfortunately, they were not the answers she wanted. She could see on the girl's face a look she knew too well, a mingle of confusion and betrayal, disbelief.

"Let her go, Malinka." But the girl was already moving in the other direction.

"Oh, shit," said Cody when he reached the stairwell. The space was filled with rubble, no way through. Panic constricted her chest. They were trapped.

"There's got to be another way out," said Adele.

"There is." A form moved from the darkness, slim, young. A boy—no, a young man—in cargo pants and a rain jacket, heavy boots, a pack on his back, phone in his hand.

"Are you Adele?" Thick dark hair and a wide smile. He seemed like a dream, from another universe. "I'm Hugo. Blake sent me."

"Blake?" said Adele, confused, incredulous. "My son?"

"Come this way," he said. "We can get out through the tunnels. But there's not much time."

She turned to Cody, who gave her a look. "What choice do we have?"

"I'm going back for her," said Malinka, backing away.

"No," said Adele reaching for her hand. "She left. She ran."

Malinka was shaking her head. "I've spent a year looking for her. I can't leave her now."

"Don't do this," pleaded Adele. Cody put a hand on Adele's arm.

"We have to go *now*," said Hugo. "It's falling."

Behind them another beam crashed into to the ground. "I'm sorry," said Malinka. "I love her."

And then she turned, running, splashing through the rising water.

"No," yelled Adele.

"Let her go. We all have to do what we have to do," yelled Cody. "Let's get you home to your kids."

Then Adele and Cody were following Hugo down a hallway, through a doorway, and into a tunnel nearly thigh-high with murky water. They waded after him, a series of crashes behind them and only darkness ahead.

48

ANGELINE

Angeline pulled away from Maverick. She spun around trying to orient herself. A large free-floating piece of wood smashed into her ankle, and she wailed with pain. The ceiling above them was coming apart, caving in places with water pouring through.

They were going to die down here. She grabbed Maverick's hand, but he was looking at something behind her.

The soldiers, two of the men from outside, carried flashlights and were waving at them.

"Over here," one of them yelled. "Come quickly."

They both froze. Was it safe? Were they really trying to help? Finally, one of the men ran toward them. "Come now or this place will be your tomb."

It broke some kind of spell they were under. He led them toward a dark doorway which was mercifully unblocked.

They ran, limped, struggled, with the men behind them, up the shallow steps that wound up and up, walls covered with rot and graffiti, decades of neglect and vandalism. It seemed like it would never end, that they were trapped in the spiral, and this was it for both of them, for all of them.

Finally, when they were in the lobby, running toward the exit, the men turned around and ran back into the building. She heard voices shouting, saw flashlight beams in the darkness. The soldiers were helping everyone out of the building. Footsteps behind them, running, voices, cries. Groaning, crashing.

And then she and Maverick were out in the rain, and it felt like a gift, a blessing. A storm they would have normally run from, hidden from, felt like freedom. Angeline turned to see who else got out behind them. But they were alone.

"Run," she heard someone call from inside. "Keep moving. Clear the building."

Who would get to safety? Who, as Maverick liked to say, would live to play another day? The thought made her laugh, hysterical, then start weeping.

Maverick dragged her farther, farther away.

"Holy shit," he yelled over the wind and the rain. "It's coming down. Enchantments, it's falling."

Angeline stood rooted, staring at the building, which seemed to be shrinking. Ahead of them, the Range Rover sat waiting. The line of men guarding the exit was gone.

Petra had said that the men weren't there to protect the land, they were there to keep people from hurting themselves. She'd meant it. They must all be inside the building, helping people out.

She kept watching—for Hector, for Gustavo. No one emerged from the entrance. Oh, God, what had they done?

Angeline sank to her knees, wailing, and finally Maverick just picked her up and ran for the vehicle. Stunned, she climbed inside. A glance to the back seat revealed the two duffel bags, undisturbed in the back. The key fob was in the center console. Maverick gave her a look and started the engine, then peeled out.

Behind them, with a final, seismic groan, a roar of crashing wood, stone, concrete, plaster, Enchantments fell.

Angeline watched, horror dueling with disbelief, as Enchantments folded in on itself and collapsed with a roar.

Maverick never looked back, kept looking ahead, the Rover easily moving through the swamped roads.

"Oh, my God," she whispered. Who got out? Who didn't? The tragedy of it all settled over her, and her tears became sobs. When she turned back toward the road, what she saw there caused her to issue a scream.

"Maverick, stop!"

A woman, ghostly white, stood glowing in the road. Robed, erect, staring.

Maverick brought the truck to a screeching halt. "What? Angeline, *what*?"

Angeline stared; the other woman's eyes bored into her with a kind of sad judgment.

"Petra," she whispered at Mav, who just shook his head.

"No," he said, putting a hand on her arm.

When she turned back to the road ahead, it wasn't Petra at all.

It was a giant bird, using its powerful beak to rip at the flesh of its prey. A buzzard, tawny feathers glistening wet from the rain. Startled by the headlights, it lifted its wings in a show of anger and let out a high-pitched cry, eyes glowing, beak bloodied. Then it flapped off into the storm.

Maverick and Angeline just stared at the road a moment, then at each other. Finally, Maverick gunned the engine, and they roared away into the night.

Part Four

Home Base

"In the end, maybe Maverick Dillan was right. Maybe he's not the villain. Maybe we are for watching him."

HARLEY GRANGER,
Stranger Than Fiction: A Podcast
"What Happened to Chloe Miranda?"

49

ADELE

"Are you comfortable, Adele?"

She *wasn't* comfortable, hadn't been since Falcão Island.

Her body ached. Her back, an injured neck, leg, and elbow were all healing slowly. She struggled with flashbacks, was in therapy for trauma. She hadn't slept through the night without vivid, terrifying dreams in months.

But she was alive, thanks to Blake. Both her kids were okay. Miller, for all his crimes and betrayals, had come back when they'd needed him. And he was now in custody. And after it all, the healing had begun. That was enough.

So it was truthful when she answered, "Yes, I'm okay."

"Thank you for being here," said podcaster Harley Granger.

He was younger than she thought he'd be, slim and unassuming in a long-sleeved black Vans T-shirt, a beanie over dirty-blond hair, jeans. They sat in a quiet, dim recording studio. It was nicely appointed with ergonomic chairs and a big walnut table between them. The professional mics hung from the ceiling, monitors and a soundboard blinked on a table lining the far wall. There was a pleasant quietude to the place as if nothing outside existed and nothing mattered as much as the conversation that was about to begin.

Through the glass window, Harley's producer, Roger, tapped on a keyboard. Finally, he gave Harley a thumbs-up, and a light box glowed red, reading *Recording*.

"Folks, today I'm sitting down with Adele Crane, who was at the heart of the Extreme Hide and Seek scandal and what I like to think of as the final chapter in the Chloe Miranda story."

She'd heard a lot about Harley Granger, that he was unethical, tricked people into saying things they didn't mean, not honoring the victims in his reporting. But there was something easy and warm about him, the inquiring gaze of his heavily lidded eyes. She felt like she could tell him anything and whatever it was it wouldn't surprise him. She planned to tell him everything she knew.

"Adele, is it fair to say that you went to Falcão Island expecting one thing and found something else altogether?"

Adele had to think about that for a second. What *had* she expected when she signed up for Extreme Hide and Seek? A game. A challenge. What *had* she wanted? Money, first of all. No point in lying about that. But also, she wanted to prove something—to her kids, to herself, to the world. That she was more than just a survivor. That she was a winner. That Miller hadn't won, that he hadn't deceived her for years, then left her broken and struggling to care for her kids.

"That's fair, yes," she said. "I went there expecting a challenge, to play a game I thought I had a chance at winning. Instead, I walked into a storm—literally and figuratively."

"Malinka Nicqui calls you a hero. She says you saved her life."

Adele had to laugh at that. "I'm no hero. And I had help saving Malinka. Cody Bryce, who most people know as Wild

Cody, saved us both, literally pulling us back from the edge. He sacrificed his own win and his life when we needed him."

She held back tears, took a deep breath, remembering those terrifying moments when she thought the world was going to end.

"He helped me save Malinka. He stayed with us until the end, when Hugo Silva found us and showed us the way out through the tunnels as Enchantments collapsed. So if we're looking for heroes, I'd choose Hugo and Cody."

Harley tapped his pen on the notes in front of him. "We're always looking for our heroes, aren't we?"

"I think it helps to believe there are people around without flaws, someone to come in for the rescue when things go *FUBAR*, as Maverick Dillan likes to say. But I don't think there's a person alive without flaws, someone who doesn't make mistakes."

He turned an intense gaze on her. Harley Granger, she knew, had faced down his own scandals. "What mistakes have *you* made, Adele?"

She smiled. "Too many to count. Leaving my kids behind to chase after a cash prize, for one. Before that, not seeing my husband for what he was. For relying on him for the life I thought of as my own but couldn't sustain without him."

He folded his hands together on the table between them.

"Your husband, Miller Crane, the biotech engineer accused of embezzling funds, stealing ideas from junior scientists. As the authorities descended, he fled and remained missing until he was recently captured."

"That's right," she said. "But he returned to face his crimes and make amends to his kids. He turned himself in to authorities."

That was partially true, without being the whole truth.

"There are people who say you knew where Miller was all along," said Harley. "That you helped him get away and stay hidden."

She bristled at that, shifted in her seat. "That's not true. Anyway, this podcast isn't about Miller Crane, is it?"

"No," he said, flashing her an apologetic grin. "Maybe next season?"

"I hope not," she said. "The truth is all out there now. Miller is in jail. He's confessed and is awaiting sentencing. He's working on making amends."

"And what about you? How will he make amends to you?"

"All I want is for my kids to heal, to find a way to forgive their father if they can, to love him in spite of his flaws. He is a man who did bad things, but he loves his children. That's... something. And that's all I can say about this."

He gave her an assenting nod.

"So let's start at the beginning," he said. "Tell me when you first decided to apply for the hide and seek challenge."

Adele started at the beginning and ended at the collapse of Enchantments. By the time they'd finished talking, more than two hours had passed. It was healing to tell the story, to relive that day and night, to take it all apart, question it, analyze it.

When she was done, she felt better than she had in months.

How are you doing with it? Cody had texted her last night.

Moving through it, she'd answered. **You?**

One day at a time.

Exactly.

Can I see you again?

I'd like that.

"Lives were lost on Falcão Island," said Harley. "Alex Tang's body was found washed up on Falcão Island's north shore. Gustavo Bello did not make it out of the building before Enchantments fell; he is presumed dead. According to island officials, the site remains unstable and recovery efforts have faltered. His body has not been recovered."

How close she had been to meeting the same fate, leaving her kids forever. That sudden wash of sadness, the tingle of dread, the hallmarks of trauma's aftermath made themselves known, and Adele felt heat come up her throat. She breathed through it.

"It's a tragedy," she managed. He gave her a moment to collect herself.

"Let's talk about Chloe Miranda and Hector Cruz. They claim that they were on a year-long mission to reveal all the fraud and corruption at Extreme. Chloe, with Hector's help, staged her disappearance to draw scrutiny to the organization and expose all their wrongdoing."

"Hmm," said Adele.

She'd watched Chloe make the interview circuit, explaining herself, trying to paint herself as a hero and a crusader for good. Apparently, she spent the year on Falcão Island, squatting at Enchantments. *Men like Maverick Dillan can't keep getting away with hurting people and stealing. Good women, strong women have to expose them.*

Adele hadn't heard her talk about the pain she must have caused her family, or how they might heal now that she'd returned home. Maybe Chloe thought it was worth it. Or maybe she didn't think about it at all. Adele couldn't help but compare her to Miller, someone else who'd put his own interests before the people who loved him.

"Chloe faces charges now for blackmail, falsifying a crime, among other things," said Harley. "Neither Chloe nor Hector will speak to me for this podcast. Attorneys I know think she could serve prison time."

Violet told Adele that Chloe's following had more than tripled, that online she was hailed as a hero and a female crusader against men who use and ghost women, who lie, steal, and cheat.

"She's like a feminist icon, now," said Violet, quite sincerely. Adele wasn't sure how she felt about that. Any of it. But *feminist* wasn't a word she'd use to describe Chloe Miranda.

"Meanwhile, Malinka Nicqui has used the scandal to come clean about her own business failings," said Harley, looking down at notes in front of him. "She has admitted that she would not have been able to climb all Seven Summits without the help of her father, who died several years ago. She said it was you who helped her see that a lot of what she did as a kid was to please her dad. He wanted her to climb. So climb she did."

Adele thought about Malinka a moment, what she wanted to say. She and Adele were in regular contact. A few weeks ago, Malinka had sent a box of clothes to Violet who practically lost her mind with joy.

"Maybe a lot of us, women especially, go through life pleasing people. First we try to be what our parents want us to be," said Adele, thinking of the place she was in when she met Miller. Unformed in a lot of ways, ripe for the taking. "Then maybe our boyfriends or husbands. Then *everyone*—social media, our kids, the neighbors. It's not even conscious all the time. It often takes a moment of reckoning before we ask ourselves, *Who am I? What am I doing here? What do I want?*"

She paused a second, took a breath. She noticed how Harley gave her the space to finish her thoughts. How much of this interview would wind up on the cutting-room floor? Probably a lot.

"I think that's what happened for Malinka," she went on. "She is a young woman who has accomplished a lot—for her father, for her fans. I think what happened at Enchantments helped her to see herself in a new way. Helped her look at her past from a different perspective and forge a truer path forward."

She nodded to indicate that she was done.

"Malinka and Chloe continue to support each other online, and have a message of facing the truth, mental health, honesty, and self-love," said Harley. "Between the two of them, they have more than three million followers, and they are launching their podcast *Grrl Power: Yes I Can* in January. The outpouring of financial support for Malinka has allowed her to save her company and the foundation which continues its work of empowering women."

"That sounded like spon con," said Adele. Harley just smiled. That, she figured, he'd edit out. She remembered that last moment in Enchantments when Malinka went back for Chloe. Petra Arruda's men then helped them both to escape before the collapse. "I wish them both well. I hope they both face down their demons while they're young."

If Malinka was her daughter, she'd have had advised her to stay away from a woman who'd lied and hurt countless people with her so-called crusade to expose Maverick, who then bailed on everyone when Enchantments started to fall, including Hector Cruz and Gustavo Bello, her supposed partners in trying to bring down Extreme. But Malinka was a grown woman, and like everyone, she'd have to make her own mistakes.

Harley kept his eyes down a moment, then said, "And finally, let's spend a little time talking about Maverick Dillan and Angeline Alba."

"So much to say about those two," she mused.

"Indeed. Maverick Dillan, founder and CEO of Extreme, and Angeline Alba, COO, escaped Enchantments that night. They somehow managed to get to the airport, though roads were washed out. Dillan's jet was the first to leave Falcão Island once the storm had cleared with just the two of them and the crew on board. What do you think about that?"

What *did* she think about that?

"It's easy to think that they got away with something," she said. "Supposedly there was money, right? Cash in the back of one of the Range Rovers?"

"That's the rumor. The jet, corporately owned by Extreme, landed at a private airport outside Toronto. And now Dillan and Alba are off the grid. Gone. No one has heard from them since. Maverick Dillan is wanted for questioning in the murder of Alex Tang. Angeline was caught on film along with Dillan and Gustavo Bello disposing of Tang's body and is also wanted by police. Thoughts?"

"There's something I know for sure," she said after drawing and releasing a breath. "We don't get away with things. We can run and we can hide. We might escape justice or the law, for a time. Like Miller did. But he said that he was never free, knowing what he'd done, that he was on the run, how badly he'd hurt his family. That his life was a kind of hell of looking over his shoulder, separated from everything he ever loved."

"We can't escape the truth of ourselves?"

"Something like that."

"Online rumors abound," said Harley. "There have been Mav-and-Angeline sightings all over the world. One or two of the photos are convincing."

Blake filled her in daily on the latest. It was his mini-obsession.

"Sounds like you have the subject of your next podcast. *The Rise and Fall of Maverick Dillan and Extreme*."

"And fall it did. Hector Cruz, the last shareholder still accountable, filed bankruptcy for the company. A pending multimillion-dollar deal with BoxOfficePlus imploded. Extreme is being sued by sponsors who paid for advertising they never received. A group called Moms Against Mav, who demand compensation for their injured children, has filed another suit. No fewer than ten charities say that money raised for them was never received from Extreme. The company that made it seem like their Extreme Games was simply a fun way to do good in the world. But that's not the whole truth. What would you say to Maverick if you had the chance?"

Adele didn't have any anger toward Maverick or Extreme. Since her trials on Falcão Island, her followers had more than doubled. She hadn't won the prize money, but her income from her WeWatch page had tripled. She had a raft of new sponsors— from apparel to camping and climbing gear to organic, vegan protein bars. Her interview with Malinka and Chloe would be the premier episode of their new podcast. *Adele Crane: Mom, Tough Be-atch, and Survivor.*

Adele had gone to Falcão Island for something she didn't get. But she walked away with other things she never expected.

She would keep her job at the school because the work meant something to her. In her heart, what she'd wanted as a younger person, before she met Miller, was to help people, as cliché as it sounded. With her job as a school counselor, her blog, and her WeWatch channel, she felt like she was doing that. Finally.

"I'd tell him to come back," she said. "To face the truth. To make amends. It can be terrifying to face the consequences of our actions and choices. But it's no easier to spend your life running."

Harley looked down at his notes.

"The most recent headline is that Hector Cruz has been arrested for the murder of Alex Tang," said Harley. "Apparently there's security footage that shows them in an altercation, ending in a fatal fall."

Adele nodded; she'd heard the news last night. That, at least, was one question answered. They dove into other open items like: Who had been hiding in the hotel leaving items that reminded her of Miller? Who had put that flask in Cody's tent? The consensus was that it was just one of the Extreme team, doing what they did best: keeping things unstable. It tracked with claims from other challenges. But Adele thought that maybe it was Chloe, though she'd denied it. Adele had become adept at understanding that some questions didn't have answers. And you just had to live with it.

"There is one other thing I wanted to get your opinion on, Adele."

"What's that?"

"There are some people that say the whole thing was a plan cooked up by Maverick, Malinka, and Chloe, something to get more views. All of the drama with Petra Arruda, the radical shaman as she calls herself on Photogram, and her private security team, the abduction of Angeline—that it was all theater. And then things just got out of hand when the hotel collapsed."

Adele shook her head. The storm, the building collapse. She remembered the fear, the anguish. She remembered, too, how those men who seemed so menacing were responsible for rescuing everyone who survived, leading the way out of Enchantments.

"I don't believe that," she said, shaking her head. "It was real."

"You're sure."

"Positive."

Harley gave her a look she couldn't read.

"What's true is that people were hurt and died on Falcão Island," she went on. "Maybe we all went there for different reasons. We all believed that we were playing a game of one kind or another. But the game turned deadly real. I just feel lucky to be alive."

Did he think she was naive? What did he believe? She didn't bother to ask. She wasn't sure he'd tell her the truth.

Back at the house, the kids were home, Violet making dinner, her famous one-pot baked ziti. Blake was on the couch playing *Red World*. Adele didn't give him a hard time about the game anymore, or about the people he met while playing. If it wasn't for Hugo Silva and Blake's ability to reach him via the game, she might not be here right now. Although, Violet was always quick to point out that Adele might not have gone to Falcão Island at all if it wasn't for Blake's "stupid virtual friend."

Blake and Violet both had a million questions, about Harley Granger, about the interview. She told them everything while they set the table together, then gathered to eat. They'd spent some time in therapy together in the months since she returned from Falcão Island—where Blake confessed to communicating with his dad on *Red World*, and Violet felt crushed that Miller hadn't also reached out to her. And Adele told them about the money Miller had left, and the house she had a feeling he'd return to someday.

She'd also admitted that after she took the money from the safe, that she reported the house to the FBI. Even though she'd said otherwise, she'd always suspected Miller would one day return there and try to contact them. The FBI was monitoring the house, so even if Agent Coben hadn't been trailing Violet, they would have found him when he came home. Miller claimed that he knew that. He'd returned to help Adele and reconnect with his kids before the FBI came for him.

Blake, Adele, and Violet made a promise to each other: no more secrets between them, ever. Just the truth, however uncomfortable, however unpleasant.

Blake intended to maintain a relationship with his father, even though he'd likely be in prison for a long time. Violet had so far chosen not to speak to him again since he'd been taken into custody while the kids watched. Adele hadn't decided whether or not she wanted to confront Miller. She was working through it with Dr. S. *Sometimes closure is a thing we find within,* he'd said. *It's not necessarily given by another person. It can be something we give ourselves.* She was all about moving forward now. She didn't want to go back to the person she was—*before.*

As they were cleaning up after dinner, she had one more thing to tell her kids.

"Hey, so," she said. "Wild Cody?"

"Yeah," said Blake, mildly interested. Enough to look up from *Red World.* He'd finished clearing the table and returned to the couch. "What about him?"

Violet was wiping the counter, and Adele started the dishwasher.

"In about five minutes," said Adele, "he's going to ring that doorbell."

Violet and Blake both stared at her, confused.

"He's, uh…" She felt herself blushing, unable to go on.

"Oh. My. God," said Violet, drying her hands on a dish

towel. Outside the sun was setting, washing the kitchen in its final golden glow.

"He's a friend now," said Adele, clearing her throat.

"A friend," said Violet flatly, frowning.

"What?" said Blake. He closed the lid on his laptop. "Are you *dating* Wild Cody?"

Was she? Not really. Maybe? She wasn't sure of anything yet. She hadn't been with anyone but Miller in almost twenty years. What did the kids say these days? Adele and Cody were *talking.*

"He just wants to be called Cody now," she said instead of answering.

Blake's jaw dropped open. "That's…nuts. I don't know how to feel about that. I mean—you mean—he's coming here? Like now. Like…he's your boyfriend?"

"He's just a friend right now. I'll let you know if that changes."

"Wait," said Violet. "Have you…*kissed* him? Ew, gross! He's so old."

"He's not that old!"

"Does that mean you *have?*"

"That's private. Not a secret. Private."

"That means you did!"

The doorbell rang, and they all stared at each other. Then Violet started shrieking and ran up the stairs. Blake gave Adele a look, amused, curious, but then he followed his sister. She didn't call them back. She knew curiosity would get the better of them.

This was going to take time.

She walked toward the door, toward her future. And for the first time in a while, she smiled.

50

ANGELINE

After the Game

She stood on the edge of the dock and looked down into the cold, gray water. Above her the sky was cerulean, towering cumulus clouds piled high. She loved this moment, before the plunge. The water, she knew, would be freezing. When she dove into its depths, a shock would move through her. She'd emerge to draw breath more awake, more alive than she had been before. Still, she waited, counting her breaths, feeling alive in her body.

"Are you going in?"

Maverick sat on the Adirondack chair behind her. She didn't turn to look at him.

Instead, she looked out at the island closest to theirs. Had she seen movement on its shore? It was far, a good ten minutes by boat. There was a house, bigger than theirs, all windows that glowed golden in the early morning. It belonged to some tech billionaire, according to the gas-station attendant at the marina. Hadn't been there in years. Anyway, it was too far for anyone there to see her, naked on the dock.

She'd grown used to it quickly. Living without eyes on her, without voices, without chatter.

It had taken Maverick longer.

She turned back to him, and his eyes were closed. His body was toned and tan, wearing a sweatshirt and the navy blue swim trunks they'd picked up at the general store in the nontown on the mainland. He might join her in the water. Or maybe not.

She took a long, deep breath, put her hands over head, and dove into the gray, the cold. There was always that moment going down, breath held, when she wondered if she'd break the surface again.

When they'd first arrived, part of her had wished that she could just keep swimming deeper and deeper until the world was just a memory, a trick of light.

As soon as the storm had cleared on Falcão Island, they'd bribed the air traffic controller to let them leave. As the plane taxied down the runway, she half expected to see Petra and her men chasing them in their ATVs. But no, nothing. Just a smooth liftoff.

The dirty secret about private airports like the one they landed in outside Toronto was that no one asked questions. There was a kind of person that came and went at places like this, passage greased with hundred-dollar bills. There was no stop at customs. No passport control. When they landed, there was a car waiting for them—a beat-up old Land Rover, sky-blue and with a definite cool factor despite its age, the rust around the wheel wells, the tilted bumper.

Maverick handed the pilot an envelope stuffed with cash. They exchanged nods. And Angeline didn't ask what had transpired between.

Maverick threw the two duffel bags in the back. And other than what they were wearing, that's all they had with them.

"Were you planning this?" she asked.

He laughed a little. "Not this exactly, no. But I did promise you a retreat, right? Just the two of us?"

"I didn't think you meant it."

"I meant it."

They drove past the city in silence. And then they were on winding roads through thick forest, night falling. And they drove and drove, Angeline drifting, dreaming about the masked person on the trail, the falling building, Alex's body broken, falling. She dreamed of him washing up on some beach, body turned to flotsam, everything he was to them gone. She woke up crying.

Maverick put a hand on her leg. "We're here."

A marina. It was late, past eleven, so the shop was closed. The harbormaster showed them to a boat at the end of the dock. Another envelope of cash changed hands.

The water was dark, but Maverick seemed to know what he was doing, where he was going. And she trusted him when it came to things like this. He could drive the thing, whatever vehicle it was. Get them where they were going. When she needed him, he came in for the rescue, guns blazing.

In the huge lake, there were islands. Windows from homes glowed like embers in the night. It was quiet, so quiet—just the boat engine and the water and the vast silent night. The sky was alive with starlight, and the water glimmered and danced all around them.

There was nothing.

They'd both ditched their phones in Falcão Island.

She'd texted her mother: **I'm okay. I love you. Whatever you hear about us, it's not true. Not the whole truth.**

Then Maverick had taken it and dumped it with his in a garbage pail. Neither one of them had a device of any kind now.

The world and whatever consequences awaited them receded for a time. A deep calm came over her.

Finally, after about twenty minutes on the water, they came

to a dark island, and Maverick pulled their boat up to its wooden dock and tied them off.

"What is this place?" she asked. With the engine quiet, there was no sound except the water slapping against the hull.

"You know, up here in the middle of nowhere, islands are pretty cheap."

"You *bought* an island."

"Yeah," he said. "It's an engagement gift. Don't get too excited. It's nothing much. The house needs a lot of work."

Then he was down on one knee, and from his pocket he produced a small velvet box. Inside was the biggest diamond she'd ever seen.

"If not now, then when, Angeline?" he asked. "Will you marry me?"

She said *yes*, and he slid the ring on her finger. It was a perfect glittering pink star. She didn't imagine that they'd ever get married, not really. Because they were both probably going to prison at some point. So—why not?

He carried her over the threshold of a modest wood house that smelled a bit musty but was comfortably furnished with big couches and chairs and a decent kitchen—a pantry and refrigerator stocked with food. There were instructions about the water, and flushing the toilet, and the generator that would need to be kept gassed up. Too many trips into the marina could be a problem, she thought.

"It's pretty rustic," he said from the loft landing.

"It's perfect."

The master bedroom had a huge king bed, neatly made with enough pillows. There were clean towels in the bathroom, soap and shampoo.

"They'll find us eventually," she said.

"Or we'll go back and try to put things right," he said. "But not tonight."

They made love and slept deeply.

In the morning the sunrise washed in the big bay window and the lake and the trees and the other islands. It was the most beautiful thing she'd ever seen.

She made coffee. When Maverick woke up and joined her in the kitchen, she said, "Maverick, tell me everything."

He released a big sigh, took a swallow of the coffee she'd poured him.

He told her about the night in Iceland with Chloe. About the pictures she took. How she started blackmailing him. How he started taking money from the business accounts to pay her. Small amounts at first, then more and more.

Finally, they'd struck a deal. She would come to the Haunted Hide and Seek Challenge, and he'd make sure she won. And that would be the end of it. She promised.

Then she disappeared.

After that he started getting threats online, via email. He felt like someone was following him, trying to kill him. He was scared all the time. He bought and learned to use a gun. He didn't feel like he could tell anyone because he'd stolen so much money from Extreme. He was afraid the scrutiny might draw attention to all the other things he'd done wrong.

He kept stealing money, planning an escape. He bought this island with cash under an old company name. It wasn't perfect. If they were looking, and they probably were, they'd eventually find him.

Then came the BoxOfficePlus offer, which he and Alex knew was a lifeline, a way out. But who was he without Extreme? What would Extreme become if they had to answer to a corporate overlord? He fought the deal, found reasons to turn down every offer. He held the majority shares. No one could take Extreme; he'd have to give it.

Alex, still hopeful, was getting the books ready for review. That's when he realized that money was missing—a lot of it.

"How much is in the bags?" she asked.

The black duffels were sitting in the bedroom.

"There's a little under a million dollars."

She walked over to the window, looked out into the vista. Like this, they could live on that money forever. She steeled herself to ask the question she most needed answered.

"Did you kill Alex?"

She had to know. If the answer was *yes*, then Maverick was one thing. If it was *no*, he was another. Maybe she could love him either way, but she wouldn't know unless he told her the truth.

"No," he said, walking over to her. He spun her around and took both of her hands. Her ring cast glittery rainbows on the wall. "Look at me. I swear to you, I *did not* kill Alex."

Did she believe him? Or did she just *want* to believe him so badly?

"Then, who?"

"I don't know. But the truth is that if Alex and I were out of the picture, all our shares and the money would go to Hector and Gustavo. Hector was with Chloe. He was the last person to leave the hotel that day. So maybe that was the plan. Ruin me, kill Alex when they realized he was going to cover for me, and take Extreme to BoxOfficePlus. They'd all be rich—even Hector with his small share. Like megarich."

"It makes a twisted kind of sense," she admitted. The logic was off, the risks were too high. But if you were stupid, you might think it could work. Hector and Chloe wanted to be the new Maverick and Angeline of Extreme.

"Except in the process, they destroyed Extreme," he said. "Now it will be one of those stories—a great thing that was ruined by scandal, murder, fraud. BoxOfficePlus, with their whole woke, squeaky-clean image, won't touch Extreme now. Without the deal, the company is bankrupt. Hector, the only one standing, gets nothing."

His eyes filled then; he turned away so that she wouldn't see. But she pulled him back and wrapped her arms around him.

"They're gone," he whispered. "Everyone's gone."

He meant the guys, but also his audience, all the people that fed him back the version of himself he'd needed to survive. Who was he without that? Without Extreme? Angeline supposed they were about to find out.

"It was Hector. Hector killed Alex," she said.

He looked up at her.

"Think about it," she said. "You're right. He was the only one there after we went to the site."

Maverick considered it.

"Maybe there was a fight," she said. "Maybe it was an accident."

She remembered how Hector had cried in the trailer. Had it been an act? Or had it been true grief, remorse, or even shock that Alex was dead? She knew Hector—or thought she did. She couldn't see him murdering anyone in cold blood, even for money.

It was hard to recast him. Hector, the mom of Extreme, to Hector, killer, destroyer, betrayer. But everyone had their secret selves.

Now she swam deep, the water murky. Sometimes when she was down here, she saw things. Figures in the dark. Just a play of shadows and light, she guessed. But sometimes she was startled by their size, their closeness. Today, there was nothing, just that swirling gray.

She emerged finally, drawing a big breath of clean air.

Maverick was standing on the end of the dock. How long had she been down?

But he wasn't looking for her. He was looking out into the distance.

A boat approached, still far off in the distance. But close enough to see the flashing red light and the word *Police* emblazoned on its side.

Angeline emerged from the water, climbing up the slim ladder, and walked naked up the dock to go get dressed. She knew they couldn't run forever, that eventually they'd have to return and face everything broken they'd left behind, try to piece it back together. Pay the bill that had come due.

As the boat drew closer, she heard the wail of its siren.

Ready or not, it seemed to say, *here we come.*

★ ★ ★ ★ ★

Acknowledgments

Every book is a journey. This one started with an actual trip across the ocean to a magically beautiful archipelago in the Atlantic Ocean called the Azores. These stunning volcanic islands are characterized by dramatic vistas, primeval forests, charming fishing villages, and wild riots of blooming hydrangeas. Honestly, we chose the destination in part because of the short flight from New York, but we fell immediately in love with this autonomous region of Portugal that manages to be elegant and sleepy, moody and welcoming, dramatic and relaxing all at once. Falcão Island is a fictional rendition of this special place.

Toward the end of our trip, my husband, daughter, and I were rained out of a hike around the rim of a volcanic lake. And as we returned to our hotel, we happened upon a huge abandoned structure. The Monte Palace Hotel on São Miguel was built in the 1980s, a very poor French investment that closed in less than a year. Once intended to be a grand European destination, it's now a ruin. So, of course, in spite of the giant signs that read "DANGER" and "DO NOT ENTER" in multiple languages, we had to explore. That island excursion was the seed for this book, though again the place in my novel is totally fictional.

We write alone. But the journey, from the seed of an idea on a family vacation to publication, cannot be successful without a network of supporters.

My husband, Jeffrey, and our daughter, Ocean Rae, are my home team. They keep me laughing, offer endless love and support, and are always down for the next adventure. My husband is my partner in crime, the love of my life, and my best friend. Sorry, honey! I know it's not easy being married to a writer! And our girl, about to head off to college at the time of this writing, is the pride and joy of our lives, our North Star. I wouldn't want to be on this wild ride without them to remind me daily what truly matters. Our beloved labradoodle, Jak Jak, is my faithful writing buddy and foot warmer, and a constant nudge to finish up work so we can play.

My agent, Amy Berkower, of the incomparable Writers House, is rock, champion, and friend. I'd be lost without her calm advice and steady hand at the helm as she navigates the big waters of this writing life. Huge thanks to Celeste Montano, Maja Nikolic, and Maria Aughavin for all their tireless efforts on my behalf.

I say this every year, but the folks at HarperCollins, Harlequin, and Park Row Books are every writer's dream team. In everything from editing to marketing and publicity, from art to sales, they are exemplary. I can't say enough good things about the people who devote themselves to publishing my books in the most thoughtful possible ways.

What would I do without my beloved, funny, wise, and oh-so-brilliant editor, Erika Imranyi? In the business of writing, we often talk about our "ideal reader," the person we imagine in our head as we write. Over seven books together, Erika has become that person to me. I am a better writer because of her input, encouragement, and wisdom. Erika, I forgive you for "Old Bob." Sort of.

Special thanks to executive vice president and publisher Loriana Sacilotto and vice president of Editorial Margaret Marbury for their wise leadership and endless creativity. Publicist extraordinaire Emer Flounders tirelessly works to spread the word about my novels and launches me (kicking and screaming) out onto the road with endless patience and organizational genius. Lindsey Reeder, Brianna Wodabek, and the fabulous social media team help me stay on the bleeding edge of what's happening in the virtual world. Much gratitude to Rachel Haller, marketing maven, Randy Chan, independent bookstore and library whisperer, and Nicole Luongo, editorial assistant, for her organization and good cheer.

I am blessed with a sterling network of friends who cheer me through the good days and drag me through the challenging ones. They are forced to attend book signings year after year, read early drafts of my work, and endure my social media posts. But they still love me! (Or so they assure me.) And I love them! Erin Mitchell is early reader, tireless promoter, inbox tamer, voice of wisdom, and pal. Heather Mikesell has been a longtime early reader, eagle-eyed editor, and bestie. Jennifer Manfrey is always on standby to dig in deep to some obscure topic over which I'm obsessing. Her support, friendship, and wisdom are foundational in my life. And honestly, I think she buys more of my books than anyone else on the planet! Lifelong friends Tara Popick and Marion Chartoff have had the pleasure of dealing with me since college and grade school respectively. They still answer my calls! A big shout-out to Team Waterside—Kathy Bernhardt, Colleen Chappell, Marie Chinicci-Everitt, Rhea Echols, Karen Poinelli, Tim Flight, Bill Woodrow and Jennifer Outze, Celeste Van Auken (and Tucker!...even if he did eat my book), Cathy Kimber, Heidi Ackers, and Barbie Graham to name just a few—for being my home team, reading, supporting, showing up at events, and being there in every way possible. The Laymans—Andrea, Bill, and Ayers—have shared every chapter of our lives and are so often the loving faces I see first when I look out into a crowd.

My mom, Virginia Miscione, former librarian and avid reader, gave me the gift of loving story in all forms—books, film, television, and theater. She remains one of my earliest and most important readers. I mainly just give my dad, Joseph Miscione, a hard time for being the guy who told me *not* to pursue my writing dreams but to get a "real job." I usually do this onstage and it always gets lots of laughs—especially when he's there! (It's not bad advice, though. I have succeeded against all odds!) But he and my mom have been the safety net beneath me as I walk that tightrope we call life. Thanks, Mom and Dad, for always being there. And of course, along with my brother, Joe, for shamelessly bragging, facing out books in stores, and always spreading the word.

And finally, a writer is nothing without her readers. Some of you have been with me from the very beginning. Thank you for connecting, reviewing, turning up at events, engaging in social media, and generally making this writing life more fun. It means so much to me to know that my stories, characters, and words have found a home in your minds and hearts. I could not do this without you. Thank you for reading!